U Murder U
(Suicide)

Gladys Lawson

G

GLL Publishing

gllpublishing.com
gllpublishing.co.uk

G

GLL Publishing

gllpublishing.com
gllpublishing.co.uk

Dedication

Shalom means Peace or in more detail, *'Nothing Broken, Nothing Missing'*. JEHOVA, the Uncreated Creator, has many names, one of which is JEHOVA Shalom, for in Him, nothing is broken and nothing is missing.

This book is dedicated to the God of Peace in whom we are complete, we are loved, and we have true, everlasting Shalom.

To God be the Glory.

Amen.

Acknowledgement

My mother and father, Mr and Mrs J.K. Lawson

My children, Stephanie and Zack

My brothers and sister, Richard, Elizabeth and Tunde

My family and friends

My readers

Me

Books by Gladys Lawson

Despite all odds: A Dream Fulfilled Part 1
Despite all odds: A Dream Fulfilled Part 2
Truths, Lies And Untold Secrets
Blood Borne Connections
U Murder U (Suicide)

Foreword

While writing this book, I felt like throwing in the towel so many times. I constantly questioned myself. Each time I wanted to stop something pushed me on, telling me that this was a book people needed to read.

In my research, I read so many stories about people who have not just had suicidal thoughts but have actually gone on to kill themselves. People who were depressed, or who probably thought that they were unloved and that there was no hope to the mess or pain they were in. One thing led to another, and they took their own life. A lot of people cannot understand what would make someone do this, what would cause a person to manifest their suicidal thoughts. Some say it's the weak person's way out, and some say it takes courage to do it, but most people say it takes more courage to conquer it, face your problems and live!

We all go through situations in our lives, some good, some not so good and some bad. Going through a bad situation doesn't mean staying in it. Courage will take you where you need to go, and perseverance will keep you there.

I may not have gone through what you have, but I can

say this – Don't give up, give in . . . Give in to God. Why? – Because all things are possible when you believe in God and when you believe – Change happens!

Step away from your problems and look at your life as if you were just about to walk round a corner. You can't see what's coming . . . So don't stop walking. Keep on moving – Sometimes, change happens when you least expect it to.

Lx4 = Live Life x Love Life

A Story

"A story is told of an angel called Lucifer who was once given a mission of making musical sounds and was put in charge of the worship team in Heaven. He was both beautiful and gifted, so much so that other angels and heavenly creatures were enthralled by his beauty and talent. He knew he was handsome and every day he would admire himself and portray himself in all his splendour in front of the other angels. One thing led to another, and some of the angels began to worship him instead of JEHOVA, the One, who created him. Day after day they would tell him how handsome he was and how amazing his music sounded. After a while, it was as if this angel forgot who had created him and what his mission was and began to believe in the praise he was given. The 'Sound' of his music changed as he became abnormally arrogant and proud - narcissistic. One day he decided to rebel against the Creator and establish his own kingdom in Heaven where he would be worshipped day and night. But the only way he could have his own kingdom in Heaven was to overthrow the Creator. His rebellion led to him and about a third of the total population of angels in Heaven, whom he had misled into following him, being cast out of Heaven.

Today that ex-angel, now called Satan, still exists but his mission is entirely different. Today, his self-imposed mission is to capture as many souls as he can through any means necessary. He tempts people into worshipping him, and once they do, they become his. He offers them 'gifts' of riches and fame, but as these are not truly his to give, he never tells them how long they will have them or their real cost. In exchange for the 'gifts', he gives he takes their soul. For those whom he cannot tempt with riches and fame, he causes situations to arise through his many workers (demons); he sends these workers out with evil spirits of depression, anger, hate, bitterness and unforgiveness to name a few. His workers walk among people on Earth and can attach or latch onto those who open themselves up to evilness. Through these attachments, they have caused conflicts which have led to wars in this World. They have created broken families, broken communities and broken countries. When they attach to people they infect their minds, and they control their minds, and they destroy their minds. They enhance emotions, re-arrange the truth and impart death and depression, which can cause a person to think of suicidal thoughts. They know that if they can get a person to kill himself/herself, then the person's soul will belong to their leader and in return, they will be rewarded. Their leader has convinced them that the more souls they get, the more chance they have of getting back into Heaven. Their leader is a liar, a thief and a destroyer but they cannot see this. All they see is him, the way he was before they were all thrown out of Heaven and disconnected from the Way, the Life and the Truth they once knew – they believe his lies.

'There is a war going on. Evil demons and spirits of murder and suicide controlled by the evil one are the 'enemy'. Time is limited, and the battle is fierce. The deception that souls are required to buy back entry into Heaven is pellucid and is being perfunctorily implemented.' - **Quote by A. Newman 1852.**

In recent years, there has been an increase in the number of teenage suicides all over the World. This is a time of greater comfort and easier living – so why is this happening? Why do we read in the Newspapers, almost on a daily basis, stories about someone taking his own or her own life? Why is there an increase in suicide pacts taking place? This can no longer be ignored. We must pause and ask the question - What is going on?"

Part of a paper written and read by
Dr Peter D. Lewis
National Congress of Human Life Preservation
NCHLP Headquarters, Washington DC

PROLOGUE

Chicago, Several Years Ago

Her days and nights had become one. Nothing pleased her, and nothing made her happy anymore. She hated the way she felt and hated, even more, the way her husband and the doctors tippy-toed around her, talking to her like she was a five-year-old while expecting her to act like a mother and wife. She tried to tell the doctors that her poor appetite, her inability to shut down at night and sleep like a normal person and her constant feeling of low self-esteem were not right and meant that something wasn't right, not that she was merely depressed. She tried to tell her husband that the fact that she was always tired, moody and wasn't turned on sexually by him anymore since she had the baby meant that something wasn't right and not that she was just depressed. No one listened to her, and since her baby was four years old they all dispelled the thought that she had 'baby-blues'. In the past four years, she had seen three physicians and five psychiatric doctors and the only thing they all seemed to agree on was that she was showing signs of depression caused by something they couldn't identify.

They took her husband's money and in exchange gave her drugs to take (uppers and downers) which were supposed to make her feel better but often left her feeling like she was stranded on a desert island, terrified of the water around her and allergic to the sand beneath her – unstable.

The physicians took her blood and tested her hormone levels, and the psychiatrists prodded her brain with words and more words; they asked questions, and some of them answered their own questions while others completely ignored her answers to their questions and told her what they thought. They told her to write her problems on pieces of paper, put the papers in envelopes and the envelopes in a box and keep the box somewhere safe, only visiting it when she felt strong enough to deal with a problem. She never visited the box. Initially, she had tried to explain that she did love her baby but sometimes found it difficult to express the love she felt and because of this she felt guilty, was always anxious that someone would find out and was tired as a result of all the anxiety. She couldn't concentrate on things, and she was always forgetful (a thing her mother-in-law was always reminding her about).

She stared at the jug on the table. The dark fizzy liquid was lighter at the bottom than it was at the top and for a moment she wondered why. 'Ice', she thought to herself, 'it's the ice in the jug that has diluted the cola at the bottom and made it lighter'. She smiled to herself, happy in the knowledge that she had resolved the question all by herself, without the assistance of one of her many prescribed medications (she had stopped taking the drugs days ago).

"Mommy, Mommy here's my cup, can I please have some soda?" Anna Lee asked excitedly.

She turned and smiled at her precocious daughter, only four years old and as inquisitive as someone much older. She picked up the jug and poured some cola into her daughter's cup and added some ice; her daughter loved to suck on the ice. She watched as her daughter gulped the drink down then put an ice cube in her mouth and sucked loudly on it. She poured some cola into a glass until it was three-quarters full and quickly drank it then poured another glass full and quickly drank that. She burped, loudly. Her daughter looked up at her and smiled then burped. They both giggled.

The sound of a raised voice and running footsteps preceded the banging and then crashing open of the door.

A man ran into the room; he held a note in his hand – her suicide note. "What have they made you do?" He shouted, confusion and total disbelief etched on his face.

She looked at her husband, always protective, always blaming someone else, the nanny, the doctors, himself – never her. "I can't bear living like this so I'm leaving and I'm taking our daughter with me," she told him calmly. The poison was beginning to take effect . . . she felt a sharp pain in her stomach; she was dying, the cola served as a catalyst, it made the poison work faster. Soon, her emotional turmoil and her physical pain would end . . . soon, she would be dead.

"No, no, no . . . not my baby! Not Anna Lee! Think of all the things she could have done with her life . . . all the good things she could have done, think of all the people she could have helped!" Her husband sobbed as he reached for his daughter. His broken, distraught, pain-infused, shock-filled voice brought a semblance of sanity to her foggy brain.

'Oh no, oh no! What have I done? What have I done? I don't want to die! Help me! I don't want to die!' Her brain screamed as she lay on the floor, moments away from death.

The Room

Despite the presence of thousands of people in the room

The room was cold and dark

The room was quiet . . .

Each occupant seemed to be captivated by images on a screen, images that only they could see, voices that they alone could hear. They were unaware of the person standing next to them, unaware of what that person could see or hear.

The room was cold and dark

The room was quiet . . .

This room is one of many rooms, in a place where the living do not dwell. It is a place where people who have taken their own lives, committed suicide, dwell. It is said that because of what they have done they have been initially cast into this room where they watch their lives play on as if they had lived. They watch what could have been – be.

At times, so engrossed in the visual, they forget the factual; they forget that they are dead!

SIDE A

CHAPTER 1

Battersea, London

Un-suppressed, volatile, typical-teenage anger bubbled deep within Elle's chest as she watched her mother get ready for her date. How her mother could bear to be in the same room as the philanderer baffled her (recently, due to peer pressure, Elle often referred to him as the dick-head-led man, or D-H-L man, rarely as her father). Her mother applied some more blush to her cheeks and then applied some lip gloss to her lips and puckered them together. Next, she ran a hand through her auburn hair and scrutinised her appearance in the mirror.

Clarissa saw the scowl on her daughter's face and took a deep breath, smiled then turned to her. "Elle May Williams, why are you frowning like that, you're going to get wrinkles before you turn fourteen at this rate."

Perplexed and unable to comprehend why her mother was doing what she was doing, she jumped up and mumbled, "Why? Tell me . . . I don't understand Mum . . . why?"

"Why what, sweetheart?" Clarissa calmly asked, eyebrows arched.

"Why are you going to dinner with him? He cheated on you so many times. He left you-"

"Correction sweetheart, I asked him to leave."

"You went through weeks of depression when you found out what he'd done. Please don't let him take you there again. The last time you went to dinner with him, you came back, and you were so hurt and upset."

"That was a while ago. I'm stronger now."

"Yes, but he hasn't changed Mum, he's still the same."

"He's your father, Elle. I'm just trying to keep the line of communication open between you and your dad and your sister. She's younger than you and sometimes I think she

1

doesn't understand why he doesn't live with us anymore."

"Mum, Maddy is the wisest 8-year-old that I know, and she knows that dad is the biggest dick-head-led man this side of Battersea Bridge and-"

"Whoa, where did that language come from Elle May Williams? I didn't raise you to be disrespectful, especially towards your father!"

"But, but-"

"No, you never disrespect your parents young lady, full stop! And you know better than to use that kind of language. Listen, your father made his choices and he put me, you and your sister through hell because of his selfishness but you know what? I'm alive. I'm beautiful, and I have two beautiful daughters who I intend to teach how to respect themselves and not put up with crap and selfish men."

Apologetic, Elle smiled at her mother.

"There she is, ladies and gentlemen, there's my beautiful daughter. Come here and give your mama a hug."

Still smiling, Elle walked into her mother's open arms and hugged her tightly.

Headphones on, music pumping into her ears, Elle walked past Battersea Park with determined steps towards her friend, Jessica Carmichael's house. She ignored the joggers in the park, ignored the mothers pushing buggies and the people strolling around – she couldn't understand why anyone would want to be out in the park in this freezing weather. She increased her pace as a cold wind blew against her, biting into her skin. A podgy, blond, thirty-something-year-old man jogged towards her; he was wearing a pair of tight shorts and a vest which struggled to contain his hairy chest. Moments away from her, he blew her a seductive kiss, winked at her and slowed his pace to an almost jogging-on-the-spot pace, a lazy smile etched itself onto his flushed perspiring flabby face.

Elle's blood went cold. She pulled her headphones off, "I'm

only thirteen years old you pervert!" She shouted at him as they passed each other.

The man stumbled to a stop; her words unbalanced him. His eyes darted this way and that in search of anyone who had heard the words that now hung accusingly in the air.

"You pervert!" Elle shouted again.

He turned blindly, tripped over his feet and fell forward walloping the pavement hard. Within seconds he had picked himself up and started running down the road.

"That's right, RUN YOU PERVERT! RUN!" Elle yelled at his retreating back.

Shame-possessed, he ran faster and faster disappearing into the Surrey Lane Estates.

Elle pulled her coat tightly around her and continued on her way slightly warmed by the thought that the jogger would think twice before he did that again to some other innocent girl. She pulled her headphones back over her ears, pressed the fast-forward button on her iPod and smiled as one of her favourite songs played. She contemplated turning around and going home but decided against it knowing that she would only be bombarded by more text messages if she didn't show up. She was going to Jessica's house because Jessica had sent her several text messages begging her to come over and help her pick out an outfit for a party she was going to tomorrow. They'd been friends for ten of Elle's thirteen years and on-again-off-again best friends for nine of those ten years. Elle needed to vent about her dad and the adverse effect she thought he had on her mother – Jessica was her occasional sounding board; she listened to her, calmed her down and voiced the negative things Elle thought about her dad. Hearing the negative things she thought, spoken by someone else, gave her affirmation that she was right to think them. Jessica was the one who had coined the phrase 'Dick-Head-Led' in reference not only to Elle's father but all philandering men and insisted that Elle use it. The first time Jessica had said it a few

3

weeks ago, Elle hadn't quite understood what she meant and had watched with confusion etched on her face as Jessica had laughed at her own joke. When her laughter subsided, Jessica had gone on to explain using some new words she had discovered in her Dictionary/Thesaurus that a dick-head-led man or a D-H-L man was a womaniser, a Lothario, a man who allowed his genitals to lead him and make major life-changing, reprehensible decisions for him. Decisions which ultimately, disastrously ruined his life!

*

"Here have a sip of this Elle."

Elle took the glass from Jessica and sniffed its contents; it didn't particularly smell of anything alcoholic. "What is it?"

"A vodka martini, my mum's started drinking them in the morning now. She mixes it up in large quantities then stores it in bottles that she hides in the shed. She puts it in a glass with orange juice then sloshes it back like it's some wonder drug. The stupid cow thinks I don't know she drinks like a fish."

Elle put the glass down on the kitchen counter, "I told you before, I don't like alcohol, Jess. Do you have any fruit juice?"

"Sure, we have some in the fridge, help yourself. Are you hungry?"

"No, I ate dinner with Maddy before I left home." She walked over to the fridge, opened it and pulled out a carton of apple juice.

"So why did mother-dearest go out with the dick-head? Don't tell me she's thinking of taking him back? No, please, no, don't tell me she's going to take that piece of scum back? My mum says your dad has practically dipped his wick into every ink pot this side of London and who's to say how many damsels he's done it to in the States!"

Elle thought of her mother's earlier rebuke, she suddenly felt uncomfortable and shrugged her shoulders, "Let's talk about something else."

"Why?"

"Don't call him that anymore-"

"Why? Have I touched a sensitive Daddy-nerve? Come on, loosen up, are you sure you don't want a sip of this? It will help to loosen you up." Jessica slurred.

Elle swept her hair off her face and frowned at her friend, "I said I don't drink so let's talk about something else Jessica, or I'm going home."

"The sweeping of her graceful hand through her hair, the frown on her pretty face, here she is ladies and gents, my Best Friend Forever. The product of a once-upon-a-time, Oscar-nominated best-supporting actor, Neil R. T. Williams, a man so desperate for fame he would sell his soul to anyone and a songwriting mother, Clarissa Williams (nee Stapleton), who put up with so much bullshit from him she stinks of-"

"Look, from now on watch what you say about my father and don't you ever say anything rude about my mother!"

The silence was cold as it was harsh, it balanced precariously on a low wall, on one side of the wall stood 'change the subject' and on the other side 'continue to goad'. Not wanting to be alone Jessica pushed her drunken angry irritation out of the way and made a quick choice, "Loosen up Elle, I was only joking, gosh, don't take things so seriously, loosen up, chill out, let's talk about something else then BFF."

"You know sometimes I don't know why we're still best friends, you can be such a pain when you drink. One minute you're a mean-drunk, then you become a bitchy-drunk or a crying-drunk. You need help. I mean serious help, Jess."

"What can I say, I'm my mother's daughter, a bad tree can only produce what it knows, its DNA," she dramatically waved her hands up and down her body, "ta-dah, bad fruit."

"That's rubbish, you can change if you really want to, you have the choice, you don't have to be like her, stop drinking and get help, I'll go with you to your GP if you want-"

They both turned towards the back door as it suddenly opened and Jessica's mother, Eloise Carmichael, stumbled into the kitchen. She stood by the door holding the door handle and swaying (as if to some imaginary music).

"There's a good girl, get inside darlin', same time next week then," a man said, his cockney voice abrasively rough as he pushed her further inside and closed the door behind her.

The girls didn't see his face; all they glimpsed was the dirty yellow sleeve of the road sweeper's jacket he wore. Eloise turned to say something spontaneously sexy to the man and frowned in disappointment at the empty space and the closed door she saw. She blinked a few times as if by doing so he would magically reappear. Her blonde hair was messy, and she had dirt marks on her face. Her silk dressing gown was partially opened, and it was clear that she was wearing only a skimpy, flimsy, very low cut camisole negligee beneath it.

"Mum, what the hell are you doing? Who was that? Why are you dressed like that?" Jessica screamed in disgust.

Shocked, Eloise turned swiftly to her daughter, saw her daughter's friend and hiccupped; her guilt was quickly smothered in an elaborate smile, "Jess-si-ca! Hello, Jess-si-ca! Hello, El-le-May! How are you, El-le-May? How's your mother, El-le-May? How's your sister, El-le-May? How's your-"

"Stop it, Mother! What were you doing in the garden? Who was that man? I thought you were out. Shit, shit shit! This is not happening right now. This cannot be bloody happening right now!"

"Jessica Carmichael, what have I said about swearing in this house? No swearing allowed, swearing is banned from within these four walls," she giggled as she pointed at the walls. Unaware that her dressing gown had fallen open and the belt dangled in front of her she took a step forward, tripped on the belt, fell onto her hands and knees then collapsed onto the floor. The girls stared at her as she lay motionless on the floor.

"Is she okay?" Elle whispered.

"Who gives a bloody shit," Jessica replied.

Eloise Carmichael vomited, grunted, then turned onto her side, "Jess-si-ca, no swearing in this house. There are rules that you have to-"

"To hell with you and your rules you drunk! I hate you! You make me wish I was dead!" Jessica screamed at her mother.

"Stop it, Jessica," Elle scolded. She intermittently held her breath not wanting to breathe in the smell of the vomit as she helped Jessica's mother to sit up then propped her against a kitchen counter and gave her a glass of water.

Almost, but not quite demented, Jessica grabbed Elle's arm, pulled her out of the kitchen and up the stairs. "I need you to help me decide on my outfit, after all, that's why you came over BFF, ignore the drunk." A cold calmness seemed to have engulfed her as she stomped up the stairs with Elle in tow.

"We should call your dad Jessica we can't just leave her in the kitchen like that. She might-"

"If she can drink like a fish and act like a bitch in heat all the time then she can deal with the consequences like a dog and sit in her own vomit, my dad feels the same!" Jessica said as she playfully pushed Elle into her bedroom, slammed the door and turned her radio on – loud.

Later, when Elle had gone home, Jessica sat at the desk in her room and logged onto her computer. Her heart thudded with excitement as she typed some words that opened up doors and penetrated firewalls which gave her access to a secret chat room; her hands shook as she read the words already written.

Shy boy 1: Had a hell day today, feel like shit. Got bullied at school, can't tell anyone.
I'm Unhappy: No one understands, no one cares, I hate pretending that everything's okay when everything isn't okay.
Unhappy 2: I hate that too. My dad is having another affair and my mum is in denial again. She keeps shouting at everyone ☹. We pretend we don't know what's going on and I

hate it.

G-N: I hate that, why can't your mum deal with him and give everyone else a break?

Unhappy 2: I wish she would but she won't ☹.

Li-sa 5: I hate everything and everyone, my school is full of bitchy girls and I want out of everything. The cutting isn't working anymore. I don't feel the release I used to feel. I need to escape the pain cos it's driving me mad.

Shy boy 1: I hear you Li-sa 5, I need to end things soon, can't take much more.

Unhappy 2: How are you going to do it?

Shy boy 1: Fly off a bridge, go out in style.

Li-sa 5: Someone's knocking on my door; I bet it's my mum's boyfriend trying to cop a feel again. I wish I could kill him then myself.

Shy boy 1: Why don't you? Kill him then you can leave this world feeling good about something!

Jessica joined the conversation, she typed -

Jessy James 6: My mum's sloshed again, she really embarrassed me in front of my best friend. She is crap. I hate her. I wish I was dead. I want to die!!!

Unhappy 2: Don't worry JJ6, we'll get there soon. We're all going to get out of this world, on our terms and to hell with everyone else ☺ UREDRUMU!!!

Thirty minutes later, Jessica went to bed happy that she wouldn't have to put up with things for much longer. She and her friends in the suicide chat room had a pact – they would soon escape their pain and find the freedom they craved.

A few minutes later, she heard her mother tapping on her door asking her to unlock the door so they could talk. She ignored her, turned over and went to sleep.

CHAPTER 2

Clarissa Williams paced around her bedroom. Shocked and agitated, she bit the last remaining fingernail on her right hand as she thought about what Elle had told her moments ago. Clarissa knew she needed to do something about the situation her daughter was in, but she didn't know what to do. She contemplated calling her mother to get advice; her hand reached for her mobile phone, but her brain intervened before she picked it up. Her mother was still on holiday in New York and not back for two days. Anyway, she knew what her mother would say; her mother said it all the time.

"Your children are a gift from God – never forget that!
Don't neglect your child for someone else's child Clarissa!
Never hold someone else's child higher than your own child!
Discipline your children early and they will grow into wise teenagers and be smart adults!
Direct your children onto the right path and when they are older they will not depart from it!"

Clarissa picked up her leather tote bag, left her house and strode quickly down the road determined to put an end to the madness wrapped up as upper-class normality she had allowed her daughter to be a part of.

*

"I think you have a severe drinking problem!"

Like most functional alcoholics in denial, Lady Eloise Carmichael had mastered the fine art of deception extremely well. Being an alcoholic from a wealthy English family, she had married a handsome man of Scottish decent she thought beneath her social class and thus hoped would be easily malleable and tolerate her drinking. What she got was an oxymoron – a man, kind to and tolerant of everyone, but her. A man who acted as if he hated and resented her. What she gave back was her pain of rejection, well disguised but

9

displayed for all to see, regularly doused in whisky, vodka or rum - it didn't matter which. Lady Eloise Carmichael didn't 'do' being accountable, answering questions or taking criticism. She thought only people in her inner social/financial circle were qualified to criticise her and even then with all the tax avoidance loopholes, 'gross' (not 'net') income played a significant part in what she took onboard. Eloise looked at Clarissa with cold, irritable, angry eyes as she would something unpleasant she had just stepped on while wearing a pair of expensive one-of-a-kind designer shoes. Her foggy brain struggled to think of a rebuff to Clarissa's statement - she decided to bluff her way through. She took a swig of Dutch courage disguised as orange juice from her glass, "What do you mean? I don't have a drinking problem! How dare you suggest I do, how bloody dare you, Clarissa?"

"Elle said that you were drunk, half naked and lay right here in your own vomit! Your daughter said that she wished she was dead! Jessica is always telling Elle that she wishes she were dead because she hates you and what you've done to your family with your drinking and promiscuity. Elle thinks she might be self-harming because she's always wearing wrist sweat bands and won't take them off. And you think you don't have a problem!"

"I do not have a problem!"

"Yes you do, and you need to get help because your daughter needs you."

"I don't need help, and Jessica can take care of her bloody self. I'm not her keeper. Look, why don't you just get out of my house?"

"That would be so convenient for you wouldn't it? I just ignore everything, and you continue to drink and drag Jessica down with you."

"Listen, she's my child, I can do whatever-the-hell I want-"

"I don't think Social Services will see it like that, do you want me to call them? Shall we see if they have the same view as you?"

On hearing the 'SS' words Eloise froze, she stood dead still momentarily as fear flooded through her then her survival instincts kicked in. She plastered a condescending smile on her face, "Come on Clarissa, I think that Elle might have exaggerated a little, I was sunbathing in the garden as one does, I walked into the kitchen and stumbled on a loose kitchen floorboard, see it was that floorboard right there," she pointed. "It's happened before, in fact, the last time-"

"Really, Eloise? That's the best that you can come up with? You were sunbathing in February, one of the coldest months in England!"

"You know how emotional teenagers can get. Elle probably misinterpreted what she saw. Jessica gets like that, all emotional, hormonal and confused. I have to stuff Evening Primrose Oil capsules down her throat just to get a bloody civil word out of her sometimes."

"Look, no more excuses, I think we need to work on separating the girls. It's not just *your* drinking I'm concerned about, I'm not comfortable with the language Jessica uses which I know Elle is picking up because of Jessica's subtle bullying. Neither am I comfortable with Jessica's drinking. If she is self-harming, I don't want Elle exposed to that. I don't think that you or your daughter are people I want Elle to be around anymore. Then there's Maddy to consider-"

"Whoa, whoa, what did you just say? My daughter and I are no longer suitable companions for your precious girls? Who the hell are you to say that to me? Who are your daughters? They're the product of a broken marriage! What is your social status? At least I have echelon. At least Jessica lives with both of her parents. At least my husband isn't out there screwing everything and anything with a pulse!"

"Stop!"

"What?"

"I said stop."

"Or what? What are you going to do if I don't stop?" She took another swig from her glass and wiped her lips with the back of her hand. "You think you scare me? You think I'm intimidated by you or your threats? You stupid, weak woman, you couldn't keep hold of your bloody husband! You went all manic and depressive because women out there were giving him something you apparently weren't giving him!" The images of a broken, weepy pathetic Clarissa pouring her heart out, day after day, thinking she had an ally in her, made her smile and gave her a false sense of bravado.

Clarissa walked up to her and slapped her hard across her face, "I told you to stop! Watch your mouth around me! You were one of those women my *ex*-husband screwed remember? Or has the booze robbed you of your memory?" The images of a lying, back-stabbing friend who sat with her while she cried and poured her heart out then had one tryst after another with her husband, Neil, in tacky cheap hourly-rate motels filled her mind – she pushed them out of her mind. "I forgave you and kept quiet because our daughters have been friends for years and I didn't want them affected by you and your screwed up behaviour. So don't you dare, ever, speak to me in that manner woman or I will show you exactly what I can and will do! Have I made myself clear?"

"I'm sorry-"

"I'm not interested in your apologies. You may not care about your daughter but I care about mine, and I will not neglect her for yours. Their friendship ends! You work on your daughter, and I'll work on mine. Something isn't right with you, and something isn't right with Jessica, and I will not hold your daughter over mine. You may not give a toss about Jessica, but my children are a gift from God, and I will not back down on this, am I clear? Work on your daughter and I'll work on mine or everyone especially your psycho joke of a husband will know about you and Neil!"

"Okay, okay, I'll do it," Eloise said as a wave of fear and

nausea engulfed her and sobered her. With a shaking hand, she lifted her glass to her lips, drank some more of her Dutch courage, which had become a little lacklustre then stared at the back door Clarissa had slammed shut on her way out. She knew that she could probably end up in a body bag if her husband ever found out about the affair she had with Neil.

Her husband, Inspector Patrick Carmichael was the head of the UK Central Police Domestic Violence Unit. A job description and person specification as far away from his real character as East was from West. Why? Because Patrick Carmichael had a violent temper, was a wife-beater and made many of the men arrested by his unit for violent domestic crimes look like cherubs. He was careful; the residents of their posh cul de sac had never witnessed anything and the detached houses afforded confidentiality but somehow the neighbours knew (walls can't always contain the sounds of violence). Strangely, it was something that no one in his unit knew about, or, professed to know about. Eloise knew that if he ever found out about her indiscretion he would beat her up and put her in the hospital – dead or alive! He had put her in the hospital before for a crime less severe. It was a few years ago at her sister's wedding, she had had a little too much to drink and been a little too friendly with a man, a stranger, she had danced with him and in her husband's words 'rubbed her arse against the toerag's privates'. Members of her family watched in shocked horror as Patrick kicked, slapped and punched her like a madman with no fear of repercussion from the police. The police were called, but when they saw Patrick calmly drinking whisky and talking on his phone, no interviews were held, no notes were taken so obviously no report was filed.

With a shaking hand, Eloise lifted her glass to her lips then frowned, her glass was empty, her lackadaisical Dutch courage gone.

The Room

Unknown to them, the people in the room would soon be moving on to phase two. They had been in this phase, phase one, for some time now watching the lives they would have lived if they hadn't taken their own life, play before them on a screen. Soon they would be moved to phase two, a place much worse than where they currently were.

Unknown to the people in the room, there were four phases in total. Phase four was the worst phase – phase four was like hell.

CHAPTER 3

Neil R.T. Williams crossed then uncrossed his legs as he waited to be called into Dr Lincoln's office. He was early and had expected that being the celebrity he was the doctor would see him when he arrived but to his annoyance Neil was told, he would have to wait as the doctor was with a patient. Patience was not a virtue that Neil was familiar with. He considered himself a go-getter, a man who made things happen quickly – very un-akin to being patient. He took a deep breath as he lifted his right leg and let his ankle rest against his left knee. His right foot tapped nervously against his left knee like a woodpecker on a new branch.

The door opened, and a pretty, young, red-haired lady came out with a notepad in her hand. Neil's foot froze mid tap, he openly stared at her, as he did all attractive women. She blushed, she immediately recognised him. She had seen him in several movies and TV dramas.

"Dr Lincoln will see you now. I apologise that you had to wait. As I said on the phone when you called this morning, Dr Lincoln had an appointment with a patient who flew in from America yesterday. He tried, but couldn't reschedule her."

"Oh, that's fine, I don't mind waiting," Neil lied. "I haven't seen you here before, have you just started working here?"

"I don't work here I'm just helping my uncle out and getting some practical patient work experience for my MSc degree in Psychology." She told him.

"Your uncle?"

"Dr Lincoln is my mother's brother."

"Oh."

"He'll see you now, Sir."

Neil stood up and strode towards her. He stopped in front of her, produced a dazzling 'TV' smile and tilted his head seductively to one side. "Will you be here when I'm done?"

"No, I won't Sir."

"That's a real shame. What did you say your name was?"

"I didn't say."

"No, you didn't say, did you? So what's your name?"

"It's Gennifer, with a G."

"Genny with a G," he said, his voice low, teasing, almost seductively musical.

Embarrassed she coughed, "You can go through now Sir. Dr Lincoln is waiting in his office."

"Thank you Genny with a G," he said and headed towards the doctor's office.

Neil walked into Dr Lincoln's plush office. The doctor rose from behind his mahogany desk, walked towards Neil and welcomed him. They shook hands then both sat down facing each other. Dr Lincoln sat in his soft, dark brown leather armchair which his wife had bought for him as a graduation present fifteen years ago. He had moved offices three times, each time an upgrade and each time his armchair had been the first thing to be packed from the old office and the first thing settled within the new office; the rest of the furniture was always comfortably tossed around it. Neil sat in the leather two-seater and crossed his legs. He paid no attention to the art deco or beautiful view of the river Thames, which the large windows afforded. His eyes stared blankly at the cream coloured wall opposite him.

Dr Lincoln picked up a pen and notepad, "Neil, let's talk about you and what's going on with you. Why did you want this extra session today?"

Neil's thoughts left Genny with a G and wandered along empty corridors in his mind until it came back to the reason he was here. He took a deep breath then exhaled as sadness engulfed him. He suddenly sat forward in one fluid movement and appeared to be about to launch into dialogue but said nothing.

"Neil?"

Neil stared at Dr Lincoln blankly.

"Neil, what happened?"

"I had a date with Clarissa yesterday, and we talked about some of the things that occurred in the past. She said some things last night that shook me up." He paused and studied his hands. Moments passed.

"What did she say, Neil?" Dr Lincoln coaxed.

"She said that she didn't want our daughters to grow up thinking that they had to put up with someone like me, 'Crappy Men' she said, men who cheated and lied. She said no one, not even her worst enemy deserved to go through what she had gone through. She read somewhere or heard something about how daughters tended to go for men similar to their fathers, and she didn't want our daughters to have to suffer with a husband like me, the way she had suffered. She said that my selfish philandering actions didn't only break her heart but that it had broken Elle May's heart and broken Maddy's heart as well. It had destroyed the relationship between my family and her family. Our divorce meant that her family and my family were also divorced, disconnected, no longer family. She said she felt sorry for me because of people like my mother, brothers and sisters who could never tell me the truth and had failed me. She said they were scared of me as I was the primary breadwinner in the family and they all lived in a house I had bought. She said that they didn't care about me, or her, or our children, because whenever one of my brothers had a problem with a wife or girlfriend I always helped mediate. But when we had a problem not one of them spoke up or tried to help, that they were all a bunch of hypocrites who knew that my actions would leave me alone in my old age but hoped that I would die soon, so that they could get their hands on my money. She said I gave my siblings money and provided a place for them to live not because I loved them but to oppress them, and to get them to do what I wanted. When I tried to dismiss her accusations she asked if I remembered the time I didn't talk to my mother for over four years because of a family disagreement. And, how none of my siblings wanted to cross me so didn't intervene. And, how my mother had to plead with people to plead with me to accept her olive branch and talk to her. And, how in the end, it was only because she, Clarissa, had said that I had to be wicked and evil to put my mother through all the humiliation of having to plead with people to plead with me, that I eventually called my mother. She said that my siblings didn't love me, they just wanted what they could get from me and were scared of losing everything I had provided. She said she didn't hate them or me anymore, she just felt sorry for us and prayed that one day we would know and experience true love. She said she felt so sorry for the miserable couples she saw day after day and was so glad she no longer had to put up with me and the consequences of my behaviour." He stopped talking and stared at his hands, but the silence couldn't hide his words; his words stood in the room, naked, unembellished and demanding to be acknowledged. They made him uncomfortable and anxious.

"How did hearing *all* of that make you feel?"

"Honestly?"

"Yes, honestly Neil, no lights, no cameras, tell me how hearing that made you feel? It has obviously affected you."

"I feel like I'm the worst person in the World like I've harmed my children who I love. Like I'm the biggest loser in the World."

"What in particular makes you-?"

Neil jumped up cutting Dr Lincoln off, he walked to a window and looked out, "It's like the time I worked my arse off for a movie role. I starved myself for weeks, and I went to the gym and lost two stones. I shaved my hair off and gave one hundred and ten percent of my soul. I gave everything there was to give. I sacrificed my family – I missed family birthdays and school plays." He turned, excitement shone in his eyes. "The critics wrote reviews for weeks about my excellent, ground-breaking performance and said that I was sure to get the award for best supporting actor. My agent said I would get the award. He promised me that award . . ."

"Neil?"

"I had my acceptance speech in the breast pocket of my tuxedo. I'd rehearsed it so many times that I was word-perfect and time-proficient. You know, nominated actors say they don't mind when the award is given to another nominee, that isn't true, at least not for me. I minded! In my head that award was mine, it was sitting in my display cabinet. It was going ahead of me opening up doors of opportunities for bigger and better roles – it was everything! When I didn't get it, it was like I had nothing, I was empty!"

"And, the way you felt when you didn't get the award is the same way you felt when Clarissa told you what she did?"

"Yes!"

"Why?"

"Why do you think?"

"Neil, you know how this works, you have to tell me what you honestly think so that I can help you."

"I know, I know, I'm sorry."

"Tell me the truth."

Neil nodded, "During our marriage, Clarissa was loyal, reliable and completely dependent on me. You know she writes songs, right? Well, when I first met her she was Clarissa Stapleton, and she had already written some excellent songs, she had a couple of top ten hits, and she was studying Music and History at University. Clarissa had big dreams. She said her songs were going to change the World! But then it was only expected with her coming from the family she does; her father was a gifted, award-winning musician and singer, and her mother is so artistic, fashionable and talented. After we got married and she got pregnant she put her career on hold to work with me on mine. She put her big dreams on the back burner and stoked the embers of my dreams. As the years went by Clarissa took care of the girls and our home, and allowed me to do whatever I wanted. I got my strength from her dependence on me. The more dependent she was, the more I felt that I could do what I wanted. When she told me that she was completely over me, stronger without me and putting her and the girls first from now on. I felt like I had nothing, like I was weak, like I was empty. Clarissa was my safety net, someone I could always go back to when I messed up." Neil fell onto the couch and hunched forward then dramatically buried his face in his hands. "I'm empty. I'm so empty. I'm so full of emptiness. So heavy, so overly burdened with emptiness! What's the point of carrying on? I might as well end it. That'll make them regret not giving me the award! I could end it right now and be an icon! I could be a modern day 'James Dean' or a 'Kurt Cobain', I could go out on top. Lights dim but not dead, my movies would be watched again, and I could be nominated for awards posthumously."

Dr Lincoln observed him; he was used to Neil and his overly dramatic ways. He knew that there was a fragile line in Neil's mind separating his real life from his acting life and that sometimes the line became blurred and other times it simply faded into non-existence. He wrote some things down on the notepad then placed the pad on the table next to him and started on the journey of pulling Neil out of his current state of depression. He had an array of actors and singers as patients, he was good at his job and was highly sought after, but he had lost an actor a few years ago. The young man had been rejected for a movie role and went on a three-day binge of drugs and alcohol (self-medication for depression) and had been found dead in his apartment – contracts for two new movies were found in his unopened mail. The tragedy had affected Dr Lincoln more than he cared to admit. He focused on Neil, as he did with all his patients, now, determined never to lose another patient to what he called the evils of fickle fame, peer-pressured-prestige and un-solicitous-society, again.

CHAPTER 4

They worked together side by side. Flour scattered on top of the kitchen counter; chocolate chips, chocolate chunks and sugar intermingled with the flour. Elle mixed the muffin batter and hummed a song her mother had written a few years ago, and Clarissa sang the words. Elle tossed a couple of chocolate pieces into her mouth and fed her mother a piece. Clarissa smiled as the chocolate melted on her tongue.

"The cookies smell great. I love the smell of baking cookies."

"You love the smell of baking full-stop, Elle."

Elle smiled, "That is so true. How many muffins are we making?"

"Twelve, which should give us four each, unless someone I know decides to sneak more than her fair share."

"Who would do that?"

"Oh, I don't know, who do you think would do that Elle May? Who has a tendency of doing that Elle May?"

Elle smiled sheepishly at her mother. She loved making muffins and cakes and bread and savoury dishes (containing secret ingredients) with her mother. It was one of her favourite things to do. It filled her with anticipation of something exciting. Her mother would tell her to close her eyes when she made a pie or casserole and while Elle's eyes were closed she would add some secret herb or spice. Elle never knew what she added only that afterwards the dish would smell and taste like something out of this World. Elle carefully spooned the muffin batter into the twelve muffin cases then licked the wooden spoon.

Madeline Stapleton paid the taxi driver and thanked him as he helped her wheel her suitcase to the front door of her daughter's house. Madeline, a famous former model in the days before the supermodels were called supermodels, was a classical beauty. She was highly sought after for guest appearances on fashion segments for several daytime TV shows, and she was also a favourite judge on an American nationally syndicated fashion TV show. With all this, she still ran her own modelling agency and enjoyed her life to the fullest. She sighed contently as she fished her key out of her handbag and opened the front door quietly. Intent on surprising her family she wheeled her suitcase through the front door then quietly closed the door and tip-toed towards the front room. She looked inside and saw Maddy doing homework; she tip-toed towards the kitchen and looked inside. The sight of mother and daughter standing by the stove cooking brought a surge of warmth to her heart. It brought back memories of when Clarissa was young, and she used to have cooking/bonding sessions with her.

"I smell something good in here!" Madeline exclaimed as she walked into the kitchen and dropped her handbag onto a chair.

"Grandma!" Elle exclaimed and rushed over and threw herself into her grandmother's outstretched arms. "When did you get back from New York?"

"Hello sweetheart, I just got back. I was on my way home when I remembered that I don't have anything delicious in my fridge for dinner, so here I am. How's my little angel doing?"

"I'm okay Grandma, how are you? You look really nice, did you get your hair dyed?"

"I'm fine thank you darling, and in America, it's called colouring your hair not dying it. This colour is called Cool Gorgeous Grandma Auburn," she swept her head from side to side then puffed her hair up.

Elle giggled.

Clarissa rushed over and hugged her mother tightly, "Mum, I missed you! You look beautiful as usual."

"Thank you, dear. I missed you too. How are you?" She hugged her daughter tightly then released her and studied her.

Clarissa smiled warmly at her mother. They could pass for sisters, a thing her mother was very proud of. She knew her mother was checking to see if she was okay. "I'm really good Mum, really good. I like the highlights they suit you."

Madeline ran a hand through her hair, "Thank you, I think so too, I'm quite pleased with this new cut as well, it knocks off a few years don't you think?"
They both giggled.

"Grandma, guess what, Mum said she'd teach me how to make her special cottage pie next week. We're going to go out and get the ingredients from the farmers' market and then she's going to show me how to make it step by step!"

"That's great darling, but if my memory serves me well, she stole that recipe from me."

"Mum, I didn't steal it-"

"Did I give it to you Clarissa?"

"No, but I found out where you hide your recipes and copied it and added a few of my homegrown herbs and spices and-"

"There you go, it was stolen."

They all laughed. Three generations laughed warmly together.

"Grandma!" Maddy squealed, rushed over to the three of them and hugged her grandmother tightly.

"Hello Mademoiselle Maddy, how are you, sweetheart?"

Maddy stood back and bowed as accustomed, "I'm fine to thank you Grandmother, and may I enquire, how are you, Madam?"

"I'm very well thank you Mademoiselle Maddy," Madeline playfully curtsied, and Maddy bowed again. They asked a few more questions of each other and performed a few more dramatic curtsies and bows.
Clarissa and Elle looked on, both amused at the *Downton Abbey* like display of etiquette playing out before them. After a few moments, Clarissa edged Elle back towards the stove where the vegetables were nearly boiling over.

"Look Grandma look. Another tooth came out yesterday!" Maddy opened her mouth wide and showed her grandmother the gap where the tooth had once resided.

"Oh look, that is so cute."

"Grandma, may I speak to you in private please?" Maddy asked as a serious expression etched itself onto her face.

Clarissa and Elle looked at each other and frowned as Maddy pulled her grandmother over to a corner of the kitchen and spoke to her in a low voice, her hands moved in the air as she seemed to be describing something or some things. When she finished, she looked at her mother with a knowing smile then sauntered out of the kitchen.

"What did she say?" Clarissa asked her mother slightly puzzled.

"That is one of the wisest little negotiators I know. She asked me to have a quiet word with the tooth-fairy and ask if she can have £2 instead of £1 this time as the tooth that has recently fallen out is a big tooth and must weigh far more than the others which she previously got £1. She said that if I do this 'one thing' and she gets her asking price of £2, she will split the profit with me. She will give me 50p for my effort, and she will take £1.50. Did you notice all her little hand gestures?"

"Yes," Clarissa nodded.

"That was so cute. It was her emphasising how big the tooth is and how much she wants me to understand why she felt the need to ask this 'one thing' of me. Oh and she asked if I felt that the negotiation was fair as she wants to make sure that I'm happy with my cut because she feels that it is very very *very* fair."

Again three generations laughed warmly together.

Mother and daughter sat facing each other at the kitchen table. The girls were in bed, and the house was warm and peaceful. Donny Hathaway's version of *Song for You* played on the kitchen radio. A wine bottle sat in between two wine glasses. The bottle was three-quarters full – neither of the women were particularly heavy drinkers.

"I love this song, the piano riffs are amazing," Clarissa said as her fingers danced elegantly in time with the riffs.

Madeline smiled as she relaxed and listened to the song and her daughter sing along with Donny. The song ended, and she clapped – her daughter had a beautiful voice and each time she sang Madeline was reminded of her husband and his soft baritone voice.

"I missed you, Mum. I'm glad you're back."

"I'm glad I'm back too. Everyone asked about you and the girls, they all send their love. I had a fantastic time, I took a carriage ride in Central Park, I saw a play on Broadway with your Aunt Maxine, and I went on a day trip to Niagara Falls with your cousin Priscilla and her new husband."

"Sounds like you had an excellent time."

"I did, and you would have loved it, you know what, let's organise a trip over there when the girls are on a school break."

"I'd like that. The girls would too. I'll start arranging things then we can surprise them. The girls and I could catch up with all our family over there and maybe go and see Niagara Falls too. I've always wanted to see that, Elle and Maddy would love to see it too. You know every time we went to America I only did what Neil wanted, which was always something that would make him visible to directors, producers and casting agents, anything that would enhance his career. I never did what I wanted to do . . . well, that era is over now, and it's not just time for a change, it's time to live the change, time for change manifestation."

Madeline clapped her hands again, this time, more loudly and tears shone in her eyes.

"What?" Clarissa asked.

"In the words of the various diverse women in my church's

prayer group, 'You're there', 'You've arrived', 'You've landed'. Clarissa, my prayers have been answered, you're much stronger than you were before, sweetheart, and I'm glad. You've crossed that invisible line that so many women get stuck on; the *'I'm so lonely and bored, I'll put up with anything just to have my unfaithful unrepentant husband in my bed'*. Or, the women who say, *"It gets so cold at night, I need someone to keep me warm, anyone will do"*. I say to those women – Pray to God for His Will to be done in your life and while you wait, go get yourself a hot water bottle for the cold and a couple of good, intellectually stimulating books to read."

Clarissa laughed.

"Look at you – you look great, and you sound confident and happy. Remember when you said to me that you were all alone, and you had to take care of the girls by yourself? And that you had to take care of the house by yourself and manage the finances by yourself? And, make sure the girls got to the dentist for regular check-ups and all the other one-hundred-and-one things that you had to do when Neil first left?"

Clarissa nodded then frowned, "Why?"

"Remember what I said to you?"

She nodded again, "You said, 'So what's changed?'. I remember we were in the front room, and I had all these bills in my hand, and I was crying."

"You didn't understand what I meant at first, and I could see in your eyes that you thought I was cruel. What I meant at the time was that you already did all those things without Neil. He never helped you. You did everything, even though you made him believe that he did everything. You're a strong, beautiful woman, Clarissa, and I'm so proud of you. The way you've come out on top, gotten over your heartbreak and depression and the way you're bringing up Elle and Maddy to be confident young women. It makes me so proud!" Her voice broke, she sniffed and wiped away a tear that had started to roll down her cheek.

"Mum, I learned from the best, I learned from you. I know your prayers have kept me and the girls safe and strong. Thank you for being there for me when I lost myself when I . . ." her tears fell freely, she didn't wipe them away. "When I thought that I couldn't go on, you pushed me forward, supporting me along the way . . . Is this the wine talking or me?" She sniffed and wiped her tears with the back of her hand.

"It's the wine. You never could hold your alcohol."

They both smiled.

"I never really liked Neil. And, I hated the way he strung you along for months telling you that he was going to get a marriage counsellor to help iron out the problems in your marriage but only when he was ready to find one. Then he said it couldn't be a Christian counsellor but only one that he was comfortable with. For months he made false promises knowing full well that he had no plans of even looking for a marriage counsellor let alone making any appointments. He told you he didn't believe in divorce but refused to do anything to work things out because he was shacked up with one girlfriend and having it off with several others. He was committing adultery but had 'divorce' issues? Then in the middle of his coming and going he signs divorce papers without telling you so he could get engaged to that actress whose father produced his last movie. The cheek of that man! I read in a magazine in New York last week that she's dumped him because he was cheating on her." She sighed, "You know I always thought you should have married that medical student you dated when you first started university. Tall, dark brown hair, gorgeous piercing greyish eyes, cute smile and dimples. He was humble and had a great personality, I liked him."

"Steve Truman!" Clarissa exclaimed, slightly shocked that her mother still remembered him.

"Yes! He's probably Dr Steve Truman now. I remember when you first brought him round to meet us, I could see that he was so into you. He worshipped the ground you walked on.

The way he would lovingly call you '*Rissa*' and you would smile and light up like a Christmas tree. Only he could shorten your name and get away with it. Each time he came round, I would think to myself, 'Clarissa Truman, the doctor's wife'. You were so cute together. I used to watch and smile as you both finished each other's sentences. Or, you would say something cheeky, and he would reply or vice versa. Or you would say something, and he would repeat it word for word but make it sound different, sort of complementary to your words. What was it your dad used to call that?"

"Counter-saying," Clarissa murmured.

"That's right, counter-saying! You know I always thought he was the one for you, and that he would take care of you and put up with your musical mentality-"

"Mum-"

"Then one day Neil R.T. Williams showed up like a bad penny with his bleached blond hair and sinisterly handsome face that couldn't hold a sincere emotion . . . but you know what?" She waved her hand dramatically, "All is not lost. You have two beautiful well-grounded girls and for that, I tolerate Neil, although I have to state the obvious, Elle and Maddy both clearly take after *our* side of the family."

Clarissa giggled. She sat back and listened to her mother reminisce some more. She was glad her mother was here. She knew that she would only spend a couple of nights with them then she would return to her own home where memories of Clarissa's late father would be waiting.

Forty minutes later Clarissa bid her mother goodnight and watched as she walked towards the guest bedroom on the ground floor. She washed the wine glasses and put the unfinished bottle of wine away. She turned as something on the table caught her eye. She smiled, picked up the £1 and two 50p pieces her mother had left on the kitchen table, turned off the light and headed upstairs towards Maddy's room.

As Clarissa got ready for bed believing both her daughters to be sound asleep, Jessica was bombarding Elle with text messages.

Jessica 00:10
√ Why can't you come to my house tomorrow? Want to give you a necklace.

Elle 00:12
√ B'cos I want to spend time with my family. I told you my Gran is back from her hols. Plus don't want your necklace, got my own necklaces.

Jessica 00:12
√ Okay forget necklace!!! I need to talk to you. What about me?

Elle 00:14
√ What about you? Why don't you stop drinking and talk to your mum?

Jessica 00:14
√ Y'know I can't talk to her, plus she's drunk again

Elle 00:16
√ I'm not coming round tomorrow

Jessica 00:17
√ Please and pretty please, I need you to come here – girl power

Elle 00:19
√ Nope

Jessica 00:20

√ Why do you have to be such a cow??

Elle   00:21
√ Still not coming over – Mooo. You can come over here if you want to.

Jessica   00:22
√ I can't your mum hates me, she wants to keep us apart.

Elle   00:23
√ My mum doesn't hate you. She doesn't like you calling her by her name, so stop it cos it's rude.

Jessica   00:23
√ Yes she does hate me, my mum said that you and I need to spend some time apart. Where did that come from if not your mum!

Elle   00:24
√ My mum just wants me to get serious with my piano lessons. She thinks I'm good

Jessica   00:25
√ LOL, you are so rubbish at playing the piano Elle. She just wants to control u, come over to my house instead!

Elle   00:27
√ No

Jessica   00:28
√ Aww, r u upset cos I said u r rubbish ☺

Elle   00:30
√ Since when did what you say matter

Jessica   00:30
√ Be like that then

Elle   00:31
√ Okay I will

Jessica   00:32
√ Oh get lost

Elle   00:34
√ Stop texting, u r getting on my nerves now

Jessica   00:34
√ Why can't you come over???

Elle   00:36
√ Read text I sent mins ago dummy. G'night, turning phone off now zzzzZZZZ

Elle switched off her phone.

'Bitch' Jessica thought but didn't dare text her thought to Elle. At fourteen, Jessica was smart enough to know that Elle was not only her best friend; she was one of her only few non-virtual friends.

CHAPTER 5

Conference Room, Large Bookshop in Oxford Street, London

"Mrs Lewis, there are nearly two hundred people in the conference room waiting for you, are you ready?" The bookshop's posh divisional manager asked, interrupting Anna's soliloquy. He studied the attractive woman, whose head was bent; dark, luxurious curls framed her tanned, pretty face. She opened her eyes and looked at him, and he felt his breath catch at the back of his throat as he stared at her un-matching eyes. One eye was greenish brown and the other a bright greenish blue, he was unsure if they were real or contact lenses and even though he had read that she had heterochromia iridum (mismatched eyes), seeing them in the flesh took his breath away.

Anna Lee Lewis nodded then opened the gold locket which hung from a chain around her neck. She looked at the picture of her late mother enclosed and smiled. "I'm ready," she said, pushed her curly hair to one side and walked to the conference room with firm, confident steps.

"First of all, I want to thank you all for coming today, and I also want to say, no matter what you've read or heard about me, unlike the little boy in that movie – I don't see dead people," Anna told her audience.

Some people in the room laughed, others stared openly at her, not sure what to expect.

"My name is Anna Lee Lewis, I was born and raised in Chicago, I co-founded the charity Talk To Someone, known more commonly as TTS, four years ago with my husband. We work closely with counsellors, psychiatrists, doctors and other healthcare workers all over the World," she paused and looked around the room at her audience. It was usually at this point she was able to judge potential reactions and work out what she would say and how she would phrase what she would say – from the look of expectation (or lack of it) on the faces of her audience. "I co-founded Talk To Someone with my husband shortly after I read about a sixteen-year-old girl who was bullied because she went on a date with a classmate's cousin who already had a girlfriend. The persistent bullying instigated by the girlfriend was so severe and brutal and when she couldn't bear the pain it caused her anymore she somehow managed to get hold of one of her grandfather's handguns, shot herself in the head and died. This happened in a town in Connecticut in America. The girl's name was Tammy, and she was a beautiful girl who had her whole life in front of her but, unbeknown to her parents, she was in so much pain she felt that she couldn't continue with her life. I never knew Tammy when she was alive. I never met her parents when she was alive. I knew nothing about her until she died. Then something happened . . ."

"What?" Someone asked.

"What happened?" Another person asked.

"What happened was Tammy started talking to me in my dreams two days after she died," Anna said.

"What?" Some of the people gasped, some shivered and others continued to stare openly at her.

"But, you just said you don't see dead people," a man said.

"I don't see dead people. I hear dead people. And, Tammy wasn't the first dead person to talk to me." Anna replied.

Department of History & Cultural International Studies, University of London

Several students rushed into the DHCIS building. They weren't late, but they wanted to get a place near the front to sit and hoped that the lecture theatre wouldn't be packed like it was the last time. The last time so many students turned up for the lecture and due to a lack of space, a lot of students were refused entry.

*

The lecture theatre *was* packed. The striking lecturer, Dr Peter Durojaiye Lewis smiled to himself as he set his papers down. He thanked his assistant and took the remote control from him. His dark eyes twinkled as he looked at the students; some he had never seen before, and he realised that word had spread about the shocking nature of this lecture. He pressed a button on the remote control. A picture of a dead baby boy appeared. The baby had a cut on the side of his face, a mark inflicted by a native doctor after his death. The picture was thirty years old but still had the power to shock people. The students in the lecture theatre gasped.

"As I've said in the past, there are many cultures in the World where superstitious beliefs rule peoples' minds and actions. This picture was taken in South America. The family of this child believed that the child was a reincarnated child, a child who had been born many times and died many times. A child sent by evil spirits to bring misfortune to the family because of a family curse or something that someone in the child's family had done wrong."

"Is that similar to what people in Nigeria call Abiku?" Jumoke Daniels asked.

"What do you know about Abikus, Jumoke?" Dr Lewis asked her.

"My mother is Nigerian, and she used to say that they were children who died early, I think she said before they were teenagers and that their mother would get pregnant again and give birth to them again, and the cycle would repeat itself. It was a bad omen if this happened in a family as people associated it with witchy-witchy, a curse or plain evilness."

Dr Lewis smiled, "Witchy-witchy, I haven't heard that phrase in a long time. Your mother was right Jumoke. Abiku is a Yoruba word. For those of you who don't know, the Yoruba people are located mainly in the south western region of Nigeria, a country located in West Africa. Abiku means one predestined to death. It is derived from two words, *abi* – something that possesses and *iku* – death. Some say that Abiku refers to the spirits of children who die before they reach puberty. In the Igbo language, these children are known as Ogbanje aka children who come and go. They are in and out of peoples' lives causing pain and misfortune, they deliberately die and then come back only to die again. Some people believed that evil spirits or *Iyi-uwa* plagued the family. These evil spirits were strategically placed and served as a portal, which allowed these children to come and go."

"How often did these children come and go?" A male student asked, his pen poised, ready to write the answer down.

"As often as they were allowed to," Dr Lewis answered.

"Who allowed them to come and go?" The male student promptly asked.

"It wasn't so much as who allowed them to come and go as how people stopped them from coming and going. As you can see in this picture, the child has a mark on his face. It was believed that when the child died if a visible mark was made on the child, the child would not be able to leave the World of the dead and return to the World of the living. Some parents were so stigmatised and traumatised by events that they went as far as mutilating their dead child to stop them coming back again." He pressed the button on the remote several times and each time allowed a few moments of digestion for each of the pictures on the screen to tell their own story. Silence and gasps were the only sounds heard. After the tenth picture, he looked at the students and waited for their questions.

"I don't understand. Why would marking or mutilating the child stop the child from coming back?" Jordan, a third-year Sociology student, asked.

"It was believed that only unmarked children, children with no markings on their skin, could be reborn. I don't have all the answers, but I have read that in several cultures it is said that children can only be born if they are unmarked."

"Are these markings the same as birthmarks?" Ken, a medical student asked, his stethoscope hanging proudly.

"No, birthmarks are skin discolorations, which at times can be linked to melanin issues or other pigmentation issues. The markings I'm talking about are physical indents in the skin."

"Are they linked to disabilities?" Jumoke asked.

"No," Dr Lewis quickly answered. He had ventured on that road before and did not want to go along it now as it had taken nearly two hours of intense discussions to extrapolate himself from the questions and counter-questions that had arisen the last time. He had somewhere he needed to be in less than an hour. "Research has shown that birth-disabilities have nothing to do with these markings, a child born with Down's syndrome or some other genetic disorder has nothing to do with Abikus."

"So a marked child can never be reborn?" A female student asked.

"No, some children have been born with a mark on their skin which was identical to the mark given to the dead baby that preceded them."

"What?" The female student whispered.

"Watch this," he said in answer to her whispered question and the questions he saw on faces looking at him. He pressed the button on the remote and a short film played on the screen. It showed several children of various heritages with their faces blacked out but all having various marks on a part of their bodies which their parents said that they were not only born with but which had been inflicted on an older dead sibling of the child. One mother, clutching a photo of her dead child in her hand, said that her new baby smiles just like her dead child used to smile. Another said that her toddler always sits in the corner of the kitchen and plays with invisible friends – talking to them and sharing his food with them – just like his brother, now dead, did before him.

Dr Lewis waited for the final clip then nodded for his assistant to turn the lights back on. "The reason I find this topic interesting is that my father was said to be an Abiku and, as the child of an Abiku, superstition, which I don't believe, says that I have access to the world of the dead, a world that not everyone has access to."

"What?" Jordan said.

Dr Lewis removed the cufflink from his left shirt sleeve, rolled it up and revealed a mark on his forearm. "My mother said I was born with this mark on my arm. My father has a similar mark. One of his names is *Durojaiye,* which means *'stay to enjoy life'* in Yoruba and is also my middle name. My mother miscarried three pregnancies and had three stillbirths before I was born. She said because my father was an Abiku, the evil spirits didn't want him to have a child because that child would know their secrets and reveal them to the World."

"Dr Lewis, are you saying that you're the child of an Abiku?"

"I'm saying that my middle name depicts certain things, this mark on my arm also suggests that what they depict might be true, but I'm not a superstitious person." He decided to end his lecture by playing with their minds. "My names were given to me; I didn't choose them. Am I the child of an Abiku also known as an Ogbanje? I don't know. I want you to do some research and tell me what you think. Let me know your findings based on what I've said. For those of you who are actually taking my course, I want a two-page report on Friday the thirteenth, ladies and gentlemen. And on that note, I need to get to a bookshop in Oxford Street so I don't end up with some spousal-inflicted-marks, before our next class," he joked.

Some of the students laughed others stared at him, unsure if he was what he had just implied he might be.

CHAPTER 6

Conference Room, Large Bookshop in Oxford Street, London

After an hour and a half of talking to her audience, Anna had opened the floor up to a question and answer session. The questions were coming fast and furiously.

"Is it true that people who talk about wanting to die by suicide are only seeking attention and don't try to kill themselves?"

Anna shook her head, "No, people who talk about wanting to die by suicide often do go on to kill themselves. Psychiatrists say that when people talk about it, it is often a cry for help and people shouldn't ignore this cry because some people are actually looking for a way forward, a way through their pain without dying."

"Does suicide always occur without any warning signs?"

"There are almost always warning signs, we just need to know what to look out for in people," Anna replied. "You'll be surprised at the number of parents I've spoken to who've said that they were completely blindsided, they didn't see it coming. Parents who've stated that they were completely shocked and distraught at their child's unprecedented action of suicide. Then you ask them a few pertinent questions, and you find out that their son or daughter had started locking themselves in their bedroom and had not been communicative for weeks before their death. Or the child had been depressed for weeks then suddenly became happy, which is usually when they've devised a plan to kill themselves, or a child suddenly starts to give away his or her most prized and treasured possessions. A mother would look back on her intuition and say:

'I knew that something wasn't right.
I felt that something was up, but I didn't know what it was'."

"But surely if someone is intent on killing himself there is nothing you can do to stop him, or are you saying there is?" A man asked.

Anna thought for a few moments, "Yes, I'm saying that suicide can be prevented. Most people who are suicidal do not want to die. You have to understand; it takes a lot for someone to think that there is no way out of their situation, usually they are in so much pain, and they just want their pain to stop."

"Anna . . . , I'm sorry Mrs Lewis, I'm sorry, do I call you Anna Lee or Mrs Lewis? I'm sorry I'm really nervous," the lady said, her hands were clenched, and her feet tapped nervously on the floor.

"Please, call me Anna."

She took a deep breath then exhaled, "Anna, my fiancé killed himself last year. He got into so much debt trying to pay for our wedding. Kieran . . . that is . . . that was . . . his name wanted me to have a fairytale wedding. He never told me how much money he owed. He never told me that he'd lost his job and that he had debt collectors threatening him. I thought we were so close, and I thought that nothing could shake us. But Kieran didn't tell me a thing about what was going on or how much trouble he was in," she started to shake. The woman who sat next to her put an arm around her and said something in her ear. "I'm fine Mum," she said to the woman then turned to Anna, "There were no signs. I didn't see anything different. I didn't notice any changes."

"I am so sorry for your loss. What's your name?"

"Sandra, um . . . my name is Sandra Nixon."

"Sandra, you said you didn't notice anything different about him-"

"Nothing at all," she shook her head vehemently.

"Did you used to call him at work?"

"Yes, I used to call him every day, why?"

"Did he ever tell you to stop calling him on his work number or to call him on his cell phone – sorry his mobile phone?"

"Yes, two weeks or so before he died he said that he was busy and not always at his desk, he asked me to call him on his mobile but only if it was urgent, why? How did you know that he told me to do that?"

"Prior to him telling you only to call his mobile, was that normal?"

"Normal? In what way?"

"How long had he worked for his company?"

"About three years."

"Had he ever, in the time you were together, asked you to do that?"

She thought for a few moments, "No, never, he always used to insist that I call him on his work number during his lunch break because sometimes there was no reception on his mobile phone. He used to joke and say that it was the only way he could get through the rest of the day and that he wouldn't take one step further into the day unless I called him. Oh my goodness! That was it! I should have seen it, I was so engrossed with the wedding arrangements, I should have seen it!" She gasped and choked back her sobs at the same time.

"Calm down Sandra, please calm down sweetheart," her mother said as she gathered her sobbing daughter to herself.

Anna tried to move forward to comfort Sandra but found that she couldn't, for some reason her limbs seem to fail her. She felt a sudden chill then she felt the presence of something strange. Her mouth went dry, and her vision became heightened way beyond anything she had ever experienced before. By the time she was able to lift her head and look at the back of the room to where her eyes were drawn she was shaking.

"Are you okay?" She heard someone ask.

"Mrs Lewis, are you okay?"

Anna looked at the back of the room, the little girl dressed in a white dress, bright red woollen hat and matching scarf looked back at her. Anna noted that she was there but not all there physically. She wasn't an apparition, but she seemed to be there and then not there. Anna was scared. She knew that everyone was staring at her, and she couldn't understand why they weren't looking at the little girl who was emitting enough light to draw everyone's attention.

"Mrs Lewis," the divisional manager of the bookshop took hold of her arm, "Mrs Lewis, are you okay? You look like you've just seen a ghost," he joked.

"Who's that little girl over there? What's she doing here?" Anna asked him.

He turned, he looked around the room. He didn't see a little girl, "What girl? I can't see a little girl plus this meeting is only for adults so there aren't any children here. Guests were specifically asked not to bring any children today. I can assure you this is one of the many branches I oversee, and I run a very tight ship."

Confused, she looked at him for a few moments then turned and pointed, "She's right there." She froze; the little girl and the bright light were gone.

CHAPTER 7

Dr Peter Lewis walked into the conference room and saw a man holding his wife's arm and talking to her. He saw the look of fear on his wife's face which she was trying desperately to conceal. With slight trepidation, he walked up to them and turned his wife round to face him, "Anna, what is it?"

"Peter, thank God you're here. I just . . . I just saw a vision of a little girl, she was standing over there, and there was this bright light around her," she whispered then collapsed against him. He held her close. He could feel her shaking.

A short time later
"Ladies and gentlemen, my wife is not feeling well and will not be able to continue with this conference. She is aware that some of you have come a long way to be here today and has asked me to continue on her behalf and answer whatever questions you might still have. My name is Dr Peter Lewis, and I co-founded TTS with Anna some years ago."
Completely ill at ease, Dr Peter Lewis rubbed his forehead nervously as he tried to make the transition from university lecturer mode to conference speaker mode. "*Suicidium* is a Latin word from which *sui caedare* is taken from, which means to kill oneself or the act of intentionally causing one's own death. World organisations estimate that each year approximately one million people die from suicide. These organisations have said that in the last 45 years suicide rates have increased by 60% Worldwide, and it is among the three leading causes of death among 15-44-year-old men and women. In the UK over 6000 people committed suicide in 2014 and the numbers increased in 2015. Studies have shown that mental health disorders such as depression as well as substance abuse are associated with some cases of suicide."
He looked at the faces wearing frowns and coughed as he

realised that he had lost some people along the way as he quoted facts to them. "You know what, I'm going to take my lecturer hat off and stop reeling out points and trying to define words. It might be a better idea if you ask me questions, and I answer them."

"Will Anna be okay?" Sandra asked.

"She'll be all right, thank you."

"She was in the middle of telling me that there must have been some signs I didn't see before my fiancé killed himself. I told her that Kieran asked me to call him on his mobile and not on his office number a couple of weeks before . . . he died."

"There are usually always signs, but some are so subtle that they can easily get missed among the hustle and bustle of life. It's the people left behind who suffer when someone dies. The suffering is escalated when someone commits suicide because you always wonder if there was something you could have done to prevent it. Something you could have said or something you shouldn't have said that could have given them fifteen minutes to think things over and change their mind. Your fiancé made a choice that didn't involve your input. It was something he chose to do. There may have been several signs. There may have been only one sign but don't replay things, don't look for what you missed because the guilt will destroy you and the unanswered questions will paralyse you."

Slowly, still struggling with the unwanted answers, Sandra nodded, "Okay."

"Why did you just mention fifteen minutes?" A man with a nervous twitch asked, his eyes glued to Dr Lewis.

"You've heard of fifteen minutes of fame, well some psychiatrists believe that it takes just fifteen minutes to 'talk someone down from a suicide ledge'. They've compiled a series of questions which they've found engages the person on the brink of suicide and can pull them back."

"And this works?"

"Some studies have been published online. Log on to the TTS website, have a look at them. See what you think."

The man wrote something down. "Thank you, I will."

"Dr Lewis, is it true that people who commit suicide make several attempts?"

"Studies have shown that some people have attempted suicide as many as twenty times before they eventually kill themselves. On the other hand, some people die at their first attempt."

"Why do people say that only crazy people attempt suicide?"

"I don't know why people say that, and I'm not going to say that some people who commit suicide are not crazy. A lot of studies have shown that some people are in so much pain they probably have a chemical imbalance in their brain. What I've learnt over the years is that some suicidal people do not want to die; they're in so much pain and just want their pain to stop by any means necessary."

"What do you mean?"

"A teenage boy being bullied who feels that there is nowhere to turn. He thinks his father will look at him as a wimp for not standing up to the bullies, and his mother won't understand. She'll just march down to the school and embarrass him in front of everyone and give the bullies more ammunition to use against him. A middle-aged woman drops her children at school, cleans her house, pays all the outstanding bills then takes a rope and hangs herself. A beautiful teenage girl breaks up with her boyfriend and is so distraught she poisons herself. A thirty-something-year-old woman breaks up with her partner and sets herself on fire, burning 80% of her body – she lived for a week in excruciating pain before she died. A teenage girl gets involved with a man via the internet, a man she thought was a teenage boy. A man who calculatingly grooms her. When she finds out that the private 'revealing' pictures she has sent to him have been displayed online, she becomes so ashamed. Some other events occur in her life, and she kills herself. Those are all real stories. All those things happened, and they are still going on in one form or another now. The list of names of people who have committed suicide is getting longer and longer. We can no longer sit back and let it continue to grow. We have to stop this from continuing to happen!"

"Is it true that you should never ask people who are suicidal if they're thinking about suicide, or if they have thought about a method because talking about it will give them the green light to go ahead with it?"

"No, that's a myth which needs to be exposed as a myth. In fact, asking a person if they're thinking about suicide does not give them the green light to go ahead with it. It is important to talk about suicide with people who are suicidal because you will learn more about their mindset and intentions, and allow them to see things from another perspective," Dr Lewis replied.

"Is it true that people who are suicidal do not seek help?"

"Many people who are suicidal do reach out for help and many don't. Sometimes it takes an expert to really see beneath the projected layers, and when that expert is not available, things get missed. People are busy and might not see things until it's too late. That's why we set up TTS. It's a safe-haven for those who reach out for help. We make that help available through our staff and various organisations."

"Everyone has good days and not-so-good days. So what are the exact symptoms of depression and how do you help someone who is depressed to the extent of suicide?"

"I listened to a CD lecture once, and the doctor talked about something called the dot test. They take a clean sheet of paper and mark it with a dot, and then ask the person to look at it. He said that usually the depressed person will only see the dot and focus on the dot, but everyone else will see a clean sheet of paper with a dot on it. Depressed people focus on negatives, and everyone else focuses on positives. Taking this literally and using things in everyday life, talk to the person and see from their response how they're feeling. If they're tending to feel down, negative, over-emotional, sad, disappointed for reasons that they can't explain. Or if they can explain them but the reasons don't seem reasonable then they could be depressed, and the way to help them is by getting them to talk to someone before that depression goes undetected, untreated and leads to suicide."

"What if you can't relate to someone who's depressed?"

"You don't have to relate to them, all you have to do is try to help them. You may not understand what they're going through just try to understand that they're going through something. Don't be judgemental because that only causes them to shut down and camouflage and tell you what you want to hear. Listen to them. Talk to them. And, if you can't do that, call TTS. People are manning the phones at TTS 24 hours a day, every day of the week, who can talk to them. They are in thousands of locations and can physically get to people quickly and talk them out of committing suicide. They can help them through whatever it is they're going through any time of the day. TTS works with patients as well as families and friends of the patients."

"What about when someone has an illness, and they want to go out on their own terms instead of being sick and a nuisance to their loved ones?"

"I um . . . .," Dr Lewis hesitated.

"What about when they think that suicide is the only solution and a way that will see they die in good health, while they still have their wits about them?"

Again he hesitated then decided to continue. "Something happened in my family a few years ago, and I'm not going to make any excuses, I'm just going to tell you what happened. I had a cousin who was a footballer, and he was doing really well. He got signed to a premiership club at a young age, and everyone in the family was so proud of him. He went for a routine check-up for insurance purposes, and they found some tumours. It was completely unexpected. He never got sick. Long story short, I was in America when I got a phone call from my mum to say he had killed himself. My whole family was distraught. During the autopsy, they found the tumours, but when they ran some tests, they concluded that they were all benign. My cousin was just twenty years old. He had his whole life ahead of him. He killed himself because he wanted to go out on his terms. He thought he was going to die, but the tumours were operable and wouldn't have killed him if they weren't removed," he paused as he struggled with his emotions. "He wanted to go out on his terms, but his terms didn't come with all the facts. I don't know what hurt his parents the most, his lack of faith in God or his lack of faith in them. Faith that they loved him and would do anything for him take care of him and love him regardless of what he had or didn't have. We don't know what tomorrow will bring, and we don't know what new drugs are out there that can help. In this life, we need to have faith. I don't see dead people. And, I don't hear dead people. But, I've been woken up on many nights to hear Anna talking in her sleep and nine out of ten of those times, she's trying to console a person who is trapped in a room watching their life play on a screen. The life that they could have had if they hadn't killed themselves and those are on good days. Sometimes the people she talks to are watching the people they left behind suffering and other times they can actually feel the pain they've caused. From what I've heard, when these people die, their pain doesn't stop. Unresolved pain doesn't go away when they die, like matter, it just gets transferred!"

Anna tossed and turned as she slept on a settee in a side room of the bookshop. She could see fish swimming on a wall and the little girl she had seen earlier reaching out to her, asking her for something with silent words. Her heart pounded in fear as she tried to move forward. Her feet were rooted to the spot, and the girl seemed to be moving further and further away. It was as if she were floating backwards. Anna saw the girl's lips moving, but she couldn't hear what she was saying. Her heart was pounding so loudly she thought it would explode. "No," she called out, "wait, don't go, who are you, what do you want from me?" Then she heard words that made her heart freeze.

"Help me. Please help me! Help me to help them!"

CHAPTER 8

Elle and Maddy sat at the piano playing one of their mother's compositions that had once been voted 'Best Song used in a TV commercial'. Elle led while Maddy stayed two or three notes behind. They smiled at each other and shoved each other lovingly as they played. Maddy tried to catch up, but Elle played faster moving ahead of her. Maddy giggled as Elle missed a note and tried again to play faster but again Elle picked up speed and stayed a few notes ahead. They played to the end then Elle gave a count to three, and they started the song together, this time, Elle playing upper keys and Maddy playing the lower keys.

Clarissa listened to her daughters as they played, she smiled. Her babies were growing up. Each morning when she woke up and every night before she went to bed she was thankful, and she prayed for her girls. She prayed that they would grow up to be better than her and achieve more than her and marry the right men (never experience separation or divorce) and be so happy. Be so happy that each day they woke up and each night before they went to bed, they would be thankful and pray for their own children to be better than them and achieve more than them and marry the right people and be so happy.....

Clarissa listened as Elle and Maddy played another song then the music stopped.

"Okay enough warm-up you need to practice your recital now Maddy," Elle said as she moved further along the piano stool and allowed her sister greater access to the keyboard. "How many weeks do you have before the big recital day?"

"Six weeks and that Rebecca Marshall thinks that she's the best piano player in the class, she's mean to us, and she won't let Miss talk, and sometimes she gets obscene. Do you think I should do something, Elle?"

"No, let your teacher deal with her, you concentrate on learning your piece and kicking Rebecca's arse by being magnificent. We Stapleton-Williams girls need to use our brains, let the bad guys fall into their own pits!"

"Yeah! Yeah!" Maddy snarled as she jumped up and high-fived her sister.

Elle smiled, she knew her sister so well. She knew that she was trying to avoid practising, "Down girl, I mean sit down and practice your piece."

"Oh, okay Elle," Maddy replied unable to hide her reluctance. Her little fingers hovered over the keys briefly. Then she started to play.

Elle turned caught her mother's eyes and winked. They both knew Maddy didn't like practising for recitals; she loved playing the piano undirected, she loved playing from her heart, *'making music from my heartstrings'* was what she called it.

The phone rang.

Clarissa quickly picked up the receiver, "Hello," she answered.

"Hello Clarissa, can I speak to Elle please?"

Clarissa cringed and frowned; she clenched her fists tightly to stop herself from getting angry, "Jessica, Elle is busy right now helping Maddy with a piano recital she has to play at school. I'll get her to call you when she's done."

"Thank you, Clarissa," Jessica said sweetly.

"Jessica, I've spoken to you about this before, and I've spoken to your Mother, can you not address me as Clarissa. I'm not one of those liberal mothers, and I'd prefer if you called me Miss Stapleton or Mrs Williams."

"Oh yeah, you did mention that didn't you, sorry I forgot. But . . . technically you're not Mrs Williams anymore, are you? Anyway, can you make sure Elle calls me back, thank you," Jessica said then hung up.

Clarissa took a deep breath then exhaled, replaced the receiver and marched into the kitchen fuming.

"Who was that on the phone?" Her mother asked noting the

suppressed anger on her daughter's face.

"It was Jessica Carmichael. She wants Elle to call her back. She had the audacity to call me Clarissa even though I've specifically asked her not to. She can be so rude sometimes, and she's just like her mother, she drinks like a fish-"

"What? How old is she again?"

"Fourteen, she's only four months older than Elle, but sometimes I think she's forty-something."

"She's probably seeking attention, but I'd separate the girls if you think she's a bad influence on Elle. You know my thoughts on putting someone else's child over your own. Children are a blessing. They don't ask to be born, but they do deserve to be loved. Love your own child, and then you can love other children."

"I find it so hard to like her let alone love her-"

"Why don't you start by praying about the situation. You know I never really understood why you and Lady Eloise Carmichael were friends, you're so different. She's such a prima-donna, and you're so realistically realistic."

"Praying?" Clarissa asked as she dipped her finger in the sauce her mother was cooking and tasted it. "Ummm, that's so good."

"Yes, praying. Remember, troubles can be compared to big mountains and big mountains started off as little hills in 'prayer-less' environments once upon a time."

"Dad used to say that," she smiled, "you're right Mum but what about Elle?"

"Separate the girls, pray for Elle not to miss their friendship and get her to hang out with some of her other friends."

"Okay, I'll do it."

"Good, dinner is ready, get the girls, I'll set the table."

Jessica   22:05

√ Why haven't you called Elle? I asked your mum to tell you

to call me. I've called your mobile so many times! Call me!!!

Jessica   22:20
√ Are you avoiding me Elle, I've called you a million times!!!

Jessica   22:25
√ Did you get my text messages? Answer your bloody phone or text me!!!

Jessica   22:27
√ I've called you so many times, answer your bloody f---ing phone!!

23:36
Elle reached for her mobile phone in her bedside drawer to set her alarm and give Jessica a quick call. Her mother had told her that Jessica had called earlier when she was helping Maddy. She saw that she had 14 missed calls and 4 text messages from Jessica. Elle read the last text and frowned, she was sick of Jessica's swearing and aggressiveness. She turned her phone off and put it back in the drawer. After reading the last text message, she had no intention of calling Jessica back tonight or receiving any more calls/text messages from her.

CHAPTER 9

Unable to sleep, very drunk and infuriated because Elle hadn't called her back, Jessica rifled through some papers she had taken out of the secret desk compartment. She kept the compartment locked and the key to unlocking it hidden in a pendant on a chain around her neck. She glanced at the papers as she desperately looked for one in particular. She read words like, *'Death is a friend of mine'* and *'We're going to leave this World on our terms when the time is right for us'*. They made her smile as did the gothic-like art that surrounded the words. These words usually gave her comfort in her sobriety pending the time she could get hold of a drink. She found the paper she sought, relief flooded through her, igniting her nerves and sending her pulse racing; she clasped it to her chest for a few moments. She turned her iPod on, selected a song then clambered onto her bed. She closed her eyes momentarily absorbing into her soul what can only be described as morbid, death-like music. Chanting embraced and caressed the music as it spewed out from the speakers. Each syllable seemed to conjure up spirits, evil and agile spirits that pandered to her mental state of mind – they danced to the music, decadence rife. Her heart beat faster as the chanting picked up a pace and the music became almost maniacal-like. Jessica swayed this way and that, her eyes rolled backwards in her head. She felt herself floating higher and higher.

The banging on her bedroom door served as a light in the dark bringing Jessica back to shore. It severed the hand of darkness which had taken hold of her with its fierce grip and had pulled her to a place she had not ventured to before. The banging persisted. Jessica's eyes snapped open, and she turned to the door thinking it was her mother, "WHAT?" She shouted.

"Turn that bloody demonic music down!" Inspector Patrick Carmichael shouted back in response.

"Sorry Daddy, turning it down now," Jessica said as she turned the volume down. She waited until she heard him close his bedroom door then sat and read the words on the sheet of paper in her hand, savouring each word as a desert plant would morning dew:

Shy boy 1: Had a hell day today, feel like shit. Got bullied at school, can't tell anyone.

I'm Unhappy: No one understands, no one cares, I hate pretending that everything's okay when everything isn't okay.

Unhappy 2: I hate that too. My dad is having another affair and my mum is in denial again. She keeps shouting at everyone ☹. We pretend we don't know what's going on and I hate it.

G-N: I hate that, why can't your mum deal with him and give everyone else a break?

Unhappy 2: I wish she would but she won't ☹.

Li-sa 5: I hate everything and everyone, my school is full of bitchy girls and I want out of everything. The cutting isn't working anymore. I don't feel the release I used to feel. I need to escape the pain cos it's driving me mad.

Shy boy 1: I hear you Li-sa 5, I need to end things soon, can't take much more.

Unhappy 2: How are you going to do it?

Shy boy 1: Fly off a bridge, go out in style.

Li-sa 5: Someone's knocking on my door; I bet it's my mum's boyfriend trying to cop a feel again. I wish I could kill him then myself.

Shy boy 1: Why don't you? Kill him then you can leave this world feeling good about something!

Jessy James 6: My mum's sloshed again, she really embarrassed me in front of my best friend. She is crap. I hate her. I wish I was dead. I want to die!!!

Unhappy 2: Don't worry JJ6, we'll get there soon. We're all going to get out of this world, on our terms and to hell with everyone else ☺ UREDRUMU!!!

"There's something not right with her," Eloise said to her husband as soon as he closed their bedroom door. "She's been locking herself in her room, playing that satanic music, laughing and talking to herself for days now, do you think I should take her to the GP?"

"You need to take her to a psychiatrist and book an appointment for yourself while you're there," he replied coldly.

"You think that's funny? I've read about people like her who go on to kill people in their school or shopping centres. We need to do something!"

"So why don't you bloody do something instead of tip-toeing around her all the time? Get your head out of your arse, get dressed for once and stop prancing around in your silk dressing gown like Lady Muck and sort her out!"

"Why don't you do something Mr big-shot Inspector? What is it they say – when a child does well they belong to the father but when they do wrong they belong to the mother. You've always wanted her to belong to you so help her to do well. You've always smothered her and given into her every whim. She calls me 'bitch' and 'cow' and tells me to 'f-off' but with you, it's 'yes Daddy' this and 'okay Daddy' that and 'Oh Daddy, you're home, I missed you today!' It's all peaches and cream with you! All sweetness and honey! I've always been the outsider, the bad guy in this family. So why don't you take her to the psychiatrist? No one in my family has ever been like her so it must be something from your side of the family, which means that you should be able to explain to the psychiatrist your family history and help him reach a diagnosis quickly. Plus, I can't take her, in my family we don't venture outside for help."

"In your family, you don't venture outside for help? You're having a laugh, aren't you? Your whole bloody family is nuts. Your dad, Lord of the pubs, is a bloody alcoholic. Your mother lives in cloud-cuckoo-land reliving days when she ate at the Palace as a child and how your great, great grandfather was a Duke of some sorts. And, your brothers are delusional dodgy businessmen living on hand-outs from hard working tax payers and through the various tax evasion scams they do under the questionable guise of them being Lords. The only semi-sane one is your sister, and she wants nothing to do with any of you! She moved thousands of miles away just to get away from the lot of you. Have you looked in the mirror recently? When you look in the mirror, you should see Jessica looking back, you stupid woman!"

"Mockery of the elite, that is so typical of you, so lower class. That's all people like you know. You really are uncouth to the bones aren't you darling?"

He moved towards her menacingly, "Maybe I should slap some sense into your thick head so you can see that you ain't exactly royalty."

"It's 'are not' not 'ain't' dumbo-" she stopped as he moved towards her then as if suddenly bitten by a 'senseless' courage bug she braced herself, "why don't you then, why don't you slap some sense into me? That's obviously all you know, how to beat your wife up one minute and the next collect awards for bravery in the line of duty. They award you for saving battered women from abusive partners who are just like you! You make me sick, you big hypocrite!"

He grabbed her, shook her hard then pushed her roughly onto the bed, "You want me to hit you, don't you? You're really asking for it tonight. You're begging for it?"

"You uncultured buffoon! Only you can make wife beating sound like a sexual proposition. Hit me, go on hit me! I'm sick and tired of being scared of you. Kill me, why don't you just kill me and get it over with!"

"You're drunk again, aren't you? You pathetic drunk bitch! Maybe I should just kill you!" He moved swiftly, grabbed her by her throat and squeezed. She struggled against his grip and scratched at his face and hands until he let her go.

They both turned as they heard the bang on their door then saw the door open slowly. Jessica fell into the room. Blood pumped out of her wrists and squirted onto the door, wall and carpet of their room. Both her wrists had been slashed – she was moments away from death.

CHAPTER 10

The two people hated each other but the one thing which held them together albeit loosely, spurred them into action, dissipating their hate, if only momentarily. Eloise's screams had been short-lived as her husband had slapped her and calmly instructed her to call for an ambulance. He had grabbed a towel and tore it into two as if it were mere tissue paper then using each piece had firmly bound each of Jessica's wrists. Now, he held his daughter to him and spoke to her, willing her to live, willing her to try, "Don't die, Jessica, don't leave us, please don't die," he whispered.

The sound of the siren preceded the flashing lights of the ambulance.

"They're here! Patrick, the ambulance is here!" Eloise said as she let go of Jessica's hand which she had been rubbing and ran downstairs to open the door for the paramedics.

"Up here!" Patrick shouted. "Please hurry!"

The paramedics, a male and female, rushed in with medical bags. "How long has she been unconscious?" The male paramedic asked. He knelt down next to Jessica's lifeless body and felt the side of her neck for a pulse.

"Two maybe three minutes," Patrick replied.

"What's her name?"

"Jessica," Eloise answered.

"Okay, we'll take it from here," the female paramedic said as she firmly moved Patrick back and took his place. "Jessica, can you hear me, sweetheart? Jessica, can you hear me, love? Squeeze my hand if you can hear me, Jessica."

Jessica didn't respond.

"Oh my God, she's dead, isn't she? She's dead this time!" Eloise screamed.

The female paramedic put the ear pieces of the stethoscope in her ears and pressed the metal end against Jessica's chest. She listened then shook her head, "There's a heartbeat! She's alive! We need to bag her and get her to the hospital asap!"

"I'll call it in," the male paramedic said.

The Room was waiting.
It pulsated.
It trembled in excitement as it waited for someone new.

It is said that the angels in Heaven rejoice when someone repents and becomes born again. It is also said that the demons in hell rejoice when someone dies who isn't, and are jubilant when someone commits suicide.

The Room was waiting.
It pulsated.
It trembled in excitement as it waited for someone new.

CHAPTER 11

From the periphery of the A&E operating room Patrick and Eloise Carmichael watched as doctors and nurses worked quickly to save their daughter's life. Wires were connected. Monitors checked. A tube inserted down Jessica's throat. And, blood taken from her arm. Amid all of this, Eloise's sobs were not acknowledged by her husband. He offered her no comfort, and he allowed himself none either. Suddenly Jessica went into cardiac arrest, and as the doctors and nurses hurried to shock her heart, a nurse ushered the Carmichaels out of the room.

Sergeant John Kelleher parked his unmarked squad car on a double yellow line on the road outside the hospital (he mentally dared any traffic warden to give him a ticket – he was looking for a reason to let off some steam). He hadn't been able to find appropriate parking on the hospital grounds, and he was irritated that he had to attend to the family of yet another suicide attempt, his fifth in two weeks. Not all his cases were suicide attempts; some were actual suicidal deaths. Yesterday a young man had jumped from a bridge in front of a high-speed freight train. Police officers had tried unsuccessfully to talk him down for twenty minutes. The minutes were used asking him his name, asking him about his family, what his favourite food was, where he lived and where he worked. Intermittently, they begged him not to jump. He had calmly answered the questions as he sat precariously on the bridge overlooking the rail tracks. Below, trains speed along the tracks ferrying passengers who were unaware that he was moments away from death. The police had radioed for the train operators to stop the trains and that must have been what tipped the man off. He must have noticed that the usual number of trains which ploughed the lines had started to reduce in number. He jumped amid the police asking if he liked football and what team he supported. The train company had sent out a message to passengers delayed by the disruption on the trains which said *'Trains have been cancelled or delayed because a man has been hit by a moving train'*. That had ticked Sergeant Kelleher off because he knew that the train had not suddenly come off the tracks and knocked the man off the bridge, the man had made the decision and thrown himself in front of the moving train, had been struck and crushed by it and instantly killed.

Sergeant Kelleher couldn't understand why people killed themselves. He loved life, and he intended to stay alive as long as he possibly could. He wasn't always happy with the things that happened in his life, like most people he had good days and bad days. But he had seen his father lose his battle with cancer a year ago, and that had completely changed his perspective on life. His father would have given anything for a few more years of life, and he would have given anything for him to have them. Luther Vandross' song *'Dance with my Father'* was now one of his favourite songs. To him, it depicted a man like him asking God to bring his father back to life so that he could dance with his father again if God granted him his wish he would put a record on that would never stop playing and as a result, he would have his father back forever. The song made Sergeant Kelleher smile wistfully and often brought tears to his eyes. He would play it over and over. In the pockets of his mind, areas he kept to himself, he hoped the request would be granted to the singer then he could make his own request for the same thing and have his father back.

That last year had brought Sergeant Kelleher closer to his father. When his father had first been diagnosed, he had moved back home. His older sister lived in Australia with her family, she had been pregnant with her second child and couldn't visit often but telephoned or video called every day. He didn't mind looking after his father; they had always had a good relationship, the death of his mother five years ago had brought them even closer. He had taken time off work and taken his father on short trips to places on his father's bucket-list. When his father had been too weak to walk long distances they had played crazy golf in electric wheelchairs, and they had both gone shopping on mobile disability scooters laughing and crying together – mostly laughing at Sergeant Kelleher's attempt at a two-wheel-wheelie or at his father's struggle to drive his scooter in a straight line. His father, once a handsome, virile engineer and a pilot, who had once flown planes for the air force now struggled to handle a simple device – it made them cry but a quick joke conjured up by father or son soon had them laughing.

"If the enemy saw you now Dad you'd be a sitting duck, a goner", Sergeant Kelleher would say.

"If I flew my planes in that Second World War the way I'm driving this contraption you'd be called Hans, and we'd all be speaking German", his father would quip. And they would laugh at the poignant poetry of life as they knew it.

It was the laughter that he treasured, the laughter that made him value his own life and count every living moment as precious. He couldn't understand why someone would throw away what his father had so desperately wanted – to live – to breathe – to exist.

Sergeant Kelleher looked around A&E then walked up to the first nurse he saw and asked her a few questions. She answered them and when he asked for the family of the suicide attempt patient she pointed towards the Carmichaels. He walked briskly towards the couple.

"Mr and Mrs Carmichael, can you tell me what happened?"

"It's Inspector Carmichael, officer," Patrick corrected.

"I'm sorry, Inspector and Mrs Carmichael can you please tell me what happened?"

"And you are?" Patrick asked.

"My name is Sergeant Kelleher and this is just a routine

question and answer session, Sir. You know how it is. The hospital has to call us when there's an attempted suicide." He pulled his notebook and pen out of his pocket and waited.

"This is not a routine question and answer session Sergeant, my daughter is in that room fighting for her life, and I'm not going to waste my time answering your questions." Patrick stormed off leaving his wife standing next to Sergeant Kelleher nervously wringing her hands.

Sergeant Kelleher turned to Eloise, "Do you want to tell me what happened?"

"I don't know what happened," Eloise lied.

"I was told you came down in the ambulance with her."

"She's just seeking bloody attention again," Eloise said then walked off in the direction her husband had gone.

CHAPTER 12

48 Hours Later

"How's she doing today?" Eloise asked Preeti, the nurse looking after Jessica.

"She's stable Mrs Carmichael. She woke up in the night asking for you. I told her you were at home and would be here in the morning." Preeti looked at her fob watch attached to her uniform and noted that it was past midday.

"I'm sorry, my husband had to go to work, and I don't like general public hospital wards. We're planning to get Jessica moved to a private room." She nervously ran a hand through her hair.

"The social worker is waiting to talk to you. I told her you'd be here this morning at 9am as you told me you would and she's been waiting for you since 8.45am. Shall I go and get her and bring her here or do you want to use the family room?"

Again Eloise ran a nervous hand through her hair, "What does she want to talk to me about? I've never spoken to a social worker about anything before?"

"It's routine when a child attempts suicide. She probably just wants to know why Jessica did it, what's going on with her, what could have prevented her doing what she did. Has she been depressed and if so how can Social Services help. I'm sure it will just be your bog-standard routine question and answer session."

"Why she did it? How do I know why she did what she did? How does any parent know why their child attempts suicide? It's not like we're given a chance, like we have a chat where they say, 'Mum, Dad, I just want you to know that I'm thinking of killing myself tomorrow, what do you guys think?' Or 'I've had some strange suicidal thoughts, and I want to share them with you so that when I give into them, you'll understand!' It's not like they care enough about us to stop and think of the damage they're doing, the pain that they'll leave behind, the shattered lives that can never be put back together because of the selfish act they carried out. Their death usually means the death of the family! You get shunned, and you become stigmatised you know! People see you and automatically see death around you. You lie and make excuses, 'Oh that's so-and-so in the picture, we don't talk about her because she died young and we don't want people to know how she died!' People look at you and think, 'How did they not know?' Or 'How did they miss the signs?' Like parents know everything!" She was becoming hysterical.

Preeti put a reassuring arm around her, "Calm down Mrs Carmichael. Jessica is still alive. She still has a chance to get through this. Look, why don't you go and see Jessica, I'll go and get the social worker and take her to the family room, and you can come along in say five minutes, okay," she told her.

"Was this Jessica's first attempt at suicide?" The social worker asked Eloise.

"What has that got to do with anything?" She answered.

"I need to know if we need to section Jessica-"

Eloise held a hand up, cutting her off mid-sentence, "Section my child? Are *you* crazy? You can't section her. She isn't mad, and this isn't the eighteenth century! You can't send people to the mad house in this day and age! What would people say about me if you section my child?"

"She could be a danger to herself and others Mrs Carmichael. We need to make sure that she doesn't harm herself again or anyone else."

"You will not section my child and in answer to your question, NO, she hasn't attempted suicide before. Her father and I were having an argument, and this was Jessica's way of getting attention. She's an ordinary teenager, full of life and she has never, ever, done this before."

"Are you sure? She may have done it secretly, maybe with poison or a large number of painkillers?"

"Where would she get painkillers from? You can only buy

two packs of painkillers in any one transaction nowadays," she avoided the answer.

"Has she ever self-harmed?"

"No."

"Are you sure Mrs Carmichael? Nowadays teenagers know how to cover their self-inflicted cuts. She may be cutting herself somewhere not visible-"

"If that were the case, how do you expect me or my husband to know?"

"I know, it's difficult, but there are signs, like staying in the bathroom too long, bloody bits of tissue paper in the bathroom bin or the bin in her room or missing razor blades. Her not wanting you to touch her arms is also another sign."

"I rarely touch my daughter. We're not a touchy-feely family."

The social worker sighed, "What about any strange behaviour?"

"Define what exactly you classify as strange behaviour?"

"Staying in her room, locking her bedroom door, wanting to be alone-"

"That's normal behaviour where Jessica is concerned."

The social worker studied Eloise for a few moments. Words came to her mind, but she quickly bit her tongue and diverted her thoughts. "Does Jessica go online a lot? Are you aware of any chat rooms she visits?"

"No."

"Has she been depressed?"

"Why would you ask me that?"

"You'd be surprised at the number of young children who are diagnosed with depression nowadays. There was an article in the newspaper the other day which said that severe depression is affecting the lives of over 8000 children under ten years old. Can you imagine the number of undiagnosed teenagers that might be clinically depressed nowadays?"

"You make it sound like a good thing! Children nowadays

have so much given to them, why the hell should they be depressed, they're a bunch of ungrateful brats if you ask me, they have X-boxes, PSPs, games, trainers, money, holidays!"

"They may have a lot of things given to them, but they're impressionable and also exposed to a lot of things-"

"Here we go," Eloise murmured, "things like what?"

"Like sex, the image of half-naked women on billboards affects both boys and girls in a negative way. Then there's the alcohol, drugs, peer pressure, bullying, cyber-bullying, trolling and more alcohol."

"Why do you keep going on about alcohol?"

"What?"

"Why do you keep going on about alcohol? What have you heard about me?"

"Excuse me?"

"Oh, forget it," Eloise snapped.

Confused the social worker shook her head, "Is Jessica depressed Mrs Carmichael?"

"If anyone should be depressed in my house, it's me. Jessica acts strangely all the time it's always one thing or another with that child."

"What exactly do you mean by strange?"

"Strange like girls her age!" Eloise snapped again unable to conceal her irritation. "Look, if all you're going to do is ask irrelevant questions about *that* child, I might as well leave."

"What did you just say?"

Realising she had over-stepped the mark Eloise smiled sweetly, "I'm sorry, do you have any more questions to ask? If yes, please ask them, if no then I need to get home."

Most social workers would have given up, written a few notes and left by now but something compelled this one to stay and keep digging. "Does Jessica smoke, drink alcohol, take drugs or binge eat?"

Eloise hesitated, she studied her nails and noted that the red polish on one nail was chipped, 'when did that happen?' she wondered as she rubbed a finger along the chipped nail, 'it must have happened when Jessica tried to kill-'

"Mrs Carmichael, I just asked you a question."

"What? Oh, the answer is no to all of those things."

"Does Jessica communicate with you or your husband?"

"She talks to her father and she shouts at me . . . they always make me out to be the villain, it's always about them, never about me-"

"Mrs Carmichael, do you even love your daughter?"

"How dare you ask me that, of course, I love her, I tell her all the time."

"Love is a verb, not a noun. Love is an act it's something we do, something we show to another person."

"So what about me? Who shows me anything?"

"Mrs Carmichael, this isn't about you now, this is about Jessica. Now I need to know what's going on with her and why she did what she did."

"Excuse me a moment. I need to call my husband who's a Senior Inspector in the police force. He can come over, and you can talk to him."

"Mrs Carmichael, I need to speak to *you*, this is crucial. You don't seem to comprehend the magnitude of what's happening here."

Eloise held her index finger up indicating that the social worker is quiet and give her a moment then walked out of the family room and called Patrick's mobile number. "Can you please come down here now Patrick, it's an emergency," she said as soon as he answered.

"Is it Jessica? Is she okay?" He panicked.

"It's worse than that - a woman from Social Services is harassing me!"

"She can't harass you, it's standard procedure, just answer her questions," Patrick said.

"You answer her bloody questions! Get down here now, Patrick and answer her bloody questions!" Eloise screamed.

CHAPTER 13

Bright blue eyed, dark haired, Murray Nelson aka The Charmer, was a serial wife beater. He was one of those men who beat his wife in front of his children to keep his whole family submissive. He often joked with friends at his local pub that he killed two birds with one stone. His wife was scared of him. His five children were scared of him, and he was happy – there was peace and discipline in his abode, and he was the king of his mansion. His mansion was a three-bedroom council flat located on the tenth floor of one of the many tower blocks scattered like tentacles over the Wandsworth area in South West London. Murray's neighbours hated his bullying loud manner and the way his wife allowed him to control his family with his fists.

Murray had grown up on a council estate in Birmingham; he was the product of an Irish father and Yorkshire mother. He grew up with four siblings, his parents and his paternal grandmother, Nana Colleen, in a three bedroom council house in Dudley. His early life hadn't seen much violence at home. His parents quarrelled as some parents do, and he and his siblings squabbled as most siblings do. At nineteen, unemployed and not qualified for much in the job market, Murray had joined the army. He didn't talk much about his tour of duty; he didn't talk at all about the people he had killed or the friends who had been killed. The army tattoos were the only things that identified him as an ex-service man, and they only came out in public on sweltering days. Most of his unemployment money was spent on helping him forget the army; most of the child benefit money the family received was devoted to assisting his unemployment money with this mission. He topped up his benefits with petty theft and fencing the stolen mobile phones and other electrical gadgets (he called them gad-jits) he obtained from his teenage workforce. A customer wanted a high-end phone or electronic device, they told Murray the type and colour, Murray sent a text to one of his nifty teens and within hours both his teen and customer were happy – modern day Fagin-ism he called it (he fancied himself an entrepreneur). In his spare time, when the anti-depressants consumed him and the Indian hemp spiked with crack cocaine took his mind to places non-users could never imagine or visit, he beat his wife and children. He always had a reason – his tea wasn't hot enough, or his tea was too hot, someone had left the heating on, or someone hadn't turned the heat on. The meat in his dinner tasted like boiled cauliflower and smelled worse, or the meat in his dinner was too small, too hard, too fatty or too stringy. The excuses for the beatings were many, varied and a joke to normality but in his mind, they were very valid, 'to ensure peace and discipline in his mansion'. He had been arrested several times for domestic violence and each time his wife had refused to press charges so he had walked out of the police station angry that his valuable time had yet again been wasted.

Murray was here again, in Battersea police station waiting for his legal aid lawyer. He knew he was about to walk out of the station a free man despite the fact that he had damaged his neighbour's new car with the cricket bat he kept in the boot of his twelve-year-two-door BMW. His reason being, his neighbour, had parked his car, a brand new Volvo, in Murray's spot. Amid a torrent of swear words, Murray had slapped his long-suffering wife and punched two of his children when they had tried to get him to go up to their flat and not get into a fight with the neighbour.

Inspector Carmichael walked into the interview room where Murray sat alone at the table waiting for his lawyer to make an appearance. He looked coldly at Murray; the red mist which had descended when Eloise had called three hours ago still taunted him. As soon as he had hung up, he ran to his car, put his blue flashing light and siren on and drove through the streets of London at 70 miles per hour. Thinking that his daughter was moments away from death while Eloise was playing 'silly-buggers' with a social worker instead of being there for Jessica made him run through every red light in his path. The red mist mocked him when he arrived at the hospital and was confronted by a social worker determined to section Jessica. Eloise was hysterical. After he had used his authority to get rid of the social worker (a phone call to her boss). He saw Eloise standing by the nurses' station looking at him as she always did, as if he were scum, as if by the nature of his low-birth status, he was not worthy to breathe the same air as her. *'She thinks you're scum',* the red mist mocked him.

Now, as he looked coldly at Murray, he could feel a tightness in his chest, he could feel the red mist still taunting him, telling him that he was weak, scum, a bad father who was unable to protect his daughter from herself.

Murray smiled, "Inspector Carmichael, good to see a familiar face, you got any smokes on you, boss?"

"You've been here enough times. You know the rules Murray, you can't smoke in here. Look, the sooner you plead guilty, the faster my boys process your paperwork, the sooner you'll be out of here," Inspector Carmichael told him.

"I'm innocent Inspector, I told your officers that it was all a misunderstanding. I didn't touch that car and my wife walked into my fist like she always does, we both know how clumsy some women can get," he winked. (A drunken football brawl had landed Murray in hospital on the same night a battered, bruised and bloodied Eloise Carmichael had been taken there by her husband – the night of her sister's wedding).

"What about your kids, you were seen punching them."

"I didn't lay a finger on those pathetic kids, Inspector. Ask them. They'll tell you I didn't touch them. Ask them."

"Are you saying you're not guilty Murray?"

"I didn't do anything, Inspector, you know me, we're like

kindred spirits you and me, like two peas in a pod, we wouldn't hurt a fly," Murray smiled sheepishly. "Not one of those prats will say I touched them. They're all a bunch of idiots. The only good one out of that bunch is Shane, the kid is 9 years old and already a genius. He's smarter than the whole bunch put together, you should see him on a laptop. He's my little man, from the moment I saw him, two days after he was born, I said to hell with the rest of them," Murray continued to gush about Shane and verbally abuse the rest of his family unaware that the inspector had stopped listening and was clenching and unclenching his fists.

Suddenly, the red taunting mist exploded around Patrick.

Moments later his hands were covered in blood, and Murray Nelson lay curled up on the floor protecting his head while screaming that he would plead guilty.

Inspector Carmichael washed his hands, threw a damp towel on the floor next to Murray and told him to clean himself up. He stood and waited until Murray had done so and was re-seated at the table.

"What happened to you, Murray?"

"I fell Inspector, I fell and caught my face on the side of a table in the pub."

Inspector Carmichael nodded then walked out of the room, closed the door and turned the camera linked to the interview room back on.

CHAPTER 14

New York

A cold wind bit into his face and refused to let go as he walked swiftly towards the bakery/coffee shop on Lexington Avenue. His hands were painfully frozen inside his leather gloves and even though he knew it was fruitless he stopped, cupped his hands together and blew warm air into them. He smiled as the warm air appeared to freeze before his eyes and like a tennis-ball-sized puff of air, wait, confused, unsure of the reason it was created – then it disappeared. Resuming his pace he continued down Lexington.

Moments later, he pushed the door of the bakery/coffee shop open and walked inside. Almost immediately, disco lights came on, and people cheered. He was shocked to the core as he stared at the people in the shop.

"Yeahhhhh! The doctor is in the house!" Someone cheered.

"Dr Park is in the building!" Another person said.

People clapped and cheered as he stood completely dazed.

Toney Demiro, fake-tanned, dark curly hair and slightly overweight, the owner of the shop, smiled and walked towards him with a cake-sized bran muffin, which had two candles alight on top. "Dr Park, we just want you to know that we'll miss you and Josh, and we wish you both a safe journey to Australia and the UK."

"Thank you, Toney, but you didn't have to do this."

"No worries Dr Park, now blow these babies out before they burn me."

He blew the candles out and smiled, "You do know that Park isn't my real name," he told Toney.

"I know that Doc, we all know that, we all just call you that cos you're always jogging in Central Park." He returned the smile. He liked the doctor; even though he worked in a private hospital, he also worked in a free clinic and gave free medical advice to Toney and some of his customers. Each Tuesday and Thursday lunchtime rain, hail or snow, Dr Park would come in for his English tea and bran muffin, and each time he came in there would be people waiting to see him. People with ailments that they couldn't afford to take to a private clinic or have the time to wait for hours and be seen at a free clinic. They knew Dr Park would see them right. He would give them advice, or send them to a doctor who would help them free of charge (they didn't know he paid their bill) or he would personally treat them right there and then if possible. It was these customers who had come today to wish him well. They came with the only gift they knew he would take from them, a card scripted with their best wishes.

"Ladies and gentlemen," Toney started, "Dr Park first darkened my doorstep eight months ago. He came in here with his young son, Josh, and asked me for a glass of soda, a cup of English tea and a bran muffin, all this I might add, in his English accent. I remember thinking 'English tea. This is New York, why is this dude asking for an English tea?' That was eight months ago, and I speak for all of us here today when I say, Dr Park, thank you for taking the time to be a decent human being and for always making time to take care of those of us who needed a hand. Some of us wouldn't be alive today if you hadn't . . . " Toney stopped, choked-up, he looked away and coughed; he was Italian and Italian men didn't get emotional in public.

Dr Park smacked Toney playfully on the back, "You need a hand there Toney."

"No, I'm good Doc. Joe you wanna read your poem to the Doc now?" Toney asked a young man who stood near the counter shuffling from one foot to the other. The man looked at the ground as if searching for something engrained in the wooden floor. He was painfully shy and scared to look up at the people he knew were now staring at him, waiting for him to say something – so he stared at the ground.

"You've written a poem, Joe?" Dr Park asked surprised.

"I tell you Doc, it's beautiful, a real tear-jerker. And you know what Doc, he worked on it for days, isn't that right Joe?" Toney encouraged.

Joe nodded still searching the floor with his eyes, not moving or saying anything.

"You can give it to me later if you want Joe," Dr Park told him sensing his nervousness.

Head bent, Joe shuffled over to Dr Park and held a sheet of paper up. Dr Park took it from him. Joe shuffled back to his spot and fixed his eyes back on the wooden floor. Dr Park read the words written on the paper.

You changed my life and made it mine
Loss is only profitable to the found
Sadness is only profitable to the happy

He is strange and weird. He must be mad
He acts like a person who is always sad
Why is he here, why not a loony bin?
Was it his mother's or his father's sin?

Before I met you, I had confusion guised as a long hopeless rope
Now, you've changed my life and given me hope
You've shown me, I'm not weird, I'm not mad, I may act a little bit strange
But I'm a person. I can do things, and I can change

The sun pushed the moon to one side and claimed the day
The rain drenched the desert, and new life came to stay
On the day I met you

Loss is only profitable to the found
Sadness is only profitable to the happy
You've changed my life, and now it's mine

Dr Park re-read the poem and choked back his emotions.

Toney playfully smacked him on the back, "You need a hand there Doc?"

He shook his head and walked over to Joe, "Hey, this is excellent Joe. I'm impressed. I'm going to take it with me." He reached into his pocket and pulled out a business card, "Joe, here are the contact details of the doctor I told you about, Dr Fleming, she's looking forward to meeting you so make sure to contact her tomorrow okay."

Joe nodded. He didn't look up, but he smiled.

Dr Park patted him on his shoulder, on a spot he knew he was allowed to touch. Joe was bipolar, and when he took his medication he was fine but without it, he could sway between manic and passive so quickly that he was originally misdiagnosed as schizophrenic. Before meeting Dr Park, he'd been ostracised at school and college. His peers thought he was mad, but he was harmless, he did well academically and as such was allowed to be one of society's 'weirdoes', aka a geek or a freak. Dr Park found that with the correct dosage of a new drug Joe could live a normal life but he needed monitoring, and the level of the drug in his blood checked regularly because sometimes he forgot to take his medication.

"Make sure you take your meds Joe okay and go and see Dr Fleming, she's not as cool as me but she rides a Harley Davidson, and I told her you like bikes-"

"What?" Joe's head shot up, "Really? She rides a Harley D? Cooooool!"

"Promise me you'll take your meds, and I'll have a word with her and see if she'll let you have a look at her bike."

"Scouts' honour Doc, I'll take my meds, and I'll go get my blood tested regularly for the drug levels like you told me, I promise. Scouts' honour Doc!"

"Good man," Dr Park told him and patted his shoulder again on the same spot.

Twenty minutes later Dr Park left the bakery/coffee shop and headed home to his son. His card and poem were tucked away safely in his coat pocket. A cold wind bit into his face and refused to let go as he walked. He didn't feel the cold.

*

"Dad, are we really gonna come back to New York?" Josh asked.

"Yes, we will, in six months we'll be back in New York."

"So after you do this toxaco, um, toxicolololigy, um, Dad what's it called?"

"Toxicology research."

"Yeah, so after you do this tox-i-co-lo-gy research in Australia and England, we're gonna come back?"

"Yes, God willing."

"Promise," Josh insisted.

He hated making promises. "Josh, as long as things go to plan, we should be back here in six months."

"Good enough I suppose. Why don't you ever promise anything anymore Dad? You used to promise all the time."

Once, he had promised he would bring his wife and new baby home, they both died - he stopped making promises. He changed the subject, "Guess who called me today asking what you want for your birthday?"

"Aunty Kate?"

"No."

"Uncle Matt?"

"No."

"Cousin Luke?"

"No."

"My teacher?"

"Why would your teacher call me and ask me that?"

"Oh, I just said that so that you would hurry up and tell me."

He playfully grabbed his son and wrestled him onto the bed then tickled him, "Oh, you just said that huh," he mimicked his American accent.

Josh laughed so much that tears formed in his eyes, "Okay, okay Dad, I give in, tell me who called?"

"Your Grandmother and Grandfather in England."

"I can't wait to see them again, do you think they miss me?"

"They miss you so much that they're going to visit us a lot more when we get back to New York."

"Really! I'm glad," he nodded affirming his gladness.

"Okay young man, brush your teeth, say your prayers then bed, chop-chop."

"Chop-chop, chop-chop," Josh mimicked as he climbed off the bed and went to brush his teeth.

CHAPTER 15

Anna Lee Lewis says –
'I DON'T SEE DEAD PEOPLE, I JUST HEAR THEM!'
Chris Plummer
Freelance Writer for the Sunday Newspaper

Sandra Nixon, 26, says that her life has been turned upside down by thoughts that her late fiancé, Kieran Brown, 28, might have communicated things to her about his suicide intentions before he died. She attended a meeting in Central London where American Anna Lee Lewis, whom some critics have dubbed *'The hearer of dead people'*, told her that Kieran must have displayed some signs that all was not well with him before he took his own life. Mrs Lewis said that most people displayed signs that all was not well or that they intended to kill themselves. Sandra said that after Mrs Lewis had questioned her about Kieran's behaviour before he died, it became apparent that Kieran had indeed acted in an abnormal manner before his death. He usually insisted that Sandra call him at work at lunch time every day but before his death, he had asked her not to call him on his work number only on his mobile. Had she called him at work she would have discovered that Kieran had been sacked and also discovered that he was in fact in serious debt and being threatened by debt collectors! What is so heartbreaking about this story is Sandra's mother, Denise Nixon 49, won a substantial amount of money with her work syndicate lottery colleagues two days after Kieran's death. Enough money to clear Kieran's debts, pay for Sandra and Kieran's wedding and their honeymoon and still have enough left over to buy a couple of houses as well. If she had won the money two days earlier would Kieran still be alive? They say your spirit doesn't die. Is Kieran's spirit watching somewhere thinking, *'If only I had waited for 48 hours, things could have been so different?'*. You know it is stories like this that make you think that *'Help is always on the way – all we have to do is be patient and wait for it to arrive!'*

'What happens when we die?' Or more importantly 'What happens when we die by our own hand?' Some religions believe that when you kill yourself, you go to a place where you are neither dead nor alive, some liken it to the place mentioned in Dante's Inferno. Others say you remain in purgatory because killing yourself is a sin against God. They say that life is a precious gift and when you take your own life or another person's life you are committing both a crime and a sin. One thing I do agree with is that life is precious. It is not something that should be discarded simply because we cannot cope with the current 'hand' we have been dealt with. No one knows tomorrow, who's to say that the 'hand' won't change, who's to say that tomorrow won't be a better and brighter day. I read once that when we have problems we should pray because 'Yesterday has gone, Today is a 'present' and Tomorrow is a 'future gift'. Sometimes with gifts, we have to be patient as we wait to get them, which means that we have to wait and ride out whatever is happening right now. We can't give up and throw in the towel if we want to get the gift! Anna Lee Lewis and her husband Dr Peter Durojaiye Lewis, genuinely have a calling to help people see that life is indeed a gift. They have helped to save some lives via the numerous Talk To Someone – TTS call centres. In these call centres, counsellors, psychiatrists and volunteers are available 24 hours a day to listen to and help the thousands of people who call asking for help. From military personnel (ex and currently serving) to civilian men, women, teenagers and surprisingly children as young as ten years old, some of whom are moments away from killing themselves – hundreds of people have been pulled back from the brink of death, have got the help they required and are alive today! How does it work? According to Anna and Peter, by getting people to re-focus their lives and to take their eyes off themselves and their problems and to be the light and salt, they were created to be.

Studies have shown that as many as 14 teenagers take their own lives each day.

This is more than 5000 per year. Which means that somewhere in the World, a person gives in to bullying, stress, depression, hurt, rejection, grief, anger, hate, etc. and takes their own life.

'Murder Within' is how Anna Lee Lewis describes this act. Murder Within, Suicide, *Sui caedare*, whatever you call it, means the end of life to a person who could have been helped.

Anna has said on some occasions, 'I'm not here to help the dead. They're gone. I'm here to help the living. I hear dead people, and I'm here with a message from the dead. A message I have heard for so many years from so many people. This message is always filled with fear, pain and regret. This is a summary of what I have heard over the years – *'Death is final! Death means you can't go back to the living! DON'T DO IT!' Don't take the precious life which God has given you and discard it like a dirty rag! Pain is temporal! It might seem at the time that there is no way out of your painful situation – believe me, there is. Pain is temporal! Death is final!!'*

Anna Lee Lewis advises - there are a number of organisations out there which offer support to people and help them to fulfil their dreams. Organisations like the Samaritans, Kidscape, NSPCC, Anti-bullying, ChildLine, The Prince's Trust and others that you can find out about online. If you need help, don't suffer in silence, please, please, please, *talk to someone*!

Chris Plummer also writes for Times Magazine

The Room

Phase two is a section in the room where empathy is heightened. Here the gentle breeze of summer is like a tsunami which rips at the skin. Tears are not only seen, but the pain in the breaking heart which produces the tears is also felt. It always comes as a shock to the people who are moved here from phase one because in phase one they felt nothing. Phase one was like the calm before the storm. Phase two hits them like a sledgehammer. The people in phase two watch their loved ones discover their dead bodies. Over and over again they feel the pain of their loved ones.

They feel the pain they see on the faces of the people they have left behind, unrelenting, the pain rips through their hearts again and again . . . and again.

A mother screams at the discovery of her child hanging from a beam rafter – dead.
A father cries as he cradles his son, an empty bottle of painkillers on the floor, his son – dead.
A husband screams in pain as he discovers his wife in a bathtub of blood – dead.

They feel the pain they see on the faces of the people they have left behind, unrelenting, the pain rips through their hearts again and again . . . and again.

CHAPTER 16

Task Force

"My father was a good man. He would have given anything to have a few more years, but he didn't get that, he died!"

"I understand Sergeant Kelleher. I wouldn't ask you to do this if I didn't believe that you can make a difference. I know that you can do something," Inspector James replied.

Sergeant Kelleher looked at his commanding officer sceptically, "Why me?"

"Because I know that what you went through with your dad has made you value life because I knew your dad and I know it's something he would want you to do, something that would make him proud of you."

"No, no, no, don't use my father like that. You think I feel sorry for a bunch of individuals who believe that they can just throw their lives away like used toilet paper? People who don't understand the value of life and living! I don't give a toss about selfish people like that. You know what, I hate them, I hate that they can just discard something my father wanted."

"You can't hate the dead Sergeant. They're gone. I know how you feel, believe me, I share your feelings but some of these people are children, and we have to do what we can to stop them-"

"How? How do you stop people from throwing themselves off a bridge, or from shooting their brains out?"

"By giving them an alternative, by helping them through whatever is making them feel that they need to commit suicide."

"No disrespect, Inspector, but don't we have enough crime to deal with."

"Sergeant-"

"There are decent tax payers out there, who need our protection, why spend our time on deaders? They want to die, so let them."

"You know that things are not as simple as that."

"Why? Why can't they be simple?"

The inspector sighed; he knew under the stubbornness a good heart resided, and he was determined to get through to it. He decided to sideline him, "What's a deader?"

"What?"

"You said 'why spend our time on deaders?', what's a deader?"

"Someone who has attempted suicide a number of times, they're already dead in their head and determined to die physically, no matter what. A person who's unreachable who in my mind is a complete waste of space!"

"That's a bit harsh. A lot of people don't want to die. They're depressed or lonely or vulnerable and desperately crying out for help. Look I think that you know what it feels like to lose someone you love and maybe you can help talk to some of these people-"

"And tell them what exactly? Tell them not to do it? Tell them to get help? Tell them to pull their heads out of their arses and deal with life, because life can suck, because every day might not be perfect but at least they're alive!"

"I've known you since you were a little tearaway. A twelve-year-old wannabe 'hard-man' gang member hanging out on the Surrey Lane Estates in Battersea with your little cronies. Your parents thought butter wouldn't melt in your mouth. They didn't have a clue that you and that posh friend of yours were up to no good and trying to get initiated into a gang. Where is that posh boy you got caught with attempting to rob the corner shop? Coleman or Colton? What's his name again?"

"Colwell, his name's Tommy Colwell."

"Thomason Colwell, that's right, posh little Tommy. Private school educated Richmond boy, wasn't he? He was a hard nut to crack that one, even at twelve. Where is he now?"

"The Scrubs," his voice was just above a whisper.

"That's right he's in Wormwood Scrubs Prison at Her Majesty's leisure, doing time for armed robbery, assault and battery."

Agitated, Kelleher got up and walked to the window, "What has he got to do with deaders?"

"Absolutely nothing whatsoever. I'm just trying to show you how people, with help, can change their lives. You could've been sharing a cell with Colwell, but you got a second chance, you took that chance, and you turned your life around."

"Inspector-"

"No, wait a minute, let me finish, your parents brought you down here when you were twelve and told me to put you in a cell when they found out that you were hanging out with a gang. They said that if you felt you needed to muck around with a bunch of low-life boys and not listen to them then they would spare themselves years of pain and disappointment and for me to lock you up then and there and throw away the key, remember?"

Sergeant Kelleher lost the battle with his smile, "Why are you bringing that up now? That was years ago, old man."

"But it made a difference, didn't it. I locked you in a cell for an hour, just one measly hour and you cried and blubbered like the baby you were, and I let you out. That one hour changed your life. Do me a favour, give me one hour, and come to a task force meeting I've organised tonight. Listen to a lady called Anna Lee Lewis and her husband Dr Peter Lewis talk about the work they've done with the police in America and Europe and the number of lives they've saved and see if you change your mind. Who knows, you may help not only to change some lives but also to save some lives."

"One hour?"

"One hour, that's all I'm asking for Sergeant."

"Okay, for old times' sake, I'll give you one hour."

CHAPTER 17

Nine-year-old Shane Nelson's hands ran confidently over the keyboard of his laptop. He occasionally paused as he read something from a book on the table then he typed some more. The laptop was second hand, but it served its purpose well. He was the only one in his family who owned a computer – it was a gift from his father, Murray Nelson (one of his stolen gadjits). Shane was his father's *Joseph* and Shane's siblings *like Joseph's brothers* hated him because of this. His two older brothers and two older sisters were never openly cruel to him and always over-attentive when their father was around. They played with him. They read him stories from books he pretended he couldn't read, and they treated him like he was royalty. Sometimes their father would look on sceptically (wondering what the catch was) but approvingly. Shane's two brothers shared a bunk bed, a broken wardrobe and one-half of their bedroom while Shane had the other half of the room which housed a single bed, a TV, a study table and chair, and a large wardrobe.

One day, when Shane was seven, his mother sent him to fetch his brothers and sisters in for dinner. Shane went to the large park adjacent to their tower block in search of his siblings but didn't find them. As he walked back to the building something fell on the stony grass a few feet away from him. He looked at the broken gin bottle then looked up and saw his eldest brother Robbie standing on the roof of the building. He turned, ran inside the building and took the lift up to the twenty-first floor. When the doors opened, Shane stepped out and stood and stared at the stairs leading to the roof. There were twenty steps (ten then a small landing followed by another ten) that led to a dark brown metal door, which opened onto the roof. He had been on the roof with his brothers and sisters several times. Tenants were not supposed

to go onto the roof. There was a deterrent, a big yellow sign by the stairs leading to the roof which read:
'DANGER – Residents Must Not Go Onto The Roof!!!'
But, for some reason the door was never locked and the deterrent ignored. Not only was the door leading onto the roof never locked, but it was also always slightly ajar. The slightly open door served as a magnet to most of the children who resided in the many council flats below. Four apartments served like the corner of a box on each floor. The centre was a hollow which housed the lifts and emptiness – bleak emptiness, which engulfed the entire building – Shane's mum often said, 'true friendships, for some reason never seemed to be found in council tower blocks.'

Each floor, like a box, was placed one on top of another until you got to where Shane stood – (in the centre of the twenty-first box), staring at the steps that led to the roof.

Shane was on the fifteenth step leading to the roof when he heard his brothers and sisters laughing. He heard Robbie tell the others that he wanted to put poison in their father's food and hoped their father would die a slow painful death, and his guts would turn purple and rot while he was alive to see and feel everything then he would die and leave them all in peace. Siobhan, Shane's eldest sister, said that if he did this their mother would be arrested for the crime and she would go to prison because the spouse was always the guilty person. Their loyal, docile mother, who wouldn't hurt a fly, would know one of them had done it. She would agonise then take two steps forward and two-and-a-half steps backwards as she always did, accept the blame and die in prison. Robbie agreed and said that he didn't want their mother suffering because of their father anymore. They all agreed that they needed to get rid of their father and his brat and discussed other ways they could achieve this without implicating their mother. Shane had been confused; he didn't understand who their father's brat was. He didn't want his brothers and sisters to think that he had been spying on them. The last time they had found him spying on them, they took him to the roof and locked him out there for what felt like days to him but was, in fact, twenty minutes. They told him that if he told anyone what they'd done, they would do it again. Shane waited for a few moments then called out to them that they needed to come home for their dinner.

Still confused, the following day Shane had asked his father why his brothers and sisters wanted to get rid of him and his brat. He asked his father who the brat was.

As a result of Shane's questions and his father's military-style interrogation of his siblings individually at 3'oclock in the morning, Shane's mother was beaten for producing wicked and ungrateful children. Shane's brothers and sisters were beaten for mutiny and treachery towards their father. Shane's father called them 'the enemy' and 'traitors' and said several times that Shane was his only loyal soldier.

Loyalty to his father meant disloyalty to his mother and siblings. If they disliked him because of the attention and favouritism his father showed him in the past, after that day Shane knew the only thing his siblings felt for him was pure unadulterated hatred.

Shane stopped typing.
He smiled.

CHAPTER 18

Mother and Daughter

"What were you thinking Jessica? You know the family I belong to is very private! We don't do things like that. We don't draw attention to ourselves in that way. What were you thinking? What if this gets out and people find out what you tried to do, how will that make me look?" Eloise Carmichael asked her daughter.

"I'm sorry," Jessica whispered.

"Well, sorry doesn't mean anything anymore. You said sorry the last time and the time before that. How many times must I go through this with you, how many bloody times do we have to show our dysfunctionality to the World?"

"Do you think I like doing this? Do you honestly believe that this is something I like doing Mother?"

"If you didn't like doing it, you wouldn't do it!"

"What do you want from me, Mother?"

"I want to know why you insist on putting your father and me through this, why do you do these things then leave us to pick up the pieces. I had to listen to a social worker tell me that you need to be sectioned. No one in my family has ever been sectioned. Do you know what would happen if I allowed her to section you? Do you know what shame and humiliation it would have brought on my family?"

Jessica smiled; a cold empty smile that didn't reach her eyes.

"You think it's funny, don't you? You tried to kill yourself, and you think it's funny," Eloise said as she threw her hands in the air, "I give up."

"No, I don't think it's funny that I tried to kill myself, I believe that it's bloody pathetic, more so because all my mother seems to be concerned about is how it affects her and her precious fake aristocratic family. Something is wrong with me, and I don't know what it is, maybe they *should* section me, maybe they *should* put me in a padded room and throw away the key. Then at least I won't have to put up with a crazy alcoholic like you for a mother!" Jessica screamed.

"Just because I drink occasionally doesn't make me an alcoholic. You trying to kill yourself is not linked to me having a few drinks. The truth is it's not about my drinking this is about you-"

"So stop telling me about your family and give me some attention for a change!"

"This is what you wanted all along, isn't it? You want everything to be about you. Jessica this and Jessica that. You gang up on me with your father, you both reject me and lock me out of your precious father-daughter circle. Do you ever wonder why I drink? I drink to feel something. Anything, I don't bloody care."

"If you want to feel something go to marriage counselling, go to parent counselling and while you're there ask them where the nearest Alcoholics Anonymous is. You know what, I think you should leave! Sometimes I don't understand why you gave birth to me! Sometimes I think that you don't know how to be a mother."

"What? How dare you talk to me like that-"

"Mother, Newsflash! I've been talking to you like this for years. You've just never listened. Go home and screw the road cleaner in the shed again and when you finish go and drink yourself under the table!"

"Listen to me young lady. I am sick of you talking to me as if I'm stupid or don't count in this family. From now on you talk to me with respect, you hear me?"

"Or what? Are you going to drink twice as much? Oh, I know what, you're going to get a bloody life as a sober person aren't you?" Jessica laughed.

"When did you become such a little shit? I don't recognise you anymore!"

"Mother dearest you're just looking in the mirror when you look at me. Don't you recognise yourself anymore, you made me like this!"

"Why don't you stop attempting to kill yourself and get it right, why don't you put an end to all this rigmarole!"

"What?" Jessica gasped.

"Eloise!" Patrick Carmichael's voice cut through the heated silence.

Eloise turned and stared at her husband. She hadn't heard him come into the room. The silence that ensued wasn't as awkward as it was dangerous. Words had been voiced which couldn't be taken back. "Oh my goodness, I didn't mean it. Patrick, I didn't mean it. Jessica, I didn't mean it, I'm sorry."

"Go home Eloise!"

"Please, Patrick-"

"Get out of here Eloise-"

"But-"

Patrick grabbed hold of her arm pulled her towards the door and threw her out of the room. "Don't come back here unless you're sober," he warned, his voice dangerous, quiet and full of unspoken intention.

Eloise landed hard on the ground. She hit her head on the wall opposite the room. The last thing Eloise saw before she blacked out was the door to Jessica's room slam shut. The last thing she wondered was why none of the nurses or doctors came to her assistance . . . then darkness.

CHAPTER 19

Task Force Meeting

A heated discussion was taking place as Sergeant John Kelleher walked into the conference room. A screen on one side of the wall displayed several graffiti walls embossed with unreadable words. Beside it on a smaller screen was a list of computer IP addresses. He looked at his watch then took a seat next to the door. He had said he would give an hour of his time, as far as he was concerned they had fifty-nine and a half minutes left, and he wasn't going to give them a second more.

"This is ridiculous! We need to shut the sites down." A woman seated at the head of the table said.

"It isn't that easy." A man dressed in a dark suit seated midway down the table replied.

"Why isn't it that easy? The government can shut anything down if they want to shut it down, if there's a bomb threat they can shut networks down, they have the ability. How many children have to die before they do something to stop this from happening?" The woman insisted.

"When I said it wasn't that easy, I didn't mean that the government can't do it, I meant that the people or person hosting the server to these sites is very tricky. Each time we think we have them in our sight, they shift location. We don't even know if they're in the UK or some remote hole in some distant country," he replied.

"Fair enough, but I still think that more can and should be done!"

"We all feel that way-"

Inspector James held a hand up, "Can I just interrupt for a minute? The officer I mentioned earlier has just walked in. I'd like to introduce Sergeant John Kelleher to you. I know I asked him to come down here for an hour but in fact, I've a confession, I've been heading this task force now for some years and truth is I'm getting old. I want him to take over - I want him to lead this task force."

"What?" Several people said at the same time, Sergeant Kelleher's voice was the loudest.

"Hear me out. Sergeant Kelleher and I go back many years, he's smart, diligent and he gets results, he doesn't like to admit this, but he cares, deep down inside, he really cares."

"What exactly do I care about?" Sergeant Kelleher asked. Shocked to the core and angry he stood by the door, in flight mode.

"You care about a person's soul, you care about life, John, I know that, and you know that. Sit down - I still have about fifty minutes of your time left."

He looked at his inspector, his eyes searched for answers, "Why me?" He asked.

"John, we have to stop this, somehow and some way we have to stop this senseless killing, this profuse adherence of hopelessness. You love life, and you know the value of life, help us to put an end to this."

Sergeant John Kelleher sat down, his eyes fixed on the wall, "You make it sound like this is some plot or organised plan-"

"That's because it is. My name is Gennifer Cookson, Genny with a G, I work with the police as a psychological profiler, and I'm doing my MSc in Psychology."

Sergeant Kelleher looked at the pretty, young, red-haired lady. He saw her blush and realised he was staring openly at her. He adverted his eyes, "What do you mean exactly? People commit suicide every day, how is this part of some elaborate plot or organised plan?"

Genny's fingers flew swiftly over the keyboard in front of her, and the computer IP addresses were replaced with a map of the United Kingdom. She continued to type, and red dots magically appeared - hundreds of them. Several lines moved across the screen linking the red dots. However, there was no central point, and the lines didn't form a pattern or spell a word, in short, the red dots didn't reveal anything. "We've been working with computer geniuses all over the World trying to make sense of this pattern."

"What do the red dots represent?" Sergeant Kelleher asked.

"They account for the locations of some teenage suicides in the United Kingdom in the last six months," the man in the dark suit replied. "Genny let him see some of the details."

The details came on the screen, one after another – life after life – once here now gone, lives cut short by a weapon no one had seen to contain – their own hands.

14-year-old girl bullied about her weight committed suicide
14-year-old girl hanged herself after she was targeted by cyber-bullies
16-year-old girl overdosed on drugs after visiting website
13-year-old boy kills himself after being bullied about his sexuality
12-year-old boy expelled from school kills himself
18-year-old boy argues with parents and jumps in front of train
16-year-old girl hangs herself after visiting online suicide sites
19-year-old girl breaks up with boyfriend and hangs herself
18-year-old boy jumps in front of high-speed train
12-year-old girl tormented by trolls kills herself
15-year-old girl jumps in front of train, described as gifted young lady
17-year-old boy drinks himself to death on purpose after online bullying
19-year-old girl shoots herself dead after emotional turmoil
13-year-old boy bullied for years kills himself, leaves note telling Mum he could no longer cope with the bullying
16-year-old boy concerned about his GCSEs kills himself after a number of attempts

The man in the dark suit studied Sergeant Kelleher, "You

heard about what happened in *Jonestown* in 1978?"

"Yes," Sergeant Kelleher replied a little shocked by the information he had just seen on the screen – there were no pictures, but the ages and the reasons were in one word – painful. ·

"Well, unlike Jonestown where over nine hundred people died in what was reported as a mass suicide by some and mass murder by others. And, which took place in one main location, what we see here is mass suicide in different places all over the country, and we think there might be a central control point, someone somewhere pulling the strings-"

"Are you serious?" Sergeant Kelleher asked; unbelief etched its way across his face, and doubt reflected in his eyes.

"Serious about what?" The man asked.

"About someone pulling the strings? About someone telling these people to kill themselves?"

"Sergeant Kelleher, suicide is the third leading cause of death for 15-24-year-olds in the World. A significant portion of these deaths are linked to internet bullying or cyber-bullying as it's called, emails, mobile phone photos posted online, suicide and self-harming chat rooms, fear about not achieving, depression, family fall-outs, the list is endless. Research has shown that at least 25 attempts are made for every completed teen suicide, ranging from subtle to extreme. 'Self-Elimination' is not a video game! Nearly every day when you open a Newspaper you read that someone has been killed and the police are not looking for anyone in connection with the killing, or it is not suspicious, or there are no suspects – these are all usually codes for suicide. Weapons of choice are guns, drugs, hanging, jumping from a height or jumping in front of a train. It's become so commonplace now that it seems society has become disaffected."

Sergeant Kelleher shook his head as if to stabilise the information that was bouncing around inside it, "I'm sorry, you are?"

"My name is Dr Tristan Cookson, and I work for the Department of Health. We've been looking at the connection between suicide and mental health for years now. Believe it or not, the government is trying to combat this problem and throwing everything possible at it in an attempt to stop it from happening."

Sergeant Kelleher looked from Genny to Tristan, a question on the tip of his tongue.

"Siblings," Genny quickly voiced. "Tristan is my older brother. He asked me to get involved when I told him about the work I was doing for my degree." She felt strange at the need to clarify this fact so that he would know she was single.

"With all due respect doctor, the people who kill themselves want to die, full stop!" Sergeant Kelleher said with the conviction in his voice backed up by the many dead 'suicide' bodies he had seen.

Tristan sighed, "Sergeant Kelleher, I know that's not true and you know that's not entirely accurate. People are being influenced by forces that we don't yet fully comprehend, but we do know that there is an evil entity out there-"

"Whoa, whoa, slow down there, what do you mean by an evil entity? Are we dealing with voodoo or magic here?" His voice couldn't conceal his amusement.

"Sergeant Kelleher, there is a battle going on for souls-"

"And, you are?" Sergeant Kelleher interrupted the man.

"Dr Chang Lin. Young man, you have to understand that the enemy tries to stop people fulfilling their destiny because he knows that if they get where they were created to go, God, has amazing things in store for them, and they can help others. The enemy tries to stop people by getting them to use their own hands – this is because no one can prevent people from fulfilling their God-given purpose but them, be it through suicide, alcohol or drugs."

"And this enemy is?"

"The devil and his co-workers Sergeant Kelleher, they work

by getting people to tell you that you're nothing, you're worthless, and you'll never achieve anything so you might as well not bother trying – they present reasons to die. At TTS we say you're not who people say you are! You're who God says you are! People may call you many things, but you decide what you call yourself. We have helped thousands of people by presenting reasons for them to live."

"That's all very 'Inspirational Speaker' jargon. However, I find that stuff like straw, good when mixed with something reliable but useless by itself."

"Sergeant Kelleher, my name is Dr Peter D. Lewis, and I've seen things that show this increase in suicide rates is not coincidental. It is not related to a lack of the sunshine or a severe bout of cold weather or too many rainy days. It is directly linked to the fight going on for souls. There's a story in the Bible, in the Gospel of Mark, Chapter 5, about a man who had a legion of demons within him. He would cut himself and try to harm himself – some say that similar to that man, some people who commit suicide are possessed by evil spirits."

Sergeant Kelleher looked around the room at the faces which all seemed to agree with Dr Lewis' statement, "You *all* believe this? You *all* think that like in that film 'Constantine', demons and evil spirits are flying around trying to get people?"

"There are good and evil forces in the spiritual realm Sergeant Kelleher and there is a battle being fought. Genny, play the South American video for the Sergeant please," Dr Lewis said. He pressed a button and the lights in the room went off.

The screen on the wall went off momentarily then jumped back into life. The face of a young man appeared on the screen and then the camera moved and focused on something behind the man. A figure dangled from a tree. The camera zoomed in and focused on the figure. The figure was a woman hanging from a tree; long, dark hair covered her face, and her neck was at an angle which indicated it was broken. Her body swung around slowly as if being moved by a slow circulatory breeze. Suddenly, dark figures appeared below the body. They were shapeless but seemed to be jumping up and down and dancing. A strange chant emerged as the figures appeared to revel in the woman's death. After a few moments, the camera moved again and focused on the man's face. The man held up a newspaper. The camera zoomed in on the date. Then the screen went dark. Suddenly the screen came to life again, an old South American man with wrinkled skin, white paint on his forehead and wearing an animal skin shawl spoke for several moments then the screen went dark.

"What was that?" Sergeant Kelleher asked as the lights in the room came back on, he was a little un-nerved.

"That was Mustafa Keen, a former student of mine filming in South America. He was there researching evil spirits for his PhD thesis when someone took him to that village and showed him the woman's body in the tree. The native doctor in that area forbade anyone to go near the body until the evil spirits left. He said that if they did the spirits could identify someone who was vulnerable and attach themselves to the person, and that person without substantial intervention could end up the same way. That short narrative by the native doctor is him talking about a fallen angel, an angel who was once so handsome and musically gifted who allowed himself to be worshipped by other angels in heaven. This angel tried to overthrow his Creator and was cast out of Heaven with the other angels who had become his followers. Now, the fallen angel also known as the Devil or Satan and his followers (demons) roam around looking for souls. His followers attach themselves to people with suicidal thoughts who voice their thoughts or make an attempt to carry them out or people with evil intentions and do whatever it takes to get their soul. To get a person's soul means taking their life! Satan has deceived these fallen angels into thinking that the more souls they get, the easier it will be to buy their way back into Heaven. Are you familiar with the Theologian, A. Newman?"

"No," Sergeant Kelleher answered.

"In 1852, after years of research, Alfred Newman was said to have uncovered the Dark Deception. He said the demons in hell had been deceived into thinking that they could use human souls as currency to buy their way back into Heaven. The native doctor mentions this. He also says that the only way for humanity to be saved is if humanity turns back to the Uncreated Creator, JEHOVA, repents and asks Him for forgiveness, salvation and protection."

Sergeant Kelleher shook his head, "Are you serious?"

"I'm very serious, Sergeant."

"All that mumbo jumbo was about fallen angels who are now wicked demons?"

"I can assure you, Sergeant; that wasn't mumbo-jumbo as you call it, and some people would find your use of those words politically incorrect!"

"Then they need to check a thesaurus and not dwell so much on meaningless words," he paused then decided to back down and keep the peace. "What were the dark images and what was that chanting about?"

"According to the native doctor, those dark images are the evil forces and the chanting them rejoicing at the woman's death and claiming her soul. The native doctor quoted John Chapter 10 verse 10 and some other verses several times in his dialogue. John 10:10 says – *The thief comes only in order to steal, kill and destroy.*"

Stunned, Sergeant Kelleher shook his head again, "You're joking right? A native doctor quoted a section from the Gospel of John in the Bible?"

"He also quoted from 1st John Chapter 4 verses 7-21, 1st Corinthians Chapter 13 verses 1-13, Matthew Chapter 22 verses 37-39 and John 3 verse 16," Dr Lewis added.

Sergeant Kelleher frowned, "1st Corinthians Chapter 13 versus 1-13! A native doctor quoted the bit in the Bible about love! Love is patient, and love is kind, and love is eternal and so on and so on. My dad read that passage at my sister's wedding – a native doctor quoted that, I don't believe that, how would he know that? I find this whole thing very amusing."

Dr Lewis sighed softly; he could deal with sceptics. He had done so for years. It was people who knew the truth but refused to accept it that he had problems dealing with, but he had patience, and he was always ready to exercise it. "Sergeant Kelleher according to Mustafa the native doctor knew a lot of Bible passages he knew that 1st John Chapter 4 verses 7-21 talks about God being Love and how we are to walk in Love. He knew Matthew Chapter 22 verses 37-39 speaks of the Great Commandment – to love God first, yourself and your neighbour. And, he knew that John 3 verse 16 talks about God loving the World and giving His only begotten Son Jesus, for the salvation of man. But let's go back to the unfortunate woman. The woman you saw in that video was called Loretta. She had been married for eight months and had recently found out she was pregnant. Her husband had gone to visit relatives in the city to break the good news to them. There was an accident involving the bus he had been travelling on. It was reported that all the passengers had died. On hearing the news, the woman hung herself. Three days later her husband was found alive, he was the sole survivor and had been thrown clear from the bus when it crashed, his only injuries were a broken leg and concussion. She killed herself because she thought he was dead and probably saw no reason to go on, not even for the sake of her unborn child. There is nothing amusing about that Sergeant."

"I'm sorry Dr Lewis, I mean no disrespect but I deal with crime daily, and I get sent to mop up after someone commits suicide, it's not something I enjoy doing, and it's desensitised me a little. I'm sick of the waste, tired of the deaders, people who have no respect for the life they've been given that they think they can just discard it as and when they choose to! From what you're saying, it sounds as if this has nothing to do with the individual because there are a bunch of demons running around making them kill themselves. It's almost like you're making an excuse for them doing what they've done!"

"No, I'm not making an excuse. I hate the fact that someone feels they can take their own life instead of choosing to fight. I hate the fact that life has become valueless to certain people, but I'm aware that in some cases the suicide attempt is a cry for help. Sometimes the person is in so much pain they feel the only option they have is to end their life. I've seen first-hand and have heard stories of people suddenly acting as if they were possessed by evil spirits, of people being overcome by a sense of depression which science is unable to explain. These people have gone on to commit suicide, and I don't make any excuses for them. Suicide is wrong! There is always something that can be done to prevent it. We need to understand that what we may be dealing with in some cases cannot simply be explained away by science and formulas. And, understanding brings enlightenment and the ability to think outside the box. That's the only way we can help! That is why I'm here. To give a person an educated choice and to stop this happening! A person in pain needs help to see that life can get better. It might involve them taking time away from their current situation, and it might involve them talking to someone about their problems so that they can get help. For me, it's about getting people to stop and think, to choose life and see that once you're dead – you're dead!"

Sergeant Kelleher felt as if he were sinking in quicksand. Everything he thought he knew about suicide was being squashed, and he felt uneasy. He held his hands up as if to ward off what he knew was true and what threatened to expose his dark thoughts about suicide. Thoughts that allowed him to hate and remain detached.

Anna could tell that Peter was getting frustrated at Sergeant Kelleher's attitude and quickly jumped in, "Genny can you play two short clips of success stories and the before and after clip by the poet please?"

"Sure," Genny replied, undecided if she liked Sergeant Kelleher or not. She opened up a file on her computer then pressed the play button. "For confidentiality purposes, there are no faces and no names but the voices are real, and the people chose the background screens and in some cases music to accompany their words."

Sergeant Kelleher leaned back in his chair, "Wow, this comes with music?"

"Yes, Sergeant, it does," Genny snapped.

"Look, I admit I'm a sceptic. I grew up watching Houdini movies. I read about how he exposed spiritualists in 1925. I saw movies of his mocked séances, and how he revealed how they were done, it fascinated me, so all this stuff doesn't impress me."

"We're not trying to impress you, Sergeant, we're just trying to get through to you, to make you see that some things are not what you think they are," Genny said.

Sergeant Kelleher shook his head, "Okay, play the clips," he conceded.

CHAPTER 20

Clip 1 – Atlanta, Georgia, USA

"For two weeks I cut my arms with a dirty razor blade because I hoped that I would get an infection and die. One day I ended up in the hospital with septicaemia and nearly died. The funny thing was when I was faced with the possibility of death. I didn't want to die. When the doctors discovered all the cuts on my arms they told my parents who contacted TTS, and a counsellor came to see me in the hospital. It was weird; it was a bit like in the Matrix movie where Neo was told to choose a pill. I was told to choose life over death and that in order for me to get over my own problems I should try and help other people. My counsellor took me to the children's cancer unit in the hospital and showed me some children who had various types and stages of cancer. Suddenly, my trying to kill myself because my boyfriend had dumped me seemed so pathetic and incomprehensible. My TTS counsellor kept in touch with me every day for weeks. She checked that I was going to school and spoke to my parents about any concerns for me they might have. She still calls me and still makes sure that I focus on my dreams and work towards them. I want to become a Clinical Research Scientist and help people with cancer get better. I go to the cancer ward every week, and I love talking to the children there and taking them on trips with the hospital staff. I love that they are fighters and want to live, and I thank God every day for the man who talked to my mom at her job days before I nearly died and gave her and her work colleagues the TTS card with their emergency number on it. You know what's strange, my mom said he was a Black man, but one of her work colleagues insists he was an Oriental man while another said he was a White man. My mom says that she had never seen him before, and she has not seen him since. She thinks his name was P. Holister, but she isn't sure. I know he was a God-send, and I now see that life is precious, and

when I was faced with death, I didn't want to die."

Clip 2 – Surrey, UK

"Boys don't cry, boys slug it out and don't go crying to mama. Boys become men in the playground. No one actually says these words to you when you're fifteen but by the time you get to fifteen you've heard them so many times that you feel if you don't man-up and live up to them then you're not a real boy, you're a wimp. My family moved because my dad got an excellent job and I had to change school. Changing school meant leaving the security of my friends and going to a foreign territory where I had to make new friends. My dad said that the new school would be better as it was higher up the league table than my old school. The first day I went there I hated it. There was a group of boys who seemed to run the school, and I hated them. One day they were hitting this boy two years their junior and no one stood up for him so I did. They waited for me after school that day and kicked the shit out of me. I went home and said that I had been hit several times during rugby, and no one questioned me. My dad actually said 'that's my boy!' He was so proud of my bruises. They bullied me for weeks until I couldn't take it anymore. I remember waking up, getting dressed and the next thing I was at the train station standing on the platform waiting to jump in front of the fast train from Euston to Northampton. The automated voice warned people to move away from the edge of the platform as the fast train would not be stopping at this station. Eyes closed. I waited. The train didn't come. I waited some more then I heard shouting and running. I turned and saw the boy I had helped at school running towards me with this woman right behind him. The boy grabbed my arm and pulled me back from the edge of the platform. He told me he used to come here when he thought of ending things but then he had talked to someone, and they had put him in touch with TTS. He introduced me to the woman who he said was his counsellor.

He said he had just come to show her the platform he used to stand on waiting for the fast train. He said he would come ten minutes earlier and by the time the train was a few minutes away he would chicken out and go home. He also said that the train was never late. That it was one of the few trains in the country that was always on time. That day the train was seven minutes late! The whole thing still gives me goose bumps when I think of it. TTS have changed my life. I'm in another school studying for my GCSEs, and I'm loving it all! Life is too good! I got evidence against the bullies and pressed charges against them, and I followed through and made sure that they were punished. I can't believe that those boys could have taken me to such a low place in my life where I thought that I couldn't go on living. When I think of all the good things waiting for me in my future, I can't believe that I almost threw everything away. What would my parents have done? What would my brother and sister have done if I'd killed myself? I would have destroyed my family!
I work with TTS as a youth support worker, and I talk to other kids and tell them my story, and they listen. I tell them what TTS have told me, 'Bullies want to make you a victim but you don't have to be a victim.' I believe that by Talking To Someone, you can save your life!"

Clip 3: Before and After – Newcastle, UK
"I heard once that when you say you want to die enough times a spirit of suicide takes hold of your mind and this spirit plagues you with suicidal thoughts 24/7 until you actually do it, kill yourself. I read some of the poems I wrote before talking to someone at TTS, and I can't believe that I wrote them. I'm not that person anymore. I have everything to live for now. Listen to this."

There is a pause then the words of the poem appear on the screen as she recites them:

"I don't want to live anymore – I want to die

I can't bear this pain
Feeling depressed and unworthy
Feeling abandoned and full of shame
I have tried everything to make me have a little bit of peace
Drugs, parties, drink
The more I do, the more I think
That I don't want to live anymore – I want to die.
If I died today
Who would care?
I would end everything
There would be no more pain and fear
I don't want to live anymore – I want to die
I can't bear this pain
Feeling depressed and unworthy
Feeling abandoned and full of shame."

There is a pause then:

"Oh my gosh, literally, OMG, that sounds so dreary and full
of despair. That was when I left my passion for singing in my
church choir because my boyfriend at the time convinced me
to have sex with him then chucked me after a couple of
months. I'm from Newcastle, a city in Tyne and Wear, and all
my family is here, but I felt so cut off from everyone at the
time. I was ashamed. I let him use me just cos he said he loved
me. He's sixteen, what does he know about love and what do I
know at fifteen? He couldn't even change a duvet cover or
separate his coloured clothes from his whites before washing
them without his mum's help, and he was telling me he loved
me and wanted to marry me, take care of me and set up home
with me just to get into my knickers and I let him. That was
then, and this is now. I've gone back to church, and I've
changed my life around after talking to a counsellor at TTS. It
wasn't until all this happened that I understood the meaning of
the prayer of repentance – **Lord Jesus, I repent of my sins,**
please forgive me, come into my heart today, I make You my
Lord forever and my Saviour always, Amen.

U MURDER U (SUICIDE)

*I wrote this song for the choir at church a few days ago, and I
want to share it with you, so this is like an exclusive, peoples!"*
She giggles infectiously.
Music starts to play then:
♫ *"Fill me with Your Love Oh Lord*
Fill me with You
For I want to live a life full of You
A life where I can be all, You want me to be
For I want to do all the things in my life
That bring You the Glory and Praise

Fill me with Your Love Oh Lord
Fill me with You
You are all I have. You are all I need
In You, nothing is impossible, in You I can achieve
All that You said through Your Holy Word
I can be all that I've read and all that I've heard

Fill me with Your Love Oh Lord
Fill me with You

No longer a sinner, no longer in sin
In You, my life is renewed, and I can begin
Now that I am empty of me and full of You
Through my Precious Saviour all things can, I do

Always fill me with Your Love Oh Lord
Always fill me with You ...." ♫

The screen went black.
Anna turned and looked at Sergeant Kelleher. She saw him
blink several times then look away. "Sergeant Kelleher, the
aims of TTS, are as follows:
To stop people killing themselves
To make people want to choose life

To shut down suicide chat rooms and self-harming sites
To replace every one of those evil sites with sites containing
our message and connect people to other people or like-
minded groups who can help them. I'm talking about
organisations like the Samaritans, NSPCC, Kidscape,
ChildLine, Centre Point, the Prince's Trust in short anywhere
these people can contact or go to and get help. This is just a
fraction of our group if you're going to head this task force
you need to know who we all are and what we do. My name is
Anna Lee Lewis, and this is my husband, Dr Peter Lewis.
You've met Gennifer and Tristan Cookson and you know
Inspector James. The gentleman over there is Dr Chang Lin,
he is a medical doctor, one of our senior counsellors at TTS
and is also a consultant for New Scotland Yard. The lady on
your left is Geeta Singh, a psychiatric consultant and part-time
counsellor at TTS-"

"TTS?" Sergeant Kelleher asked.

"It stands for Talk To Someone."

Suddenly it clicked, "I thought I recognised you! You're the
lady I read about in the newspaper the other day. It was an
article written by Chris Plummer in the Sunday Newspaper.
The article said that you don't see dead people, you just talk to
them in your sleep!" He stood up, "Inspector James, you *really*
want me to head this task force? You know me, Sir. You know
the sceptical me inside out! Do you really think that I can
work with someone who talks to dead people?" The humour in
his voice simmered.

"Sergeant Kelleher, you don't have to believe in what I don't
see or what I hear, but you *do* have to believe in saving lives
because that's why we're all here. If you don't believe in
trying to save lives, then my question is, does Inspector James
have the right man for this job?"

"You know, I think you and I are in agreement about that
Mrs Lewis," he turned to the inspector, "do you really believe
that I can do this?"

Inspector James cleared his throat, "Yes, I think I have the right man for the job John. I wouldn't have asked you to come if I didn't believe you were the right person."

Anna felt a slight chill as she stared at him for a few moments; she blinked as a voice said something. She heard the words clearly and was not surprised that no one in the room heard what she had, she was used to this happening. "Sergeant Kelleher, what will it take for you to believe in me?"

"Tell me something that no one else knows?" He joked.

"Okay, but when you're freaking out, remember you asked me to do this."

"Believe me, one thing I do not do is freak out Mrs Lewis-"

"Call me Anna."

"Okay Anna, tell me something no one else knows?"

Anna studied his handsome face for a few moments, "The last thing your father said to you before he died was *'Johnny, make every minute of your life count, help those who can't help themselves and enjoy your life'*. He called you Johnny, the nickname he's used for you since you were nearly 5-years old and fell off the bike he was teaching you to ride. He says he had taken his eyes off you for mere seconds to light a cigarette and you went riding off by yourself and landed in a rose bush. He was upset because he was not supposed to be smoking and had told your mom that he had quit but would take you to the park and sneak a cigarette. Even after all these years you still blame yourself. You feel that if you hadn't kept your father's secret and told your mom, he would have quit smoking and wouldn't have died from lung cancer. He says to tell you that you were the child, and he was the adult, you shouldn't blame yourself for his actions and his bad choices."

Blood rushed to Sergeant Kelleher's head, and he found that he couldn't breathe. Fear manifested itself as a strong pressure in his chest. His blood went cold, and he felt sick, "How did you . . . How the hell did you know that?" He whispered.

CHAPTER 21

"How the hell did you know that?" Shock etched itself into his being and resonated on his face. Fear engulfed him – it paralysed him as he stared at her different coloured eyes.

"He just told me-"

"My father just spoke to you!" Scared he looked around the room for the sign of a presence, "what the hell are you doing?" He asked Anna, his eyes scanned the room again, a trembling hand ran through his hair. "Why would you do this to me?"

"I'm telling you something that no one else knows," Anna answered, concerned at his response, "just like you asked me to Sergeant Kelleher."

"Are you a psychic? I don't understand, what the . . . My late father just spoke to you? My dead dad just told you all that?" His voice broke as tears rushed into his eyes.

"Sergeant," her voice was empathetic, "I'm not a psychic, but I hear things from a variety of people who have died. One day I'll tell you why I'm the way I am, that is if you decide to stay. I hope you stay."

Sergeant Kelleher tried to compose himself but (in Anna's words) he was freaking out. He didn't like dabbling in the world of the dead or getting a message from a deceased person. Such things gave him the chills, even watching a movie about such things had him sleeping with the lights on for days. Reading about how Houdini had exposed fake séances when he was a boy and watching old movies about it growing up made him regard all messages from the dead as fake and not worth the time it took to voice them. He had never allowed himself to be exposed to messages from the dead before – until now. He tried to compose himself and reclaim his nonchalant air; he could hear people talking quietly.

Peter: You can't keep doing things like that Anna, he looked like he was going to have a heart attack.

Anna: He needed to hear that Peter, how else was I supposed to convince him that we're legit.

Peter: By being a little bit more sensitive, he probably didn't need to hear what you just said in front of an audience.

Anna: I wouldn't have told him if his father didn't want him to know. His father is still concerned about him blaming himself and wants him to stop. Plus he was getting a little too smart with you.

Peter: I'm a big boy Anna, I can handle him.

Sergeant Kelleher could feel his breathing stabilising and the pounding of his heart taking on a slower rhythm - normalising. "I have one condition if I stay, I don't want to hear any more messages from the grave, I don't want to be reminded of my loss," he said.

Anna rubbed a hand across her brow, "I'm sorry Sergeant Kelleher. My husband's right, I shouldn't have just blurted that out in front of everyone like that I should have been a lot more sensitive. I needed to get your attention. If everything Inspector James says about you is true, we could use you."

He nodded. Genny placed a glass of water on the table in front of him and squeezed his hand. He smiled his thanks. He hadn't seen her get up to get the water and realised Anna's words had hit him hard and for a few moments had winded him and made him close in on himself like a wilting plant. He refocused his thoughts – he took them away from his father's last words to him, which Anna had just voiced verbatim.

He straightened up and looked at the screens on the wall, his eyes scanning the graffiti walls and the red dots. He heard voices in the room; Anna and Peter were talking about something with the others – it was as if they were all intentionally giving him time to breathe. He wondered how he would enter into the conversation taking place in the room. Truth be told, he was intrigued by Anna and her ability to converse with dead people; when he had first read about her, the possibility of her being able to talk to his father had crossed his mind. But he didn't *just* want his father's words he wanted his actual father back. He knew he was still grieving, and he was aware that Anna's words – his father's last words to him, were said to help him deal with his grief. *'Johnny, make every minute of your life count, help those who can't help themselves and enjoy your life'*. The image of his father laughing as he struggled to manoeuvre his scooter in a straight line came into his mind; his father had loved life, and his father would want him to save lives.

He looked at the symbols next to the pool of letters. He knew them well and what they represented. He had seen them drawn on the bodies of dead people or on suicide notes that had been written by dead people before they killed themselves. Notes often written in minutes which tried feebly to explain why they had done what they did – why they couldn't go on living. What the notes never explained was why they couldn't trust in God, their families or friends to help get them through their dark moments; why they couldn't believe in love.

The symbols were used in everyday life, and if you didn't look too hard you wouldn't pay attention to their hidden meanings:

∞ - infinity

Ω - the end

Θ - death

Next, his eyes went to the pool of letters embossed in the graffiti – they were in no logical or sequential order. He again wondered how he would enter into the conversation taking place in the room. Reluctantly, he turned away from the graffiti but was immediately pulled back as letters suddenly jumped out at him. Unconsciously his mind receded to a time when he was younger, and word searches were second nature to him – a hand moved the letters around – a hand he recognised: his father's hand. His father had spent hours teaching him, then seven years old, how to find hidden words.

"UREDM?" Sergeant Kelleher said almost to himself but

loud enough to attract attention. He walked over to the screen on the wall displaying the embossed graffiti. Silence filled the room. All eyes stared at him as he stood in front of the screen. The eyes couldn't see what he saw. They couldn't decipher what he had. "Right here on the screen," he circled the letters, "I've seen this before. There was a jumper. A young man jumped in front of a moving train last week. I had to take his rucksack to his family. Inside his bag was a notebook, it was unused, but there was one word written on the first page. UREDM, no one knew what it meant, not his parents or his friends. At the time I didn't think anything of it, I just thought it was gibberish, written by someone who was about to kill himself. Seeing it here on this wall like this with all the other symbols around it - it's so unbelievably clear."

No one said anything. They stared at him and the inscrutable letters he had circled – they didn't move. They had tried for weeks to break the code. The same excited thought probably dangled in all their minds – 'Has he done it? Has he really done it? Make sure he's really done it before you move because it might be a fleeting fluke!'

"Sergeant Kelleher, do you know what the letters stand for?" Anna asked.

"Individually, no, it isn't that obvious but with all the other letters and symbols it all makes sense, it's all really clear."

"What do you see?" Anna asked.

He didn't answer directly, "When I was young my father, and I would do cryptic puzzles together, he taught me how to read puzzles and how to decipher the clues. He was always leaving word puzzles for me. I would get the answer and a small prize, and there would be another puzzle with the hint of a bigger prize. Sometimes it would go on for hours until I found all the prizes. I wouldn't stop looking until I found everything."

"But we've had some of our analysts look at those images and no one's been able to decipher the message," Genny said.

"That's because the message is 'simply' hidden in plain sight," he told her, "pull out your vowels then work with your consonants, go left to right first then right to left," he said his father's words to himself. His eyes did as they had been trained to do until they found what they sought. He noticed that some letters were superimposed on themselves once or twice and some were not. His heart began to pound as he saw the simple pattern.

Genny was staring at him, "You've figured it out haven't you?" She asked.

He nodded, "UREDM, stands for U MURDER U. The U has been superimposed twice and the R once. Each layer depicts how many times that letter appears in the word. It's written backwards to read, UREDRUMU. Over here EDICUS is SUICIDE written backwards, the letter I is superimposed once. With these letters and those symbols which indicate suicidal tendencies, I think you're right, someone is putting this out there and probably waiting for people to take the bait."

"The message is hidden in plain sight," Genny repeated softly. "Our analysts have spent numerous hours on this."

"EDICUS? EDICUS! – Wasn't there a Greek myth about a person with that name? He thought he was the most handsome and intelligent person in the World then one day he found out he wasn't. Some say the shock of that revelation drove him insane and made him kill himself, while others say his pride made him fall." Tristan said. "I'm sure that's how the story went," he added.

"I've heard about that myth but I thought it was fake," Dr Lewis said, "it's in Somerville's book of fake/factual legends and myths. You can only get reference copies of that book in libraries nowadays. It's been banned in some countries because of all the contradictions and misinterpretations that surround it. Some people have taken the book as factual, and some serial killers have quoted from it during their trials."

"Hidden in plain sight," Inspector James said almost to

himself, "someone or some people are brazenly going out and putting these words on walls or websites or chat rooms instigating weak-minded people to take their own lives. What kind of hellish society are we living in?"

"A society that aids evil forces to do this, knowingly or unknowingly, a society that is leaving out the only One who can protect them from the evil forces!" Dr Chang Lin replied.

Genny grabbed her mobile phone, moved to a corner of the room, pressed some numbers and waited. "Hello, Miguel, this is Genny. Sergeant John Kelleher might be taking over from Inspector James as the head of the task force. He's here with me, and I think he might have just broken the code." She listened for a few moments. "We're coming over now," she said, grabbed her bag and indicated with her head that Sergeant Kelleher follow her as she continued to talk and walk. He was about to protest, to tell her that he hadn't officially agreed to work with the task force let alone head it but something in her eyes stopped him. Instead, he followed her. She hung up and told him that they needed to get across London quickly then started to run.

"Whoa, slow down, are you planning to run all the way?" Sergeant Kelleher joked.

She stopped running and started walking, "No, smarty-pants, there's a car waiting to take us to Canning Town then we have to take the ferry, which leaves in thirty minutes."

"Where are we going?"

"A secret location, we have our primary server hidden there, and we have people working on hacking into websites all over the World." She strode quickly ahead of him, and he had to walk fast to keep up. "Is this pace easier for you Sergeant?"

He nodded, "It's better."

"Well you need to take it up a gear slowcoach, look alive, put some grease in your cogs and move it, we have urgent business to see to," she said and smiled as she strode quickly ahead of him.

CHAPTER 22

Elle sat in the assembly hall with the other children and teachers and listened to the speaker, a member of the Inspirational Mentors, talk about microbiology, biochemistry, haematology, blood transfusion and histology. The speaker, a pathology manager, talked about what she did on a day to day basis at work and the mandatory GCSE subjects and A-level subjects required to study one of the sciences at university and get a job in pathology. Elle wasn't interested in studying science. She wasn't sure what she wanted to do, but she knew it would have something to do with music, drama and writing. The speaker also wrote novels and had come with a friend, a secret surprise guest speaker, who also wrote books. Elle couldn't wait for this surprise guest to talk about her books. One of the teachers had let it slip that all of them were now blockbuster movies.

The room was plunged into darkness as a video about pathology started to play.

A whispered voice asked if there was any popcorn going.

Another if there were any nachos, M&Ms or dolly mix sweets.

Several children giggled in response.

Mrs Fletcher, the class teacher, coughed loudly. It was a warning cough that carried the weight of detention behind it.

Silence immediately ensued as everyone watched the video.

A questions and answer session followed.

"So enough about Science, has anyone read any of my books?" The speaker asked.

Several hands flew up, lingered then fell.

"Who would like to tell me about their favourite one?"

Elle's hand shot up first.

Later than evening Elle told her mother about how she had

been picked out in assembly and asked to talk about a book she liked written by the visiting speaker. She told her mother that at first she had felt nervous and when she had seen some people in her class snickering and making faces she had felt angry and upset but then the speaker had gotten off the stool she was sitting on and asked Elle to sit there. She told everyone to listen to what was about to be said and jokingly added that she had a white belt in karate and would sort anyone out if they didn't listen. Wide-eyed, Clarissa looked at her daughter as she talked about what she had said and how even though everyone was looking at her, at that moment she hadn't felt nervous. It was as though something took over her when she sat on the stool. She had felt brave and confident. Clarissa noted the light sparkling in her daughter's eyes. It captivated her and drew her completely into what Elle was saying.

"And Mum, Mum, then she said that I had described certain sections in the book so well it was as if I had written it myself. She said that I had such a vivid imagination and my clarity of expression was exceptional and that I should apply for a writing scholarship at her friend's writing academy, and she would give me a reference. Then her friend who must have come in when we were watching the video and sat at the back stood up and started clapping for me and everyone was shocked at who it was. Then her friend talked about her books, and everyone was like 'OMG, is that really her?' We couldn't believe who her friend was and that she was actually standing in our school's assembly hall. It was like, 'Noooo. That isn't really her is it? That can't be her!' Then they both talked to me after assembly and asked if I was interested in applying for one of the writing scholarships. Then the original speaker had to leave, and her friend said to my teacher that my applying would be a formality as she would set a scholarship aside for me today! Aaaarrrrrrrrh!"

"What?" Clarissa asked, taken aback by Elle's excited

scream and the news which had preceded it.

"She said that if I was interested, I was to talk to my parents and ask them to contact her," Elle pulled a business card out of her pocket and held it out to her mother.

Clarissa stared at the name on the card. She felt sensations of dizziness assault her first, excitement quickly followed as it tried to wrestle her away from dizziness and claim her to itself. She took the card from Elle and looked at it properly. She rubbed a finger against the lettering almost as if trying to make sure that the letters were actually attached to the card. The handwritten mobile number and a smiley face written by the author took her breath hostage.

"Elle, this is . . . this is . . . she's sold millions of books all over the World . . . she's really famous . . . she's," words failed Clarissa as gobsmacked she stared at her daughter.

"The next writing school programme starts soon in North London and since I have a scholarship, can I go? I really want to go, Mum, can I go?" Elle pleaded.

"Elle, this is . . . J . . . this is J.K., . . . Elle, this is," Clarissa couldn't breathe.

CHAPTER 23

JaneDoe2B: Can you believe I took 12 painkillers . . . they didn't kill me ☹ . . . still here ☹

Li-sa 5: That really sucks, take more next time.

Unhappy 2: I'm going to do it with a rope in the garage in the middle of the night.

Doeboy: I've got some Heroin . . . I'm going to use it to OD. I'm going out on a high ☺

Jessy James 6: In the hospital, cut wrists, felt death nearby but got pulled back by my dad. Help . . . I'm still here in the land of the living!!

Shy boy 1: Oh man, that close to death it must have felt awesome! Wicked!

Jessy James 6: I felt like I was floating to a better place.

Shy boy 1: I wish that was me and no one found me, I'd be free from this hell house, free from this life. UREDRUMU ΘΩΘ

Li-sa 5: I wish it was me too. Maybe next time JJ6.

Jessy James 6: Next time will be it, I just know it, the next time will be final.

Shy boy 1: What method?

Jessy James 6: Poison!

Shy boy 1: Have you got it?

Jessy James 6: I'm in the hospital, it's everywhere you look. Got some stuff out the nurse's trolley-thing-a-mi-jig, that they keep the drugs in. Got loads of cool stuff.

Shy boy 1: Enough for me as well?

Li-sa 5: Enough for me too?

Jessy James 6: More than enough, @Room 15, third floor.

Patrick Carmichael knocked on his daughter's door and walked into her room. Jessica quickly lowered the top of her laptop and looked at her father with cautious eyes.

"How are you feeling Jess?"

"Much better Daddy," she replied a little too sweetly.

He frowned and proceeded cautiously. "Were you on your laptop just now? You know the doctor said that he thought you shouldn't do anything that might trigger certain emotions."

"I was just sending an email to a friend-"

"Which friend Jess?" Before she could think of a name, he walked swiftly up to her bed leaned over and grabbed the computer out of her hands.

"Dad, what are you doing?" She tried to grab it back, but he pushed her away and raised the top. The dark screen jumped into life as it lit up and revealed words.

Patrick Carmichael's frown deepened as he read the words on the screen, he had heard about chat rooms like this. He had read about suicide pacts and how the internet was a place to connect with like-minded people. But for some reason, he never actually believed that such a place would have anything to do with him, that he would be linked with such a place. Yet, here he was reading words written by people who wanted to commit suicide. Not only that, in this latest chat, his daughter was the primary 'chatter' the one talking about how her next attempt would be successful and how she had stolen enough drugs for herself and Shy boy 1, and all her potentially soon-to-be-dead Jane Doe and John Doe friends to use.

He looked at the last entry written by Shy boy 1 and his heart went cold:

Shy boy 1: I'm nine years old, and I think you're a hero Jessy James 6, not sure how to get to the hospital, but I'll find a way then we can die together ☺

"NURSE!"

"Dad, what are you doing?"

"NURSE!" Patrick screamed again.

The door swung open, and Nurse Preeti rushed in, "Inspector Carmichael, what is it? What's happened?" She looked from father to daughter and then back to father.

"Jessica has stolen drugs from the nurse's drug trolley. She's planning another suicide attempt."

"What! Sweet mother of God, Jessica, why would you do that?"

"It's a lie. My dad is lying, I didn't steal anything!"

Patrick walked towards her, grabbed her arms and shook her hard, "Where are they? Where are the drugs?"

"Oww, oww, I don't have anything," Jessica sobbed.

"Where are they?" He shook her again.

"Mr Carmichael, um, Inspector Carmichael, let her go, we'll find them, please, you're hurting her, let her go," Nurse Preeti's voice was low but firm.

Patrick looked at his daughter as she sobbed. He tightened his grip. He was scared that if he let her go then, she would be lost forever. He would never find her again, and all he would have were cold pictures of her once warm laughter. Baby pictures full of so much hope, toddler pictures, pre-teenage pictures and early teenage pictures – that would be all he had, this warm living girl would be cold and dead. "Why would you do this to me? You selfish bitch, why would you do this? Haven't I always been on your side, haven't I always supported you? Why would you hurt me like this? You selfish, selfish, cold hearted bitch!" These words came out from his mouth, but they were not the words that ripped through his heart, these were the words which cut through his heart, *'Jessica, I love you so much, please don't do this, please, want life! Want to live! Please, Jessica, don't hurt me like this anymore but most importantly, don't hurt yourself. I love you so much. I'm your father. I'm supposed to look after you, and I'm meant to protect you from external harm. But no one ever told me how to protect you from hurting yourself.'* These words no one heard, only his heart.

"Inspector Carmichael, please let go of her, we'll find the pills and anything else she might have and get rid of them."

As quickly as he had grabbed hold of Jessica, he let her go. He stared with unseeing eyes as she fell onto the bed and scream-cried. The sound she made was similar to that of a banshee he had seen once in a horror movie. He didn't try to comfort her. He didn't move towards her; frozen, he watched her scream-cry.

Nurse Preeti pressed a bell on the wall and within seconds two nurses rushed into the room. "We need to strip search this room for drugs or anything else that might be used by Jessica to harm herself. And, we need to get Jessica over to Psych for evaluation then into a room on an open ward so she is more visible – STAT!" She told them.

CHAPTER 24

Sergeant John Kelleher hated many things, but one thing had the biggest portion of his hatred – telling a family that a loved one was dead, not by accident or another person's hand, but killed by their own hand – suicide. The blank look of complete disbelief, the pain filled screams, the collapses and the tears were things that he hated to see, not because they hardened his heart but because he felt they made him too vulnerable, he pretended they didn't, but he knew they did. Times like now, he had to detach himself and get on with his job.

He sat in the front room of the family home of Geoffrey Gollantz-Cole, a warm cup of tea on the table next to him, which Geoffrey's 'new' widow had insisted he have, and he hated being here. Usually, he made these visits with a partner but several of his colleagues were off sick with suspected Norovirus, and he had to do this by himself. He had done some visits by himself recently and tended to stick to a protocol which saw him in and out within forty-five minutes. He looked at his notes. Up until this morning, Geoffrey had been a top City investment banker; he had a wife and three children and lived in this beautiful house in Hampstead, one of the wealthiest locations in London. Last night he had been home, he had eaten dinner with his family and even discussed the holiday they were going to take next month. This morning he had eaten breakfast with his family, helped his youngest son with his maths homework and told his only daughter to make sure she brought her cello home so he could hear her practice tonight. He had told his eldest son, 11-year-old Jake, to make sure that his room was tidy by the time he got home from work this evening, and he had told his wife of fourteen years that he would prefer fish instead of chicken for dinner tonight. She had given him the choice of chicken or fish.

Geoffrey Gollantz-Cole had acted as if he had every intention of coming home this evening, but all the evidence gathered showed he had no intention of doing this.

His wife, Valerie, had insisted that John have a cup of tea after he told her the news. First, she had insisted on hearing how Geoffrey had died; she wanted to know every single detail, wanting nothing to be left out. Sergeant Kelleher told her that her husband had gone to lunch in a trendy restaurant situated on the roof of a fifteen-floor building in Central London, ordered his meal with his work colleagues then calmly got up from the table and threw himself off the roof. He hadn't died immediately. It had taken about ten minutes from the time he hit the ground next to a popular pub for him to be pronounced dead by the paramedics. Some of the pub's clientele had tried to help him, but he had landed on his back, broken his neck, legs and numerous other bones in his body. Thirty seconds after hearing all of this, Valerie had risen and dashed out of the room. John had gone after her to make sure that she was okay and had watched as she made tea. He had seen this reaction before, and experience told him not to say anything until she had done what she set out to do. So he watched her get two cups out, place them on a tray, get the teapot out and place tea bags in it. When the water had boiled, she stumbled as she turned to get the kettle and John just stopped himself from moving forward as she held onto the side of the kitchen island and steadied herself. She quickly finished off, and John helped her to carry the tray into the front room where he now sat ten minutes later, his tea untouched and him having no intention of drinking it.

"What do I tell the children, what do I say? Geoffrey left this morning saying that he wanted to eat fish tonight. I have the fish marinating in the fridge, I've used spices I saw Lorraine on the telly use . . ."

"Lorraine?"

"Lorraine, from the TV, the pretty Black lady, I think she used to be a model, she bakes and cooks. She makes amazing cakes you know. I always watch her cooking show on TV. I have her cookbooks as well."

"That's nice, um, is there anyone I can call for you, Mrs Gollantze-Cole?"

"I will be ostracised because of this you know, people will shun me, my children will be socially scarred because of this, I will have to take them away, take them out of the country . . . I can't let them be exposed to the press and the questions."

John took a deep breath and tried again, "Is there a relative that I can call, is there someone who can sit with you, a close friend maybe?"

"What happens to a person when they commit suicide Sergeant? Do they go to hell? I read somewhere once that when a person commits suicide, they go to hell."

"I don't know what happens to them, Mrs Gollantze-Cole."

"I hope he goes to hell for what he's done to the children and me."

He thought about the task force and what Dr Lewis had said about what happens to a person's soul when they commit suicide; he changed the subject. "How old did you say your children are?"

She suddenly sat up under her heavy load and smiled, "Jake is eleven, Baron is nine, and Juliet is eight. You know, on the way to school this morning they talked about what they would get their father for Fathers' Day. They added up all the money they had and decided that it had to be something he would treasure."

"What did they decide to get?"

"Juliet said they should get him something he could take to work and put in his office so that he would always know how much they loved him. Jake agreed as long as it wasn't too girlish and Baron said 'cool', like he always does," she chuckled, "his way of agreeing. They decided on a framed picture of them with his mother." Suddenly her hand shot to her mouth, "My God, how could he do this to them? How could he leave them to continue without him?" The howl that escaped from her heart hit him hard. It suffocated him. He hated this but much more than this he disliked the people who caused this to happen. The people who thought it convenient for themselves to die by their own hands but gave no thought to their loved ones. The Valerie(s), Jake(s), Baron(s) and Juliet(s) - People who loved them and who they wittingly left behind. He grabbed hold of some tissues from a box on the glass coffee table and pushed them into her hands then tried to comfort her as best he could. He waited. He couldn't leave her alone, and she had not given him the contact number of a friend or relative to call. His next step would be to get the number of her GP and get someone from the surgery to come down and give her something to calm her and possibly come with the phone number of a relative he could call. He waited.

Valerie gulped as she struggled to breathe and calm herself, she tried to focus her mind on something, anything. "You know he never really got over the mess he caused for himself with that woman."

"What woman?" John asked.

"He had an affair with a woman last year. They met at some art function or Alcoholics Anonymous thing. I'm not sure which. He said it wasn't serious, and he was under a lot of stress from work and had started secretly drinking. His job required that he managed several portfolios worth millions of pounds which he had to build upon and make a profit. He wasn't sleeping at the time, and he was always on his computer looking for investments. Then one day he told me he'd been seeing this woman for a few weeks but had ended it. I forgave him because of the children."

"Do you know her name?"

"No."

Sergeant Kelleher frowned, "I have to ask you again, is there anyone I can call to come and stay with you? Or maybe I can call your GP."

"My GP? No, no you mustn't call Dr Doherty, you can call

my sister and my mother, their numbers are on my phone."
She reached forward picked up her mobile phone and handed
it to him. "Tell them everything you told me and tell them to
come over now, please. I can't tell the children by myself."

*

"Thank you for staying with her until we got here, Sergeant
Kelleher. Thank you so much. Do we need to go and identify
the body now?"

John shook his head as he looked at Valarie's younger
sister's tear-stained face. "Someone will be in touch with you
shortly about that. There will be an in-depth autopsy and then
the coroner will release the body. Things get done differently
in cases like this."

"Thanks for letting me know, Sergeant. I'll make sure
Valerie knows. I'd better get back inside," she indicated with
her head towards the room where her mother and sister were
sat – in mourning.

"I'll see myself out."

As he walked down the steps towards his car, every step he
took made him more resilient, he wasn't going to do this job
anymore. He hated it. He took his mobile phone out of his
pocket and pressed some numbers.

"Hello, Inspector James you're right, this has to stop, count
me in," he said.

Inspector James put the receiver down and jumped up,
"Yes!" He shouted.

The people in the outer office stopped what they were doing
and stared at him through the glass door. He quickly moved to
the door and pulled the blind down then grabbed his mobile
phone and called Anna Lee Lewis.

CHAPTER 25

It was a school day. Jimmy Duncan didn't go to school today; instead, he went to the local internet cafe and sat in front of a computer for hours. This was his safe place – here there was no bullying, no hateful words, no hitting and no laughing at him. Here he played games, listened to music and chatted with virtual friends online. He spent six hours in the internet cafe and during that time he ate ten packets of crisps, five chocolate bars, five packets of sweets (500g packs) and he drank a litre of cheap cola. At 3pm he left the cafe and walked home choosing not to take the bus and face public humiliation.

Jimmy closed the front door. He heard sounds coming from the front room; the TV was on. He walked into the front room and saw his mother asleep on the settee. A half full one-litre bottle of cider was next to an empty cider bottle under the settee – they had not been there this morning. He retrieved both bottles and crushed the smouldering cigarette that dangled precariously from an empty beer can which served as a makeshift ashtray. He carried the bottles to the kitchen, threw the empty bottle into the bin and put the half full bottle on the counter next to the fridge. There were no pots and pans on the stove and no dinner ready for him. There never was any dinner when he came home so he usually ate out. He heard his mother cough and went back into the living room. She had turned over and now had her back to the TV. She snored softly, and he knew she was drunk, he had seen her like this so many times when she was sad and depressed. He saw something white on the floor, 'it must have fallen from under her when she turned' he thought to himself, it looked like a letter. He rushed forward to retrieve it, hoping that it was the letter his mum said would come from Social Services offering him help with his weight. He picked it up, unfolded it, saw it was a letter and quickly read it.

Children's Services
Social Services Department
Liverpool

27th May
Our Ref: 2X7770 112Y

Dear Miss Duncan,

Ref: Assistance Request for Jimmy Duncan

We have reviewed your request and have decided that there is nothing that we can do for your son Jimmy at this point. We advise that you contact your GP again and find out if there is any medication that can be provided to help Jimmy with his issues. We understand that Jimmy is currently on anti-depressants but feel that this is not something we are qualified to deal with and strongly advise you contact your GP. Regarding the government assistance you mentioned in your letter, I feel that this finance should be used for children who are salvageable and as such feel your son does not qualify.

Yours Sincerely

Mr N. Bolton
Manager Children's Services

Note:

Katie can you print and then send the letter above to Miss Duncan. It regards her fat son who keeps stuffing his face with crisps, chips, pizza and fizzy drinks. The woman is deluded if she thinks that we will use our budget to cater for her ignorance. If she would stop allowing that 13-year-old tub of lard to stuff his face with crap then maybe he would have a chance at a decent semblance of life. She is such a stupid, uneducated, ignorant waste of space and should have kept her legs closed when she was sixteen then we wouldn't have to deal with this. Her fat stupid son is also a waste of space – talk about ignorance breeding ignorance.

Send the letter out asap Katie to get the idiot woman off our backs!

Thanks

Nicolas

ps

Fancy grabbing a bite tonight?

New joke

Q. How useless is it trying to do something for these fat dummies?

A. As useless as building a prison – all that hard work for nothing ☺ ☺ ☺

It was a school day. Jimmy Duncan didn't go to school today; instead, he went to the local internet cafe and sat in front of a computer for several hours. He went into a new chat room, one he had heard of but never been on before. He answered some questions then clicked on a symbol - Ω.

It was a school day. Jimmy Duncan didn't go to school today; instead, he went to Liverpool Lime Street train station and took a train to London. He had a photocopy of the Children's Services letter in his pocket.

CHAPTER 26

Danielle and Ryan – Milton Keynes Central Train Station

Ryan Kean, born in Essex, worked as the mid-west territory manager (newly appointed) and Sales Representative aka Sales Rep for a company that supplied microbiology testing kits to microbiology laboratories. His company didn't actually make the kits. However, they were the sole UK distributor for the kits which were manufactured in France. So what did these kits do? They did, albeit not so well, what it said on the tin. One kit detected Hepatitis B surface Antigen, another HIV 1&2 and another Hepatitis C antigen in human blood samples. Each kit had three parts in three separate boxes – the reagent kit, the calibrator and the quality control. A set of all three had a list price of over seven hundred pounds for the Hepatitis C kit, nearly seven hundred pounds for the Hepatitis B kit and six hundred pounds for the HIV kit. They were not the only kits in the UK; there were many different types of kits supplied by other companies, manufactured in other countries, which used the same or similar principles. In fact, the kits that Ryan's company sold was middle of the road, they worked, but they were not that good. But, in Ryan's mind, his kits were the best in the country, and he made sure everyone knew this. His Economics teacher once described Ryan in secondary school as '*a person who can sell snow to Eskimos and coats to keep them warm in the same transaction – he has the gift of the gab*'. This gift had helped him to get his kits into numerous microbiology laboratories all over his territory and some beyond. Ryan would phone a lab manager and say that he was in the building and wanted a quick word about new techniques and developments and how he was going to save them bundles of money in line with NHS efficiency policies. He never asked if he could have an appointment, never asked if the manager was busy managing their budget, managing their staff or making sure that their test-analysers were functioning properly or the many other things that managers had to do. Why would he? These things were of little or no consequence to Ryan. He expected to see a lab manager whenever he wanted to see one. After all, he was doing them a favour and saving them money and providing them with kits which were in his mind the best in the country. And, most importantly – despite his busy schedule he was making himself accessible to them *and* giving them his valuable time *and* his attention. Ryan was very forceful and egocentrically wired like that.

Danielle C. Brownlow was heading home to London. She was a second-year architecture student in Cambridge. She had spent the day with friends who lived in Milton Keynes and was now on platform one waiting for the train to Euston. Danielle had recently broken up with her boyfriend of six months and was happy about it. He was always calling her and texting her and distracting her from her studies that breaking up with him had brought so much relief she was buzzing. They had met in London at her friend's twentieth birthday party. She had liked him at first sight. He had wooed her and flattered her with gifts and dinner dates initially, but there was something about him, something she felt he was hiding. Yet, like many twenty-year-olds in the first throws of crazy love, she had ignored her concerns and rushed in. She put up with his smoking and the designer-cough thing he did of coughing often and with his mouth open but after a few weeks she found out what he was hiding. He was a Spitter, and he spat everywhere. For Danielle, the spitting issue was too big a thing to ignore and after a while, it started to get to her to the extent that when he spat it made her skin crawl. He would kiss her one minute then turn away the next and spit. He spat out of the car window while driving. He spat on the beach in Brighton. He spat outside a restaurant after dinner. When she asked him why he did it, he shrugged and said it was a habit. She never spat. She couldn't stand people who thought they needed to share their saliva with other people so much so that they had to display it on pavements, in shop entries or on public steps. Individuals who spat in public or in private (when they thought no one was watching), people who spat from car windows and quickly drove off before the spittle could settle. To her it was a disgusting habit and, like people with dogs who had to go around picking up their dog's poo, to keep the environment clean and disease-free, she felt that Spitters should clean their own mess. Comically, for some reason, she continued to date a Spitter who smoked, which made him spit even more - crazy.

Danielle watched as a train pulled onto platform two. She listened to the announcements of cancellations and delays and mentally calculated the new expected time of arrival (ETA) for each of the delayed trains.

Ladies and gentlemen the train arriving on platform two terminates here.

The seventeen twenty-two is delayed by fifteen minutes.

We regret to announce that the seventeen thirty- five has been cancelled.

The seventeen forty is delayed by ten minutes.

Ladies and gentlemen do not board the train on platform six it has a minor fault and will be removed shortly.

We regret to announce that the seventeen thirty-five has been cancelled.

The seventeen fifty-five is delayed by twenty minutes.

We apologise for the delay in your journey.

Then –

There is a good service on all trains!

Danielle smiled to herself. After Spitters, the poorly run overpriced train service was high on her list of dislikes.

"DANIELLE! DANIELLE BABES!"

Danielle felt her heart stop then kick-start itself in her chest. She didn't move. She hoped that the person who had called her would think he had made a mistake. She kept her head down and sat still. She reasoned that the voice had come from the furthest platform across three sets of tracks and if she sat dead still and the person hesitated, unsure if it was her, her train would come, and she would be gone.

"Danielle, wait there babes!" Ryan shouted out to her and grabbed his bag. He dropped his file, "Shit-bloody-shit-shit-shit," he grabbed the file, "wait there I'm coming over."

Danielle got up and grabbed her bag determined not to get caught in a scene. They hadn't given an updated ETA for her train yet. She checked the departure board. "Where is the damn train?" she said to herself then followed this with, "shit, sugar, sugar, sugar." She hated the fact that he was making her swear. He always said that 'shit' wasn't a swear word but she believed that any word you couldn't use in a letter to your grandparents, mother or father was a swear word. She heard feet pounding down steps then he was in front of her, and she had no means of escape.

"Danielle, I can't believe it! It's like that *Casablanca* film babes! Of all the coincidences in the World who would have ever said this would be one of them!" Ryan said as he dropped his overnight bag on the ground, dropped his file on top of it and gently cupped her arms with his hands.

Almost involuntary Danielle stepped back, and Ryan lowered his hands. "Ryan, what are you doing here?"

"Working. I was just in a meeting with one of my clients in Bedford. I got her to buy a load of stuff, as usual, then I had another meeting with a client at Milton Keynes, and now I'm going to Northampton to meet up with friends and celebrate my huge bonus. Where are you going, Danielle?"

"To London, I just heard that my sister isn't well."

"Tough," Ryan said.

She was used to this from Ryan. A thing was either tough or

sad, nothing more, when it came to her family and friends. He never wished anyone well or hoped they felt better. When she had questioned him about this once he had replied, 'what's the point in saying more? I can't help them can I love'.

"Danielle, I've been meaning to talk to you about our separation. I think two weeks is long enough. We need to move on now and get back to how things were-"

"Ryan, we are not on a break or brief separation, you're not Ross, and I'm not Rachel from *Friends*, we *have* broken up. There is no more 'we' Ryan, there is you, and there is me, we are both single, free agents-"

"I don't want to be single, and I know you can't want to be single either," Ryan protested.

"Actually, I do want to be single. I need to get on with my University work, and I need to be there for my family, and I need to take care of me."

"I can take care of you, Danielle. I'll always take care of you if you let me." He moved to the side of the platform where a plastic transparent bin liner swayed in the breeze. He spat on the ground next to it. He moved back towards her and stood in front of her, leaning in, his body language saying in Essex swagger, 'please take me back – babes'.

"Now's not the time for this Ryan, my train will be here soon, and you need to get back over to your platform and get your train."

"Danielle, I am begging you, please take me back, I can't live without you, please," his voice broke, and he struggled to hold himself together, "I'll do anything you want, just take me back Danielle, give me another chance, please. I don't even know what I did!"

Shocked, Danielle stared at him as he continued to plead. She could see that people on the platform were looking at them; a couple of old women had wandered closer to them and were blatantly listening. "Ryan stop this, people are looking-"

"I don't care!" He shouted. "I love you, is this what you

want from me, you said I don't show my feelings, I'm showing them now, PLEASE DANIELLE!"

"Ryan, I'll call you later. You need to get back over to your platform."

"What's the point of living without you? I might as well just jump in front of the next train and end it all-"

"Don't even joke about doing anything so sick, okay, that's not funny, and I'm not impressed!"

"If I can't have you I have nothing, don't you get it?"

"Before we met didn't you have a life? Do you think talk like that makes you look good?"

From the corner of her eye, Danielle saw a train coming along platform one. It was now seventeen thirty-seven.

Ladies and gentlemen the train approaching platform one is the delayed seventeen twenty-two . . .

CHAPTER 27

Madness is:
A. Doing the same thing over and over again and expecting a different result?
B. Doing something once and when it doesn't work give up and get angry?
C. Jumping in front of a moving train and hoping that your ex-girlfriend who is standing next to you will feel so bad at what she's made you do that she'll forget about the breakup and take you back?
D. All of the above?
Answer: D – All of the above, definitely – All of the above.

   Ryan was wallowing in self-inflicted madness. He saw Danielle as his sanity, and he was losing her (it). Danielle's train was moving along the platform towards them. His heart was beating fast and his mind racing with various scenarios. Each scenario involved Danielle taking him back and Danielle loving him again. He needed to make her see that they belonged together: she was his Victoria, and he was her David.
17:37. 20 "Danielle, I'm begging you to take me back."
17:37. 32 "Ryan, my train is here, I need to go. We can talk later today."
17:37. 47 "Danielle, please, just give me a bit of hope that we can work things out."
17:38. 01 "Ryan, we can talk later today, I need to go."
17:38. 10 "I can't live without you, Danielle."
17:38. 30 "Ryan, I will call you."
17:38. 37 Ryan's mind went blank. He watched as the train came nearer and nearer and he prepared himself to jump.
17:38. 39 'JUMP, JUMP, JUMP!' The voice in his head said.
17:38. 40 Danielle placed a hand on Ryan's shoulder, "Ryan, are you listening? Ryan, I'm talking to you!" She hit his arm.
17:38. 45 'JUMP RYAN!' The voice in his head screamed.

17:38. 48 "Ryan, my train is here, I have to go."
17:38. 55 'Jump Ryan, she'll feel sorry and take you back, she'll love you again – JUMP RYAN, JUMP!'

Ryan moved towards the edge of the platform.

Danielle grabbed his arm and pulled him back. "Ryan, listen to me, my train is here, and I'm going to get on it. Go back to your platform and wait for your train. I'll call you later, okay?"

Ryan jerked himself back into reality and stared at Danielle's retreating back as she climbed into the train that was now standing on the platform. He had zoned out and lost a few seconds. He hadn't seen the train stop at the station or the people disembark from it. His mind had been focused on jumping; now the train was here, stationary, he couldn't jump in front of it, and Danielle wouldn't feel sorry for him and take him back. He would have to think of something else. "I'll wait for you to call me Danielle but if I don't hear from you soon, like in thirty minutes, I'll call you." He shouted out.

From inside the train, Danielle nodded, waved then found a seat by the window and sat down. Unseen by him she turned her phone off then she held her phone up to him, mouthed that she would call him soon and smiled.

As he sat on the bench and watched her train pull out of the station he psyched himself up – he had wooed her before, he would woo her again. 'What was it that my Economics teacher said about me when I was in school? *Ryan has the gift of the gab. He can sell snow to Eskimos and coats to keep them warm in the same transaction* – I'm unstoppable, and I will get her back even if it kills me,' he thought to himself. He chuckled at his ironical macabre thoughts.

CHAPTER 28

Ryan's eyes stared at the granulated cemented ground of the platform and yellow line which was more of a yellow hump than a flat line; he smiled to himself. He noted things like that. An untrained eye would see a flat yellow line, but he saw that it was a yellow raised hump of a line. Next came a row of coloured terracotta tiles. Each tile had thirty-six small raised circular bumps. He knew there were thirty-six circular bumps on each tile because he had counted them several times. He read the words MIND THE GAP written in white capital letters and looked at the white paint which lined the edge of the platform. The edge was where the trains aligned themselves with the platform, and he wondered why the colour on the edge was white and not yellow. The white colour made the edge seem so safe as if venturing beyond it would not leave you mangled by the train that would not only crush you but rip the flesh off your bones and spill your blood all over the dirt and debris on the track. Yellow would warn you off he thought wisely, yellow or red. He often found his mind wandering to things others thought insignificant; like how many tiles were in a ceiling or how many cubes of ice were in a margarita. Or, like the number of small circular bumps on the tiles at the train station. Not many people would have bothered to count them. In fact, most people found them a nuisance and a pain to walk on. And, short of jumping over them to get onto a train, you had to step on them at some point during any train journey which involved using train stations where they were in place. Ryan had reasoned a while ago that they were in place to alert people how close they were to the edge of the platform. Ryan tended to simplify things to make sense of them. He often said things were 'tough' or 'sad' because quite frankly he was often given information of which there was little he could do regarding helping with the situation. Ryan found it hard to break down and cry in empathy when someone cried. Apart from thinking that this line of action was fake and fickle, he didn't see the use, and it wasn't the Essex man's way of doing things. Danielle said her sister wasn't well and to him that was 'tough'; he wasn't a doctor or a nurse – he couldn't do anything to assist in her prognosis. He had never met any of Danielle's family but from what she had told him he thought her sister was a spoilt brat. He thought her unbelievably pampered by parents who should have given her some common sense to work with when she was little, that or some proper discipline instead of catering to her every whim financially. He thought it sad that Danielle's mum initially had to work two jobs to look after Danielle and her brother before she remarried. He found it strange that no one voiced the obvious where Danielle's sister was concerned – Danielle's dad had once been married to Danielle's mum and for social elevation, the 'Mug' had abandoned his family to shack up with and then marry a strange bit of fluff, and produce the spoilt brat. Now the spoilt brat wasn't well and Danielle the 'abandoned' child was rushing down to London to see the 'usurper' child. He credited himself with being a person who paid attention to detail and, as far as he was concerned, that didn't make sense to him.

He found that a lot more things didn't make sense to him since his twin brother Dylan had died in Florida. He found he had to simplify things to survive. He was deep in thought when his train pulled into the station on platform six. He was still deep in thought when the announcement asking passengers to board the train to Northampton was made. A pigeon pecked at a piece of croissant near his foot, and the cooing noise suddenly jerked him back into reality.

.....train on platform two calling at Bletchley, Leighton Buzzard, Tring, Berkhamsted, Hemel Hempstead, Harrow and Wealdstone, Wembley Central.....

He saw his train on the distant platform, grabbed his bag and file and started running. On the bridge, he looked down to make sure that the train hadn't left and ran straight into a woman walking in the opposite direction. He nearly tripped over. The woman dropped the folder she was holding and stumbled backwards.

"I'm so sorry, are you okay? I was trying to get my train. It's still on the platform-"

"Go, I'm all right, I'll sort this out," she indicated her papers which had spilt out of her folder.

"Are you sure?" Ryan asked, moving towards the steps.

"Yes, go, I'll be fine."

"Thanks," Ryan said then ran down the steps.

"Are you okay?" A handsome ginger-blond-haired man wearing the rail network uniform asked. He didn't wait for an answer; he bent and started picking up her papers and shuffling them together.

"I'm fine thanks, thank you for helping me."

"No worries Miss, all part of the service." He picked up her identification badge and looked at it. "Miss Sophie Adams. You're a reporter with-"

"Thank you," Sophie said and held her hand out.

He gave her the badge and papers. "No worries Miss Adams." He looked around, "looks like we got all your papers. I wouldn't want you to lose your exclusive story."

Sophie frowned, "How do you know I'm writing an exclusive story?"

"Aren't you reporters always writing exclusive stories and bugging peoples' phones?"

She smiled and looked at the name on his ID badge, "No Bob. We don't all go around writing exclusive stories and bugging peoples' phones."

"That's not what I read in the papers," he joked.

Sophie chuckled then quickly looked through and arranged her papers and put them in her folder, "Thanks, Bob."

"Again, no worries Miss Adams. You know . . . " he paused.

"What?"

"I'm not sure if anyone has told you this before, but your accent is lovely. And, I love your braids," slightly embarrassed he stopped.

"In the part of Scotland where I was born, we pretty much all sound like this, so no, no one there has ever said anything like that before as for my braids what can I say," she joked.

"I'm sorry . . . I didn't mean to be forward."

"No worries Bob," she smiled and walked towards the exit.

Sophie Adams *was* writing an exclusive. A story that she had tried to write before but each time she had tried one issue, or another stopped her. She was writing about the 'Power of Unity' in the Church. Having an African mother and Scottish father, she had been brought up in the church and believed in One God, One Jesus Christ and One Holy Spirit, and believed there could only be 'One Church', which resulted from the unity of all churches. She believed that if churches united, there would be a demonstration of such power in the World that many real Christians had never seen. She had seen firsthand the manifestation of such power in Scotland when four churches of different denominations united in prayer and dramatic changes and miracles took place. And so, like Alchemists researched and worked at transforming base metals into gold. Like they had dreams of attaining the mysterious Philosopher's Stone. Sophie had ardently with much tenacity studied the Bible and correlating historical documents and found pure gems. She found scriptures in the Bible that talked about the power of unity like Deuteronomy Chapter 32 verse 30 which says that one can put 1000 to flight, and two can put 10,000 to flight. And, Matthew Chapter 18 verse 19 where Jesus said that when two or more people gathered together and prayed about something, it would come to pass. Sophie felt that the constant division among churches due to man-made doctrines was resulting in the lack of power that unity brought. And the lack of unity within some churches caused the ineffectiveness they had in their communities, towns, countries or indeed World. People outside the church saw these divisions and lack of love and as a result didn't want to join. The divisions contradicted what Jesus said in John Chapter 13 verse 35 that people would know His disciplines by the love they had for one another. The lack of unity and love in churches made it hard for people to see Jesus (the Head of the Church) let alone who His disciples were and Sophie hoped that her exclusive would highlight this and get people loving each other and uniting with each other. She knew that there was evil in the World but also knew that people who belonged to Christ (like sheep knew the voice of their shepherd) knew His voice and when called upon to unit were capable of uniting and driving the forces of darkness back – where they belonged.

The papers that Bob had helped her to pick up contained information gathered over several months from several churches in different countries. Her editor loved her first and second drafts. And, from the excited buzz in her office, she knew that this story was already causing ripples which were anticipated to become huge waves. Four weeks ago, Sophie had attended a church in South West London. It was a big family-oriented church which also catered for single people, single parents (divorced/separated), teenagers and seniors – people who were at times ignored in some churches. She found that there was unity and love within this church which touched the community and other churches. This church came with church fathers and church mothers. Sophie was given to two church mothers. A lady she called Aunty T, one of the funniest people she had ever met who was also a prestigious lawyer. And, Aunty M, one of the kindest people she had ever met who took the time to check up on her and make sure she was included in functions. She felt loved and at home here. Sophie's final draft was nearly finished. She just wanted to test her theory on the power of unity before submitting it.

CHAPTER 29

Ruth Valencia and Clarissa Williams were more like sisters than best friends. They had been roommates at University and remained in close contact ever since. Ruth, born and raised in Los Angeles, came to London as an international student to study Law. Her mother was English, and her father was from the Caribbean and a well-known lawyer who had worked on some high profile Celebrity Murder cases in LA. Her childhood, spent in America and London gave her the best of both worlds. Ruth, like her father, was a lawyer. In contrast, however, she was what she called a 'behind the scenes' lawyer. She exposed illicit charities set up by people who had little or no intention of helping the cause they had been established to help. Instead, they collected millions but paid less than 5% to the cause. Ruth made it a point in her work to get the money back from these charities and hand it over to the beneficiaries. The last few weeks had seen her go after a charity set up in London where, despite the fact that well-wishers had donated over half a million pounds, less than twenty thousand pounds had been given to the beneficiaries. After tying the charity's finances up in legalities, Ruth had collected four hundred thousand pounds from its frozen account and personally seen that it was handed over to the cause – the families of injured soldiers. The money would be used to provide a job re-entry centre, a recreational facility and a family counselling service for the soldiers. Tears were shed by several of the soldiers' wives when they realised how the money would help their husbands re-adjust to society and live somewhat semi-normal lives. Ruth was affected by 'Injustice'. She hated it and fought it in any which way she could. Home for Ruth was St Lucia where her part St Lucian, part English husband, a paediatric doctor, worked and her sons Bryson and Jermaine went to school. She loved the people and the weather and even though she didn't originate from that particular

Caribbean island she had no intention of leaving it.

Ruth worked as a freelance agent, but most of her work came to her via a large corporate organisation located in central London. It was to London she came every few months to submit her evidence, attend court or get information sourced by the company's investigators. When she came to London, the company housed her in one of their luxurious town homes. They tried to entice her to move to London and work for them permanently, but nothing could entice Ruth from the warm weather and beautiful beaches of St Lucia long term.

Ruth was Elle's godmother, and Clarissa was Bryson, Ruth's eldest son's godmother. Both friends took their responsibility seriously. Whenever Ruth was in London, she and Elle had a date-day. It was a day that Ruth used to spoil her goddaughter and catch up on her life. She knew that Elle told her things she felt she couldn't tell her mum. And, when Clarissa had a semi-nervous breakdown after the collapse of her marriage; it was Ruth who had rushed back to London to take care of Elle and Maddy with the help of their grandmother, bringing Elle and Ruth even closer. It was Ruth who had helped Clarissa see that she wasn't to blame for the collapse of her marriage, she wasn't a bad person, and she had so much to live for. And, if Neil chose not to attend couples counselling, chose not to fight to save his marriage and, chose to continue with his philandering ways then she had to move on with her life for the sake of her sanity and her children.

Today was a date-day. Ruth and Elle had just returned from a trip to the cinema; it had been Elle's turn to choose the film. The last movie selection had been Ruth's; she had taken Elle to a French black and white cultural film with English subtitles. Elle had fallen asleep, and her snoring had drawn embarrassing attention to both of them. Ruth had recorded Elle's snoring on her mobile phone and often threatened to expose Elle on YouTube – they were that close.

As Ruth studied Elle sending a text message she knew something was wrong. Elle had read a text and suddenly appeared agitated then proceeded to reply. Ruth waited for her to put her phone down. "What's going on Elle?"

"A friend of mine is in the hospital," Elle said then stood up and went over to the table, picked up a muffin and took a big bite. "She sent me a text to tell me."

"And you don't know if you should visit her or not and feel guilty for thinking that."

"Yes," Elle sighed, grateful that her godmother got her; she was finding that not many adults understood her since she turned thirteen. "Is it bad if I don't go?"

"No, not if it makes you feel uncomfortable. Is it that girl who's rude to your mom and keeps calling her Clarissa?"

Elle nodded

"From what I've heard about her and her mom, they sound like trouble. I wouldn't go if I were you. There's enough trouble in this World. You don't need to go looking for more, baby-girl."

"You sound like mum," Elle said then took another bite of the muffin, "Ummm these are really yummy. How did you make them again, Aunt Ruth?"

"I used the usual basic muffin mix your mom uses but I also used some super-secret oil I picked up in Dominica, it has myrrh, cassia, cinnamon, calamus and nutmeg in it. It's supposed to bring out the flavour of food but can also be used as a healing oil as well. I'm glad you like them I was going to send you home with some muffins for your mom and Maddy, so stop eating them all. You've had three already. I don't know where you young people put all the food you eat. You're just like Bryson and Jermaine - you guys eat so much but are so skinny. The only thing that seems to be getting any bigger on you Elle-belly is your bum."

Elle laughed and did a dance, more a constipated bum-jiggle than a dance.

"Whoa, whoa, what was that?" Ruth asked.

"The booty-jig, it's a bit like twerking but more classy," Elle replied and did it again.

"Stop!" Ruth grabbed a cushion and playfully hit her on her bum, "enough booty-jigging young lady, get some fruits from the fridge, we're going to make some smoothies."

"Okay," Elle said and skip-hopped to the kitchen.

Ruth tried to copy Elle's dance and quickly gave up, "You need to learn how to dance properly, keep that booting-jigging thing up and you're going to do yourself an injury." She pressed the play button on her iPod; a Mary J. Blige song started. She danced and mimed the words of the song.

"You have strawberries, apples, bananas, melon, kiwis, oranges, tangerines and pears. Do you want me to bring everything out?"

"Yep, bring them all out. We're going to make two healthy smoothies after I show you how to dance without giving yourself a back injury. Come on hurry up. Oh and if I see you do that booty-jig thing again young lady I'm going to put you on YouTube – Headline 'Elle May and her Indecent Dance with a Dangerous Weapon'."

Elle laughed. As she copied her godmother's dance steps, she felt a sense of love and being loved. She loved her godmother. She loved her coolness and her kindness which were wrapped up in a package that said, 'this here is my godchild - don't mess with her'.

***

About thirty minutes after Elle left Ruth's house Clarissa called Ruth to see if she wanted to come over for dinner. They talked about their children and how they were all growing up and becoming independent. Ruth mentioned that she had asked Elle if Jermaine had confided anything to her (Elle and Jermaine were the same age and kept in touch via the internet). Ruth was worried about Jermaine and how he had recently started acting 'closed' and moody. How he had suddenly gone from a very talkative boy to a not-so-talkative boy and neither she or her husband could figure out why. Each time they asked him if he was okay he said 'yes', which perplexed her because it was evident that something was wrong. But she didn't know how to tell a nearly fourteen-year-old boy that even though his mouth said yes she didn't believe him without him getting into a strop and becoming more secluded. His older brother Bryson, who was sixteen, had never been like this, and she didn't know what to do. Clarissa talked about some of the prayers in Stormie Omartian's book *'The Power of a Praying Parent'* that her mother had recently given her and how she had started using some of the prayers to pray over the girls, Ruth's children and all her nieces and nephews. She promised to get a copy of the book for Ruth. Clarissa smiled as she told Ruth that on handing her the book her mother had said, *'Things happen when you pray that won't occur when you don't pray because prayer is the language of Love and God is Love'*. And when she had tried to take the book from her mother's hand her mother had firmly held onto the book until Clarissa promised that she would read it and say the prayers – only then did she let it go.

Just before they hung up, Ruth remembered that she needed to ask Clarissa for a favour. "I need a favour, Clarissa," Ruth started, "I'm just about to start a case which means I have to go home for a few weeks and might not be able to attend a conference I've been scheduled to speak at next month. You know my speech. You helped me to edit it. If I get tied up, will you attend on my behalf and do the speech for me?"

"I thought you said you were going to give that speech at a conference about children not receiving money collected on their behalf? Children of flood and famine victims! You said that you were giving it to some World leaders!"

"A few World leaders, nothing to panic about, plus it's a mother's speech Clarissa, and I know if I can't get there you'll do it justice, you're like me, a mother who'll go the distance, you'll do anything for your children. Will you do it?"

"Only if you can't get there Ruth, you know how nervous I get when I have to give a speech."

"Yeahhhh! Thank you, thank you, thank you."

"Hold on, and, only if you do something for me."

"What?"

"Give a talk to some of the Year 10 students at Elle's school. I promised the careers officer that I would ask some of my friends."

"No, no, don't do this to me Clarissa, the last time I helped with the careers fest at Elle's school I got so mad at the students for not paying attention and the teachers for being so negative that I nearly gave them a piece of my mind. You know it winds me up to see ungrateful children, those kids have so much they don't know what suffering is, yet they go around acting like they're oppressed. Give a child in India or Africa half of what they have and they'd do wonders with it."

"I agree with you but . . . you help me, and I'll help you, Ruthie," Clarissa said and smiled.

"Please don't do this to me. Look, if I tell them what I think they're going to throw me out of the school and then they're going to be mean to you and Elle. I'm just trying to save you a lot of grief."

"You help me, and I'll help you, Ruthie," Clarissa repeated.

"Stop calling me 'Ruthie', I've told you before, when you say it like that it sounds like an illegal drug."

"Say you'll do it, and I'll stop calling you Ruthie, Ruthie."

"Okay, it's a deal. I'll do the careers fest thing, and you'll do the speech if I can't get back, but if I do get back and do the speech I'm not doing it, you hear me?"

"Loud and clear. However, I'll give your name to the careers teacher and your contact number so you can tell her yourself."

"Wait a minute, is it that teacher with the swollen ankles who's so sweet?"

"Yep, the one who makes those lovely shortbread biscuits with real coconut."

"You know I can't say no to her, she's adorable."

"Just sent her a text with your details so don't worry you won't have to say no to her," Clarissa replied and laughed as she heard Ruth protest.

Ruth smiled to herself. If she had to suffer in front of a bunch of secondary school students, she was going to take someone else (down) along. She had a friend whose husband helped her with some private accounting work and who had talked about accounting and working for the London Underground at school events in the past. She reasoned that if they both went then, it would mean less time for her and less time for him. She sent him a text and waited. A few minutes later he sent her a rude reply, she laughed.

CHAPTER 30

Paul Dayo-Johnson re-read Ruth's text and frowned. He didn't mind going to schools and talking to willing-to-learn children, but he didn't like going to schools to talk to kids who couldn't be bothered. He sent a rude text to Ruth in reply; warning her that he was only doing it because she was his wife's friend, and if anyone fell asleep while he was talking she would be sorry she asked him. He smiled to himself. He liked Ruth. She had a passion for people which inspired him to care. His wife, Grace Dayo-Johnson (nee Sanusi) and Ruth had worked on a couple of investigations which involved children's charities and finances which had not gone where they were supposed to. Together they were able to retrieve the money and re-direct it appropriately. Grace and Ruth were similar in nature; they were both feisty women who hated the injustice they saw in the World.

Paul and Grace had relocated to London over twenty years ago within a year of each other. They had both been born in London and taken to Lagos in Nigeria when they were young. Their parents repatriated to Nigeria at a time when things were not stable, and Paul and Grace removed from what they knew to a country where electricity and clean water were seen as a luxury and not as necessities. It probably wouldn't have mattered so much if everyone was the same and had to face the same struggles and so had the same goals. But in this country of the 'Haves and the Have-nots', this was not the case. The rich were too rich while the poor were unbelievably poor and the group in the middle consisted of a spectrum of levels – those who were nearly rich, those who were okay and those who were poor and hated being poor. Outside of all of this sat the wealthy! The rich, try as much as they could, were never accepted as wealthy. The rich rented ostentatious homes in areas like Ikeja, from the wealthy. And some of the wealthy lived in homes that were not as ostentatious but built on land in Ikoyi that secured their status in society. They believed that to be too opulent in their choice of abode might attract armed robbers or Government inquisitions. In Nigeria, some people lived on money that they stole; money that was supposed to be used to make the country better and provide a form of civility for its occupants. These people travelled 'overseas' often and wore expensive clothes which cost more than a security guard working for them earned in several years. Without any remorse, they stole money and lived lavish lifestyles evidenced in their pictures which adorned colourful magazines. The poor bought these magazines and admired the lavish pictures of the rich adorned in clothes that cost more than they earned in several years bought with money that was meant to make the country better and provide a form of civility for them. It was a vicious circle that Paul and Grace were flung into. A time not far from the independence of the country that was coloured by corruption. A time depicted in a lot of the songs sung by Fela Kuti like *ITT* and *Zombie*. Corruption ran rampant and deception and fraud followed in hot pursuit. Corruption was something that the rich and poor both participated in: the rich to get richer and the poor to 'have a bite'. Contracts were awarded, and millionaires were formed overnight while the contracts remained unfulfilled. Strikes were rampant as government workers, teachers in secondary schools and lecturers in universities were not paid for months at a time. It amused Paul how the West referred to Nigeria as a Third-World country when many Nigerians were richer (be it via corruption/fraud or hard work) than those who originated from their First-World countries. And also how, behind most of the corruption in Africa, stood a White man pulling the strings. And also how, the West condemned corruption in Africa but were the ones from whom the Africans had learned the art of corruption and the ones who laundered/banked the money of the corrupt. Still, Paul had a love for Nigeria and the honest Nigerian men and women who thrived in Nigeria and all over the World because of their discipline, hard work and the 'seeds to succeed' which were embedded in them at birth. Men and women like his parents and Grace's parents.

"Nigerians are like seeds with fertiliser embedded in their DNA," Paul's father would laugh, "plant Nigerians anywhere in the World, be it Russia, Alaska, Mount Everest or even Timbuktu and they will not only grow, they will thrive - BAMN!" (By Any Means Necessary)

Grace had lived with her family in Maryland, and Paul had lived with his family in Phase 2 Complex in Victoria Island. They had so much in common but lived separate lives until the forces of nature worked its magic, and one thing led to another leading to them meeting at the University of Lagos. Because of the strikes by university lecturers (due to non-payment of their salaries) and the riots by the students (usually just before exams), they both spent over five years doing courses that should have taken four years to complete. Grace had studied Psychology and Economics, and Paul had studied Accountancy. They tell people that they met at a mutual friend's party one night and clicked – that was the official story – a little far from the truth but it served its purpose. In fact, a disagreement over a parking space had initially thrown them together, and he had thought her too feisty when she called him 'Mr Man' and told him to move his car. He had told her that she had more than enough space to park her car, and his name wasn't Mr Man. To which she had quipped – "Look Mr Man, I don't know you, you don't know me, you're a male hence Mr, and I don't know your name hence Mr Man, now kindly move your car, my friend!". 'Way too feisty' he had thought but for some reason found he couldn't stop thinking about her. However, as fate would have it, they were both at the same party on campus later that day. Someone had started the usual University of Lagos chant of 'Great Akokite' to which every true-blooded University of Lagos aka 'Unilag' student (past, present or future) replied 'Great!' And at the end of the third 'Great Akokite', everyone did an extended 'Grreeaatttttt!' And, he saw her. As soon as he saw her, he swaggered over to her and dramatically made the sign of the cross with his fingers and mockingly backed away from her. She had sought him out later and apologised then explained that she was trying to get to the bank before it closed and he had parked at an angle which made it difficult for her to park her dad's car. She had just started to drive her dad's car after months of begging him and didn't want to get it scratched or bumped because if she did he wouldn't let her drive it again.

That was over two decades ago. They now had three children: Maria Sinmisola 16, David Temitope 14 and James Jide nearly 9, aka JJ. They all lived in a four-bedroom house in North London where Grace worked as a social worker and Paul, a qualified accountant, worked as a train driver for London Underground, a job that paid him almost double what he had earned when he worked as a junior accountant for the same company. Each Sunday the family went to church and each day the family lived a good life in what Paul Dayo-Johnson often described to his children as 'free from corruption'. Paul Dayo-Johnson was a hard-working man and before taking the job as a train driver had worked as a junior accountant and had to subsidise his pay by taking a second job as a security guard. Why? – Because he wanted to provide a good life for his wife and children and he wanted his children to make a good life for themselves and provide for their children. He often told them that he could have gone back to Nigeria and joined the band-wagon of corrupt government officials and businessmen but one day he would have to face God and wanted to do so with a clean conscience. He didn't want anything to do with stealing money and directly causing poverty, suffering and death among his people. Growing up in Nigeria he had seen firsthand how babies and children had died from various ailments ranging from severe malnutrition to malaria. How adults had died due to a lack of proper medical care and from illnesses and diseases that were curable with the right medication. These deaths were all due to the misappropriation of government funds. He loathed people who took money meant for the development of their countries and used it to line their own pockets and couldn't understand why the poor people who the money was supposed to go to, often took it upon themselves to worship the corrupt people. They held these thieves in such high esteem, thinking them better than other people because they had money. *"That person is a Governor O"*, the poor people would croon. Or *"Hah, look O, look at the Governor's wife, look at her beautiful dress O"*, they would say while looking at a glossy magazine (the letter 'O' is generally added to the end of sentences to emphasise a point in Southern West Nigeria). Sometimes he wanted to shake them and say to their inner mind, 'That dress she's wearing cost thousands of pounds – money that should have been used to develop Nigeria, to provide good hospitals, schools and roads and you sit there admiring her dress!' But he had long ago learned that poor people admired what they couldn't have, and most of them never ventured to try and get to a place where they could attain the things they never had – it was a mindset. Their minds were shackled with 'cotton-wool-like' chains, which kept them bound in their 'wall-less' poverty. That was why he knew that his children, who although like him were born in London, would achieve greater things than he had because he would see that by the Grace of God they had the right mindset and were put on the right path. He was doing for his children what his parents had done for him – making sure they got a good education. He often told his children that education was the key which opened doors to so many levels of life and racism though rampant was a force of ignorance carried around by ignorant people who couldn't rise to estimable high levels – levels that mattered – levels that education took you to. He kept clippings from Nigerian newspapers and copies of Nigerian magazines with historical stories which he brought out from time-to-time and showed his children. They would listen intently as he recanted stories of his and Grace's years growing up in Nigeria and their hope that things would one day change for the better in the country they loved. They had hopes that a new generation of Nigerians with an uncorrupted mindset would take over the reins of the country and catapult Nigeria to the great, corrupt-free, united nation that it was created to be.

That Sunday after Church

Paul Dayo-Johnson parked the car in front of his house. Almost immediately the back door flew open, and the children jumped out of the car. JJ ran up to the front door first followed by David and then Maria. He looked at his wife and shook his head. She looked at him and smiled – they didn't say anything, after years of marriage they spoke in silent loving words.

"I won, I won, I get to watch what I want tonight," JJ sang as he danced to the silent Azonto music in his head.

"JJ we've just got back from church, stop dancing like that," Maria scolded.

"What's wrong with dancing like that?" David asked deliberating winding his sister up by dancing in front of her and doing his 'I'm not touching you so you can't touch me' face.

"Get out of my face," Maria warned him.

"Or what? We've just got back from church so you have to love your brothers and sisters, you can't do anything, sister."

Maria pushed him out of her way and walked to the front door.

"Maria, no pushing my friend!" Her mother scolded.

"But he was annoying me."

"How can your brother annoy you? He's your brother," her dad said as he followed his wife up the path. "Why are you all standing there, open the door."

"My key is in my room," Maria said.

"I left my key at Paris' house yesterday. He said he'd bring it round-"

"And, I don't have a key," JJ interrupted, his tone implying he thought he was old enough to have a key, and this wouldn't have happened if he did.

"What's the point of giving you both keys if you leave them in the house or at your friend's house?" Their dad reprimanded.

"I don't have a key, Dad," JJ said again.

"I have my key, everyone move to one side, I'll open the door," Grace said, her key poised in her hand ready to open the door. Before she could get to the door, it opened, and David's friend stepped out. Everyone stared at him and, flushed face and embarrassed, he looked at David.

"Paris! What are you doing in our house? Hold on, how did you get in? Where did *you* get a key from?" JJ asked.

"I brought David's key over. I let myself in . . . I hope you don't mind Mr and Mrs Dayo-Johnson, I was sitting in the front room waiting when I heard you."

"Everybody inside, it's chilly out here," Paul told his family. He had known Paris Haughton and his parents for some years. Paris had been in David's class in primary school and had spent the night here several times and was constantly here when David was home but he was not comfortable with him being in his house by himself. He knew he wouldn't take anything but the thought of him wandering around, looking through things that had nothing to do with him, personal things – irritated him. However, for his son's sake, he pretended that it was okay, but it wasn't okay. He would discuss it with his wife later; now he wanted to get something to eat and catch up on the football.

CHAPTER 31

"I don't think my dad was too happy about you letting yourself in Paris. He may have been born in London but he's a Nigerian at heart, and his business is his business – his home is his home, you get me, bro?"

"Yeah, sorry bro, it was freezing out there, and I didn't want to go back home. I came to give you your key and the books you borrowed me. I thought you finished church at eleven?"

"We normally do, but there was a guest singer and my mum wanted to buy a copy of her CD, then Maria saw one of her friends from school and went to talk to her, and my dad started talking to someone, by the time we all got together it was nearly twelve. Have you been waiting long?"

"Since ten thirty," Paris replied.

"What's up?"

"Nothing, I'm just really feeling like crap."

"Wanna talk?"

"I think my dad's a racist," Paris blurted out.

David sighed; he knew that Paris' father was a racist. Paris' father, Mr Haughton, was a teacher at the local high school he attended, and he couldn't stand him. He had once been the deputy head teacher at Paris' secondary school, a private school but had resigned when the school governing body brought in a new Headmaster from outside instead of giving him the job when the old Headmaster retired. Mr Haughton had worked in the private school for ten years and had already appointed himself as the Headmaster in his head. The reality of being thrown over for an external candidate had devastated him. Mr Haughton taught Economics and Politics and was well known for his racist views among the students, although he pretended to conform in front of the other teachers. In front of the students, however, he openly mocked single parents. He often said he thought that Black men who abandoned their children were a disgrace. This wasn't a bad thing to think because even Black people thought this. What ticked David and other Black students off was that he pooled all Black people together and would say negative things about the Black boys in the school. He would say that he didn't expect much from them, and they were too busy impregnating girls who opened their legs at the drop of a hat and had babies that taxpayers had to raise while the fathers were off impregnating some other poor cow. He would say that it was a waste of time educating people who didn't value the education and would only end up stacking shelves, sweeping floors or guarding someone else's property. He said it in such a way that the meaning, though clear, was like an onion, wrapped in 'layers'.

"Why do you think your dad's a racist Paris?"

"Apart from all the stuff you've told me in the past. The other day I heard him on the phone talking to the leader of that party in East London about how he could corrupt the minds of ethnic children and get them to think that they won't amount to much and at the same time promote the English kids. Then he said that he couldn't stand the way the 'ethnics' were taking over things and how they just elected another one of them 'ethnics' into the government."

David frowned.

"You're lucky to have a dad like yours, D. You're fortunate to have your family."

The door opened, JJ walked in, sat down on the couch next to his brother and smiled.

"What do you want?" David asked him, pretending to be annoyed.

"To hang out with you guys, Mum's in the kitchen with Maria and Dad's watching football. I thought we could have some D, P and JJ time."

"We're talking," David said and rolled his eyes.

"So, I can talk too, what you both talking about bro?" JJ asked as he sat back and settled himself, preparing his mind to talk.

"Things that don't concern you," David replied.

"Let him stay bro," Paris said.

"Thank you P. Oh yeah, I made you both something," JJ told them and handed them each a shiny coloured stone.

David looked at his and frowned, "It's a stone! How do you make a stone?"

"I had to file it into shape and make it colour-adaptable then colour and gloss it over to preserve it. Then I put your initials on them. It took a long time to do."

"JJ, it's a stone!" David repeated, baffled.

"It's the thought that counts, thanks, JJ it's really cool."

JJ smiled at Paris, frowned at his brother then walked out of the room. Moments later he was back with two cans of cola. He handed one to Paris who thanked him. He then settled back on the couch, opened his can and drank from it.

"Where's mine JJ?" David asked.

JJ ignored him and continued to drink from the can in his hand. David got up, took the drink out of his brother's hand, put it on the table then picked him up. In one swift movement, he tucked JJ under his arm and marched to the kitchen with him. David went to the counter and told his struggling brother to stop wiggling and pick up a drink. JJ refused, and David tickled him until he did. He marched back into the front room, put a laughing JJ down, took the drink from him and thanked him for the drink.

"As I was saying, bro, before this mite interrupted us, let him deal with his issues and don't let them contaminate you, okay? Anytime you're feeling down come over here, and we can hang out. We might be at different schools now, but we're still good friends right?"

"Always," Paris said as he blinked back unexpected tears.

"Maria's making roast potatoes for you," JJ told Paris, "she said that you might not like the jollof rice cos she put a lot of pepper in it today."

"I'm starving, I'll eat anything, even Maria's jollof rice,"

Paris said.

"I like roast potatoes you like Maria's 'too much pepper' jollof rice that burns your tongue and makes you cry," JJ grimaced, "we can swap."

"Don't let her hear you," Paris warned him.

"If she does she'll say what Mum does, she'll say 'my friend by careful O!' Or the classic, 'I'm not playing with you O!' like Dad says," JJ laughed.

David smiled. "My mum says she has to practice cooking for when she gets married, but I think that she might poison us all with a salt overdose before that day ever comes." He saw something flash across Paris' face and heard the sound of something rushing past his head then felt the newspaper hit his head. "Ouch!" He cried out.

"I heard that David," Maria said, "and I'll be putting extra salt in your portion!" She threw the newspaper on the table and walked out of the room.

"You better watch yourself, bro, she'll get you with the salt or the newspaper," JJ whispered, "either way you're in big, big, trouble."

They all laughed.

Maria walked back into the kitchen and tasted the jollof rice. It tasted as if it needed a bit more salt so she picked up the salt and was about to put some more in when her mother grabbed her hand and took the salt out of it.

"Did you taste it, Maria?"

"Yes, I just tasted it, what's wrong?"

"Too much salt isn't healthy," her mother avoided a direct answer.

"David just told Paris that I use too much salt when I cook. Is that true?"

Her mother studied her for a few seconds sensing that this was one of those make or break moments. "You don't always use too much salt. You just need to make sure you taste food properly as you cook it. A good cook knows when to add salt and when not to. You're a good girl Maria. I thank God that you're my daughter, and I also thank God that you listen. No more salt sweetheart, if anyone needs to add more salt they can add it at the table, okay."

"Okay Mum," she smiled.

Grace smiled at her daughter and silently prayed that she would always listen and be respectful. She thought momentarily of the family she had visited in the hospital recently and how dysfunctional the entire family were – alcoholic mother, abusive father and suicidal daughter. She had seen many horrors in her life as a social worker and in one way or another, they all culminated to make her value and love her own family with a resolve that could never be broken. She smiled as she heard her sons and Paris laughing in the front room.

"Tell him about Mum and Dad and the bird noises," JJ encouraged his brother.

David rolled his eyes and tried to protest, but JJ insisted; he liked listening to his brother telling funny stories especially stories where he spoke with a Nigerian accent to emphasise a point.

"What happened?" Paris asked.

"We were all talking last week about dating and my dad says that nowadays guys chirps girls-"

"Your dad knows about chirpsing?" Paris asked surprised and amused.

"I tell you, I was shocked when he said the word 'chirps', it sounded so strange coming from him. Anyway, he went on about how in his days it was called 'toasting', that a guy toasted a girl when he liked her-"

"Not sliced bread toasting," JJ quipped already on the periphery of laughing.

"Obviously JJ," Paris laughed.

"So he and my mum started talking about how they met and how they fell in love and dated and all that stuff. Then my dad turned to her and said if they had to do it all again in this day and age he would have to chirps her-"

"Hahahahaha," JJ laughed.

"I haven't got to the joke yet JJ," David scolded jokingly.

"Hahahahaha," JJ continued, the thought of the words to come made him laugh even harder. It was an infectious laughter that tickled Paris. It made him smile as he tried to keep his own laughter abated and concentrate on David's words.

"Next thing we hear is my dad telling my mum that guys today chirps girls and my mum asked if it was called chirpsing because guys refer to girls as birds. My dad looked at my mum like he knew more about something than she did and started to explain that chirpsing was American slang."

"American slang!" JJ said and giggled.

"So my mum said that he should chirps her and-" he started to laugh.

"What happened?" Paris asked him now openly laughing.

"My dad turned to her and said with a Nigerian accent, 'Hello darling, Chirp Chirp Chirp'."

"No way," Paris said laughing. "You're joking right?"

"I joke you not," David said, "he was serious as well."

"Tell him what Mum said David, tell him," JJ laughed.

Laughter tears were bubbling in David's eyes as he looked at Paris' laughing face. "My mum smiled at him and said 'Tweet Tweet', hahahahaha, she said 'Tweet, Tweet'," he laughed as Paris, laughing, fell off the couch and rolled around on the floor saying "Tweet, Tweet".

CHAPTER 32

They waited for JJ to pray.

JJ waited as he basked in the power of being the centre of attention.

"Start the prayer, JJ, I'm hungry," Maria told him.

"Patience, Maria," her mother told her, "JJ, say the prayer, now," she told her son, the look on her face said he had seconds to obey.

"Can we all hold hands please," JJ told everyone around the table.

"You said the prayer yesterday, and we didn't hold hands," David protested.

"We didn't have a guest yesterday," JJ replied.

"Paris is like family, he's not a guest," Maria said, "plus he's had lunch and dinner here before, and we didn't hold hands."

"He has never had lunch with us when it's been my turn to pray, so this is a new experience for all of us. Hold hands so that I can say the prayer please." JJ replied reverently.

"Everyone, hold hands, come on, I am hungry, and I want to eat, come on come on, hold hands quickly," their father said. Paris smiled as they all held hands.

"Dear Lord, Hallowed be Thy Name. Thank You for this food that You have blessed us with today. As we share it with our guest, we thank You for keeping us safe. And um, we are grateful to You for Your wonderful gift of our family. We pray that You continue to bless us and keep us safe. Amen."

"Amen," everyone said.

"Salt anyone," David joked.

"Mum," Maria protested.

"David," their mother warned.

Paris smiled, he loved it here. He wished this was his family.

"Paris, pass the plantains please," Maria said.

"Sure, here you go," he handed her the dish.

Grace Dayo-Johnson looked at the large elegant frame which held over a hundred photographs in the family room. The photos were beautifully and cleverly arranged in a collage-like family tree display. It featured the lives of Grace and Paul before they met, life after they met, their wedding, the birth of each of their children and their 'now' days. She knew every picture well and would often stand for long moments savouring the memories which formed them, happy in their existence and their presence which evidenced her history. She traced her history then her husband's then lovingly looked at each of her children. Suddenly a frown appeared on her face; it took root – it gave her a puzzled look – like someone who knew something was missing – knew what it was – but didn't know why anyone would take it. Her eyes searched the ground beneath the picture frame thinking that maybe someone had accidentally nudged the frame causing the picture to dislodge and fall. Her eyes moved this way and that in search of the photograph she knew was missing; it wasn't there.

"What are you looking for, Mum?" Maria asked her, as her own eyes automatically searched for what her mother was looking for as she waited for her mother's reply.

"I don't know, Maria, I think that a picture is missing, in fact, I know that a picture is missing, but I don't know which one it is. Have a look at the frame and see if you know which one is missing."

"Mum, there must be over a hundred photos in the frame, how do you know that one is missing? Some of them are the same and look. There aren't any gaps."

"A mother knows when something isn't right, Maria, trust me."

Maria smiled then got on her hands and knees. Her mother knew everything, about everything and if she said that one of the pictures was missing, then it was missing. Her mother had spent a long time getting the photographs just the way she wanted them. She had lovingly placed every picture in place to tell a chronological story of their lives.

"Not on the floor and not under the couch. Do you think it could have fallen out and someone picked it up and put it somewhere safe?"

"Probably," her mother answered, not convinced.

CHAPTER 33

♫ *"Order my steps, Lord, order my steps*
Let me be the one You created me to be
Order my steps, Lord, order my steps
Let Your Will be done, Lord. Lord order me.

Called but not calling
Blessed but not blessing

How can I be all You've called me to be
If I do things that are not worthy of Thee
If I journey alone, if I go my own way
How can I be all You've called me to be today

Order my steps, Lord, order my steps
Let me be the one You created me to be
Order my steps, Lord, order my steps
Let Your Will be done, Lord. Lord order me ...."♫

Gentle strings played on a guitar accompanied by soft
humming, then:

♫ *"Purify me, Lord, let me live a life that brings You Glory*
Lead me in the way that I can really love and make a
difference
I want to do, all that, all that You've called me to do my
Father
I want to be, all that, all that You've called me to be my Lord

Here I am, Lord
I want to do as You command
Order my steps, Lord
And always lead me by the hand

Here I am, Lord
I want to do Your every Will
Order my steps, Lord
Take me through every valley and over every hill
Here I am, Lord
Here I am ...."♫

Grace listened to her daughter playing her guitar and singing; she smiled. Maria had a beautiful voice, and she wrote amazing Gospel songs. She had learned how to play the guitar when she was ten-years-old. At Grace's insistence, all of her children played an instrument. It took strong determination on Grace's part to stick to her plans of getting them to find out if they had any musical gifts, and help develop them when they discovered what they were. David played the piano and had passed his grade 5 exams recently, which was an achievement for a fourteen-year-old as far as she was concerned. JJ loved to play the violin but hated practising at appointed times. At five he had chosen the violin and would spend so much time cleaning the strings with chalk then plucking the strings to make sure they sounded perfect but then to sit down and play a piece was something that he didn't think was required. Several times she had threatened to take the violin back to the shop if he didn't practice playing it, and he would beg her to let him keep it and look after it.
"I clean the strings, I polish the wood, and I make sure the bow is working properly – I take care of it, Mummy. My teacher said we must all look after our instruments." He would proudly tell her.
It wasn't until a couple of years ago when he stopped looking after it and started playing it that she was glad she hadn't taken it back to the shop. Now he loved playing it, and now he played it extremely well.

CHAPTER 34

Maria was practising her new songs, and the boys were setting up some new weights with Paris in the section of the conservatory which served as a gym. Paul had set the gym up a few years ago; it served a dual purpose; a place where both Grace and he could work out and keep in shape and also a place where he could bond with his boys.

Paul carried two glasses of wine into the living room and set them on the table; he was determined to spend some quality time with his wife. He pressed the play button, and the Nigerian movie started. He snuggled down on the settee and rested his head on his wife's lap. Her hand went immediately to the back of his neck and began to massage it gently. He sighed, he loved this. He loved his wife, and he loved the way she took care of him. After twenty years of marriage, he was still in love with the wife of his youth, and he was enjoying the blessings that this brought – It was Biblical. They made God the head of their marriage. And, they also put each other first, which meant that they had a win-win marriage. Grace enjoyed watching Nigerian movies (Nigeria was now one of the leading movie-making countries in the World and as such, in the manner of Hollywood and Bollywood, now had its own brand – Nollywood). He enjoyed lazing around on Sunday afternoons/early evenings, head on her lap and her massaging his neck and his head. He had read somewhere once that *'a person is happiest when they have God within them'* and *'when you're in love everything makes sense'*. He had friends who like him were still happily married, and he also had friends of various races who had been tempted by a philandering lifestyle which had cost them their marriages and the love and respect of their children. The sad thing was that once they had broken free of their 'ball and chain' as they had joked and gone off with their 'bit of fluff', they saw that the grass wasn't greener on the other side, far from it, the grass was bitter, dry and fake. When everything had been counted, the price paid was way too high and not worth it – but their pride had prevented them from going back home. Instead, they resisted interventions, went on a downward spiral and lived fake, single lives trying to tell people that they were happy. They went to fancy restaurants to eat, dated younger girls who only saw them as 'Sugar Daddies', 'Too-Many-Issues Men' or 'Bobo Nice' – men okay to semi-date and take money from in exchange for emotionless-sexual acts and nothing more. The girls took their money and lived lavish lifestyles while the men lived fake lifestyles full of debts. It saddened Paul that he knew men who turned to drugs, sex, gambling and alcohol to fill in the holes that the 'self-inflicted' loss of their families created. He saw how miserable his philandering friends were and he thanked God that he had a beautiful wife who loved him and whom he loved, and children who, in his eyes, were the salt of the Earth – stable.

Had he been tempted to cheat? Yes, he had. There had been times when out with the guys he had seen some fake grass but had recognised it for what it was – fake. And, the thought of hurting his wife who would throw him out of the house if she ever found out, and of his children living with their mother while he lived by himself, scared him so much. But what frightened him the most was knowing that he would not only destroy his family if he did cheat but that he would offend God – and that was one thing that he didn't ever want to do.

One thing his grandmother, a strong Christian woman who was never afraid (unlike so many mothers) to tell her three sons the truth, had passed on to him via his father, was a message about marriage. She often said the following. *'Don't get married unless you're sure you can't live without her. And, once you've decided to get married don't ever, ever second guess that decision. Your wife is the mother of your children and your children will treat and love you based on how you treat and love their mother!'* It was sound doctrine, and Paul's father and uncles all had healthy marriages and their children all had good marriages – it worked.

"Hahahaha," Grace laughed softly, and he looked at the TV and smiled. He loved to hear her laugh, and he loved to make her laugh, it made him feel good.

Paul closed his eyes, floated for a while, then dozed.

CHAPTER 35

Terry J. King, TJK as he was known to his fans, had just returned from a tour which had seen his pop group performing in sell-out venues all over North and South America. His group K-A-Y 3 consisted of him, Melvin Andrews and Simon Young. Three eighteen-year-old boys who had been friends since they were at primary school together in South London.

K-A-Y 3 was the brainchild of Terry's mum, Maya, who had seen the potential of the boys when they diligently rehearsed for a five-minute musical slot for a school play – they had performed during the interlude of Romeo and Juliet the musical. Maya, once a singer herself who had shot to fame twenty-years ago with her breakthrough R'n'B album titled *'Girls Are Doing It Too',* saw something in her son's group that oozed of potential success and reminded her of herself. As a Black woman trying to make it in a predominately male industry it had been hard for her but she didn't give up, she kept plugging her stuff, and one thing led to another which saw her opening for A-list performers then having her own tour. Her career had been short-lived, but while it lived it exposed her to a lot of money, first class air travel, stays at prestigious hotels and the consumption of food and wine that she could barely pronounce. After her career had died she was sure of one thing – having had those luxuries and lost them – she wanted them back.

Now that her son's group was a sensation, as the group's manager, she had the luxuries back. She was the sole manager of the group and everything had to be approved by her or it didn't happen. The group was worth several millions, and she was constantly looking for ways of increasing that amount. It had been her idea for the group to do a documentary movie (now a box-office hit) about how the boys had come together and how she and her husband had re-mortgaged their home to invest in the boys. Maya was very crafty. She had initially insisted on getting a famous actress to play her character in the doc movie and negotiated a hefty payment for her then just before the contract was signed insisted that the actress wasn't right for the role, and she play herself for the same payment.

It had been at the premiere of the doc movie in Leicester Square that Terry had met Sunflower Mackay, a striking model and actress. Maya saw the financial 'potential of the package' that was her son and Sunflower and she did everything she could to throw them together.

Yesterday morning Terry did interviews which his mother had told him not to do but which he had wanted to do to clear the air. His girlfriend of six weeks, Sunflower MacKay, had dramatically dumped him, and magazines and newspapers wanted to know why. His mother had thought that he was in too much of an angry place to speak detachedly, and the reporters would twist his words if he said the wrong thing. She and his father had asked him to wait for a few more days before doing any interviews. He had agreed to wait and would have done so if his friend, Damien Grey Jr., hadn't given a stupid drunken interview to the press. Damien had been the first person he had called after Sunflower had dramatically and publically dumped him at a nightclub. They had gone there to celebrate her nineteenth birthday and a role she had just won in a movie. While they posed for photographs a seductively dressed female singer came over and hugged Terry. He, not wanting to be rude to her had casually embraced her and kissed her on the cheek. The singer had grabbed Terry's face and kissed him on the mouth, throwing her weight behind the kiss. Suddenly flashes from cameras and mobile phones went off as Terry came to his senses and pushed her away. He had grabbed Sunflower and tried to leave the club. But the damage was done. Sunflower, insecure, still trying to juggle modelling and acting and being on a cocktail of slimming and anxiety pills had angrily thrown her drink at the singer and pushed

Terry out the way telling him that it was over between them before she stormed out of the club. Terry had left the club and gone to a bar and gotten drunk. He was angry that his mother had set him up with a ticking time-bomb like Sunflower in the first place and didn't call home. Instead, he called and texted Damien and was full of lamentation as he told him Sunflower had dumped him and he was going to put the whole 'dating of women' to one side and concentrate on his career. What he didn't say was how scared he was that Sunflower would go crazy and tell people about his Body Dysmorphic Disorder issues and what they did in secret. If people found out, they would hate him. He had sold books on fitness and done two fitness dance videos which had made him millions of pounds and also a role model to thousands of children all over the World. So many people believed him to be something he wasn't, and Sunflower could expose him for the fraud he was.

Wine Bar Central London: Damien, plied with alcohol bought by a reporter from a national newspaper gave an interview in exchange for £3000, which he asked for upfront and said would go to his favourite charity. In the interview, a drunk Damien stated that his best mate Terry J. King was off women and would not be dating any more women. He showed the reporter several text messages Terry had sent him. These text messages were in themselves mere words which made no sense because they were created in a place of alcohol infused mindlessness. However, in the eyes of a reporter trying to climb the ladder via a hot exclusive story, the words could be twisted to suit a purpose. For an extra £500 Damien sent the reporter Terry's text messages. After the reporter had left, Damien spent all the money in his favourite charity – the lap dancing gentleman's club next door. The next day that reporter's story 'Terry J. King is Gay' went viral. Yesterday morning Terry did interviews denying the story, but magazine and newspaper reporters wrote that he was in self-denial. They called him 'Bi-Curious' and 'Bi-Sexual' or outright Gay.

CHAPTER 36

Gia Mishra's GCSE Course Work Presentation

Some teenage girls were in the corner of the hall reading a story in a gossip magazine and talking about it – well, more like making childish remarks about the story.

Charmaine: I can't believe he's gay, man. Look at how buff he is plus he's a brother man, how can a Black hottie like that be gay?

Kerry: Why are all the cute guys gay, man?

Nita: I think it's a big con, his group K-A-Y 3 sang that song, *'Girl of my Dreams'*, I bought that song, now it comes out he's gay. So was he singing that song to some guy?

Charmaine: He should have called it, *'Boy of my Dreams'*. They all giggled.

Lola: But that's what these record labels do they get these guys to pretend they're straight so that they can sell records then when they want more money they allow them to come out so that the gay community buys their records as well.

Charmaine: Man look at him, though, he's cute and look at those dimples, how's a Black brother gone and done that man, gone and be gay!

Kerry: Terry J. King is gay! I can't believe it, man, what a waste! We could have had some cute kids, man!

Lola: I'm surprised his parents let him come out like this. Black celebrities don't tend to come out unless there's serious evidence that can be used against them.

Nita: Well it's in the magazines and national newspapers so the story must be true.

Charmaine: I can't believe it, man, look how cute he is, look at those dimples-"

"Girls, put whatever that is you're looking at away please, the presentation will start soon," Mrs Thakur told them, she lowered her voice, "I overheard some of your comments, I don't want to hear comments like that again, okay?"

"Yes Miss," they chorused sweetly.

The lights were turned off, and all of the thirty students in the hall sat back to watch the short documentary. Mr Gregory Haughton, Paris' dad, sat at the back of the hall, already bored, he pulled out his mobile phone. He heard someone cough, saw it was the deputy head teacher, Mrs Thakur, and quickly returned his phone to his pocket, irritated.

David Dayo-Johnson sat near the back. He had seen Paris' dad take out his phone; he was used to him doing this when one of the non-English students showed their documentaries. When one of the English students showed their documentaries, he sat in the front and made encouraging noises.

The face of a young, attractive Indian girl appeared on the screen; she smiled, and everyone in the class except Mr Haughton clapped. It was something all the students did in support of each other – skin colour didn't interfere. The words 'God's Way or the highway' suddenly popped into David's head and he smiled at their relevance. It was something a youth pastor had said some weeks ago at church, and it meant what it said – people will have to do things God's Way or take the highway to hell (the highway being the fast track). The youth pastor had said that God is Love. And, children were not born racist or hating anyone it was a thing their parents consciously or unconsciously taught them. And, for God's Way of Love to be spread throughout the World, it would mean that a lot of people, if they didn't change would be taken out – as simple as that. He said it happened before when the Israelites were wandering around in the wilderness for forty years. Those who were not obedient to God and didn't do things God's Way died in the desert and a new generation of people were the ones who entered the Promised Land. 'God's Way or the highway' David thought as he looked at Mr Haughton, hoping he would change.

The pretty face on the screen smiled, and dimples appeared on either side of her face. She pushed her thick dark hair off her face which suddenly took on a sombre appearance, "Hi, my name is Gia Mishra, and I would like to take you into this hospital behind me located in Goa India. For data protection purposes I will not reveal the name of the hospital, and I will not be speaking to the mothers on camera who have recently had babies here. I have explained my project to the mothers, and they have given me permission to film their babies. I'll meet you inside." The screen went black for a few moments then the crying and gurgling of babies could be heard. The screen lit up with images of babies. There were about twelve, all in individual bassinets and all of the various shades of brown. Some of the girls watching gave out little gasps and oohs and aahs as they looked at the beautiful babies. Soft music started, and the camera went from one bassinet to the next and, almost as if on cue, some of the babies smiled as the camera zoomed in on their faces which sent out another ripple of oohs and aahs among the girls watching.

The camera swung around professionally and focused on Gia's face, "They're all so beautiful, so cute and yummy aren't they?" She crooned. "Did you see the little fat one in the middle over there? His mum said he weighed over nine pounds when he was born, my goodness that's massive," she giggled. Her giggle was infectious, and some of the students giggled as well. The screen went black, and Gia spoke in the darkness, "Can you imagine being born and being told on the day you are born that you will never amount to much, that society has already determined your destiny. Can you imagine being born into a society that once had laws in place to make sure that you never succeeded in life because you were worthless? Your personality, your skills, your smile, your uniqueness didn't matter because you were born into a Caste society, also known as Jati, and if you were not part of the four main Castes you were an Outcaste, an Untouchable, a Dalit, one of the many 'Nothings' in society. And, because you were nothing, you could be murdered, raped or robbed and nothing would be done – Nothing done for Nothing!" The screen remained black for a few moments as if giving the viewers time to digest the words that had been spoken; time to recover from being wrenched from a thing of beauty to one of ugliness in seconds.

A map of India appeared on the screen. The words beneath the map listed the four main Castes in descending order:
1.Brahmanas (Brahmin) – Seers, Reflective ones, Intellectual and Spiritual leaders
2.Kshatriyas – Protectors of Society but formerly Nobles, Rajahs and Warriors
3.Vaishyas – Skilful producers of material things, Businessmen, Craftsmen
4.Shudras – Semi-skilled and Unskilled Labourers
Note: If you did not belong to one of the four main Castes you were an Outcaste, an Untouchable also known as a Dalit.

"Some records state that the British Colonial Regime introduced the Caste system in India, but others state that the Caste system was already in place before the British arrived in India to colonise the country. However, both records agree that the British encouraged the separation of Indians by Caste, granting administrative jobs and senior appointments only to higher Castes. The lower Castes all had glass ceilings, and it was difficult, almost impossible in fact to go from a lower Caste to a higher Caste. You would think that someone from a lower Caste who aspired to break the glass ceiling by working hard could do so, wouldn't you? But unfortunately, in those days your name depicted who you were and how much you could achieve." Gia paused.

"People have tried to help the people classified as Outcaste, most people have heard of Mahatma Gandhi, he was a man who wanted peace in his country and fought just like Martin

Luther King Jr and Nelson Mandela against injustice. He gave the name Harijan, which means 'Children of God' to the Outcastes and I like to think that he was trying to get all Indians to love each other and treat each other the right way – as human beings and not animals." The screen went black for a few seconds then the image of Gia, harnessed to an open-back slow moving pickup truck, filming a city in India appeared. The cameraman filming Gia zoomed in on her hands as she manoeuvred her camera. He then zoomed in on Gia's camera and as if by magic the images Gia was filming appeared on his camera. "Today the Indian Constitution has outlawed the practice of the segregation of Dalits. I just want to clarify that Dalits are not one Caste of people, they historically comprise of different groups of individuals, not in the four main Caste groups. Today, we like to think that it was once upon a time that the status of the Dalits was historically associated with their occupation, which was ritually impure." Images of Dalit people appeared on the screen, some historical, some recent. "Leatherwork, butchering, removal of rubbish, removal of animal carcases and waste removal, manual labour, cleaning the streets, cleaning latrines and cleaning sewers were all jobs done by the Dalits, and they were considered to be polluting to the individual, and this pollution was contagious. I have been told by many people in India who do not want to be filmed, that as a result of their professions the Dalits were commonly segregated and banned from full participation in Hindu social life. They could not enter the temples or schools and were required to stay outside the villages." Suddenly a sweeping view of green lands and animals scattered here and there appeared. "As I mentioned before, the Indian Constitution has outlawed the practice of Untouchables but in beautiful rural parts of India, this practice still exists. I spoke to a young man called R. Patel earlier today, and he said that he knows people who have converted to Christianity and changed their names to escape the Caste system. He asked me not to film his face for the safety of him and his family. The following clip is of him, but his voice has been disguised."

The darkened image of a man appeared. "The Caste system is a hell system for people at the bottom and those who have no Caste. To be conceived and then born into a society that regards you as 'dirt' or something that is beneath dirt is a horrible thing. The Caste system still operates today and for those at the top it might seem that you have no problems but one day you will have to answer for your actions or your lack of actions – one day," the disguised voice said.

The image of Gia appeared on the screen, her face sombre. "My mother was born into a lower Caste than my father and his parents nearly disowned him when they married in secret. The fact that he is their only son and they are from the highest Caste, which is the Brahmin, probably limited what they could do to him. But I saw how my mother was treated by her in-laws when my father wasn't present, and I know first-hand that people today still hold on to customs. To really change things we need to change peoples' mindsets."

The image of the babies in the hospital reappeared, "Can you imagine being born and told on the day you are born that you will never amount to much, that society has already determined your destiny. Can you imagine being born into a society that once had laws in place to make sure that you never succeeded in life because you were worthless? Your personality, your skills, your smile, your uniqueness didn't matter because you were born into a Caste society, also known as Jati, and if you were not part of the four main Castes you were an Outcaste, an Untouchable, a Dalit, one of the many 'Nothings' in society. And because you were nothing, you could be murdered, raped or robbed and nothing would be done – Nothing done for Nothing!"

U MURDER U (SUICIDE)

Historical images of Mahatma Gandhi embracing the Untouchables appeared on the screen accompanied by music and soft humming. Images of rejected people all over the World appeared as the song *'Come as you are'* sung by the award winning singer Elizabeth played.

♫ *Come as you are. Come as you are*
Friendless – I'll be your friend
Hopeless – I'll give you hope
Joyless – I'll give you joy
Bound – I'll set you free

Come as you are
I'm waiting for you
My love is eternal
And I'll see you through

Loneliness, pain, ashamed of the shame
Living without hope
Thinking thoughts with no joy
My love is eternal. I'll set you free
Come as you are, come follow Me

Come as you are. Come as you are
Friendless – I'll be your friend
Hopeless – I'll give you hope
Joyless – I'll give you joy
Bound – I'll set you free ♫

The song ended. The image of a young boy carrying a rucksack, homeless looking, with a large, yellow, smiley face badge on his jacket appeared. His image merged with other images. Suddenly there were hundreds and then thousands of homeless people from all over the World on the screen. Then the screen went black. Everyone heard a soft sigh and then

Gia's voice said: "The following poem lays beneath a mural at what use to be one of the worst prisons in America. A prison that was well known for racist attacks amongst the inmates. Laurel Matthews, the lady who did the mural, spent two weeks painting it. She gave her time and her gift free of charge. Since the mural and poem were revealed in the prison, the warden of the prison has said that 'the racist crime rate among the inmates has dramatically dropped.' The screen lit up as an image of a mural appeared which took up a large section of a wall. The colours dazzled the eyes; the colours embraced beautifully and gracefully as they seduced the viewer. The camera focused on the words beneath the mural as Gia read them.

"The eyes are a 'window' to one's soul.
When you look directly into a man's eyes, you cannot see the colour of his skin.
I believe that one day, one day soon, all men will be one man. All love will be one love. Hate will be hated and love embraced.
One day, one day soon, the love of God will flow, touch, change and uplift all.
One day, one day soon . . . and that day shall be called –
Today!"

The lights came on.

The students stood up, some very emotional as they cheered and clapped for Gia.

Gia Mishra had tears in her eyes as she stood up and thanked her classmates.

"That was excellent, Gia, really great work!" Mrs Thakur said.

"Yes, well done Gia," Mr Haughton said, "But I don't think you can blame everything on British colonisation, people have to take some responsibility for their own mess."

"I don't think that was the point of the presentation, Mr

Haughton," Mrs Thakur told him, "Gia's work is just pointing out and I might add explaining to people who don't know that a system is still in place which detrimentally affects certain people. The Indian government are trying to combat things. And, some individuals in the Dalit group have broken through the glass ceiling Gia mentioned and have become politicians and other professionals, which a number of years ago, wouldn't have been the case. Quotas are in place to make sure people from this group have access to schools and universities which again never used to be the case. Again, Gia has hit the nail on the head by saying that to change things we have to change people's mindsets. The poem at the end summed it up. We should never judge and condemn people because they are perceived as being different from us."

"Yes, um, in a way, I see that. I just find it rather annoying when people go around blaming the British for colonising them and stealing all their treasures-"

"And I find it annoying when students work hard and present such stellar work, and you poo-poo it," she whispered to him then turned back to the students, "Gia, excellent work, thank you so much for sharing that with us. Students, before you leave can we have another round of applause for Gia please."

Everyone in the room clapped. Mr Haughton, slightly embarrassed, managed a soft, silent clap. Mrs Thakur waited for all the students to leave the hall then turned to him.

"How dare you behave like that? You're on the board of governors, and you're supposed to be a Christian! I read somewhere that as a Christian your life is meant to preach the Gospel and only when necessary should you use words! How is your life preaching to anyone? Where is the love and compassion you're supposed to have? I've heard about your racist comments to the students and how you put some students down publically allowing those that should be disciplined to get off. Do you think you're helping the English students? You're teaching them how to live without rules and one day when they have to face those rules in the real World they won't survive."

"What are you talking about?" Mr Haughton huffed.

He taught Economics and Politics so she decided to switch her tactic, "There was a little boy who-"

"For the love of God woman, give me a break."

She took a calming deep breath and continued, "little boy who lived in a city and one day at school his teacher described the characteristics of Jesus Christ. He said that Jesus was loving, kind, forgiving, compassionate and always ready to help others. And, He came and showed the love of God to sinners for them to see that God wasn't cruel, wicked and judgemental as people had believed for years. But a Loving God with open Arms always ready to welcome them home like the father who welcomed the prodigal son in the Bible. He said that Jesus died for our sins, and the little boy asked him if that meant that the person who did all those good things was now dead. His teacher said that now Jesus was in Heaven but also alive in our hearts. The boy frowned. His teacher, concerned that he hadn't explained things well, asked the boy what the matter was, and the boy told him that he was confused because he knew someone who had all those characteristics but that man, a neighbour, was alive and lived on his road. This neighbour, he said, was kind and generous and once when his dad left the car window open, and it rained, this man came over and helped his dad clean out the car. That this man had helped his mother when she locked herself out the house, and his dad had travelled; he called the locksmith and paid him because his mother didn't have the money to pay. When his dad got back, this man refused to take money from him. Everyone spoke well of this man and called him a real child of God. He concluded that as far as he was concerned the man Jesus who his teacher had mentioned was very much alive and lived on his road!"

Mr Haughton studied her as shame tried to engulf him. He quickly shrugged off the shame before its roots took hold and dug deep, he frowned, "Look I really don't have time for this right now."

Mrs Thakur took a deep breath, "You don't get it do you?"

"Get what?"

"Your character will always speak words. The reason the Caste system hasn't been eradicated is because of peoples' mindsets. People are born into societies that think that they are better than others. That may keep them warm in their little environments, but when they go out into the real World, they can't deal with the reality of someone whom they regard as beneath them doing better than them and achieving more than them. You see it now in this country with EU people coming in and working hard and the English getting resentful. Times are changing, and mindsets need to change, or they will be eradicated – that's how the universe works. Doctors take an oath to 'First do no harm'. As teachers, what we say to our students will affect their lives, and we need to make sure that we do them no physical, emotional or intellectual harm! We need to educate and inspire them to do the right thing!"

Mr Haughton looked at her as she walked towards the door, "Are you saying that I'm a racist? Because if you are, I take serious offence at that!"

Mrs Thakur stopped, turned and looked at him coldly, "You know what you are, I don't have to tell you what you are." With that, she walked out of the hall and slammed the door behind her.

Mr Haughton heard a noise and turned, his eyes locked onto Aisha Patel who was trying to walk quietly to one of the side exits. "What are you doing there?" He shouted at her.

"I . . . was . . . I was waiting to talk to Mrs Thakur, Sir," Aisha stuttered.

"Well she isn't here is she, get out of here, get back to your classroom RIGHT NOW!" He screamed at her.

She froze as she waited, thinking that he was going to hit her like her father had when he shouted at her last night because she had said that she wanted to stay in school and not go to India to get married. Her father had never hit her before, but then she had never refused to do what she had been instructed to do before. Mrs Thakur was the Pastoral Care Officer for Aisha's year, and she needed to talk to her. She knew Mrs Thakur had helped several students with various problems in the past. Aisha knew Mrs Thakur genuinely cared about her students and stood up for them when other teachers backed down. Every child mattered to Mrs Thakur – she believed that every child had potential and should be allowed to fulfil their potential. Despite knowing this, Aisha was terrified, she feared it was too late – the air tickets for mother and daughter had already been purchased online. Aisha feared that her life was on the verge of being over.

"Are you deaf or just stupid girl? Get out of here right now!"

"Yes Sir, sorry Sir," Aisha said, as she ran to the exit.

CHAPTER 37

Clarissa felt a cold breeze blow against her face and shivered. She turned to close the window but just as her hand closed around the handle she heard Elle's voice calling her. "Elle, are you okay?" The words had popped out of her mouth before she realised their fruitlessness. Elle wasn't home. She was at the local hospital with her grandmother visiting Mr Douglas, an elderly man who had recently had surgery for prostate cancer. Thankfully he had survived the operation, but he was seventy-eight years old and as such not as able to recover as quickly as a younger man. His recovery had been slightly marred by his contracting the hospital-acquired or nosocomial infection Methicillin-Resistant Staphylococcus Aureus also known as MRSA. When this bug was isolated from his swab samples in the microbiology laboratory, he had been moved to a side room and a decontamination process implemented. He was now MRSA free and back on an open ward. Clarissa liked Mr Douglas; he had been a teacher for fifty years and had been a friend of her late father. When was diagnosed with prostate cancer last year, Mr Douglas formed a group called 'Well-Life-Man' online and had gone about educating men about prostate cancer (not commonly talked about at the time), how to prevent it using natural herbal remedies and what to do if you developed it.

"*Mummy, help me!*" Elle's voice screamed.

Clarissa froze momentarily then adrenaline took effect, "Elle, where are you? I can hear you, Elle. Tell me what you want me to do." She ran to Elle's room, pushed the door open and looked around. She knew Elle wasn't in the house, but she looked. She opened the wardrobe and looked under the bed. "Elle, tell me what you want me to do, how can I help?"

"*Pray for me,*" Elle's voice whispered. "*Don't worry, just pray. Now you have to wake up Mummy! Please wake up!*"

Clarissa jerked out of her slumber and sat up. She turned and looked at the window. It was closed. Her breathing was laboured, and fear coursed through her making her heart pound. "My God, was that a dream? It felt so real. God, please help me, please don't let anything happen to Elle." She looked at her watch. Elle would still be at the hospital with her mother and Maddy was at the cinema with her dad. She couldn't shift the anxious feeling in the pit of her stomach and reached for her mobile phone. Her mother answered on the third ring.

"Hi Mum, is Elle nearby?"

"Hi, sweetheart, yes, she was talking to Mrs Douglas five minutes ago. I told her not to wander off too far."

Clarissa could hear her mother's voice cutting in and out and pictured her turning this way and that as she looked around for Elle. "Can you make sure she's okay, Mum, I had a strange dream-"

"The reception isn't that good, Clarissa. I can just about hear you," Madeline interrupted. "Hold on, there she is, I can see her talking to someone, wait a minute."

Clarissa heard her mother call out to Elle then seconds of silence ensued.

"Clarissa, sweetheart, you still there? Elle is down the corridor. She's going to use the visitors' toilet. I told her not to wander off too far."

"Thanks, Mum, I'm coming down there now. I'll give you a lift back home."

"Are you sure? You don't have to we can take a taxi."

"I'm sure. I'll be there in about thirty minutes."

"Okay, thanks, sweetheart, see you soon."

In the pit of her stomach Clarissa felt a stirring that she didn't understand, she started to pray. She prayed for God to look after Elle and keep her safe – from what, she didn't know – but she felt such a stirring that the words as if on a loop, were said over and over again. "God look after Elle and keep her safe – God look after Elle and keep her safe – God look after Elle and keep her safe – God look after . . . . ."

CHAPTER 38

Task Force vs. Scotland Yard

The tension was building as neither side wanted to back down from what they each perceived as the right thing to do. Raised voices and bickering from both sides was persistent. It was as if the police commissioner didn't want to accommodate the task force but just to cover his back had agreed to have this meeting, and, his officers had picked up on this. The task force members sat in a group at the back of the conference room while the police officers sat in front of them. In between both groups were two rows of empty seats – symbolising an invisible wall that seemed to push both sides further and further apart.

Inspector James sat with his rank equivalent based at Scotland Yard, Inspector Mason who had just returned from a two week holiday in Majorca and was still in holiday mode. Police Commissioner Pike, an East London man who had worked his way up the police corporate ladder through hard graft, sat in-between both inspectors. He was their direct commanding officer and didn't suffer fools kindly. He said what he thought, usually without thinking.

All three sat at a table facing the others. Inspector James had laid all the findings from the task force on the table. A screen on the wall behind the inspectors and commissioner displayed the red dots which represented the location of every suicide in the United Kingdom in the last six months. The code that Sergeant Kelleher had broken was on another screen.

The police officers, stoic in their ways and their investigation methods could not comprehend the theory of someone remotely instigating the suicides. They regarded such things as voodoo and magic, un-relatable, and things that they could not relate to in their professional lives they tended to scoff.

"With all due respect, Sirs, I think that this is a complete waste of time. I don't see how one person is pulling the strings, and everyone else is merely a puppet in these events, I think that these people here have formed this task force illegally, and it needs to be disbanded." One of the police officers voiced, again.

"Why do you keep on insisting that we disband? It looks like you're scared that we might get things right and outshine you lot," Dr Chang Lin said.

"That will be the day!" Another officer said.

"You guys get paid to do what we do for free, and you still haven't got any answers to the increased suicide numbers have you?" Dr Chang Lin said.

"Why don't you suits go and be suits somewhere else and leave policing to the police?" The first police officer said.

"We will when you lot stop pissing about in the wind, pull your flies up and get some police work done!" Tristan said.

"That's rich coming from you lot, this is all smoke and mirrors if you ask me. You say that someone has a laptop with the main IP address, and you think that this is the laptop sending out the messages but the owner says it was nicked months ago, and you don't know where it is. And someone maybe using it as a front to bounce messages. Your guys are supposed to be computer freaks, how comes they can't locate one lousy laptop?" The first police officer said as he walked up to Tristan and stood in front of him, fists clenched.

Tristan stood up, "Our guys are working on it. We're not like you guys. We do things properly. We don't go after soft-touches because we can't find the real criminals or stand around scratching our arses while dangerous criminals walk out of prison right under our noses."

"STOP!" Genny almost shouted. She touched her brother's arm. He had a black belt in Taekwondo, and she knew he could floor the police officer in seconds. "I can't believe that with everything going on out there this is what we're doing, taking chunks out of each other. We need to work together, can't you see that the more we attack each other, the less we pay attention to what's happening and the more it will continue. Our Scientists have said that they believe with the recent online activity something big might be about to take place-"

"Something big, like what?" Inspector Mason asked.

"They're not sure, but-"

"If they're not sure what it is, how do you know that they're even sure it's going to take place?" Commissioner Pike added.

"It might be an idea to let her finish," Sergeant Kelleher said, almost to himself but loud enough for his commanding officers to hear.

Genny continued, "Our Scientists have said that there has been a lot of online activity between certain IP addresses recently. The problem they're having is dealing with all the firewalls that have been set up. Now, your officers may not see what we see or believe what we believe but can we agree that we are all here to save lives?"

Silence ensued as embarrassed faces looked away, most of the people in the room nodded.

Genny looked around at the people in the room, "Good. Inspector James has put Sergeant Kelleher in charge, and we need to devise a plan on how to shut this thing down-"

"Why is Sergeant Kelleher in charge?" A police officer asked.

"Yeah, why can't we have a vote?" Another officer voiced.

"Sergeant Kelleher broke the code so he's in charge," Genny said as she tried to simplify things.

"Hold on, I've been on the force longer than Kelleher, why wasn't I offered a chance?" A police officer queried.

"Some things are based on quality not quantity," Genny quipped.

"CODE RED! CODE RED! CODE RED AT LOCAL HOSPITAL!" An alarmed voice said over the police public-address system.

Phones and bleeps started to go off all over the room.

CHAPTER 39

"CODE RED! I REPEAT THIS IS A CODE RED. CAN ALL DOCTORS, NURSES AND PARAMEDICS MAKE THEIR WAY TO THE LIVINGSTON WARD! WE HAVE A CODE RED!" The female voice calmly repeated over and over through the speakers.

The first thing Clarissa noticed when she walked into the hospital was the alarm sirens going off inside the building. She was more accustomed to sirens going off outside – police cars, ambulances, fire brigades. The alarm was un-nerving and even though the voice making the announcement calmly requested that all the doctors, nurses and paramedics make their way to the Livingston Ward, Clarissa quickened her pace. The anxious feeling she had felt earlier returned. When the lift didn't appear within seconds of her pressing the call button she turned and headed to the stairs then ran up the steps two at a time to the third floor. Doctors, nurses and paramedics rushed up the stairs with her. On the third floor, she turned left, and the people turned right. She breathed a sigh of relief and headed towards Mr Douglas' ward.

"Clarissa, how nice of you to come," Mrs Douglas said as soon as she walked into Mr Douglas' room. "I was just saying to your mother that you must be so proud of Elle and what a lovely young lady she has become. Elle was telling me that you have taught her how to make cottage pie using unique ingredients and how she would make some of your quadruple chocolate chip muffins on Friday for Mr Douglas. She is a gem, Clarissa, and she has a heart of gold. Can you remind her, dear, not to put too much sugar in the muffins as Mr Douglas has to watch his sugar intake?"

"I will, Mrs Douglas."

"Oh and Mr Douglas said . . ."

Clarissa smiled at her as she listened. She admired the way they referred to each other as Mr and Mrs Douglas. It was as if they loved and respected each other so much that they didn't want anyone, not even themselves, to minimise what they had by over-familiarity. She didn't think that many people knew their first names. They had been married for nearly fifty years, had children, grandchildren and great-grandchildren. Sometimes Clarissa envied what they had, and sometimes she wished that she had followed her heart instead of her head and married Steve Truman when he asked her. But at twenty, she had wanted to see the World, not get married. Steve had said that they could see the World together. Instead, she had gone on a gap year and seen the World by herself, and he had moved on with his life. Instead, she had married Neil and never had a chance at aiming for fifty years of marriage. *'Spousal-ship is supposed to be for life but some people are not lifers, and others are',* her counsellor had said when Clarissa immersed in the pits of depression had blamed herself for her husband's philandering ways. When she couldn't understand how a man with two beautiful daughters who adored him could treat their mother, who also loved him, with such disregard. She had once asked Neil what he would do if (God forbid) one day Elle or Maddy came to him and said that their husband was doing to them exactly what he had done to her? What would he do or say to the man who was breaking his daughter's heart? Without blinking, Neil had responded with *'I'd kill him'* and that was when she knew her marriage was over. Spousal-ship is supposed to be for life, but some people are not lifers and others are. She was glad that Mr and Mrs Douglas' spousal-ship was for life.

Clarissa felt an arm sneak around her shoulder and turned.

"Hello, sweetheart, you look tired, are you okay?"

"I'm all right, Mum, I just have a slight headache. Mrs Douglas said you went to the nurse's station, is everything okay?"

"Yes, everything's fine sweetheart. Mr Douglas said he was a bit cold last night, so I went to ask if they could turn the heating up a little for him tonight. Oh, I reminded Elle again about what you said."

Clarissa smiled. "When I was coming up the stairs there was a load of doctors and other staff running towards Livingston Ward. Do you know what's going on there?"

"Livingston Ward?"

"Yes, it's opposite this ward, down the corridor."

"That's where Elle said she was going to visit that friend of hers. She said Ruth said not to go so she wasn't, then she got a text which she ignored then she said she felt bad and would text you to see what you thought. Did you get her text?"

Clarissa reached for her phone. She saw that she had a text and quickly opened it and read it:

Elle   17:14
√ Hi Mum, Jessica has been in the hospital for days, I didn't know. Should I go to see her? Can you text me back asap cos visiting will soon be over in the Livingston Ward.
Love you lots, Elle xxx

CHAPTER 40

Livingston Ward

It is said that the angels in Heaven rejoice when someone repents and becomes born again. It is also said that the demons in hell rejoice when someone dies who isn't, and are jubilant when someone commits suicide.

Some of the new younger doctors couldn't venture back into the large hospital room where, inside, the bloated and bleeding bodies with gargoyle faces and twisted limbs resembled zombies in a Cert 18 horror film. A few of the younger doctors had already vomited into yellow clinical waste bags outside the room. The sterner-hearted doctors, nurses and paramedics who, with experience, had seen death in many forms, went in and assessed the situation.

There were ten dead people in total in the room - six girls and four boys - the oldest was nineteen, the youngest thirteen.

The Livingston Ward was now a crime scene. Hospital security guards rushed around unsure what to do. The police had been tipped off by an anonymous caller and were frantically trying to make sense of the scene in front of them. Some hospitals had seen the odd suicide - A person newly diagnosed with cancer jumping from the roof of the hospital. Or a patient dies, and their distraught loved one jumps over the railings or through a window to the ground below. Precautions had been implemented over the years in most hospitals. Roof doors were permanently locked, windows secured so that they only opened a few inches. No one could have foreseen this. Children taking a concoction of stolen hospital drugs inside a hospital and killing themselves! *Using the tools of the health care service to kill themselves - tools that are supposed to save lives used to take lives!* The chief executive and the board of directors of the hospital knew the news would hit the ground running and push everything in its path out of the way. They tried to curtail the damage as best they could but two of the health care workers assigned to the Livingston Ward, on seeing how young some of the children were, had already fled the scene screaming and telling everyone and anyone who would listen that some kids were dead on the Livingston Ward. And, they had speculated the possibility of it being a terrorist attack.

Clarissa's phone rang. She looked at the display screen, saw Elle's number and quickly answered the phone. She listened to a stranger speak words that no mother deserved to hear then she screamed and screamed and screamed . . .

SIDE B

CHAPTER 41

Clarissa screamed and screamed and screamed . . . Then something happened inside of her, it started in her head and spread throughout her body – it possessed her completely. It had her running in the direction she knew her child, her baby, was. There seemed to be no sense or reason to it, just a knowing that Elle needed her to fight.

She ran like a crazy woman towards Livingston Ward. She saw police officers and doctors, nurses and health care workers standing around in various states of distress. She ran towards them. A police officer saw her coming and stepped in front of her to slow her down. She pushed him out of her way, and he flew across the corridor, shocked at the force behind her push. Another officer grabbed her arm, and she twisted out of his grip.

"Mummy, Mummy, where are you?" Elle's voice said.

"Don't go in there," one of the doctors said as he stood in front of the door blocking her vision. "Please don't go in there, the kids are all dead!"

"My daughter is in there, and she's not dead! Get out of my way!" Clarissa screamed with a voice she didn't recognise but didn't stop to question.

The doctor by the door held his hands up to stop her going in, and another doctor stepped in behind her and said, "We can't allow you in there, it's a crime scene."

"My daughter is in there, get out of my way!" She screamed at the doctor in front of her then pushed the doctor behind her away and moved to go past the doctor in front of her. Hearing the commotion, two police officers rushed towards her, and all four men held her back. Clarissa struggled against her human restraints.

"Madam, please listen to us, everyone in there is dead," the doctor in front of her said.

She froze as something within took hold of her mind,

strength resonated through her and within seconds she had pushed all the men off her and rushed into the room. The sight of the dead bodies in various positions stopped her but only for a second. The forensic team stopped taking pictures and stared at her. They watched her look at the bodies then rush over to a girl who was lying on her side – frozen in death. They watched as she picked the young girl up, held her tightly and screamed then suddenly stop. They watched as she opened the girl's mouth and stuck her fingers in and pulled out some vomit. They watched as she called the girl's name over and over again then gave her CPR. Moments later she placed her ear next to the girl's mouth, listened, then flipped the girl onto her side and banged her back hard several times.

"Please God, don't let her die! Elle, Elle can you hear me, sweetheart, there's something stuck in your throat, you need to breathe, Elle! Please breathe, baby!"

The doctors, the police and the forensic team didn't dare stop her or move near her; they just watched.

"Mummy, Mummy, help me I can't breathe," Elle murmured.

"She's not dead!" Clarissa screamed. "Did you hear her? She's not dead!"

One of the police officers looked at his colleague and the other men; they all shook their heads, all confirming that they hadn't heard anything. "Let us take care of your daughter, Madam, you have to leave, this is a crime scene," he told Clarissa.

"Please help me," Clarissa pleaded with him, "Please help me. SHE'S NOT DEAD! She just spoke to me. She's not dead! She's only thirteen! She can't be dead!"

When questioned later the police officer would say 'something', he wasn't sure what it was, made him push the other men to one side, tell them not to move and rush forward to help her. He saw a mother fighting to save her daughter and even though, at the time, he knew she was dead. He knew he had to try. He knelt beside Clarissa and followed the instructions she gave him to keep Elle's head steady and her mouth opened. Clarissa turned Elle onto her front then knelt over her and performed a sort of Heimlich manoeuvre on her. From behind she pressed Elle's ribcage twice, on the third time the rest of the vomit came out of her mouth and she took a weak breath. Her eyes were closed. She was unresponsive, but she had taken the breath, they both heard her, they both heard the faint sigh that followed and felt the warm breeze that blew over them. The police office looked in the direction from which the breeze was coming from and saw that it was a closed window – he trembled.

"She's not dead!" The police officer shouted, "She's not dead! Help us!"

"Thank God, thank God," Clarissa cried as the strength that had possessed her moments before left her weak and shaking.

One of the doctors tried to get her to release Elle's hand, but she held on to it tightly. She was scared that if she let it go, they would put Elle back where she had found her and write her off as another statistic, "No, I'm not letting her go," Clarissa told him.

"But-"

"She just had to fight off four men to save her daughter's life, leave her alone, let her stay with Elle," the police officer told the doctor. He was still stunned by the miracle he had just witnessed. He knew for a fact that Elle had been pronounced dead over twenty minutes ago and what he had just seen was not only a mother's sheer determination to save her child but the Hand of God made visible.

CHAPTER 42

Dr Park

He sat with his back against a warm radiator but for some reason, as hard as he tried, he couldn't seem to keep warm. Three days ago he had been on a beach in Australia absorbing the sun and building a sand castle with his son, Josh. The sky was a vibrant blue, the sea a rich indigo and the beach laden with bodies of various shapes. Now here he was back in London, the place of his birth, unable to comprehend that Australia was a place on an Earth that also housed England. For years he had grown up hearing that the weather in the UK was unpredictable; now as he sat huddled next to the radiator, almost cuddling it, he smiled to himself – he was glad to be home.

"What's so funny?"

He turned to the doctor sitting next to him, "I was just thinking about warm sunny days, blue skies and lying on the beach soaking up the sun."

The doctor smiled back, "We have sunny days here, they come and go pretty fast so don't blink, or you'll miss them."

Both doctors turned as did the rest of the people sitting around the conference table when the doors burst open, and several people rushed in. Two police officers carried Heckler & Koch MP5SF rifles and looked around as if ready to use them if provoked.

"What's going on, what do you want?" The chief consultant asked; his glasses were poised precariously on his nose as he looked at the men over the rim.

"Dr Parks, is there a Dr Parks here?" A man wearing a dark brown jacket asked.

"Dr Parks? There isn't a Dr Parks here," the chief consultant replied as he stared at the policemen carrying the rifles.

"Hold on a minute," the man turned slightly, asked someone

on his mobile phone a question and listened to the answer then turned back to the table. "Not Dr Parks, It's Dr Park! Aka Dr Steve Truman! We need Dr Steve Truman. Now! Make yourself known. This is a code red situation!" The man shouted. He held his ID and badge up and walked towards the table looking from face to face. "My name is Chief Inspector Miller of the Metropolitan Police."

Confused, Dr Park stood up "That's me, Dr Park is the nickname they gave me in New York that's stuck with me since then. What is this? What do you want?"

"Come with us, Dr Truman, we have an emergency at a local hospital and have been told that we need your expertise. It's a code red situation! Let's go!"

"What? Wait a minute, where are we going?"

The two officers with rifles moved towards him, and Chief Inspector Miller grabbed his arm and the coat that was on the back of the chair, "Is this your coat, Doctor?"

"Yes."

"Put it on. It's cold out there."

"Wait a minute, my son finishes his lessons soon, and I need to pick him up."

"Josh has been picked up. He's in a secured room at the hospital you'll see him when you get there."

"You went to the school and picked Josh up?" Perplexed, he ran-walked to keep up with the men and struggled to put on his coat at the same time. As soon as he stepped out of the building, he saw the flashing lights of the numerous police vehicles and knew that the matter was serious. He thought of a possible chemical or terrorist attack and wondered why his colleagues had not been taken with him, "Look, Chief Inspector, tell me what's going on right now?"

"We got an anonymous phone call earlier. The phone's been traced to a 9-year-old South West London boy."

"What was the call about?"

"It was telling us about a suicide pact-"

"Whoa, whoa, what? Where?"

"A bunch of kids just carried out a suicide pact at a hospital using poison consisting of drugs and chemicals which we've not been able to identify. We think one of them might still be alive, the anonymous call we got may have bought her some time. Get into the car, Doctor. We might only have a short amount of time left to save her life!"

CHAPTER 43

6pm

The task force and police force were united. They had set up an emergency office at the hospital and within the hour had the latest computing and tracking equipment installed. Information was being fed through to the numerous large screens which were stationed along the walls. Forensics was still inspecting the crime scene and journalists from every single newspaper, TV and radio station were standing just outside the cordoned area. Most TV and radio stations had a live-feed and millions of people were being kept up-to-date on the mass suicide pact which had taken place in the prominent London hospital.

Dr Tristan Cookson got off his mobile phone, "That was Chief Inspector Miller, Dr Park is on his way to the hospital, he's in a police convoy, and they're about five minutes away."

"Dr Park? I thought you said this poison expert or genius was called Dr Steve Truman." Sergeant Kelleher said.

"Dr Park is his nickname. He lived in New York for a period and was always jogging in Central Park so the locals gave him that name. He's a local hero over there – he ran free clinics and gave out free advice, etc." Genny said as she pulled up pictures of Dr Park and his son Josh taken in New York on her laptop, the pictures appeared on the large screens. "His wife died while giving birth to their daughter, who also died a few hours later. Since then it's just been him and his son. He was recently in Australia leading a toxicology research team and returned to the UK a few days ago."

"What else do we know about him?" Sergeant Kelleher asked.

"Not much, he was born in the UK and has done a lot of work on poisons and how to counter-react their effects. If anyone can save the child, he can," Anna said.

"We need to find out who these kids are, and if there are any more suicide pacts out there, these things don't usually happen in isolation." Dr Peter Lewis told the group. "Some of the bodies are now in the mortuary, do we know any specifics?"

"Yes, nine out of the ten left something. Elle May Williams was the only one who didn't leave anything and the only one with a mobile phone that was turned on. And, it looks like she was in the process of making a call, which confirms that she was just collateral damage," Genny said.

"It's currently 6.05pm, we have less than six hours to get to the bottom of this, another day usually means another set of similar occurrences," Dr Chang Lin warned.

Police Commissioner Pike flounced into the room like a man charged with carrying the weight of the World on his shoulders, "Can I have your attention people, things have just escalated to an international scale. One of the victims has just been identified as Kelly Albright, a fourteen-year-old American student. She was on a school exchange visit and had several pages of notes from her diary in her pocket. The British government has given us special dispensation and jurisdictions to solve this case. And, I have to answer the question, 'how did a fourteen-year-old American student end up committing suicide in a hospital, in this country?' Her parents are yet to be contacted, but this has been sent from her aunt, her mother's sister, to help us confirm our initial identification." He inserted a USB into a computer and pressed a button on the computer, pictures of Kelly taken in a school theatre production came on the screen; she was singing. Heads shook, and tears sprang into some eyes as they looked at the vibrant young girl on the screen. More pictures appeared, almost as if taken in particular chronological order and now being played backwards for this audience to see. The last image was of a beautiful baby girl, 'Kelly aged six months' the words on the screen said. She wore a light pink jumpsuit.

She laughed and giggled as she tried to grab hold of a furry ball that was dangling on a string. 'Come on, sweetie, you can do it, reach for the ball for Mommy', a woman's voice said, 'look at the ball, honey, reach for it darling.' Baby Kelly reached out and grabbed the ball then gave a big squeal of delight as her mother tickled her. Next, the picture of dead Kelly appeared on the screen. The gasps and exclamations sounded feeble in response to the lifeless body on the screen, which looked shocking. The poison had ripped through her body dissolving her intestine and vital organs and had caused several blood vessels in her head to burst open. She had died in excruciating pain which in death expressed itself in her contorted face, which was gargoyle-like and blood stained.

"Has anyone else been identified, Sir?" One of the police officers asked, as he purposely looked away from the image on the screen.

"Yes, a sixteen-year-old boy called Victor Jenkins. His parents are on their way in from Nottingham, something similar happened in his family about six months ago."

"They say that there's a high chance of suicide re-occurring in a family without certain measures of prevention," Genny said as she typed some information on her laptop. "I can't find anything about a previous suicide involving anyone with the surname Jenkins."

"Keep looking," Sergeant Kelleher told her, "they may not have the same surname." He massaged his forehead. "There has to be a link between all of these kids, someone somewhere got them all here in this hospital today to do this."

"I have something," Dr Peter Lewis called out, "under suspicious deaths, Colin Wolsey found dead on train tracks in Nottingham six months ago. Victor Jenkins is listed down here as Colin's first cousin!"

CHAPTER 44

Kelly Albright, San Francisco

Diary Entry: Jeremy Buchanan asked me out today!!! He came right up to me as I stood with Sarah and Julie after cheerleading practice and asked me if I want to watch the new action blockbuster showing. I tried to act real cool. I tried not to blush. I knew which movie he was referring to, but I asked him which one he meant. He told me which one and I said 'sure, why not' real cool-like. I wanted to scream 'YES! YES! YES!' But I acted real cool and said – 'sure, why not'. Sarah said I acted real cool, but Julie said that she thought he was too old for me, and my mom wouldn't let me go out on a date with him. Julie can be a drag sometimes; she is like the voice of reason to a drunken man, too drunk to care about anything. She is like heat to ice cream – she can take your tower of joy and knock it down, crushing it until it's useless to itself. Who said I was going to tell my mom anyway ☺.

Diary Entry: He kisses like butter – so smooth. Jeremy, Jeremy . . . JEREMY. My-Sweet-Prince-Jeremy. <u>Mrs. Kelly Buchanan</u>. Jeremy my ☼, the song ♫ in my heart. My love. I like that ☺ ☺ ☺ I like the thought of being his wife. XxX Mrs. Kelly Buchanan ☺
Guess what diary. We saw the action movie which was okay. Jeremy kept staring at me and pretending that he wasn't. After the movie, he walked me to Sarah's house. I told my mom that Sarah and I were working on a school science project. Julie's right, my mom and dad would never let me date, let alone date a guy in High School. Jeremy asked if we could see each other again and I said yes. I'll think of something to tell my parents on the day.

Diary Entry: We went to the mall downtown today. Jeremy

had to get something for his camera. He bought me a cute silver bracelet with little charms dangling from it. It's so cool. I love it ☺.

Diary Entry: Jeremy and I talked and talked today, feels like I've known him forever!

Diary Entry: Met Jeremy at the mall and we went to get some ice cream then we went to the park and talked. He said he wanted to be a photographer for a glossy magazine when he left school. He said that he had already taken pictures and sent them off and was waiting to hear if they liked his work. He started taking pictures of me. He asked me to pose this way and that, it started off as harmless fun. Then he suggested I take my top off so that he could get some arty pictures of me. He kept on telling me how beautiful I was and how he would keep the pictures of me secret and look at them when he was lonely. He said that he knew I was younger than him, and we wouldn't do anything more than kiss for now and that the pictures would always keep his mind on me.

Diary Entry: Strange thing happened today, I was at the mall with Sarah and Julie in a coffee bar and saw Jeremy walk past with a girl. She looked older than me. He saw me and smiled but didn't come over to our table. They went to another coffee shop nearby and sat down. Sarah looked at me and mouthed what was going on. I shrugged as I sure didn't know. I tried not to look at them. I heard him laugh and looked up. They were both looking at something on his phone. Their heads were almost touching as they sat close to each other. I wondered if she was his cousin or another family member. I know he has a few female relatives.
Julie said she's his girlfriend, and I was smart not to go on a date with him when he asked me (I never told her the truth). I heard myself gasp but didn't say anything.

Sarah told her to shut up.

Julie said she saw them together the other night when her mom was driving her and her brother back from his little league game. She said she saw them arguing outside the ice cream shop then she saw him grab her and kiss her.

Diary Entry: SHIT SHIT SHIT!!!! My life is shit. Jeremy hasn't called since I saw him at the mall with that girl. I've tried calling him, but his stepmom says he's studying and can't come to the phone.

Diary Entry: I don't feel like going to school today. My mom keeps looking at me like she knows something is wrong. Why doesn't she just ask me what's wrong and stop staring at me like the problem is written on my forehead in gibberish, and she's trying to read what it says? I don't want to go to cheerleading practice today. I don't want to do anything. I said I felt sick yesterday, and I don't think my mom will let me skip school today. I don't want to live. I can't go on like this anymore. Why hasn't JEREMY called me? WHY? WHY? WHY?

Diary Entry: Found a chat room today, got some good advice on how to deal with my pain. Is it even pain? Maybe Jeremy *is* studying and isn't blowing me off. Maybe I'm making a big phooey about nothing. Maybe I'm the heat to the ice cream x-x-x-o-o-o-x-x-x-

Diary Entry: I threw up twice. I can't even bear to look at myself in the mirror. I hate myself. The pictures Jeremy took that day in the park showed up online today. He said that someone stole his camera and must have seen the pictures and put them online. He said he was sorry, but I caught him looking at his friends when he was talking to me, and I heard them laughing as I walked away.

U MURDER U (SUICIDE)

Diary Entry: One day I was the prettiest girl in my year and the next I was a cheap slut. How does that happen in less than a week? How do you go from someone everyone wants to know to someone everyone hates in less than a week? Looking back I see that going to the movies with Jeremy Buchanan wasn't such a good idea. I see that letting him take topless pictures of me was the stupidest thing I have ever done. I have nowhere to go and no one to talk to. How do I tell my parents that everyone in the school is calling me a cheap slut and a whore? My father will see the pictures and think that his fourteen-year-old daughter is a hooker. I feel sick at the thought. He will look at me as damaged goods. OMG, I'm going to throw up, I can feel my guts churning and my hurl moving up my throat.

Diary Entry: Going to London today for student exchange programme.

Diary Entry: Started writing eulogies for myself – things that I think people who really know me will say. It's kinda fun. It's kinda freeing.

Predicted Eulogy from Sarah
RIP Kelly. You were taken much too soon.
Your light will always shine.
You are gone but not forgotten.
Sarah xxx

Predicted Eulogy from Julie
Kelly, Kelly, Kelly, I can't believe you're gone.
I miss you so much. I told you not to go out with Jeremy ☹
Anyway at least you can't hurt anymore. I miss you, Julie.

Predicted Eulogy for me from me
No more pain, no more shame
I am free. Goodbye World, you can't hurt me anymore, I am free!

CHAPTER 45

Victor Jenkins, Nottingham (home of Robin Hood)

RIP Colin - In my dreams I'm a superhero, I don't go around wearing tights and a cape, not me man, no, I go around with a samurai sword and a gun. The sword is shiny and sturdy and is to swish this way and that and kill the bad guys and the gun, like in that *Indiana Jones* film, is just to shoot the bad guys when it looks like things might take too long with the sword. For some reason in my dreams, I'm always tall, and buff like a giant bodybuilder, my muscles gleam and ripple and I can fly. I love dreams and dreaming. I wish they were real. My mum says that dreams are for dreamers, and I don't know what that means. She says she can't explain it as it's one of those sayings that didn't come with any instructions. It's not like 'a stitch in time saves nine', which means that if you do something soon enough, you don't have to do more of it later. Or like the saying Mr Jones at school consistently uses, 'to catch two birds with one stone', which means to perform one act that achieves two objectives at the same time. My cousin Colin, who's a bit older than me, says Mr Jones' saying is a personification of his (Colin's) manhood. It describes him going clubbing on a Saturday night and pulling two birds by himself. Colin dropped out of school with no secondary school qualifications. He got a part-time job at the local garage when he was fourteen and by the time he was sixteen worked there full-time.

The thing with being a superhero in your dream is that you can't bring that into your reality, you can't dream of being a superhero and suddenly wake up a superhero. No, people like me wake up as they are, in my case, a sixteen-year-old skinny boy with pale white skin, a mop of ginger hair. No six-pack, no muscular arms and a face so full of acne which my GP tells me should clear soon – but from where I'm standing 'soon' seems like a distant place, somewhere far away in the future.

My teacher, Mr Jones, asked us to think about what we wanted to study at University last week. He said that we should stop pissing about and stop using the excuse which has turned into a 'life-line' for some of us and used on our behalf by teachers, head-teachers, education ministers and some parents. He said some boys were born with this excuse wrapped around them like a comfort blanket, soothing them and making them feel that their inability to pick up a book wasn't their fault. The excuse: – *Girls are so much better academically in secondary school than boys, so as a boy don't waste your time competing with girls.* He said that this was a pathetic excuse which only served to make boys lazy.

I wasn't born with this comfort blanket wrapped around me. I loved to read books. Colin would laugh at me as I read English Literature books. He insisted that one in particular, *'Lady Chatterley's Lover'*, was not an English Lit curriculum book but a pornographic movie which he had seen several times (on loan from the local library). He got a lot of his subtle porn films from the library, which I found strange. The porn in the library wasn't hidden in a seedy room concealed behind a dirty black curtain, on top of which hung a plastic flashing sign indicating that the adult section of the video shop was behind the curtain. Dodgy looking men would look around quickly, necks swaying like a pendulum, to confirm they weren't followed then duck behind the curtain like I had seen Colin do. Colin took me to one of these video shops when I was fourteen, and he had the job of picking me up from school and escorting me to the dentist as both my parents were working. After the dentist Colin asked if I wanted to watch a movie, I said yes and we set off to the video shop. On the way, he told me that we weren't going to the local video store but a different one. When we got there he asked me to stay in the family section of the shop and choose a DVD, and I watched as he hunched his shoulders and walked quickly towards the back of the shop, he stopped quickly looked from side to side then slipped behind the disco-lit curtain.

Whenever Colin came to the library with me, I noticed he would spend a long time looking at the DVDs on display searching for subtle porn. These DVDs were there on display for mothers and toddlers, teenagers and adults to see. They were there in cases adorned with the faces of A, B and C list actors. They were there for Colin. Ten seconds or ten minutes of porn in any film made Colin happy. He wasn't concerned with the storyline, the 'arty farty' he called it. I laughed secretly to myself the first time I heard him say five minutes into a movie. I swear he didn't even blink, 'Come on get ya kit off already'. Ten close family members were there watching the movie with him. You should have seen my mum's face. She's his mum's sister right. She grew up with his mum, she and his mum once occupied the same womb (though at different times, my mum is younger). When Colin said those words, my mum looked at him like he was an alien from a place further than Neptune. For people who don't know, Neptune is thought to be the furthest planet from Earth, so further than Neptune is saying something, it implies somewhere way, way, *way* out there, it implies weirder than weird. 'Hahahaha' that's the sound of me chuckling at the look she gave him; it still can rip me up and as my Gran used to say - tickle my cockles.

It isn't just English Lit that I like to read. It's Physics, Maths, Chemistry, Biology and Economics. I have this knack of reading textbooks as though they're novels, which makes them easier for me to understand and much more enjoyable. Colin didn't like reading. He liked to watch movies. Sometimes I wonder if they have movies where Colin is. My

Gran thinks he's in limbo somewhere, and my mum doesn't talk about him at all, almost as if her silence obliterates the fact that he existed once, that he was once a living breathing human being. That he had once uttered words, which made her look at him as if he were an alien from a planet further than Neptune.

Colin stopped me from getting bullied. He was tall and buff and beat some of the bullies up a couple of times. He did it to send a message out to the others – 'No one touches my Blood'. On the night he jumped in front of a moving train some say he may have been drunk, and others say Colin was depressed because a girl he liked turned him down. His mother thinks the bullies might have done him in.

When Colin died, I set up a website in memory of him for people to pay their respects online and some people defaced it. They left vile messages and cartoon pictures of a person jumping in front of a train with the caption *'Trains will be delayed because of this idiot!* They call people who write such hateful messages online 'Trolls' – Troll 'noun' *an individual who sows discord on the Internet by starting arguments or upsetting people by posting inflammatory harassing messages online.* I call them cowards! Bloody Heartless Cowards who will one day get their just rewards! What goes around comes around and one day they will pay for the misery they have caused to families like mine!

The bullies at school have started picking on me again. They call me 'acne-face' and 'join-the-spot' face and they laugh at me and hit me. They say that now Colin isn't around to protect me I'll have to pay them protection money and if I don't pay I seriously need to think about ending my life and doing the World a favour. The teachers don't want to know, and I can't tell my mum, she'll only come to school and pick a fight with the parents of the bullies, which will mean that I get bullied even more, and I can't take that.

I wrote this letter and will put it on my site before I go:

To the trolls, the racists, the bigots, the haters,
Maybe the person you hate
Isn't Black or White or the shades in-between
Isn't a woman or a man
Maybe the person you hate is the one you see when you look in the mirror
Maybe if you start trying to understand why you're so full of hate and how to change the 'hate' energy into 'like' energy (one step at a time) then maybe life for you will change, and you will see every man as one man and hate the 'hate'.
Maybe from like you will grow to love and appreciate the differences in people. Get a little wisdom into your soul and understand that we can't all be the same. We were created differently so that when we come together we're not bland, we simply blend. In the paraphrased words of MJ – look in the mirror and do something to make that change!

I hope the people who've made my life so miserable read my letter and change.

I wonder if Dante's Inferno about the nine circles of hell is true . . .

I wonder if they have books where I am going . . .

Victor Jenkins boarded a train at Nottingham coming from Liverpool Lime Street Station. The train went through Northampton, Milton Keynes . . . final stop London.

CHAPTER 46

7pm – Press Interview

"Inspector Carmichael, what's going through your mind right now? How are you and your wife handling this?"

"My wife and I are not handling things very well and would appreciate some privacy to deal with this matter," Inspector Patrick Carmichael replied.

"Was this something you ever expected to happen?"

"What?"

"Had Jessica ever tried to kill herself before?"

"No!"

"Neil, Mr Williams, we understand that your daughter is in the ITU, how are you and your family dealing with the events of today?"

"My family and I are obviously very upset with what has happened to our daughter, and we're doing everything we can to come to terms with the events of today."

"Was this something you ever expected to happen?"

"As you can imagine-"

"Neil!" Clarissa rushed forward, clasping a newspaper with the headline, **'MOTHER WRESTLES FOUR MEN – To Save Suicide Daughter!'** "Neil, what the hell are you doing?" She shouted at him. "Look at what these people wrote about Elle, look at the lies they've written about our daughter!"

Neil Williams stood up, guilt and embarrassment quickly concealed, he addressed her. "Clarissa, I was just talking to the press-"

"Talking to the press!"

"Yes, I was just about to tell them how sad Elle could get sometimes and how angry she got when I came around-"

"She got mad at you because you abandoned your family! You cheated on me and didn't look back at your children when you left because you thought you were going off to a better life where you would be free to sleep with everyone and

219

anyone!"

"Clarissa!"

"Don't you dare Clarissa me, you think it's fine to tell these people half-truths about Elle but you're uncomfortable with them knowing the truth about you!"

"This is not the time or place for this, Clarissa-"

"Neither is this the time or place to sit down and talk to a bunch of people who don't care about our daughter, people who just want to sensationalise the truth."

"We don't know the full truth yet-"

"Yes, we do as far as Elle is concerned. Elle would never try to kill herself, never! She has so much to look forward to, so much to live for-"

"Every parent thinks that about their child, Clarissa, we might have to face some hard truths-"

"Tell me you're joking?" She whispered.

"What?"

"Tell me you're joking, Neil, this is Elle-belly you're talking about." In desperation she referred to the name they called Elle when she was a cute toddler, hoping to reach him.

He turned his head slightly, and she recognised something. He coughed then he sort of half smiled, "We all hope that Elle didn't do this to herself, but just in case -"

"Stop, don't say another word, this isn't some speech you give for an acting award. Our daughter is in intensive care fighting for her life. These people were counting her as one of the dead a few hours ago. They said she did this to herself, and you sat there talking to them!"

"Clarissa-"

"Have you seen Elle? Have you even asked to see her?"

"I . . . um, I was, um . . . .um."

"She was pronounced dead before I got here, she could have been put in a cold mortuary room, dead," she gasped as an aftershock flooded through her. "Thank God. Thank God she's alive! God, thank you for looking after my baby," she rubbed her forehead with the palm of her hand, her eyes squeezed shut she didn't see some of the cameras being raised and pictures taken or see the cameramen openly filming her.

Neil did. And, not one to miss a camera moment, he gave her his best 'camera-smile', stepped towards her, the cameras and microphones followed, "Clarissa, you're upset, you're still in shock-"

She heard something in his voice - it was a familiar cold smoothness. Her eyes flew open. "How dare you stand there and say that to me? Of course, I'm upset! Someone tried to kill my daughter!"

"Kill her? Did you say kill her, Mrs Williams?" A reporter asked.

"Yes, I said kill her, and Jessica Carmichael had something to do with this!"

"How dare you say that, Clarissa?" Eloise Carmichael whaled, "Jessica would never harm Elle! She loved her. They were best friends!"

"The last text message I got from Elle said that Jessica was here, and she wanted to know if she was allowed to see Jessica. The only reason Elle would have gone to see her was out of sympathy, she would never have done anything like this just because of some stupid friendship. Somehow Jessica forced this on Elle, and I'm going to prove it-"

"That's a lie!" Eloise screamed.

"Is it Eloise?" Clarissa asked then turned and faced the reporters, "I am calling on the Metropolitan Police to do their job and investigate this and I will fight with my last breath if necessary to make sure the truth is revealed. Someone tried to murder my daughter today!"

"Mrs Williams, Mrs Williams do you have any evidence?"

"I don't have anything more to say to any of you. And as for this man who thinks that he can speak on my behalf-"

"Clarissa, I am speaking on behalf of *our* family!"

"No, no you're not, maybe Elle does count somewhere deep

down in your mind, but right now you're speaking on behalf of your fledging acting career, what are you hoping for Neil? Are you hoping that Spielberg or Scorsese are watching?"

"That's not fair you know I love Elle-"

"Then show it, be her father and stop standing in the limelight. Someone tried to kill her!"

"You don't know that for sure, Clarissa," Neil protested.

"Of course, I do! She would never try to kill herself! She has too much to look forward to."

"Are you sure about that, Mrs Williams?" A reporter asked, "a lot of parents are in denial about their children."

"Yes, I'm one hundred percent sure that my daughter did not try to kill herself!"

"Are you sure about that, Mrs Williams? Teenagers are unpredictable nowadays," another said. "There's the teenager you think you know at home, and then there's the real teenager that the World knows on social media like Facebook!"

Neil said nothing to support her. She turned to the reporter and looked him in the eyes, "Of course I'm sure-"

The reporter intentionally cut her off, "Are you sure?"

"Will you let me finish-"

"Why don't you tell us the truth, Mrs Williams?"

Heads turned as a woman rushed forward, "Stop it! Stop harassing her! Elle Williams would never attempt to kill herself! She is full of life and has so much to live for so stop this circus now!"

"Ruth, thank God you're here, why are they doing this?"

"Because they're a bunch of low-lives trying to sell newspapers," Ruth said, hugging her friend to her. "If you're looking for some exclusive then write this, Elle May Williams is a beautiful young lady with her whole life in front of her. She told me this morning that she was recently given a writing scholarship, and she can't wait to start. Her little sister has a piano recital that she is helping her with and made me promise to stay and watch her perform. She was planning to make a family dinner tomorrow and-"

"Who are you?" A reporter asked.

"Are you even close to the family?" Another asked.

"My name is Ruth Valencia of the Valencia International Legal Firm, and I'm Elle May's godmother, is that close enough for you?"

"I'm sorry Miss Valencia."

"It's Mrs."

"You said you talked to Elle May this morning, was she okay? Did she show any signs of what she might be planning?"

"Have you just been standing there passing the time of day?"

"What?"

"Have you not heard a word that Clarissa or I have said?"

"I . . . um-"

"Elle May didn't show any signs because there were no signs to show! She did not try to kill herself and if you print one more slanderous word about my goddaughter I will sue you personally and the rag you write for!"

Clarissa took a deep breath, "My daughter did not try to kill herself."

A hush descended as the reporters looked behind Clarissa at the man who emerged from ITU. Clarissa didn't turn. She held her breath willing any more bad news away.

"Ladies and gentlemen, I've just been watching you on the TV harass Mrs Williams, and I have a brief announcement to make. I've been brought in by the Metropolitan Police to help with their investigation, and I can confirm that what Mrs Williams and Mrs Valencia have just told you is correct – Elle May Williams didn't try to kill herself. Elle May Williams was held down, probably knocked into a state of semi-consciousness and a poisonous concoction was poured down her throat!"

Several people gasped.

"What?" A reporter said.

"Are you sure?" Another asked.

"Absolutely sure," the doctor replied, "there's the start of severe bruising on her face and neck to substantiate this."

Clarissa couldn't breathe, her heart pounded within the confines of her chest. She felt his hand touch her arm, and she collapsed. It was as if the last few segments of her life fell on top of her like a ten-tonne weight and she crumbled beneath it. Before she blacked out, she felt hands grab hold of her, and she heard the panic in Ruth's voice and a familiar voice tell Neil not to touch her and Ruth not to worry. She felt familiar arms lift her up and carry her, and she felt herself moving along with his familiar stride. His voice was just above a whisper, but she heard the words he spoke, "I've got you, Rissa, I'll take care of you", then she blacked out.

CHAPTER 47

7.15pm

The nurses fussed around Clarissa. She had been carried into the private room by the mysterious doctor and placed on a couch. He had ordered them to take care of her and report back to him as soon as she regained consciousness then had immediately left.

"Is she okay, Grandma?" Maddy asked her grandmother.

Madeline Stapleton looked at the nurse who was taking her daughter's blood pressure, the nurse nodded. "She'll be okay, sweetheart," she told her granddaughter.

"What about Elle, Grandma? Will Elle be okay?"

"My dad's the best, he has loads of awards for his work, if he's looking after your sister, she'll be okay," Josh told Maddy.

"Grandma said that your dad and my mum are old friends, did you know that?" Maddy asked Josh.

"No, I didn't, but my dad never leaves me with anyone he doesn't trust so if he left me with you guys he must trust you."

Maddy smiled, she liked Josh. She liked his American accent and the fact that he spoke like she did, in a matter-of-fact way. "My name is Madison. It's a derivative of my grandma's name which is Madeline." She told him.

"Madison is a cool name. My dad took me to a place called Madison Square Garden in New York to watch a game once. Do people call you Madison or Maddy?"

"Both sometimes but mostly Maddy. What's your name?"

"It's Joshua, but people call me Josh."

"I like that name. There was a boy in my Sunday school class called Joshua once. He moved to Dublin with his family."

They both turned at the sound of a soft moan, "Look, she's waking up," Josh said. Maddy moved closer to her mother and hugged her arm.

"Clarissa, sweetheart, are you okay?" Madeline asked.

Clarissa opened her eyes. Alarm bells immediately went off. She stared at her mother, "Is Elle okay? Please tell me she's still stable?"

"Elle is still stable. There are three doctors in there with her now-"

"Steve," she whispered, "I heard his voice, that was him wasn't it?"

"Yes, it was, he carried you in here when you fainted then arranged for all of us to stay here. This is his son, Joshua."

"Hello, you can call me Josh, everyone else does," Josh told her.

Clarissa smiled at him; she liked him instantly, "Hello Josh."

"I've seen your picture before. My dad has an old photo album full of pictures of when he was young. I saw your picture in there. He takes the album out and looks through it now and then, and I see him smile when he does."

Clarissa took hold of Josh's hand and squeezed it.

"Are you okay, sweetheart?" Madeline asked again.

"I'm fine. I need to go and see how Elle is," Clarissa said as she quickly stood up. She swayed a little and reached out to her mother.

"You need to rest for a while. Ruth said she didn't think you've eaten. She went to look for some proper food for you. Steve said the next few hours are critical, so you'll need all your strength."

Clarissa closed her eyes and nodded. She pushed back the image of seeing her daughter already pronounced dead lying on the floor in a room full of dead disfigured looking children. She prayed to God that the image would leave her soon but for now she needed to keep fighting for Elle. Neil was busy trying to attract the attention of movie directors and producers, and all she had were her Mum, Elle, Maddy and Ruth, they were all she always had, until now . . . now that he was back.

CHAPTER 48

The Prom Dress – London

Eighteen-year-old Hazel stared at her reflection in the mirror. Her brother Carlton was right. She looked good. The hazel-green thread delicately woven into the gold material on the top half of the dress not only brought out the colour of her eyes it seemed to make her skin glow. She, her mother and brother had gone to Brent Cross to look for a prom dress and four hours and fifteen shops later came across this dress. They had almost given up and gone to a place in Finsbury Park as suggested by a shop assistant in John Lewis but at her mother's request to have one last look before traipsing across London, they had come across this beauty. The dress not only fitted her perfectly it covered up areas her mother had said she didn't want to see her daughter expose. The lower half of the dress was a creamy, satiny, silky fabric that gathered and flowed like a beautiful Grecian gown. When she took a step forward, the dress moved elegantly, almost as if it had its own life. She loved it.

"Are you ready H?" Carlton asked as he held the camera up, ready to take the pictures his older sister had asked him to take, of her wearing her dress.

"Take a shot of my top half and then full length," Hazel instructed.

Carlton took the pictures, and Hazel posted them online.

Twenty minutes later it seemed as if all 'Teenage-Girl' hell had broken loose . . . .
Lisa: "Mindy was going for the Grecian look, why has Hazel got a Grecian-style dress?"
Monica (Hazel's best friend): "Has Mindy bought her dress?"
Lisa: "That's not the point, Mindy told me she was going for that look."

Monica: "Grecian-style is not exclusive to anyone. We agreed to get different dresses. As long as Hazel's dress is a different cut – it shouldn't matter."

Kim: "Yeah, why should it matter, why are you always stirring things Lisa?"

Lisa: "Who asked you to butt in Kim???? I was just making a point!!!"

Kim: "No you weren't you were just trying to cause problems, and I can butt in where I want, this is on-the-line, which means free for all. So ???? and !!! back at you."

Monica: "If Mindy hasn't bought her dress yet and Hazel has then all Mindy needs to do is get something with a different cut – problem solved."

Lisa: "I'm going to call Mindy right now."

Kim: "Call her, can't wait to see what the head girl is going to say, shaking in my boots already."

Monica: "Kim, you're not helping. I'm going to call Hazel."

Mindy logs on

Mindy: "Hazel, why have you got that dress? I said I was going for that style."

Kim: "Monica is telling Hazel to get online. If you haven't bought your dress yet, Mindy go and get something different."

Lisa: "What is your problem, Kim? Mindy was talking to Hazel."

Kim: Hazel's my friend so until she gets online, you have to deal with me."

Lisa: "You are such a cow Kim, why don't you butt out."

Kim: "Why don't you?"

Maxine logs on

Maxine: "I have a similar style prom dress to Hazel's, it's a different colour, and I've just put a picture up. Don't give two - - - -s if it's Grecian style or not, I'm wearing it."

Lisa: "You have to stick to the rules! If Mindy is going for that style, you can't copy her, go and get another dress, Maxine."

Maxine: "Are you mad???? Did you buy my dress??? I'm wearing what I want. I told you the dress rule was rubbish. Not changing my dress, don't give a toss."

Lisa: "You sat in the common room and agreed to a dress rule, now cos you're too cheap to be original you want to rain on someone else's parade."

Kim: "Lisa, Lisa, Lisa, you're nuts."

Lisa: "Don't you dare call me nuts you bitch!"

Kim: "You're a psycho and a fruitcake = NUTS!!!"

Mindy: "Just had a proper look at Hazel's dress, it's not like the one I'm getting."

Maxine: "Even if it was like the one you're getting you don't have the exclusivity!"

Lisa: "How dare you call me nuts Kim?"

Maxine: "Maybe it's because you always act nuts!"

Mindy: "Stop the name calling and let's be civilised. My dress is not the same as Hazel's so there isn't a problem."

Maxine: "Again I ask, what if it was? Hazel shouldn't have to change her dress because of you."

Lisa: "I've always hated you, Kim, you're nothing but a spoilt bitch."

Tina logs on

Tina: "Ladies, just logged on, what's going on, come on we're sisters, is a dress really that important? Stop the abusive language!"

Lisa: "Of course it is! It's a prom dress – A dress that will be worn to the prom!"

Tina: "Lisa, it's just a stupid dance."

Mindy: "No, it's not just a stupid dance Tina, why do you always simplify things?"

Maxine: "And why do you always get your knickers in a twist about simple things Mindy?"

Mindy: "You know the whole purpose of this was so that we all wear different dresses, and we all shine on the night."

Kim: "Actually Mindy I think the whole objective of this was so that you could tell us what to do, you're always trying to control things and people, see how you've managed to control Lisa and get her eating out of your hand, you've done it since year nine."

Hazel logs on

Hazel: "Monica told me what was happening online. It took me four hours to find my dress – not changing it."

Maxine: "And you shouldn't have to Hazel."

Lisa: "Why shouldn't she if Mindy says she should?"

Kim: "Cos Mindy isn't Simple Simon duh!"

Lisa: "You all make me sick! Sometimes I wish I was dead so I wouldn't have to put up with you and your bullshit."

Kim: "You're pissing me off Lisa. I've seen your dress. I'm going to get the same one and really get on your nerves."

Lisa: "Don't you dare do that!"

Kim: "Or what, what you gonna do?"

Maxine: "Yeah what you gonna do Lisa?"

Lisa: "You bitches!"

Monica: "There's no need for that kind of language Lisa!!!"

Mindy: "Lisa, calm down they're just winding you up."

Lisa: "Don't tell me what to do Mindy. I was supporting you, and you've joined in with those bitches and turned on me."

Maxine: "Don't call me a bitch you arsehole."

Mindy: "Enough, stop the name calling, I'm logging off. Hazel, wear your dress, it's not like the one I'm getting. Lisa calm down, I'm going to call you now, pick up."

Lisa: "Don't call me, you're just like the rest of them, you're all bitches!!!!"

Mindy: "Lisa, calm down!"

Lisa: "I hate you all, I have real friends you know, I have real friends online!"

Mindy: "Lisa, I'm your friend."

Lisa: "No, you're not my real friend. I wish I WERE DEAD!"

Hazel's mum walked into her room and put some clean

clothes on the bed. She looked at Hazel and Carlton as they sat on the floor next to Hazel's bed reading something on Hazel's laptop. "What is it?" She asked.

"Mum, you're not going to believe all the aggro that's happened over H's dress. Come and see this." He moved over so their mum could sit in-between them and read what he felt was sheer senseless kafuffle surrounding Hazel's prom dress.

Lisa logged out and immediately logged into the chat room. She hoped that her 'real' friends were logged on. She was desperate and needed to be reassured that she didn't have to put up with the girls at her private school anymore. She was going to show those girls. She was going to kill herself and make them sorry. Make them regret the way they treated her. She would get her revenge. She would laugh in their faces when she came back – after she was dead!

CHAPTER 49

8pm

"We have another positive ID," Genny called out, "Lisa Goldstein, eighteen years old, resided in North London, the Finchley/Barnet area. She had a history of depression and eating disorders but no previous suicide attempts. The only thing her mother was aware of bothering her recently was a prom dress incident that happened with some girls at her £25,000 a year school. Her parents are divorced, but both are on their way down. Her mother's new boyfriend is currently in a hospital in North London with suspected severe food poisoning. I don't think it's related to the suicide pact as he's been in the hospital for three days now and he's suffering from Salmonella typhi septicaemia. The doctors don't think he'll survive."

"Salmonella typhi? Is that a dangerous pathogen?" Anna asked.

"It can be, it causes diarrhoea, vomiting, flu-like illness and if not treated on time can get into the blood and lead to septicaemia and death. According to his medical report, the bacteria was ingested in such a large amount that it got into his bloodstream very quickly, which is why the prognosis isn't good." Genny replied.

"He's the mom's new boyfriend? He's in a hospital near death's door, and the daughter kills herself. What was Lisa studying for A-levels?" Anna asked.

Genny typed some words on her laptop and waited a few moments, "Biology, Chemistry and Physics. What are you thinking, Anna?"

"That it could be a case of Lisa taking out her mom's boyfriend then killing herself after she was sure that he would die. I've come across a situation like that before. Dig around her school friends and see if they knew what was going on."

"Okay," Genny said.

Anna turned to Sergeant Kelleher, "You need to get the parents interviewed separately, see if there was anything untoward going on between Lisa and her mom's new boyfriend, willingly or him harassing her without her mom knowing, maybe her dad had some concerns."

Sergeant Kelleher nodded, wrote something down and handed the paper to a police officer. He turned and faced the people in the room, "Interviews will start in ten minutes, there are adjacent rooms that will be used. I want live interview feeds coming into this room so that we can assess everything in the same place. This is the central hub, and I want everything and everyone connected with these deaths interviewed and re-interviewed if necessary. Parents, teachers, friends, enemies, neighbours, everyone, is that clear?"

Everyone nodded. Groups were formed, and everyone rushed around doing what they did best and doing it as a team.

Inspector James walked over to a table and poured himself a cup of coffee, he wore a frown and seemed deep in thought.

"Are you okay, Sir?" Sergeant Kelleher asked him.

He nodded, "You're the best person for this job, and I'm so proud of you and the way you've got us all working together instead of against each other. I know I did the right thing in getting you to head this team."

Despite himself he smiled at his mentor of many years, "I bet you regret throwing me in that cell all those years ago, old man," he teased him.

"No, I don't, that was the best thing I ever did," he patted his protégé's arm and walked towards his desk carrying his coffee. He stopped and turned as the cup fell out of his hand and the contents splashed on the floor. He swayed a little and clutched his chest, "There were ten plastic cups with poison right?" He mumbled.

Sergeant Kelleher rushed towards him thinking that he was having a stroke or worse, he grabbed his arm and supported him, "Someone get a chair!" He shouted

"What are you doing?" Inspector James asked.

"Trying to help you, Sir, are you okay?"

"Help me? Why? What's wrong with me?"

A police officer rushed forward with a chair, and Sergeant Kelleher pushed the inspector onto it, "Sir, you just dropped your coffee, you were clutching your chest."

Everyone stopped what they were doing and stared at the two men.

"John, let go of my arm, I was just thinking aloud," he pulled his arm out of Sergeant Kelleher's clutches, "thank you. Now, what I was thinking was this, there were ten plastic cups in that room right?"

One of the computer technicians pulled up images of the suicide-pact room and displayed them on the walls. It gave the room a creepy feel, almost as if they were all in the suicide-pact room, standing amongst the dead. They looked at the bodies lying in different positions, some clasping diaries, some loose sheets of paper, and others nothing – their hands once full of possibilities now full of nothing.

"Can everyone count the plastic cups please?" Sergeant Kelleher called out.

"I count ten!" Genny called out.

"Seven, eight, nine, ten, I count ten as well," Dr Peter Lewis called out..

"Exactly! I counted ten before as well. Why were there ten cups when Elle May Williams was collateral damage?" Inspector James asked.

His question was met with silence. Eyes looked at the images on the wall.

"What are you implying, Inspector James?" Police Commissioner Pike asked.

Sergeant Kelleher looked at his mentor and smiled, "He's implying that someone is missing, ten cups means there were ten people expected so who is the tenth person and where is the tenth person?"

*

"I have a bad feeling about all this. I think that there might be a lot more suicide pacts to come." Anna said.

"Are you sure," her husband asked.

She nodded, "Unless we find out who these young people are and what the connection is between them more young people are going to die."

"What do you need?" Sergeant Kelleher asked her.

"I need to know everything there is to know about these children, and I need to get in to see Elle May Williams right away," she told him.

CHAPTER 50

8.10pm

Anna looked through the glass partition of the ITU door, she saw Elle May Williams lying on a bed hooked up to various machines, and she saw her mother and her godmother holding hands as they sat at the foot of her bed; they appeared to be praying. She pushed the door open and walked into the room. Both women turned.

"Mrs Williams, Mrs Valencia, I'm so sorry to disturb you both, but I need to talk to Elle May," Anna told them. She took a deep breath as she waited, knowing how crazy her words must sound. When they were in her head, unvoiced, they hadn't seemed so bad.

"What did you just say?" Ruth asked amazed at the audacity of this woman who had slipped past the security stationed outside the room and who now stood in front of them.

"I know how crazy that must sound but believe me, I have a good reason, my name is Anna Lee Lewis, and I have a sort-"

"NO, GET OUT OF HERE!" Clarissa screamed. "I know who you are! I've read about you! You talk to dead people!"

"Mrs Williams, Clarissa, let me explain-"

"No, no, no, Elle isn't dead! You can't talk to her! I don't want you near her! Get out of here, get out!"

"Mrs Williams, I agree with you, Elle isn't dead. She's a very brave girl, and she tried to save lives today."

"What are you talking about?" Ruth asked.

Anna ran a hand through her hair, this was harder than she had anticipated, "I'm talking about-"

"How did you get in here?" Ruth asked.

"I'm working with the police, Mrs Valencia, and I believe that what took place here today is just the beginning, I think that there may be other suicide pacts either taking place right now or in the process of taking place and they need to be stopped."

"What?" Clarissa whispered.

"I know this might sound strange, but I believe that I saw Elle May a few days ago, and she asked me to help-"

"What?" Ruth and Clarissa both said.

"At the time I thought she was asking me to help her but just before she disappeared she said 'help them'."

"But you see dead people!" Clarissa exclaimed, "Are you saying that Elle was dead then, or she died before and came back? What do you mean?"

"No, I'm not saying any of that, please sit down and let me explain." She sat down on a chair while both women sat on the couch next to the bed. Anna took a deep breath, "I was giving a talk at a bookshop in Oxford Street a few days ago and in the middle of it, I saw this vision which really scared me. I don't usually see things. Actually, I don't ever see things. I only ever hear things. I saw an image of Elle May at the back of the hall. She was wearing a white dress, red woollen hat and matching scarf. No one else saw her, and I thought that I was hallucinating or something, but then I saw her again. It was like a hologram image and quite scary."

"You said she asked you for help, who did she ask you to help?" Ruth asked.

"That's it, I thought she was asking me to help her but she said, and I repeat verbatim, 'Help me. Please help me! Help me to help them!' and then she vanished."

"But Elle was alive a few days ago, so how could you have seen her?" Ruth insisted.

"Her image," Anna corrected. "I don't know-"

"This doesn't make sense, what if by being here you harm Elle? What if you're cursed or worse?" Clarissa said.

"Clarissa, I'm not cursed, and I have no intention of harming your beautiful little girl. I'm just someone who hears things, and I try to make sense of what I hear and help people."

"But you said you want to talk to Elle, how are you going to do that?" Clarissa asked, moving slightly so her body protected Elle.

"I don't know. I hadn't figured things out that far. I was hoping that maybe I could sit next to Elle and hold her hand or ask her some questions and maybe she'll answer them."

"Clarissa this is crazy, I don't know if you should allow this, I've read about her, and I don't know if she can talk to Elle or not but Elle is in a medically induced coma so how will she be able to talk to anyone?"

"I haven't told you, Ruth, before I came to the hospital I had a strange dream, Elle asked for help then she said not to worry but to pray for her then she told me to wake up. When I first got here, when they told me she was dead, I heard her again, she asked me to help her and said she couldn't breathe-"

"What?"

"That was how I knew what to do because she told me. She said she couldn't breathe so I put my fingers down her throat to clear it then gave her that Heimlich manoeuvre thing you showed me years ago when the children were small."

Ruth turned and looked at her goddaughter, "Oh my God, Elle," tears clouded her eyes, and she touched Elle's hand, "precious baby," she whispered.

"What should I do, Ruth? Tell me what to do, I don't know what to do," Clarissa cried as she clung to her friend.

Ruth thought about the children who had died today and the children who could be saved and didn't have to die, "Let her talk to Elle," she said.

CHAPTER 51

8.20pm

Everyone in the room looked at the suicide letter on the screen. The handwriting was small and neat and belonged to a nineteen-year-old Australian girl called Samantha Simpson (Sammy). Several pictures of her taken from social networking media sites that Genny had managed to find were also on the screen. In one picture she was cuddling a baby Koala and smiling and in another picture, she was sitting on the beach smiling, she looked beautiful and happy in all these pictures. Below these pictures was a single picture of her lying dead, a picture taken of her as she had been found in Livingston Ward. The contrast was sickening. Before the letter was discovered in the pocket of her jeans, she had been referred to as Victim 4. This beautiful happy looking young lady – someone's daughter, someone's friend, someone's relative – had been bagged and tagged as Victim 4.

The Letter

The first time I saw you at Sidney International Airport, you were reading War and Peace by Tolstoy and seemed to be enjoying it. I had read the book the year before and had initially found it hard to get into, but I stuck with it and found myself sailing through the 1,440 pages. I don't remember who spoke first, but I do remember smiling at you and you putting the book down and smiling at me. That day seems so long ago now baby and still I think of it often. We were two ships waiting to board two different planes in the night. You were going to Thailand, and I was on the last leg of a 360 travel package. I remember our first conversation like it happened yesterday. You asked me why Australians were always leaving their country to go to the UK and suffer in the cold, why they would leave somewhere so warm and beautiful like Australia?

And, I remember telling you that it was in our DNA, our 'Did Not Ask' how things were until it was too late and we were there☺ in the UK. You laughed at my attempt at a joke. Then you told me about the riddle you heard recently in a pub, someone had heard it from someone else and by the time you heard it, it was sort of like a Chinese whisper-sort-of-joke, it had metamorphosed from its original state. You asked me how a man who was in a room with no windows or doors escaped. And I immediately enquired how he got in the room if there were no windows and doors. And you said that wasn't the point, and you hadn't heard how the man got in (I loved that about you, you were straight-up, you said you didn't know something if you didn't know. You didn't pretend). So, this man in the room with no doors or windows – how did he get out? I said that he got some mate called Arnie, to bulldoze the wall of the room down with a massive bulldozer and he escaped, and you looked at me like I was a typical Australian – all brawn, the sunshine and wide open spaces. You said that there was no mate with a massive bulldozer, but there were a mirror and desk in the room. I said that you weren't fair because you didn't give me that information earlier and now I had to rethink my answer – again that look appeared on your face, and I laughed. You smiled at me and patiently waited while I threw a number of wacky possibilities at you and even though that look lurked in the background you didn't belittle me. When I eventually gave up you told me the answer – the man looked in the mirror and remembered what he saw, took the saw and cut the table in half, put the two halves together to make a hole and escaped through the hole. You finished telling me this wacky crappy crazy answer that made no sense then you looked at me as if you had just solved a PhD mathematical problem and smiled. I remember asking you what kind of wacky answer that was and you laughed and said the guy telling the joke in the pub had downed more than a few beers. They say you can't choose who you fall in love with! That's rubbish. I believe you can choose because I chose to fall in love with you that night and I still love you so much that I can't stand to live without you.

I still have our first question and answer session recorded on my phone.

Q: Longest book ever read?

A: Both - War and Peace

Q: Favourite dish?

A: You – Chips

Me: Chips isn't a dish

You: Okay, chips with anything

Me: Kangaroo steak with BBQ sauce

You: You eat Flipper steaks and BBQ sauce?

Me: Flipper was a dolphin mate

You: Excuse me, Lassie eater

Me: Lassie was a dog, and Champion was a horse, I think the name you want is Skippy.

You: You Skippy the Bush Kangaroo eater

Me: Look, mate, I didn't eat Skippy, I ate his grandson

You: Hahaha. That was funny. Favourite song?

Me: Don't have one

You: Neither do I . . . mate

Baby, you said that was our puzzle – those were our pieces – that was us!!!!

In my mind I replay the last words you said to me over and over again, and they don't give me any warmth like they used to. You said:

Your laugh – Arrested me

Your giggle – Put me in jail

Your smile – Threw away the key

I have tried to go on. I have tried not to think of your face and the pain I saw in your eyes when you talked about how things were in America. You were good, why couldn't things work out for you and us? Why do the good die young? Why do bad things happen to good people? Why can't people be kind?

Why? Why? Why?

Mum, Dad, I'm so sorry. I can't go on without him. I've tried, believe me, I've tried but nothing has worked, and I am going to be with him now.
I love you both, Sammy x

CHAPTER 52

8.30pm

Grace Dayo-Johnson walked into the large room cautiously. She knew about the children who had taken their lives in this hospital, and she knew that one of them was a young girl whose parents she had interviewed when the girl had attempted suicide recently. Earlier, she had been shocked when she saw the four armed police officers march into her department demanding that she make herself known. But when the Inspector told her what had happened and that she was needed to help them with the investigation, she dropped everything and followed them. Now she was here. She felt nervous and sad.

"Mrs Dayo-Johnson, thank you for coming. My name is Sergeant Kelleher, and I'm in charge of this investigation. I'm sure you're aware of what we're dealing with here?"

"Yes, I am, but I don't understand why I've been brought here. I thought I would be taken to the police station."

"We've set up base here to be near the crime scene, and we're interviewing everyone who might know any of the deceased children. I understand that you filled in for a social worker last week when you visited Jessica Carmichael?"

"Yes, I did. My colleague who covers that area was off sick and we got a call from the hospital that a fourteen-year-old girl had slashed her wrists in a suicide attempt. Her father managed to stop the flow of blood by the time the paramedics got to her house, but she had lost a lot of blood, and it was touch and go. By the time I came down to see her she was reluctant to speak to me without her mother present and her mother was supposed to come in around 9am but didn't turn up until well past midday."

"Had you any dealings with Jessica or her parents before that day?"

"No, never," Grace said.

"So that was her first attempt at suicide and-"

"No, it wasn't," Grace interrupted Sergeant Kelleher.

"Excuse me?"

"That wasn't Jessica's first attempt. Have you spoken to the paramedics?"

"No, why?"

"Because when I spoke to them I was told that Jessica's father said in the ambulance that he couldn't go through this again."

"What did that mean?"

"It sounded to me as if Jessica had been in that situation before. Speak to the paramedics, Sergeant."

"Thank you, Mrs Dayo-Johnson, is there anything else you can tell me that might help me understand what happened here?"

"Only that if it were the case if Jessica had attempted suicide in the past, why was there nothing in her notes and why wasn't she sectioned? When I tried to dig, I was told that her father was an inspector in the police force and that he had asked for things to be kept confidential. I found her mother strange and more concerned about people finding out what Jessica had done than with Jessica's welfare."

"Can you give a statement to one of my colleagues, Mrs Dayo-Johnson?"

"Of course, I can, Sergeant, where do you want me to go?"

"If you can follow my colleague she'll set you up."

"Okay."

"Genny, can you take a statement from Mrs Dayo-Johnson, please. It might be an idea to get her to look at some pictures and see if she can identify the paramedics."

"I don't understand," Grace frowned, "the paramedics were at the hospital when I got here, and I saw them talking to Inspector Carmichael when I was leaving. I didn't get their names, but the hospital should have a record."

"That's just it," Genny told her, "we can't find anything on them, we don't know who they were, and their paperwork has disappeared."

"How is that possible?"

"Your guess is as good as mine," Sergeant Kelleher said.

Genny touched her arm, "Come with me. I'll take your statement then I'll get you set up at a desk with one of our computer experts, it might take a while, but we need you to look at ID photos taken from the Emergency Medical Services' computer database."

"Okay, sure, let's go. I might need to make a few calls to make sure my family's okay," Grace told her as she followed her to a desk in a side room.

"No worries, Mrs Dayo-Johnson, take a break and make the calls whenever you want to."

CHAPTER 53

8.40pm

Nurse Preeti nodded her head as she listened to Sergeant Kelleher. She understood his question but also understood the implications of divulging information about a patient without the patient's permission. She was torn between doing the right thing according to the hospital's data protection policy and doing what she knew was right.

"I understand that you have a duty of care to your patients and that data protection laws tie you, but I need to know how those kids got hold of the drugs they took. Did Jessica Carmichael supply the drugs?"

"I've been told by the hospital that I can't talk about the drugs as Management is doing an in-depth investigation-"

"I know that but-"

She held a hand up to cut him off and shook her head. "I don't know where they got the drugs, but I do know that two days ago the alarm bell went off in Jessica Carmichael's room. When I got there, her father was screaming and shouting that he had read something on her laptop, and she had stolen drugs from the nurse's trolley and was planning another suicide attempt. He was shaking her, and she was screaming and crying and saying that he was lying. I managed to get him to calm down and release her then I got some more nurses into the room, and we stripped the room from top to bottom looking for the drugs. We didn't find anything. I had Jessica sent over to outpatient's Psych for an evaluation. I asked to see a copy of their report and my request got rejected. It came out later that Inspector Carmichael had insisted that no one but him got a copy of the report."

"Wait a minute, you searched the room and didn't find anything?"

"Nothing, we found nothing in her room or bathroom."

"Did you tell the hospital authorities about the incident?"

Nurse Preeti didn't blink, "Yes, I told my direct line manager, and I wrote a report and sent it to the Chief Executive of the hospital and copied the Senior Psychiatric Consultant and the hospital's Children's Services because I was concerned for Jessica. She had some self-harm marks on her arms and when we did her blood alcohol level on admitting her it was very high. I mentioned this to her parents, and her mother queried why I had done this test on her daughter when alcoholics were getting away with murder. Then she said that I shouldn't worry about it because Jessica had a glass of wine with her dinner that night. The amount of alcohol in her blood was more than just a glass of wine! Plus she was only fourteen and shouldn't be drinking! Her parents seemed to be in denial about what her problems were, but I think Jessica was doing a lot of what she did for attention. Her father smothered her, and her mother drank too much and is one of the most self-centred women I have ever met. Her mother was found passed out in the corridor outside Jessica's room one day, and her father said she was drunk, stepped over her and went home, how strange is that? He left her on the floor and went home, and Jessica knew her mother was there and said nothing. I felt sorry for Jessica, her parents tip-toed around her and either didn't see or didn't want to see that she was lost. Jessica would say things to me like, '*No one understands*'. '*No one cares about me*'. '*I wish I could die*'. And she would cry all night and then when her dad came to visit her she would pretend to be upbeat, and when her mother came, she would be abusive."

"And with all the Jekyll and Hyde going on her parents refused to get her sectioned and appropriately mentally evaluated?"

"Inspector Carmichael declined, and Mrs Carmichael said it would make them look bad and people in her family didn't do things like that," Nurse Preeti replied, shaking her head.

CHAPTER 54

8.50pm

Sergeant Kelleher looked at Inspector Carmichael coldly. He had already been warned by Inspector James to handle things delicately as the man had just lost his daughter but Sergeant Kelleher didn't see things through his mentor's eyes. In his mind, this man's daughter might have been responsible for her own death and the death of eight other people. Plus the attempted murder of Elle May Williams and if this man had done the right thing and got his daughter sectioned and thoroughly evaluated, his daughter and all the other kids might still be alive.

"Why am I here, Sergeant Kelleher?" Inspector Carmichael asked. He said 'Sergeant' as if it were a dirty word. As if a person of that rank was not just literally beneath him in rank but also a person he didn't think had the right to talk to him let alone ask him questions.

"You are here, Mr Carmichael because your daughter killed herself and it looks as if she is the one who might have provided the drugs responsible for killing the other children-"

"First of all, it's Inspector Carmichael and not Mr Carmichael and secondly how dare you say that to me. My daughter died today, Sergeant, she was fourteen-years-old, and her life was cut short. She didn't kill anyone - she was killed!"

"You did that the last time we met," Sergeant Kelleher said and looked at him.

"Did what?"

"Dismissed me with that 'It's Inspector Carmichael, not Mr Carmichael' crap."

"Have we met before, Sergeant?"

"Yes, Inspector Carmichael, we've met before. I was the officer sent out to question you and your wife when your daughter previously attempted to kill herself."

"My daughter has never tried to kill herself before. My daughter just happened to be in the wrong place at the wrong time today."

"I think your daughter orchestrated this whole thing-"

"I will not listen to your lies about my daughter, Sergeant! And for your information, I'm going to sue this hospital for what they've done to my daughter!"

"Sue the hospital?"

"Yes, I'm going to sue their arses, the chief exec, the doctors, the nurses, all of them!"

"You are going to sue *this* hospital?"

"Are you deaf?"

"No, my hearing is excellent, Inspector."

"I am going to sue this hospital for every penny they have if that's what it takes to get the answers you and your task force can't seem to find, which is why you're clutching at straws and trying to pin this on Jessica! You can't pin it on her!"

"You think that's all it will take to cover this whole thing up and make the hospital execs close ranks with you? You threaten to sue them, and they do what you want?"

"I don't have a clue what you're talking about, but I would warn you to watch your step and not forget your place, Sergeant, I am still your superior officer. I will do whatever it takes to get answers."

"I'll give you some answers, Inspector Carmichael. Things don't happen in isolation. Your daughter tried to commit suicide several times in the past. She self-harmed, she drank, and she is the one who somehow got the drugs used to kill herself and the others-"

"No! That's a lie! I'll have your badge, and I'll sue you if you say another word. Do you hear me?" Inspector Carmichael shouted.

"You-will-sue-me?" Sergeant Kelleher asked, baffled at the arrogance and sheer un-connectivity with the real World the Inspector openly displayed.

"Yes, I will sue you," Inspector Carmichael repeated.

"Enough!" Sergeant Kelleher said, "Enough of this bullshit, you've covered up your daughter's suicide attempts, you've tampered with evidence, and you've lied. Now enough of the lies, how many times has Jessica tried to kill herself in the past? Before you answer that question I need to let you know that your wife is being questioned in another room."

He jumped up, "You can't question Eloise without me being present-"

"Why is that, Inspector? Are you her lawyer?"

"You have no idea who I am, do you?"

"It just so happens I do, you see I've done a little research, I've spoken to people who happen to know the real you, not the façade you slap everyone in the face with. Here's what I've gathered, you're a liar, a wife beater and a bully. And, I will do everything within my power to get you up on accessory to murder charges!"

"What?" Inspector Carmichael's eyes surveyed the Sergeant coldly.

"When it gets out that you knew about the drugs, Jessica had stolen, but you not only suppressed the Psych evaluation report you somehow tampered with the Paramedics' Report."

"What?" The coldness was replaced with shock.

"We *will* find the paramedics you know, it's only a matter of time before they surface and tell us what they know."

"I don't know what you're talking about."

"I think you do know Inspector. You know that if you had gotten your daughter sectioned or treated for depression and her drinking this may never have happened, so you're to blame for this, and I'm going to see that you pay!"

The transformation happened so suddenly that it took Sergeant Kelleher by complete surprise, "I loved my daughter, I tried to help her, I tried . . . Arrrrrrrrh, my baby's dead, Jessica is dead . . . Arrrrrrrrh!" Inspector Carmichael broke down and cried. He banged his hand on the side of the table several times until it bled. He stared at the blood for a few moments as if in shock then he grabbed the edge of the table and turned it over and viciously kicked out at it. Two police officers saw the blood and rushed to get some disposable gloves, which they quickly pulled on then rushed over and grabbed hold of him; they wrestled him to the ground and held him down. "She's my daughter. I was only trying to protect her! I'm her dad! I have to protect her!"

Sergeant Kelleher waited for him to calm down, "Where is Jessica's laptop?"

"I hid it in the boot of my wife's car," Inspector Carmichael replied.

"Where is your wife's car?"

"In the hospital car park."

"Take him downstairs, get that laptop and hand it over to the tech people."

"What do we do with him afterwards, Sir?" One of the officers asked.

"I want a written statement from him then I want you to keep him in the family room under police guard."

CHAPTER 55

9pm

Anna took hold of Elle May's hand and closed her eyes as she tried to tap into some sort of aura. Truth-be-told she didn't know what she would do if she made contact with anything as she had never had to deal with living people before. People called her many things. They tried to put her in a box with a preconceived label on it – spiritualist, psychic, weird woman. She stopped trying to explain herself or her gift; instead, she let her gift speak for itself. Earlier Clarissa had said that she could be cursed – in the past, Anna had thought she was cursed. She had been treated for schizophrenia and bi-polar when she was ten years old – to no avail. The treatment didn't mitigate her ability to communicate with the dead or relay their messages to the living. The messages she passed on were from an array of people (she didn't have the ability to choose who they were). The messages weren't fake, farfetched or full of so many possibilities. They were shockingly accurate. With the dead suicide people one theme ran through all of their messages, this common denominator was the thing that saddened Anna the most and kept her focussed on reaching out to living people, in order to put a stop to suicide. The common denominator was – regret.

She held Elle May's hand gently – nothing happened. She rubbed the back of Elle May's hand which was clenched in a fist. She looked at her other hand and noticed that it was lying open and flat next to her on the bed. She frowned as she turned Elle May's hand over and tried to see what was in her hand.

"What is it?" Ruth asked. She had been watching Anna like a hawk.

"I'm not sure, Elle May's right hand is clenched, but her left hand isn't."

"I noticed that but I thought that it was a reflex thing,"

Clarissa said.

"No, usually when someone is in a coma their body is flaccid, which means that their muscles are relaxed." She rubbed Elle May's hand some more, "Elle May-"

"We call her Elle," Clarissa said, "Usually when we call her Elle May it means she's in trouble, or we're being serious."

Anna nodded, "Elle, sweetheart, Elle open your hand sweetheart. We need to see what's in your hand."

The three women stared at her hand – nothing happened.

"Elle, you asked me to help you to help them remember, I need you to open your hand so that I can help you to help them, Elle sweetheart."

The three women stared at Elle's hand – as if in response to Anna's words, Elle's hand slowly opened, and a pendant attached to a chain fell onto the bed. The initials JC were embossed on the front of the pendant.

"JC, that's Jessica Carmichael's," Clarissa said.

"Open it, something must be inside," Ruth said.

Anna fumbled with the clasp. The pendant sprang open, and a single small key fell out.

*

The two government computer technical experts (techs) struggled with the firewalls on Jessica's laptop. Her parents didn't know any of her passwords and couldn't agree on anything she might have used as a password. The techs were high-level experts and earned hundreds of thousands of pounds between them, yet they couldn't hack into a fourteen-year-old child's laptop. Police Commissioner Pike wasn't impressed, and he hovered over them counting down the minutes and shouting the odds. He ridiculed them and made them nervous. It didn't help because the firewalls were hidden everywhere like a game and each wrong move caused the erection of more firewalls. They needed to concentrate on the layout for them to make headway – a thing their boss didn't seem to (or want to) comprehend.

"Come on men. A fourteen-year-old girl is outwitting you! Stop scratching your arses and sort this out!"

They were repulsed at his crude remarks, but he was their boss, and there was little or nothing that they could say to him.

CHAPTER 56

9.20pm

The police convoy of three cars, lights flashing and sirens blazing, drove fast through the streets of South West London towards Jessica Carmichael's house. Sergeant Kelleher and Anna were in the back of the first car. Ruth and Genny were in the back of the second car, while the third car was full of police officers. Anna held the pendant tightly in her hand as she focused on the task that lay ahead. Jessica's parents had insisted that they didn't know about the key or what it opened only that Jessica always wore the necklace. So Anna knew she was going in blind.

"Why do you do what you do?" Sergeant Kelleher asked.

"Where did that come from, Sergeant?" Anna queried.

"I'm sorry, this whole thing is making me sick. My stomach is literally churning right now. These kids, the parents, the system, it's all wrong."

She sighed, "I've worked with so many families who have lost people to suicide, and it's the worst thing ever. The blame parents carry around, and the guilt is unimaginable. The sad thing is when someone takes their life the pain they felt at the time doesn't go away – Peter says that, like matter, it just gets transformed or transferred. I believe that when a person takes their own life, they get to see their life play on a screen, they get to see the pain they've caused to the people they've left behind, and they get to feel that pain."

"You really believe that?"

"I've heard it from the people who've died. I've heard the remorse and pain in their voices and the regret. I do what I do, Sergeant Kelleher, to stop it happening. Peter and I and all the people at Talk To Someone do what we do to help people, to make them see that there is a way out of their pain, and it isn't by committing suicide."

Sergeant Kelleher nodded, "When we first met I was-"

"You didn't understand then, now you do, Sergeant."

He nodded again, "I'm sorry that I was the way I was back then, I'm really embarrassed at the way I behaved."

Anna studied him for a few moments, "I said back then that I would tell you the reason I am the way I am. My mom's sister came to visit us one day when I was twelve years old. That was the first and last time I ever saw her. She literally changed my life. She told me that there was a spirit of depression in her family which tended to pass from mothers to daughters. She told me that the doctors treating my mother had told her to write her problems down on pieces of paper but that she wanted me to do something different. She wanted me to write my dreams down on paper to make them real and that I was to pray for them to come true and work hard towards achieving them. She left the next day, and it was years later that I found out she had escaped from the mental home she lived in to come and tell me what she did."

"What did you write down?"

"I wrote down that I wanted to help people, to save lives and to make a difference," Anna replied.

"Is that why you're the way you are?"

"No. I was born and raised in Chicago my mother was mentally unstable and depressed when I was little. One day, after my dad had spent a fortune on private medical doctors and psychiatrists, my mother mixed up some poison and cola and drank it after giving me some to drink. She had a form of extended postnatal depression, and I think that she was having a hard time looking after me or bonding with me so she decided to kill herself and take me with her to prove that she did love me. I drank the cola, and died," she paused.

"I don't understand," Sergeant Kelleher said, moving slightly away from her.

"I drank the cola, and I died," Anna repeated.

"But . . . you're here."

"You know, sometimes I wonder if I really am here. Sometimes I feel like I'm living in someone's imagination. Not often, once in a while, I have dreams about a room where dead people are. I don't see anyone's face or anything, just a dark room with people in it. Other times I have dreams where I see my mother watching a screen with her life playing out on the screen, the life she would have had if she hadn't died. Sometimes I wonder if I'm doing the same if all this is my life playing out on my screen."

A voice came over the car rádio; it was Inspector Jámes asking if they were at the Carmichael's house yet. Sergeant Kelleher turned quickly, pressed a button and told the inspector that they were a few minutes away. Slightly stunned, he turned back to Anna, "Are you serious? What happened? How did you survive?"

"I died," Anna calmly replied.

"But, you're alive. You're in the back of this car with me."

"My Dad said I died for a few minutes then a doctor who was making a house call to a neighbour heard him screaming and came to find out what was going on. He just happened to have a small quantity of the emetic, Ipecac syrup in his bag, which he forced down my throat and which made me vomit while he gave me CPR. I was in a coma for days and woke up to find out that my Mom was dead. I was 4 years old."

"Wow, I don't know what to say."

"You don't have to say anything, just try and understand me. I believe no one should have to deal with depression or emotional pain or mental illness alone. There are so many organisations set up to help people, and the role of TTS is to get people the help they require and help them to see that prayer changes things, and God can make a way where they think that there isn't one. And, that suicide is irreversible."

The car stopped, "We're here, Sir," the driver told Sergeant Kelleher. Still slightly stunned, Sergeant Kelleher climbed out of the car then helped Anna out of the car.

CHAPTER 57

9.35pm

They searched Jessica's room inch by inch but couldn't find anything that the key opened. Sergeant Kelleher got some of the police officers to search the rest of the house and the shed at the back of the house in case Jessica had somewhere outside of her room where she kept her private things. No one knew what they would find in the confines of what the key opened, but they knew that it had to be important for Jessica to hide the key in a pendant attached to a chain around her neck and for Elle to have that same pendant clasped tightly in her dying hand. Tension and frustration grew as second mounted on second and the minutes piled up.

"There are too many people in this room," Anna suddenly said to Genny, "can you get some of them to leave please?"

"Of course. Sergeant Kelleher can you get your men out of Jessica's room please, Anna needs some space."

Anna waited for the police officers to leave then she sat on Jessica's bed. She moved suddenly and turned the iPod on then pressed the rewind button once then the play button. Morbid-death-like music came through the speakers, and Anna shuddered as she listened to it. Ruth and Genny stood by the door while Sergeant Kelleher crouched down by the bed next to Anna and studied her. He was still shocked by what she had told him in the car.

Anna looked at Jessica's desk and frowned. They had opened all the drawers and looked through all the papers. The drawers didn't have any locks on them, and the papers were harmless. The music was giving her the creeps, it was soulless, lifeless music, the type of music evil people or ignorant people used to conjure up bad spirits and the type of music played in horror movies to add atmosphere to the evil plot.

She looked at her reflection in the mirror opposite the bed.

Her eyes travelled to the large picture to the left behind her. She turned and looked at the picture and frowned.

"What is it? What are you seeing?" Sergeant Kelleher asked.

She pointed at the picture on the wall, "That picture is strange," she told him, "this room is all gothic, dark colours and morbid music, it's full of death and death-like things right?"

Still crouched down, he looked around and nodded his agreement, "Why is that picture strange?"

"It's the only picture on the wall. It's large, and it looks like an antique and classy, not something a fourteen-year-old girl would have in her bedroom."

"The police officers checked it. There isn't anything there. They took it off the wall to see if she had anything stuck to the back of it or hidden in a secret compartment at the back," he shook his head, "they didn't find anything."

Chanting came through the speakers as Anna walked over to the picture and studied it. Her eyes took in the figure seated at a large desk looking through large windows. She noted that the picture was about two metres wide and a metre and a half in height. "Look at this," she told the others, "look at the desk in the picture . . . look," she stopped then pressed her face against the side of the canvass. She closed her eyes and gently let her fingers move across the desk. The music picked up tempo and voices chanted loudly. With her eyes closed and her fleeting finger movements across the picture she looked like a blind person reading brail. In fact, that was exactly what she was doing – she was feeling her way in the darkness, trying to understand what was going on and reading the omens of darkness that she couldn't see in the light. *'Help me to help them'*, Elle's words came into her mind, and she concentrated hard, determined to find whatever it was she needed to find to help Elle and the others who needed to be helped. She was way out of her comfort zone and was not only flying blind she didn't know what it was she was looking for, and that scared her because she didn't know how she was supposed to help Elle. Something clicked under her fingers, and her eyes flew open, she pressed hard, and a small section by the side of the desk pulled away from the picture. Genny and Ruth gasped as they saw it happen and moved towards the picture. Anna pulled the piece away, and they all stared at the keyhole beneath. Heart thumping, Anna took Jessica's key out of the pendant and pushed it into the keyhole then turned it and pulled. A large panel of the picture came forward and hung on a hinge at the bottom. A gaping hole revealed itself just as the evil demonic music stopped.

"What the-" Sergeant Kelleher started then stopped as he stared at the iPod. He turned back to the picture, reached into the hole and pulled out and studied the papers hidden inside.

"There's more in there," Genny said. She reached into the hole and pulled out two mobile phones and a diary.

"We need to get all this stuff back to base right away. We may only have a few hours left," he turned to Anna, "Well done, excellent work Anna, thank you."

CHAPTER 58

10pm

The police convoy of three cars, lights flashing, sirens blazing, drove fast through the streets of South West London back to the hospital. Sergeant Kelleher and Genny were in the back of the first car looking through Jessica's papers and diary. Ruth and Anna were in the back of the second car while the third car was full of police officers.

"How did you know that the stuff was hidden in that picture?" Ruth asked Anna.

"I didn't know it was there."

"But one minute you were sitting on the bed then you pointed at the picture and jumped up when the chanting started."

"Did I? I thought I was standing next to the picture when it started."

"No, no you jumped up from the bed when the chanting started. Your eyes were closed yet you walked over the textbooks and clothes on the floor without stepping on them or tripping over them. The next thing I saw was you standing in front of the picture as if you were looking at it but your eyes were closed. Then you started pressing the picture with your eyes still closed. It was like you saw things with your eyes shut. I live in one of the Caribbean islands, and you hear about some people in some of the Islands, in South America, in Africa and in Haiti who dabble in witchcraft and Juju . . . are you . . . are you possessed?"

"What?" Anna said shocked, "No, I'm not possessed I was probably acting a little crazy because I was scared that I would let Elle down, and I wouldn't do what she asked me to do."

"Which is?" Ruth asked.

"Help her to help the others," Anna whispered.

Ruth studied her for a few moments then relaxed, "It must

be hard doing what you do."

"It's hard for anyone to do what they've been called to do but the reward comes when you see the success."

"Is what you do a calling from God?" Ruth was confused, she knew for a fact that, according to the Bible, witchcraft and sorcery were not Godly callings. In fact, most Christians regarded them as sin.

Anna sensed she needed to tread carefully, "There's a story in the Bible of a man having a vision and even though he was very old at the time and his wife had passed her child-bearing age and they were childless, he saw his descendants – his name was Abraham. There's another story of a man who had dreams and saved his people because he trusted in his dreams as being a gift from God – his name was Joseph. They say a blessing if not used right can become a curse. I can't help the dead. I can only assist the living by telling them not to commit suicide, to trust in God, to choose another option – to choose life. What I do is try to stop people committing suicide because once they do, that's it, there's no coming back. And, the sad thing is once they do it, they regret it, they want to come back but they can't." She stopped talking and looked out of the window as the car raced back to the hospital.

"It must be like that saying, 'Become all things in order to save some'. I guess that's what you're doing, protecting people from themselves, giving them a second chance," Ruth said as the magnitude of Anna's gift hit her.

"Sometimes, I wish that it wasn't a second chance, that the idea of suicide wasn't even on the table and that people would just trust in God to help them from the start and not try to do things on their own."

Ruth's phone vibrated, she read the text. "I don't need this right now Jermaine," she murmured.

"Is something wrong," Anna asked her.

"My son Jermaine was supposed to go for football practice today, but when my husband went to pick him up he wasn't there, and the coach told my husband that Jermaine had missed the last two practice sessions. He loves football but recently he's been quiet and distracted."

"How many children do you have?"

"Two boys, Bryson and Jermaine, sixteen and nearly fourteen," she replied.

"When this is all over maybe you should spend some time at home with your family. Some boys are strange. They act like they don't need their moms when they're teenagers but secretly they do."

Ruth smiled, "You're right. I'll call Jermaine when we get back to the hospital, and I'm going to spend more time working from home. Once Elle has pulled through I'll be on the next flight home."

"I find it strange that parents don't talk to their children. Most kids probably think that their mom and dad were born as mom and dad – that they started life as a twenty or thirty-something-year-old. Parents don't tell their kids what it was like growing up, the fun they had, the mischief they got up to. All they seem to talk about is the one pair of shoes they had or one meal a day." She chuckled, "My husband started recycling when he was seven years old. His dad would give him money to buy a newspaper, and Peter would go down the street and take a newspaper from someone's door and give it to his dad. When his dad finished reading it, Peter would tidy it up, take it back to the neighbour's house, put it back and keep the money."

Ruth laughed, "Are you serious?"

Anna nodded and smiled, "Don't tell him I told you. He was only seven years old at the time. He started coming back from the errand a little too quickly, and his dad got suspicious and followed him one day and found out what he was doing. He was so mad, but he sat Peter down and explained that it was wrong and why it was wrong. He told Peter some of the things he used to do when he was young and how he got into trouble.

Peter says that was the first time he recalls his dad ever talking to him on that level. Before that day he used to think his dad was cold and unapproachable. Today he has a great relationship with his dad. I believe that conversation changed his life. You've met my husband. He's one of the funniest, honest men I know. Can you imagine him stealing newspapers at seven?"

"Recycling," Ruth corrected.

They laughed.

The atmosphere in the back of the car shifted as they talked.

"When I was young I told a bunch of kids that my name was Sonia," Ruth confessed. Embarrassed, she looked at her hands.

"Why?"

"I hated my name and thought that Sonia sounded cool," she shrugged.

"Have you told your boys the full story?"

"No, I've never told anyone about it."

"When you get home, get your family together and tell them the story, it will change things. It will draw you all closer."

"How?"

"When you open up to people, they tend to open up to you. It's a natural occurrence."

The car stopped suddenly, and the back doors swung open, the police officers ushered the ladies out of the car and towards the lifts. Genny and Sergeant Kelleher were already waiting by the lifts.

"We just got an update, and it's not good," Sergeant Kelleher told them, "more of the kids have been identified, Aisha Patel 14, Jimmy Duncan 13, Paris Haughton 14."

The lift doors closed and the reporter who was hidden crouched behind a car waited for a few moments then stood up. He had written the names of the newly identified victims down. He pulled out his mobile and sent a text with the names and ages of the children to his editor.

CHAPTER 59

Aisha Patel had a dream – she wanted to study medicine. She was fourteen years old and knew exactly where she wanted to study medicine and what she wanted to specialise in when she finished her basic training. Her paternal grandmother had died of breast cancer last year, and Aisha had spent a lot of time with her grandmother before her demise and had seen firsthand how great the Macmillan nurses had been with her grandmother and how the doctors at the hospital had taken good care of her. She told her grandmother about her dream, and her grandmother had given Aisha her blessing and told Aisha that she could be whatever she dreamed. When her grandmother had died Aisha felt like a part of her had also died because her parents and three brothers never seemed to have time for her. Being the third child, it was easy to get lost and be invisible. In her family boys were valuable and girls were useful (for cooking, cleaning, ironing, washing, usually a lot of domestic things ending in – ing)

In her family: The first child, a boy, was a blessing; the second child, another boy another blessing; the third child, a girl; and the fourth child another boy, yet another blessing. Being the third child and a girl – it was easy to stay lost and be invisible.

Aisha knew something wasn't right on the day her father hit her. There had been a lot of whispering around the house prior to that day and each time Aisha stepped into a room her parents and older brothers were in, the whispering voices would get lower and lower until they fizzled out. It showed the amount of regard her family had for her, they didn't bother to stop whispering, they just made sure she couldn't hear what was being said and continued. On the day her father hit her, the whispering stopped, and the innuendos started – the 'Aisha, you must learn to wash clothes by hand now' and 'Aisha, don't waste food you never know tomorrow'. She didn't understand them.

She hoped that if her dream came true and she became a doctor they would like her and maybe be proud of her; she didn't dare to hope for their love.

On the day her father hit her, one of her aunts had presented her with a silk sari and a gold necklace. She had wondered why as it wasn't her birthday and she wasn't aware of any ceremonies that were imminent.

Diary Entry: "My Aunty Mira gave me a sari today with a gold necklace. They are beautiful, and I thanked her with a hug and kisses. She looked at me sadly and smiled. She told me to be brave. I don't know why she said that, and she wouldn't tell me what she meant. I like Aunty Mira. She is one of my favourite aunties, she married into our family and isn't like the rest of them."

Later that day Aisha understood what her aunt had meant. Her parents called her into the front room and told her that she would be going to India to get married. They had so little regard for her that they didn't trick her or lie to her like some parents did to get their daughters on the plane. Those parents told their daughters that they were going to visit granny, or going for a wedding, or going for a relaxing holiday. When they got to India, they took their daughter's passport and married her off.

Aisha's father (he spoke for the family) simply told her they were tired of looking after her and one day she would eventually leave them and get married anyway so they were hastening the event as they saw no need to procrastinate. Her father liked to use big words when he thought he was talking to little people. Aisha had never refused to do anything her parents had asked her to do in the past, but as she saw her dream of studying medicine developing wings and attempting to fly away from her right before her eyes, she spoke out and refused to get married. Her father had hit her – he had never hit her before, but then she had never refused to do what she had been told to do before.

Aisha had found the suicide chat room by chance on the morning of the suicide pact, which was the day after her father had hit her. When she saw the date and time that the event was to take place, she saw it as a sign, an omen sent to save her. She knew her family didn't love her and never had, and she wanted to be with the only person who did, her grandmother.

Diary Entry: "I gave the sari and gold necklace to Gia this morning. She is my best friend, and I know she will like them. I don't feel scared. I feel like I am free. I don't have to go to India, and I don't have to get married. I am free. I was so happy when I woke up this morning that I made my family a big breakfast, and I left them a note which I know they will probably not bother to read right away. It is sad that families like mine don't value girls ☹"

On the day of the suicide pact, Aisha walked into the hospital and found her way to the Livingston Ward quite easily. She saw this as another omen that she was doing the right thing, that the forces of nature were working together to help her do what she came to do. She quickly forgot the doctor who had asked her why she was there or the two nurses who told her to come back later. She forgot the persistent ringing of her phone and the text messages from Gia asking where she was and the text from her younger brother with two love-emos thanking her for making breakfast – she saw only what she wanted to see.

The last thing Aisha thought of before she drank the poison was her mother sitting and watching as her father hit her and rained abusive words down on her. She had wondered why her mother never supported her as other mothers supported their daughters. Her mother's face was void of any affection and she nodded as each abusive word was said as if to say – 'Speak my husband, speak!' When her father was upset with one of her brothers, her mother would always jump in and defend them. 'You know he is very smart' or 'He is just being a boy' or 'He got good marks in his Maths and English' or 'At least he is doing better than so-and-so's-child'. But for Aisha, there was never any defence. Then it had hit her even harder that her father's slap; she didn't matter to her mother. In her mother's eyes, she had died on the day she had been born!

"You stupid, selfish, ungrateful girl," her father had screamed at her. "Get out of my sight before I hit you again!"

The last words Aisha thought of were the words spoken by Mr Haughton, one of her favourite teachers - "Are you deaf or just stupid, girl? Get out of here right now!"

CHAPTER 60

10pm

He held Elle's hand and smiled at her. He had been talking to her each time he got a chance to be alone with her. He found that patients in a coma responded well to this type of stimuli, and he knew some who came out of a coma and said that they heard a voice or voices talking to them as if directing them back to the land of the living.

"Many many years ago I met your mother at university, and she swept me off my feet. She loves you and your sister very much so you need to pull through this and get better okay."

The door swung open. He let go of Elle's hand and immediately hid his feelings then stood up, "Hi, how are you holding up?" He asked.

"I'm okay, knowing you're here helps," Clarissa told him.

"Her vitals are looking good, and she's responding to stimuli, which is really good. The next couple of hours will tell me a lot more."

"Thank you," she reached out and took hold of his hand and squeezed it, "thank you, Steve."

The door swung open. Clarissa let go of his hand.

Madeline walked in with Maddy and Josh, "Ruth went to Jessica's house with the police officers," she told Clarissa. "I need to make some phone calls which I'll do just outside the door and Maddy and Josh will sit with Elle. Steve, Clarissa didn't eat the sandwiches Ruth got earlier, I tried to get her to eat something, but she said she felt sick. Can you take her to get something to eat please?"

"Of course, Mrs Stapleton," he took hold of Clarissa's hand and gently pulled her towards the door, "let's go to the doctors' lounge, it's just down the corridor."

"Are you sure it's okay to leave her?"

"She'll be fine, Rissa. We'll only be about ten, twenty

minutes tops."

Josh looked at Elle and frowned. She looked like she was cold. He quickly went over to his rucksack and pulled out his red scarf and matching hat.

("Awww, Dad, the other kids will make fun of me. Why are they so red?" He had complained to his dad on the day they were presented to him. "So I can see you in a crowd," his dad had joked pulling the hat down firmly on his head).

He put the hat on Elle and Maddy put the scarf around her neck. As Josh pulled the blanket around her, his frown deepened. He turned to Maddy, "Do you know any prayers?"

"I know the 'Food-Prayer'," Maddy told him.

"Which one is that one?" Josh asked.

"Bless this food, Dear Lord, thank You for everything You have blessed us with today, help us always to do Your Will and thank You for giving us this day our daily bread and protecting us from evil, Amen," Maddy said.

Josh frowned, "Wow, you say all that before you eat?"

Maddy squirmed, "Not really, I was just trying to sound cool. I usually say, Dear Lord, bless this food, Amen."

"Phew," Josh said overdramatically rolling his eyes, "I thought I'd been getting it wrong all these years."

Maddy smiled at him. She liked his comical expressions.

"I know a good prayer. My mom taught me Psalm 23. We could say that prayer together. Do you know it?" Josh said.

"Psalm 23, The Lord is my Shepherd one?"

"Yes."

"I learnt that at Sunday school. Where's your mum?" Maddy asked.

"She died. She took my baby sister to Heaven."

"Oh," Maddy frowned.

"It's okay, I was five plus at the time, but I still miss her."

"I'm sorry."

"That's okay. Let's pray."

They held hands, closed their eyes and prayed:

"The Lord is my Shepherd
I have everything I need.
He lets me rest in fields of green grass
And leads me to quiet pools of fresh water
He gives me new strength
He guides me in the right paths as He has promised
Even if I go through the deepest darkness
I will not be afraid Lord for You are with me
Your shepherd's rod and staff protect me
You prepare a banquet for me
Where all my enemies can see me
You welcome me as an honoured guest
And fill my cup to the brim
Surely Your Goodness and Your Mercy will follow me
all the days of my life
And Your house will be my home as long as I live."

They both said "Amen" then opened their eyes.

"Oh, I know something else," Josh said, *"Thy Word Oh Lord*
shall be a lamp to my feet and light to my path.
Let Your Word be a lamp to Elle's feet and light to Elle's path
to lead her back to us, Amen."

"Amen," Maddy said. "Who taught you that?" She asked.

"My grandma, she said that if one of my big cousins who cusses a lot used God's Word as a lamp for his path instead of swear-words he would be heading in the right direction. My dad says," he lowered his voice, looked around the room then changed his accent, "my grandma doesn't suffer fools gladly, and when she gets mad, she speaks with an Irish accent even though she's from Wales. She says things like . . ."

Maddy giggled as she listened to him.

Josh chuckled then told Maddy some of his dad's jokes as they coloured together. Finished they looked at the large picture of a Rainbow they had just made. They carefully placed the picture on the pillow just above Elle's head.

"Come back soon, Elle, I miss you," Maddy whispered and kissed her cheek.

"Look," Josh said suddenly, "Look, Elle is smiling!"

Madeline Stapleton read through some more text messages on her phone as she stood just outside Elle's room. She learned that Sophie Adams, a new member of the church had set up a POUR – Prayers Of Urgency Required. The POUR had gone viral and people in churches all over the World were praying for Elle. She closed her eyes and prayed for Elle and the children all over the World who, unlike Elle, thought that suicide was a choice they had to make. Elle was dragged into something that she would never willingly participate in, but there were children and adults all over the World who thought that if all else failed suicide was a path they would travel down. The pain that seared through her heart at the thought of a person feeling so hopeless they believed they couldn't go on overwhelmed her and brought a gut wrenching sob to her mouth and tears to her eyes. For the sake of Maddy and Josh she pulled herself together and wiped the tears from her cheeks.

Her phone vibrated, she answered it.

"Hello, Aunty M, it's Sophie from church, how's Elle?"

Madeline blew her nose then answered. "Hi Sophie, Elle is stable. The doctor looking after her said her vitals are good and the next couple of hours will tell."

"How are you holding up?"

"Me?"

"Yes, how are you holding up?"

"I, . . . I," tears sprang into Madeline's eyes again.

"Please try and stay strong Aunty M."

"I will . . . I have to."

"We're all praying for Elle and your family at Church."

"Thank you, Sophie, that's just what I needed to hear right now," she took a deep breath and closed her eyes, shutting off her tears.

"I checked my Twitter account and people in China, Russia, India, Africa, in short people all over the World are praying for Elle as well. They've started something called a 'Rainbow Covenant Prayer Chain' where they've put Elle in their prayers, and they're asking God to bring her back to us. They're also praying for any similar events to be stopped in time so that lives will be saved. The suicide pact story was all over the news earlier. It was incredible to see people from so many different churches praying for Elle and also praying for children in general."

"The news on the TV?"

"Yes, oh and I sent out a PUSH request a few minutes ago."

"What's a PUSH request?"

"It stands for Pray Until Something Happens. We used to do it in Scotland."

"Oh," Madeline said. Her heart warmed.

"You've always been so kind to me, and I just wanted to do everything I can to help you. My granny used to say 'the Hand of God is never still'. So stay positive and trust in God, miracles happen when you believe."

"Thank you, Sophie, I will."

"I'll let you get back to your family, take care," Sophie said.

"Thank you for everything you've done, Sophie."

"God bless you and your family."

"God bless you too Sophie."

Madeline pushed the door open and froze at Josh's words - "Look, Elle is smiling!"

CHAPTER 61

Neil Williams sat at a table in the hospital canteen, his hands clasping a full cup of cold coffee as he stared at the TV screen. He wasn't focused on anything in particular and saw only shadows moving across the screen.

"Excuse me can you turn the volume up?" A man said to one of the female canteen staff wiping down a table.

"Of course, let me get the remote control," she told him and walked off in the direction of the kitchen. She appeared a few moments later, remote control in her hand and turned the volume of the TV up. One by one people in the canteen stopped what they were doing and turned to the TV, eyes became glued and ears receptive.

"Something amazing is happening all over the World at this very moment. Something that many churches have described as a miracle! One little courageous girl, Elle May Williams, has brought Christians out in large numbers and got them praying in unity for her to survive what newspapers are calling her attempted murder. As you know, Elle May was visiting her friend Jessica Carmichael when she stumbled in on a suicide pact taking place in the hospital. You can image the traumatic event occurring right before her eyes! Police are still working on the pattern of events and piecing things together but think that Elle May was forced to swallow the poison so that she couldn't stop the suicide pact from taking place or alert anyone. According to her doctor, someone hit Elle, held her down, and poison poured down her throat.

Now, people from different churches all over the World are holding vigils and are praying in unity for her to survive. 'One God, One Saviour and One Holy Spirit' are being declared as Christians unite in one voice! They have put Elle May in what they are calling a 'Rainbow Covenant Prayer Chain'. United, they are praying, believing that they will see positive results.

They are also praying that any other suicide pacts will be thwarted on time. We spoke to some of the people earlier, let's go back and listen to what some of them said-"

Neil pushed his chair backwards, and the harsh sound of metal against the wooden floor drowned out the next few words from the TV. Neil quickly pushed his full cup of cold coffee away from him and stood up abruptly, spilling some of the coffee in the process. The story was everywhere, and he was angry that everyone was focused on the story and not on him. He knew it was selfish of him to be mad at the lack of attention he was getting and not thankful that his daughter was alive. He wanted not to be angry. He would give anything not to be angry right now but he was weak, and he accepted his weakness like a shield and as such sought no rectification.

He was an actor and as such in his 'self-genius' he felt he was allowed to get away with emotional inadequacies just like a successful footballer might be allowed to get away with racial taunts or molesting drunk/tipsy women. It was one of the perks of the job, completely wrong, but allowed to happen and the seconds of 'noise' which were swallowed by 'silence' kept it happening. It kept some weak actors and some ignorant successful footballers unrepentant. As Neil walked out of the canteen his phone rang, he saw his agent's name and number on the screen and quickly answered the phone.

CHAPTER 62

Neil Williams was vexed and hungry. When he was vexed, he found he couldn't eat. He had tried to drink a cup of coffee earlier but discovered that all it had been useful for was keeping his cold hands warm. The media were no longer interested in him, and his agent had said earlier that only one studio had called asking if he was available for a Celebrity Big Brother type show. They were interested in him talking about his feelings when he found out that his daughter had tried to kill herself; they wanted a candid account woven delicately into conversations during his stay in the house. His agent said that his fee would only be about ten thousand pounds, but it would open new doors for him and give him bargaining power with the movie makers. Even though he knew that Elle hadn't tried to kill herself - he was considering the offer. He had thought that by doing the interviews earlier someone somewhere would have recognised him and offered him a movie deal. Now, after Clarissa's eruption live on TV, the reporters only wanted to talk to her, and she didn't want to talk to them – to him it was irony punching him in the gut.

He showed the police officers guarding the ward where Elle was his family ID badge, and they let him into the ITU. He looked around, saw his ex-mother-in-law, Maddy and a little boy in a large side room and walked swiftly towards them. Hand on the door, Neil paused momentarily and stretched his face muscles to get his features into shape; he needed his 'concerned-father' face right now. He thought about how good an actor he was, and his vexation increased as he felt unloved and undervalued by the public. The audience he had spent years trying to please and had sacrificed so much for. Concerned-father face in place, he pushed the door open.

"Daddy, Elle's still sleeping," Maddy said as soon as she saw him. She didn't move towards him. Instead, she just looked at him.

"Neil!" Madeline Stapleton said when she saw him.

"Hi Madeline, how's she doing?"

"She's still in an induced coma. Steve, um, Dr Truman said that he would have to bring her out soon to see how she responds. Where have you been?"

"I was um, I was on the phone. I was on the phone to my um, to my . . . look does it matter where I was, Madeline?"

"Your daughters have both been through something atrocious today, and the least you could have done is be here, that's all."

"I know, I'm sorry, it's all been too much for me, I'm sorry, you're right, I should have been here."

She looked at him with sympathy, where once it had been with dislike now it was with sympathy because he was not worth hating anymore. Once upon a time, before she had joined her current church, she would think about the hurt and pain he put her daughter and her grandchildren through and she hated him. It was a pure, unadulterated type of hate that ate away at the soul, the kind of hate that left one angry all the time. Now, she lived without hate because she saw that there was no point in hating him or hating anyone for that matter because to hate someone meant you hated yourself. To her, to hate someone meant that you didn't live with love, and faith could only work by love. She had faith, and her faith worked now because she also had love in her heart and, like a candle was of no use without fire, she had found that her faith didn't work without love. "Why don't you go and get some fresh air, you look like you need it," she told him.

Neil was used to her hate; he rode on it like a surfer rides a wave and it gave him something to lighten the burden of his guilt. Her kindness was like an electric shock, like hot coals burning him. He found that he couldn't deal with her kindness, it disabled him, his concerned father face fell and try as hard as he could. He couldn't pull it back together; when it tumbled and hit the ground, he started to cry.

Maddy ran down the corridor in search of her mother. She saw her eating a sandwich in a room with Josh's dad and burst into the room. "Mummy, Mummy, Elle's upset, you need to come back," Maddy told her mother, grabbed her hand and pulled her towards the door.

CHAPTER 63

Dr Truman checked Elle's vital signs then pressed a button on the wall. Two nurses rushed in, one on the tail of the other, like a river they diverged, one to either side of the bed. They checked various things and listened attentively as they were told to get Elle's U&Es, LFTs and glucose done. One nurse took Elle's blood, and the other took her blood pressure and temperature. Job done, they merged and left the room.

"What happened?" Dr Truman asked Madeline.

"I don't know," Madeline said. "One minute she looked fine, then she went pale, and her breathing changed."

"What's wrong with her?" Neil asked.

"I'm not sure," Dr Truman told him, "I've started reducing the drug which is keeping her in the coma so that I can bring her out but she shouldn't be reacting like this. A piece of the puzzle is still missing. She must have eaten something unusual this morning that has caused her to react like this-"

"The muffins!" Clarissa exclaimed.

"The what?"

"The muffins she made with Ruth the other day. She brought some back to the house for Maddy and me. I had one and Maddy had one, but Elle ended up eating two this morning with her breakfast. Ruth said that they had put some oil that she bought at a market in Dominica in the muffin mix. The oil gave the muffins a lovely distinctive flavour, and that's the only thing that she had that's unusual-"

"What was in the oil?" He asked as he grabbed a pen and a piece of paper from the table.

"I don't know, let me call Ruth," Clarissa quickly said.

*

"I hid the bottle in my bag. I told Elle about the oil, and I saw her snooping around the kitchen looking for it so I hid it in here," Ruth said, panting from the sprint she had just made. She handed him the bottle. "As far as I know, it contains myrrh, cassia, cinnamon, calamus and nutmeg mixed in with olive oil-"

"Cassia! That's it! Cassia!" Dr Truman exclaimed as he saw the missing piece.

"What is that?" Clarissa asked.

Ruth shrugged, "I don't know per say, but I was told that the oil brought out the flavour in food and could also be used as a healing oil."

Dr Truman pressed the button on the wall and within seconds a nurse rushed in, her eyes went straight to Elle. "I need you to change the tests I requested for the blood you just took from Elle. I need iron levels and potassium levels done asap."

"Yes Dr Truman," she said and rushed out.

"What is it, Steve?" Clarissa asked.

"Cassia can act as a laxative, but it also has many other properties. I've seen it act like a sponge before. That must be the case here, it acted like a sponge and absorbed the poison in her stomach and held it there. She must have tried to force herself to vomit, and somehow the vomit got stuck in her throat. And, when you got there you pulled it out. Ruth's secret oil in the muffins and your quick thinking saved Elle's life." He gently pressed the drip bag feeding fluids into Elle through a tube connected to a needle in her arm. Her symptoms finally made sense to him. She was dehydrated and needed more fluids. Within a few minutes, he saw colour flood her cheeks and her breathing become less laboured.

"There is no way that this is all a coincidence," Ruth said. "I only put the oil in the muffin mix by chance, in fact, I only bought the oil by chance because someone, I don't even remember who said it was good for cooking and baking because it brings out the flavour in food."

"*The Hand of God is never still*," Madeline whispered Sophie's words.

CHAPTER 64

In the Land of the Alcoholics 'Denial' is King

Gregory Haughton sat with his lunch-time secret drinking buddies and listened to them bitching about the government, the lack of border control and the different EUs coming in and draining the British economy. They used to bitch about the Jews, the Blacks and the Asians, in the past (in their ignorance they grouped Indians, Pakistanis, Chinese and Japanese as Asian). Now, they had expanded their 'bitching pool' to include the Eastern Europeans with Polish people on the top of their list, followed by all the other EU countries. Gregory downed his fifth shot of vodka and grimaced as the liquid trailed down his throat burning as it went along.

"My cousin tried to get a job, and they gave it to a Polak. Don't they have jobs in Poland? Why are those people coming over here and draining the bloody NHS and the British economy? Why can't they stay in their own country?" Carl said. He was a bitter man because he had lost his job, his wife and his car in the same week. He had gone to work drunk and sent classified information to the wrong person, and things had snowballed from there.

"I tell you the government has a lot to answer for, they've opened the door and let all sorts come in, criminals, rapists, drug dealers, you name it - those EU people are up to it. This country is going down the pits!" Grant said. He wasn't bitter; he was angry. He was a graduate; he had gone to three universities, dropped out (just before he would have been kicked out) of two universities because he had been out clubbing every night and found that studying was not his forte. He eventually graduated in Human Resources and Management but found he couldn't hold down a job because he was out clubbing every night.

"These EUs come in and take our jobs and our women! They

need to be kicked out just like the Jews, Blacks and Asians. You can't go to a hospital without seeing one of those Asian or Black doctors walking around like they own the place, and now . . . and now, the EU doctors are getting their feet under the table we won't stand a chance of being treated properly as an English person." Rob lamented. His wife (a nurse) had put up with years of his drinking and finally snapped one day and kicked him out of the family home. Within days, Romel, her Spanish boyfriend (a doctor) had moved in and was playing super-daddy to his children.

Gregory Haughton didn't really have anything to say, he just wanted to drink and wanted the company. He didn't want anyone to tell him that getting rip roaring drunk before 2pm was wrong or remind him that he had school lessons to prepare and homework to mark. To him he wasn't an alcoholic; neither were Carl, Grant or Rob. They were men who liked to relax with a few drinks – they were harmless.

Gregory noticed that it had gone quiet and wondered why they had stopped talking, he looked up and realised they were waiting for him to say something – to add some ingredients to their 'hate-pot'. His mind was getting foggy. "I blame that Thatcher for letting the foreigners bring their money in and take up root in this country. She should have kicked them all out!" He said. He knew his mind wasn't engaged, and the words had not been thought through, but they got a good response.

"Here, here!" Grant said, "They should have kicked all those Jews, Blacks and Asians out of the country then the EUs wouldn't have stood a chance at coming in and draining the economy and buying up everything that isn't bolted down!"

"Speak on, Gregory mate, speak on," Carl slurred.

Again silence followed, and Gregory wondered what it was, this time, he had said his bit, surely it was someone else's turn to bitch. He picked up his shot glass and swigged back his sixth shot of vodka. He put down the shot glass and frowned as he looked at Rob who was staring at something behind him. Gregory turned to see what it was and froze. Right behind him, within touching distance, was his wife Rochelle, her dad and her younger brother. He didn't know how long they'd been there but even after six shots of vodka, he knew from the look on her face that she had heard. She had heard, *what he had said, and what he hadn't said.*

"Rochelle!" He squealed in panic. His voice sounded un-human.

"Gregory . . . we saw your car parked outside and came in here to see if you were okay. What are you doing? When did you start drinking like this?"

"Rochelle," he reached out to touch her, and she moved back. He heard her father tell her to leave, and he tried to stand up to explain – explain what, he wasn't sure – his head was heavy yet light.

"Just so that you drunks know, this man is my husband and these are his in-laws. Yes, I'm Black. I didn't know he was a racist when I married him," she looked at Gregory coldly, and he felt himself burning up with shame. "You all sit here talking about foreign people and how they're stealing your jobs – if you were at work, doing something productive instead of drinking, no one would be able to steal your job. My husband sat there while you said all that stuff about foreigners, I'm sure he forgot to tell you his mum is part Turkish and Jamaican, and his dad is part Ukraine. And, I'm sure that if they did a DNA test on all of you, none of you would be pure English. You're just a bunch of pathetic racist men in denial of the truth, hiding behind alcohol!" She turned and walked towards the exit with her dad and brother.

Feeling physically sick, Gregory followed her, bumping into tables and knocking over glasses as he stumbled along, begging her to stop and listen to him. When he got to the door her brother (an NHS doctor - who he really liked) pushed him back and told him to sober himself up as he didn't want to have to hit a drunk. Helpless, Gregory watched his wife, his father-in-law (a recently retired senior security officer - who he also really liked) and brother-in-law climb into his brother-in-law's Land Rover and drive off.

Rochelle, a computer program developer, had been head-hunted and offered a six-figure contract with an American firm which she had initially declined due to family commitments. Pleading and begging didn't work. Two days later Rochelle was on a plane to America and had told Gregory that she would settle herself there, then come back and take Paris to America to live with her.

"Dad!" Paris' scared voice called out.

"Paris?" Gregory jumped up startled. He knocked over the vodka bottle and stared at the clear liquid as it spread over the carpet. He looked around for his son and realised that he had been dreaming, and Paris wasn't home; he was at his friend David's football match. He heard voices and saw light coming from the TV then realised that he had slept on the couch with the TV on. He took a deep breath as he focused on the TV and the 10 o'clock news which was on when suddenly:

We interrupt this broadcast to give you the latest update on the hospital suicide pact. According to our reporter at the hospital three more children have been identified, they are Aisha Patel, Jimmy Duncan and Paris Haughton!

CHAPTER 65

10.10pm

The banging on the door was persistent. It wasn't one knock, two knocks, and wait for a reply it was a constant thumping away as if the person was trying to break the door down with their fist.

"I'm calling the police," Mr Thakur said as he climbed out of bed.

"Aren't you going to see who it is first?" His wife asked.

"Danger, do not enter, killer on the loose, no I'm not going to see who it is," he quipped.

Despite her concern, she smiled at his joke. The banging continued, and she went over to the window as her husband dialled 999. "Wait, I know that man, Sunil, don't call the police." She rushed out of the room and down the stairs but before she could open the door her husband grabbed her and protectively placed her behind him.

"I don't care if you know him Priya, why is he banging on our front door at midnight?" He whispered.

"It's after ten, it's not midnight, Sunil," she protested "and he might be in trouble."

Sunil held a hand up. His eyebrows shot up a few millimetres as they did whenever he wanted to humour her, "We were in bed, and this is my . . . um, our castle."

The banging persisted then they heard a man begging for help.

"Mr Haughton, is that you?" Priya Thakur asked.

"Mrs Thakur, please help me! Please help me!"

Sunil opened the door but kept the latch on, and they both had to press forward to see the bedraggled man on their doorstep. "What do you want?"

Gregory Haughton attempted to tuck his shirt into his trousers but gave up after two attempts, "I need your wife's help-"

"What for?"

"I just heard on the news that they've identified some more of the children in the suicide pact at the hospital and . . ."

Priya Thakur moved her husband out of the way and opened the door, "What suicide pact? Which hospital? What are you talking about?" Her heart pounded as she silently prayed that none of the children in her school were involved.

"I thought my son was at his friend David Dayo-Johnson's football match," he gulped as if the words were stuck to the back of his throat and he would rather swallow them than say them out aloud because saying them out aloud would validate them. "I thought he was over there, but the news on the telly said he isn't there . . . they said he's at the hospital!"

"Which hospital? Why is he at the hospital?"

"I thought he was with his best friend, David . . . I thought he was with-" he swayed slightly, as if drunk.

Sunil grabbed him, held him upright then brought him into the house; he sat him down in the living room and went to turn the TV on. "Stay with him," he told his wife, "he looks like he's about to pass out from shock. I'll get him a drink."

"What did you hear?" Priya asked.

"The news reporter said that my son Paris was involved in a suicide pact. That Paris has been identified as one of the dead children."

"Oh my God, has anyone called you?"

"No, I checked my phone, I checked the answering machine at home, I called his best friend David's home, no one answered. I don't know what else to do!"

"You need to get to the hospital-"

"NO, NO, I can't do that, what if I go and it *is* really him. Nooooooo!"

"Calm down, what about your wife, where is she? Is she at home, does she know?"

He started to cry. "She . . . she," he couldn't finish.

"Here drink this," Sunil handed him a glass of water.

He gulped it down and clung to the glass with trembling hands, "My wife left me. She called me a racist bastard and left me. I told Paris that she's working in America because she got an excellent job, which is true but I didn't say she overheard me talking with some racist people in a pub . . . I didn't mean the things I said. I just wanted company at the pub, but she wouldn't listen. She's going to come back and take Paris to America." His nose ran, tears poured down his face, and he cried like a baby.

Sunil took his wife to one side, "I'll stay with him, you get changed, once you're done, I'll get changed then we need to get to that hospital."

She nodded and rushed towards the door. She was just about to step into the hall when Sunil's voice stopped her she turned to listen to the news report on the TV:

We interrupt this broadcast to give you the latest update on the hospital suicide pact. According to our reporter at the hospital three more children have been identified, they are Aisha Patel, Jimmy Duncan and Paris Haughton!

"Oh my God, no, no, no, that can't be Aisha from my school, no, no, no!" She said as she grabbed hold of the door handle to stop herself from falling. "No, no, no, not Aisha! I was supposed to see her today, but she never turned up. Sunil, it can't be her . . . tell me it's not her!"

"Priya, baby, go and get changed. We need to get down to the hospital," Sunil told her knowing she needed his calmness to stay strong.

CHAPTER 66

San Francisco

Mitchell and Chelsea Albright sat in their daughter's school counsellor's office and listened to the counsellor tell them that everything had been done to stop Jeremy Buchanan and his friends from sending out any further semi-naked images of their daughter. Jeremy's camera had been seized by the head teacher as had all the personal computers, phones and anything that belonged to the boys which they could use to transmit pictures. The police had been informed because Kelly's pictures were not the only indecent pictures on Jeremy's camera. Four other girls had been taken in by Jeremy and his pretence of taking arty personal pictures. The youngest girl was twelve, and her parents were equally distraught. Although shocking, this was no conciliation for Kelly's parents. They had been to hell and back with Kelly and her depressive mood swings because of this whole episode. Kelly was currently on a school trip to London. Her parents had let her go because this was something that she really wanted to do and was the only thing that seemed to bring any sense of normalcy back to her. However, her mother had thought it strange when she had given a lot of her personal and favourite things to her friends, Sarah and Julie before she went on her trip.

'I'm going to kill him', Mitchell Albright thought to himself as he half-listened to the counsellor. 'I will put my hands around his neck and squeeze until every bit of life is squeezed out of him.' He hid his thoughts well as he half-listened to the counsellor talk about how Jeremy had done this to other girls, not just Kelly and how they had only just found out about it. 'Cut him up and bury the pieces', he thought, 'no one will find the body if I cut it up and hide the pieces all over the place', he suppressed a smile, 'I'm going to enjoy making him pay first', he thought. He felt a stab of pain in his heart as he recalled the look of disgust that had irked its way across his face when he had seen the seductive computer images of his daughter naked from the waist up. "How could you do this?" He had screamed at her, "How could you act like some five dollar hooker?" She had thrown up. She had gagged and thrown up on the settee. He had looked at her like he had just found out she was a lap dancer in a seedy club who turned tricks for fun; with no sympathy and with disgust.

"I know that our hands are tied with regards to the level of punishment we can give out," the counsellor told them, "but I hope you appreciate what we have been able to do."

It was here that the background noise rose to the surface, and Mitchell Albright zoned back in, "I'm sorry, did you just say that you hope that we appreciate what you have done? As far as I'm concerned, you haven't done very much! Those boys are seniors at this school, why are they not behind bars? Why are they still walking around with the ominous possibility of them doing this again to some poor innocent, unsuspecting girl?"

"Mr Albright, I understand your frustrations, I share them, but the police have said that the pictures were not taken by force. The girls chose to undress in front of Jeremy and let him take pictures of them. They succumbed to his good looks and let him exploit them-"

"The girls are young and impressionable!"

"I know, and I agree with you. I was just saying what the police have said-"

"Police who probably don't have kids-"

"Mitchell, please calm down," his wife told him.

"No, Chelsea, I'm not backing down. I know who Jeremy Buchanan is, I know his father is a wealthy businessman who gives money to this school, and I know that because of his father's wealth he thinks that he can take advantage of young girls, well enough is enough, I'm filing a civil complaint."

"If you want to take that route, Mr Albright, the school will support you. I have to admit that I personally support that action as boys like Jeremy Buchanan will not stop if you don't stop them. He'll hide behind his family wealth and keep escalating his behaviour until he seriously harms someone. Will Kelly be willing to press charges?"

"We haven't spoken to her about this yet, but I don't see the problem-"

"Mitchell, you don't know that Kelly will want to press charges. We need to talk to her about this," Chelsea told him. She had called Kelly when she landed in London, and she had sounded excited and happy. She wasn't sure if Kelly would want the things she had buried dragged back to the surface again.

"I just want to do the best for Kelly . . . I'm her dad . . . I should be protecting her from boys like the Jeremy Buchanans of this World."

"We both should Mitchell, and we both will protect her from now on, okay. As soon as she comes home we're going to have a fresh start," Chelsea told him. She opened the 'things to do with Kelly' box in her mind and stored this information away. Chelsea Albright prided herself on being a modern mom. Having been raised by an intrusive mother who wanted to know, 'what, when and where' before 'what, when and where' happened, she had opted to be her daughter's friend. The cool mom who would share her clothes with her daughter and talk to her daughter about everything, except the things that really mattered. Years ago, during a play-date, Julie's mother told her that children needed boundaries and curfews and discipline but having grown up as a miserable child with all those things in place, she thought them unnecessary. Chelsea, who had always seen herself as average when growing up and was never invited to the cool parties or pursued by the handsome jocks, now lived vicariously through her daughter. From when Kelly was little she was always first on the guest list for every party. Everyone wanted to have play-dates with her, and a party couldn't start until Kelly Albright showed up. As a teenager, she was always invited to the cool parties and always seen as an 'American Sweetheart'. Chelsea, like everyone else, saw Kelly as a gorgeous young lady who was not just beautiful with a head of lovely natural blond hair, large hazel-green eyes and a perfect figure but also an intelligent young lady who was going to go far in life. She was a cheerleader. She was popular with both girls and boys her age and she was likeable and smart. Girls were jealous of her, and guys wanted to hang out with her, both sexes felt validated by her. Because of all of this Chelsea felt she had accomplished something worthwhile in life – she was no longer average – she was the mother of a popular girl, which meant she was cool.

When Kelly had told her and Mitchell that she was going to her friend's house to study she had suspected that there was a boy involved, but she had thought it was a boy of Kelly's age who was harmless. Now she felt guilty that she had not been a little bit stricter with Kelly, a little bit like her own mother had been with her, and insisted on knowing 'what, when and where'. She resolved within herself to change things – she had time and with that time came the possibility of change.

Mitchell and Chelsea held hands as they walked towards their car. In their own way they were both positive and hopeful that they would have a fresh start and, if need be, Kelly would transfer to another school, or they would move to another state. They turned their phones on and climbed into their car. Almost immediately their phones bleeped and rang simultaneously. Chelsea answered her phone as Mitchell read through his text messages:-

The screams pierced through the car windows and attracted

the attention of people walking past the Albright's car. The screams, like a gunshot, sent birds that had nestled down on the telephone wire above the car fluttering around. It sent students on the nearby football field into panic mode, as they wondered what the heart-wrenching noise was about.

Later, teachers, students and workers looked on as the police officers helped a man and a woman out of the car. The man could barely walk. His limbs wobbled like Jell-O. And, the woman had to be carried by two officers to an approaching ambulance.

The Room

She watched as people filed past her into a room. She saw Jessica and called out to her in a soundless voice. Her lips moved, the words formed and were released but there seemed to be no life to give sound to her words and without the sound, they fell at her feet and died. She tried to move towards her friend but she couldn't, she didn't have a body. When she looked down, all she saw was a shapeless mist. She knew it was her. She knew that she was Elle May Williams, and she was nearly fourteen-years-old. She had a beautiful mother who loved her, a father she had once referred to as a D-H-L man (but now knew that was wrong), a sister who was adorable and smart, a grandmother who was her mentor and a godmother who was her loving angel.

She knew she was Elle May Williams, and she loved muffins and cooking with secret ingredients. She didn't think that she was dead, but she couldn't understand why she wasn't in her body. She remembered someone attacking her from behind as she walked into Jessica's room, something dark was held over her eyes as someone prised open her mouth and poured something into her mouth. She had tried not to swallow it, but the person had held her nose so she couldn't breathe and had to swallow the liquid – something happened, and she felt herself vomiting – then darkness.

In the darkness came moments of lucidity and moments of confusion and sometimes they entwined and other times they overlapped.

Unable to move and unable to give sound to her words she just watched as Jessica and the others stood in the dark room and stared ahead of them as if they were watching something as if they were captivated but something they alone could see completely unaware of the person who stood next to them. She couldn't see what they were watching, but they appeared completely engrossed. Suddenly dark figures appeared all around them; the figures moved vigorously, they were shapeless but seemed to be dancing, celebrating almost. A strange chant emerged from the figures which seemed to revel at the people being in the room. Elle watched them not sure why Jessica and the others couldn't see them and why they weren't afraid. And why they couldn't sense the evil and hopelessness that was emitted from the figures.

She heard a sound nearby and turned, fear gripped her and she started to shake and couldn't catch her breath – she heard a voice then everything went black.

CHAPTER 67

10.15pm

"Unless your mother specifically asks, do not tell her where we had dinner, I repeat, do not tell her," Paul Dayo-Johnson instructed his children as they left the fast food restaurant and walked towards his car. They had gone to see David play in a football match, which had ended in a penalty kick-off, which meant that they had stayed longer than anticipated, which meant that they were all starving at the end of the game and had jumped into the first fast food place they found.

Within yards of his father's Jeep, JJ ran to the front passenger's door, "It's my turn to sit in front," he told his siblings.

David ran after him, "No it's not, it's my turn to sit in front, you sat in front the last time."

"No, I didn't," JJ replied, "Maria sat in front the last time."

"I'm sitting in front," Maria told her brothers as she strolled calmly towards them as one did when one was the eldest and didn't have to fight for their right.

"Why are you sitting in front?" David asked her, "It's my turn," he insisted.

"What are you, David? Five?"

Paul Dayo-Johnson laughed to himself as he in his daughter's stance calmly strolled to his Jeep and pressed the button to open the doors – his place was secured. He climbed into the driver's seat and waited a few moments while his children did what they always did when his wife wasn't there – squabbled for the front seat. He put his key in the ignition and turned, the Jeep came alive, and his children quickly climbed in. JJ sat in front, and Maria and David climbed into the back. As JJ did his seatbelt he turned and looked at his brother, eyebrows raised in a silent 'I told you so'.

"Turn the radio on, JJ," Maria told him as the car headed

home.

"Put it on-" David started to say and stopped as his father raised a hand.

"You guys can fight over who sits where, but my radio is my radio, okay."

"Yes Dad," all three children answered and smiled.

"JJ, turn the radio on but don't touch that dial, my friend."

"Okay," his son told him and pressed the 'ON' button.

Yolanda Adams' song *'Need to Talk to You'*, was playing. Maria hummed to the chorus then sang along to the second verse as her father and brothers listened. Second verse finished and the chorus started then the song stopped and seconds of static ensued then:

'We interrupt this broadcast to give you the latest update on the hospital suicide pact. According to our reporter at the hospital three more children have been identified, they are Aisha Patel, Jimmy Duncan and Paris Haughton!'

"Dad, did they just say Paris? Was that Paris' name they said?" David asked his dad. "And, there's a girl called Aisha Patel in my class, Dad." He was suddenly scared and didn't know if he had heard the names correctly.

"What hospital suicide?" Maria asked, shocked like her brother, knowing that the radio person *had* said 'Paris Haughton'.

"Dad, what's going on?" JJ asked his father. "Is Paris dead?"

Paul Dayo-Johnson pulled his Jeep to the side of the road, turned the engine off then turned his phone on. He hadn't heard anything about a hospital suicide pact. David's football coach always insisted everyone turned their phones off during matches. "I heard Paris' name, but I'm not sure what's going on. Turn your phones on, check the news, I'm going to call your mum and see if she knows anything about this. I want you all to stay calm until we know what's going on, okay. Stay calm, David, we'll get to the bottom of this."

"Oh my God, Dad, ten children killed themselves at our local hospital!" Maria exclaimed, "They carried out a suicide pact by drinking poison. Hold on this other report says nine children, it says one survived-"

"Is Paris dead, Maria?" JJ asked, his voice just above a whisper.

David reached out and took his brother's hand, "Paris wouldn't do . . ." he stopped. He knew Paris had been unhappy recently. His mum was working in America, and his dad was a racist plus he had missed tonight's football match – he had never missed a football match before. "Dad, have you got hold of mum?" He asked.

"No, her phone keeps going to voicemail."

"We need to get to the hospital, Dad," David said.

Just then Paul's phone rang, he saw his wife's number and quickly answered as he opened the door, "It's your mum," he told his children. He climbed out of the Jeep, quickly closed the door and moved away from their hearing.

His children watched as he talked, they saw his hand go to his head, and his head tilt back as if the shock of what he heard had forced his head backwards. They watched as he put his phone in his pocket and stood on the pavement for a few moments. David's hand moved towards the door handle, and Maria pulled him back and shook her head. She had seen her dad react like this when his mother had a stroke. One minute he was laughing and joking with her mother and her mother was playfully calling him 'Mr Man' the next the phone had rung and from the conversation which was spoken in Yoruba she gleaned something bad had happened when her dad kept saying 'Oh no!' She had seen his hand go to his head then, and his head tilt back, just like now. "Wait, David, let Dad come back inside." She told her brother. The seconds seemed like hours as the children watched their father and waited.

Paul walked back to the Jeep pulled the door open and climbed in, "I've just spoken to your mum," he took a deep breath, "she's at the hospital. She had to talk to the police about a girl who was involved in the suicide pact." His hands shook as he tried to insert the key in the ignition, "there were six girls and four boys involved, one girl survived, but all the other children died."

"What about Paris?" David asked.

"We need to get to the hospital and pick your mum up," Paul said.

"What about Paris, Dad?" David asked again.

"The police think that Paris is one of the boys," he said as tears of shock momentarily blinded him.

"What?" David gasped.

"Is Paris dead?" JJ asked as tears poured down his face.

"I hope not, JJ, but let's get to the hospital," he told his son.

Maria sat back and silently prayed that the boy she had known since he was six years old hadn't done what they said he had. As the car sped along the dark London streets, she reached out and took hold of David's hand and squeezed it tightly.

David was in shock. His sister's hand squeezing his was the only thing that felt real.

Tears streamed down JJ's face as he pressed some buttons on his phone and sent a text.

CHAPTER 68

10.30pm

Shock wasn't a word to describe what people who had just read the letter felt. Shock was too mild a word. The letter had been found in the pocket of a thirteen-year-old victim who had been identified through national hospital records as Jimmy Duncan.

> *Children's Services*
> *Social Services Department*
> *Liverpool*
>
> *27th May*
> *Our Ref: 2X7770 112Y*
>
> *Dear Miss Duncan,*
> *Ref: Assistance Request for Jimmy Duncan*
> *We have reviewed your request and have decided that there is nothing that we can do for your son Jimmy at this point. We advise that you contact your GP again and find out if there is any medication that can be provided to help Jimmy with his issues. We understand that Jimmy is currently on anti-depressants but feel that this is not something we are qualified to deal with and strongly advise you contact your GP. Regarding the government assistance you mentioned in your letter, I feel that this finance should be used for children who are salvageable and as such feel your son does not qualify.*
>
> *Yours Sincerely*
> *Mr N. Bolton*
> *Manager Children's Services*

Note:

Katie can you print and then send the letter above to Miss Duncan. It regards her fat son who keeps stuffing his face with crisps, chips, pizza and fizzy drinks. The woman is deluded if she thinks that we will use our budget to cater for her ignorance. If she would stop allowing that 13-year-old tub of lard to stuff his face with crap then maybe he would have a chance at a decent semblance of life. She is such a stupid, uneducated, ignorant waste of space and should have kept her legs closed when she was sixteen then we wouldn't have to deal with this. Her fat stupid son is also a waste of space – talk about ignorance breeding ignorance.

Send the letter out asap Katie to get the idiot woman off our backs!

Thanks

Nicolas

ps

Fancy grabbing a bite tonight?

New joke

Q. How useless is it trying to do something for these fat dummies?

A. As useless as building a prison – all that hard work for nothing ☺ ☺ ☺

I'M SORRY MUMMY, I'M SO SORRY THAT THEY CAN'T HELP ME, AND NOW YOU ARE SAD AGAIN, SORRY MUMMY

"Can someone please tell me what the hell I'm reading?" Inspector James asked as he physically choked back his tears.

"It's a letter that was found in the pocket of Jimmy Duncan. Police CCTV cameras picked him up getting on a train at Liverpool Lime Street station earlier today," Dr Chang Lin said. "I checked NHS patient records and Jimmy has been to see his GP several times about his weight."

"The bit at the end, the bit written in felt-tip capitals, did he write that bit himself?" Inspector James asked.

A metal chair sailed across the room and smashed against the wall – in answer. It didn't break as it fell, slightly dented, to the floor. Everyone turned to look at Sergeant Kelleher who had thrown it, anger evident on his face. "What kind of person writes that kind of crap?" He shouted. "How can you let a child read this kind of crap about himself? Who does that?"

"John, take a break, go on, get outside and take a ten-minute break then come back in and deal with this," Inspector James told him.

"I'm going but here's what I want doing, I want Nicolas Bolton, or whatever that person calls himself picked up right now. I want him hooked up so that he can explain that bull!"

Inspector James picked up a phone, "I'll get the Liverpool police to pick him up right away, take him to their central station and get him hooked up for you to interview him."

*

Sergeant Kelleher paced around for a while then he headed down a flight of stairs. He walked through the double doors on the floor below and then walked along a corridor and stopped at what looked like a chapel. He didn't go in but sat on a seat outside its doors. His head in his hands, his elbows on his knees, he didn't see the elderly man pushing a wheelchair walking towards him or the elderly woman attached to a drip sitting in the wheelchair.

"Do you know any jokes?" The elderly man asked.

Sergeant Kelleher looked up and saw the couple, "I'm sorry, what did you say?" He asked the man.

"I asked if you knew any jokes. I've been telling my wife jokes for years, and it looks like I've run out. Do you know any good ones?"

He thought for a while as he looked at the couple, he noted their expectant faces as they waited. He smiled as a joke came into his mind. "My dad told me this joke when we were waiting for his test results, I don't know where he heard it," he told them.

He saw how the woman snuggled up to the man who now sat in a chair next to her parked wheelchair. "Tell me," she encouraged him.

"Okay, here goes. There were two middle-aged brothers who were really, really bad. They lived in an area where they controlled everything and everyone. Rumour had it that they would kill you if you so much as looked at them the wrong way. They laundered money, they muscled in on businesses and made sure that the owners paid them a tax. They extorted money from anyone they could, and they lent money out at ridiculous interest rates. No one could do anything about them so they lived the lives they did at other peoples' expense. The years went by, and the brothers got meaner and meaner with each passing year. One day the older brother died, and the younger brother went to the local church with a couple of his most hench looking bodyguards, these guys were big and mean-looking. He told the Bishop there that his brother had died, and the Bishop had to do the funeral services for his brother in two days. As he was about to leave, he turned and told the Bishop that during the funeral he wanted the Bishop to say something truthfully nice about his brother. He spoke in such a way that the Bishop knew he didn't have a choice in the matter. One of the mean-looking bodyguards moved his open hand slowly across his own throat to show the Bishop that it was a do or die situation." Sergeant Kelleher ran his open hand slowly across his own neck to make it clear what he meant. The couple nodded. "So, the younger brother left, and the Bishop started panicking because he didn't know anything nice to say about the man's older brother. The next day he went around talking to people in the community asking them if they knew anything that was truthful and nice he could say. Every single person he spoke to said – no! There wasn't one nice thing that they could think of to say about this man's older brother. The day of the funeral comes around, and the younger brother is in the front pew with family and friends, and the Bishop gets up to speak. He's sweating and shaking as he stands in front of the microphone because as a man of God he cannot lie. He looks at the younger brother who nods and smiles, and he starts the eulogy. This is what he says," he pauses then continues.

"We are all gathered here today to remember our dear brother Carlucci, who passed away recently. What can I truthfully say about Carlucci that we don't already know? Carlucci was a bad man. He was mean and ruthless, and he would shoot you if you so much as looked at him in the wrong way," Sergeant Kelleher saw the questions on their faces and paused.

Confused, both husband and wife looked at him.

"But . . . but I thought he was supposed to say something nice?" She said.

"Let him finish, Barbara," her husband told her.

Sergeant Kelleher smiled then continued. "The Bishop went on to say how Carlucci laundered money, how he stole money and how he was a mean loan shark who charged ridiculously high-interest rates. And, would break a person's bones for fun when his money (and interest) was late coming back to him." Sergeant Kelleher's face was deadpan, and he paused for effect as the couple waited. He knew he had their full attention. "So, the younger brother frowned as he listened, and the frown got deeper and deeper with each passing moment. His fists clenched and his whole persona said that the Bishop was a dead man." He paused again as he struggled to conceal a smile then he continued. "The Bishop then said, I am here today to say that we all know Carlucci was an evil man. However, the one truthful nice thing which everyone I spoke to confirmed, the one genuinely nice thing that everyone knew about Carlucci is this – compared to his younger brother sitting here today, Carlucci was an angel!"

The elderly couple laughed loudly at his punch line. The wife laughed so much as she slapped her thigh several times. Her husband laughed at the joke and his wife's laughter. His face came alive as he looked at her and laughed.

"Compared to his brother he was an angel, hahaha, that's a good one," the wife said as her husband pushed her down the corridor. "An angel, hahaha . . . ."

"That was a good joke," Genny said.

Sergeant Kelleher looked up. She was standing a few feet from him, "Glad you liked it," he told her.

"I did like it, do you know any more jokes?"

"Loads more, I'll tell you some of them, sometime."

"I'd like that," she replied.

He looked at her, "Did they get that Bolton guy?"

"Yes, they picked him up, he's at the police station in Liverpool. Inspector James asked me to come and get you. We have a live feed from the station. Also, the young boy's mother, Miss Duncan, is going to give a live interview to the press in a few minutes."

CHAPTER 69

Live TV Interview

The years of depression had rendered her eyes vacant. The years of drinking cheap cider and smoking had rendered her teeth yellow and decayed and the skin on her face limp, loose, leathery and lifeless. She was 29 years-old, but her face depicted a much older woman.

"My son Jimmy was a lovely boy. He took care of me when I got so depressed and scared." She wrung her hands together then wiped her tears away. "I have a drinking problem brought on by depression. I'm not an 'alki'. I drink and take pain killers to forget my troubles. Jimmy's dad was my teacher at secondary school; we ran off together, and he abandoned me when I was sixteen. I was seven months pregnant. I was too ashamed to go back to my family so I had Jimmy and it was just the two of us. People think that we're ignorant and stupid, but we're just trying to get by as best we can. I saw my son eating himself into an early grave, and it made me depressed so I drank then I would get headaches so I took painkillers. I'm not proud of how I've lived my life, but I tried and tried to get help for Jimmy. I went down to the Social Services and begged them to help him. I asked if they could put him somewhere where he could get access to help to control his eating. They do things like that to help drug addicts and alcohol addicts don't they, why can't they do it for people with food addictions? My son wasn't a freak; he was addicted to eating food. He tried to stop. The GP said it could be a thyroid condition, and he was going to do some more tests." She took a deep breath as if her next words were like walking on hot coals – each word burning and branding her soul. "They bullied Jimmy at school when all he wanted to do was fit in and learn. I told him about the importance of a good education and how it would change his life, but the other kids wouldn't give him any peace. The teachers were just as bad they made fun of him in front of the other children. More than once a bus driver told him he would have to pay double the amount because he would take up the space of two people on the bus. They were all cruel to my son!" She choked and a glass of water magically appeared in front of her. She tried to lift the glass with one hand, but her hand shook so badly she had to use both hands. The camera zoomed in on her shaking hands and trembling lips as she drank the water. Flashlights from cameras went off all around the room. "I went down to Social Services, and I spoke to that man, Nicolas Bolton. He said that there was some new government funding available to help obese children, he promised me he would look into getting Jimmy on a programme that would help him. I told Jimmy what he said. I told Jimmy that at last, he would get help, and you should have seen his face light up. You should have seen his little face light up . . . Arr, Arrr . . . his little face lit up . . . his . . Arrrrrrrrrrrrrrrrrr, Jimmy Arrrrrrrrrrrrrrrr, my Jimmy's dead because of that man, because of the letter Nicolas Bolton wrote. My Jimmy's dead!"

"Miss Duncan-"

"Miss Duncan what are you going to-"

"Miss Duncan-"

"Jimmy, I want my Jimmy, Arrrrrrrrrrrrrrrrrrr!" She screamed.

The policewoman sitting next to her gathered her into her arms and told the press that she would not be answering any questions at this point.

**

Scrgeant Kelleher looked at the face of Nicolas Bolton on the screen. It was the face not of a repentant man but rather of a man angry at the aspersions from people who often thought what he had written, but were too cowardly to voice it.

"Mr Bolton, you've seen the interview Jimmy Duncan's mother has just given, do you have anything to say?"

"I wrote the letter, yes, but the bit at the back wasn't

supposed to be sent out, my secretary Katie was supposed to send the top half to Miss Duncan-"

"So it's your secretary's fault that Jimmy Duncan is dead!"

"No, that's not what I said! In hindsight it was stupid of me to write that bit at the end, I didn't think that it would go out to Miss Duncan, but if I'm honest, I only wrote what everyone thinks about people like Jimmy Duncan."

Everyone who had seen Sergeant Kelleher throw the chair against the wall held their breath, not sure what he would do.

"What is it that everyone thinks about people like Jimmy Duncan?" Sergeant Kelleher asked, calmly.

"That they're a waste of space. Come on we all see the fatties wobbling around, crying about their weight then jumping into fast food restaurants like it's an Olympic event – Gold for eating a supersized meal in ten seconds, Silver for eating it in twenty seconds. Sorry, we don't do bronze! It's a joke!"

"But I understand your department received extra government funding to help-"

"Why should taxpayers pay to feed them? Why should money that can be used to help people who really need help be used to feed those fat people?"

"But Jimmy really wanted help. His weight depressed him-"

"If his weight depressed him then he should have stopped stuffing his fat face."

"You have no remorse, do you? You think that it's right for you to think that Jimmy Duncan was, and I quote, 'a tub of lard'?" He picked up a piece of paper and read aloud, *"The woman is deluded if she thinks that we will use our budget to cater for her ignorance. If she would stop allowing that 13-year-old tub of lard to stuff his face with crap then maybe he would have a chance at a decent semblance of life. She is such a stupid, uneducated, ignorant waste of space and should have kept her legs closed when she was sixteen then we wouldn't have to deal with this. Her fat stupid son is also a waste of space – talk about ignorance breeding ignorance."* He calmly put the paper down, "You have no remorse for what you've done, do you?"

"No, I don't, why should I have any remorse?"

"Then I can show you no sympathy for what I'm about to do." He nodded and one of the police officers asked Nicolas Bolton to stand up and put his hands behind his back while the other police officer read him his rights and handcuffed him.

"What are you doing?" Nicolas shouted, "You can't arrest me. I didn't do anything wrong!"

"Mr Bolton, you are being arrested for the assisted murder of Jimmy Duncan. The law has changed, if you do anything that aids a person taking their life, you pay the price. There are of course mitigating circumstances but from what you've just said, they don't apply to you. Your letter was the catalyst that led to the death of a thirteen-year-old boy."

"What?"

"There are government funds available to help people like Jimmy. You had his medical record which showed he was depressed by his weight. He qualified for assistance, but you chose to deny him the help that would have saved his life."

"Please, this is all a mistake, the part of the letter with the joke wasn't meant to be sent to his mother! I didn't know he would read the letter!"

"That explains everything, that part of the letter was a joke! Well, now the joke's on you. Maybe ten to fifteen years behind bars will help you re-evaluate what constitutes a joke."

"No! Wait! No this isn't right! You can't do this. Can he do this? You can't do this!" Nicolas shouted.

CHAPTER 70

10.40pm

"Terry J. King! The lead singer in the group K-A-Y 3! Are you serious?" Genny asked the doctor.

"Yes, we now have a positive ID from our forensic people. The reason it took so long was because he didn't have a suicide note on him just a piece of paper with what looks like words from a chat room conversation," the voice of the doctor attached to the Coroner's office replied through the speaker. "He also has a tattoo of his name on his upper right arm, and he was wearing a gold chain with his initials which both confirm his identification.

"Can you send an image of the chat room conversation to me asap?" Genny asked him.

"Sending now," the doctor told her "and one more thing, not sure how relevant to your case this is or not but the kid was seriously bulimic, he had-"

"Terry J. King is a boy, are you saying he was bulimic?"

"Genny, I spent several years in medical school, I know a boy when I see one!"

"I'm sorry, I've always associated bulimia and anorexia with females."

"Most people do, but it's a misconception, it affects both the male and female gender. This boy has been bulimic for quite some time by the look of things."

"How do you know that?" Anna asked.

"When you throw up so many times the acid in your stomach starts to erode your oesophagus, and this boy's oesophagus was really scarred and damaged. His singing days were on the verge of being well and truly over."

"Thanks for that information," Genny said.

"Glad to help, sending the image over now," the doctor said.

Seconds later Genny clicked on the email and opened the

attachment. The words of the chat room conversation appeared on Genny's laptop. She projected them onto a screen for everyone to see.

Shy boy 1: Had a hell day today, feel like shit. Got bullied at school, can't tell anyone.

I'm Unhappy: No one understands, no one cares, I hate pretending that everything's okay when everything isn't okay.

Unhappy 2: I hate that too. My dad is having another affair and my mum is in denial again. She keeps shouting at everyone ☹. We pretend we don't know what's going on and I hate it.

G-N: I hate that, why can't your mum deal with him and give everyone else a break?

Unhappy 2: I wish she would but she won't ☹.

Li-sa 5: I hate everything and everyone, my school is full of bitchy girls and I want out of everything. The cutting isn't working anymore. I don't feel the release I used to feel. I need to escape the pain cos it's driving me mad.

Shy boy 1: I hear you Li-sa 5, I need to end things soon, can't take much more.

Unhappy 2: How are you going to do it?

Shy boy 1: Fly off a bridge, go out in style.

Li-sa 5: Someone's knocking on my door; I bet it's my mum's boyfriend trying to cop a feel again. I wish I could kill him then myself.

Shy boy 1: Why don't you? Kill him then you can leave this world feeling good about something!

Jessy James 6: My mum's sloshed again, she really embarrassed me in front of my best friend. She is crap. I hate her. I wish I was dead. I want to die!!!

Unhappy 2: Don't worry JJ6, we'll get there soon. We're all going to get out of this world, on our terms and to hell with everyone else ☺ UREDRUMU!!!

"UREDRUMU!" Inspector James exclaimed.

"Wait a minute. Jessica Carmichael had a copy of this in her secret drawer!" Sergeant Kelleher said.

"She could be the Jessy James 6," Dr Peter Lewis told him.

"We need to ID all the people in this conversation asap," Anna said.

"Why?" Inspector James asked her.

"Because I think that some of the people in that conversation are still out there, and I think that other suicide pacts might take place if we don't get to them."

Genny grabbed her mobile phone, "I'll get our tech people to work on it right now," she told them.

"Put a rush on it," Sergeant Kelleher told her, "We have less than two hours to midnight!"

"You see it too, don't you?" Anna asked him.

"See what?" He asked cautiously.

"If we go into another day, the people or person behind this will think they've won, and this will all happen again and again, some other location, some other children!"

CHAPTER 71

Homeless Boy

I'm the body they will never identify. (For some reason they initially thought I was Paris Haughton – it could be because my body was found next to his fallen school bag).
But, I am me, and I could be your son or your brother. I could have been someone's husband and someone's father.

I didn't take any ID with me when I went to the hospital this afternoon because I don't have any next of kin who care whether I live or die. They will call me 'Homeless Boy' but I have a home, I just don't live in it anymore.
My mother remarried and moved her new husband into the family home I had lived in for all my seventeen years. I couldn't stand my stepfather so I packed a few things in a rucksack, left Glasgow and came to London to live with my father. When I got to London, I found my father living with a new girlfriend who had two little boys (by two different men – neither of which was my dad) and didn't want me around. She owned the council flat so my father had little say in hospitality matters. She said I could stay for a few weeks after which I would have to leave and either return to Glasgow or make my own way in London. She cracked me up with her, *'Now, there are no free handouts in life, you get what you give, and no one owes you anything'*. Can you image the cheek of this woman telling me that! She didn't work. She was always online buying stuff, and she took every penny my dad earned, and she was telling me that there were no handouts! After three weeks if she hadn't thrown me out in front of my father who was watching or pretending to watch TV, I would have walked out anyway.

She was lazy and dirty, and the flat smelled like an unshaven and unwashed armpit, with the reek of beer, fart, shit and damp thrown into the mix. Her sons were little, and I didn't understand why Social Services hadn't taken them off her, she didn't look after them. They ran around in dirty clothes all day *and* soiled nappies which she only changed once a day. They weren't potty trained so they went to the toilet wherever they felt like and sometimes ran around chasing each other with poo-poo on their hands – it was disgusting, I reckon calling it a pigsty would be offensive to pigs.

I told my dad that he needed to move out, and she went crazy, she told me I was trying to destroy her family and break up her happy home – yeah right, more like put the brakes on her gravy-train. My dad once had a beautiful home in Glasgow, a woman who would walk through fire for him and he gave it all up to come to London and live in this filthy hole with this weird woman he had met on an online sadism and masochism (S&M) dating site – why?

I packed my bags, and my dad handed me a twenty-pound note, and I left. I spent my first homeless night in an alleyway not far from the weird woman's flat. I couldn't sleep – the night noises kept me awake and filled me with fear.

It's hard being homeless in winter. There's nothing worse than having to protect your life, your rucksack of worldly goods and your dignity – all in cold temperatures. Some charities offered homeless people beds, but it was on a 'first come first served' basis which meant that you had to wait in line for hours to ensure that you got a place to sleep. Sometimes I would get there late, not get a bed and end up having to sleep in a shop doorway or on a park bench under a pile of newspapers.

Homelessness in a wealthy country makes no sense to millions of people. They look at people like me and think that we have so many options, and we choose to live the way we do. They think that we are people who turned our backs on our families and decided to take up residence on the streets. Never mind that some of us have a mental illness, were abused or kicked out of our homes – that would give us a plausible excuse which they don't want to deal with.

I've met some really nice people on the streets of London. I met a man once who asked me if I'd seen a particular play at the theatre and I asked him which theatre he was referring to (as one does), and he said that he had written several plays which millions of people had seen. He spoke with a really posh accent and said that he was a millionaire, and he was worth so much money but that no amount of money had brought him joy after his wife died. He had a small suitcase that looked expensive and a long-life plastic bag. His suit looked as if it had been expensive once and his scuffed shoes were pointy toed; all in all his attire wasn't the usual attire worn by homeless people. I stayed with him for a couple of nights, and he talked about his plays and why he had written them. He said his wife had been his muse for years but that when she died, he found he could no longer write plays. One day he had packed a small suitcase, left home, got into his car and driven for hours. When his petrol finished he got out of his car and started walking – that was over a year ago, and he has been walking ever since. Before we parted ways he gave me a big yellow smiley face badge and a poem, he said he wrote one night when he couldn't sleep. He said that particular night he met a man called Payne Holister who told him to contact his children and go home. He knew his children were looking for him but couldn't face living in his big house by himself while they lived all over the World with their families. He said that the words fought in his head and would give him no respite until he had written them down – so he did. He said he had written them down but had not read the poem in its entirety after he had written it. I remember this like it was yesterday not weeks ago. He took a deep breath, opened his suitcase and took out a piece of folded paper. He unfolded the paper and read the words to himself then closed his eyes and cried. He wept bitterly in front of me. Then he folded the paper and gave it to me to read. I unfolded the paper and read the words aloud:

Where were You?
When I was lonely and lost and had no hope
When I was homeless and when I was broke
When I cried and cried for an answered prayer
When everywhere I looked was full of despair
Where were You?

I was in the wind blowing that day, directing your footsteps towards a better way
I was in the hot cup of tea and the friendly smile given to you on that cold day
I heard your prayer before it was said and I answered it but you it misread
I too see the despair, I too feel the pain and send solutions again . . . and again.

So where are you?
What do you do with the directions I give?
How do you respond to the smile from a stranger's lips?
Why do you misread your answered prayers?
Why do you not use the solutions I send?

I am here, always was and always will be
I am in the opening of eyes and what they see
I am in the mother's joy and newborn's cry
I am in the comfort given when loved ones die

I am everywhere and in Me, there is no despair
I AM . . . Omnipresent! Omniscient! Omnipotent!
I . . . AM . . . LOVE!

Those words were powerful, and they spoke to me. They told me to go home to my mother and my stepfather who had begged me not to leave. My stepfather who had given me £100 when I had insisted on leaving to go and live with my dad. My stepfather who had given me a mobile phone with credit on it and told me to stay in touch with my mum because she loved me so much and didn't want me to go to London (someone stole the phone, I suspect it was the weird woman). My stepfather who you all thought was bad because I portrayed him as being bad. My mother who you thought had abandoned me to shack up with husband number two because that was how I wanted her to come across to you.

I apologise, I shouldn't have done that.

The poem made me cry.

The homeless man said he had called his son, and he was now going to the train station to freshen up and wait for his son who had sounded so distraught on the phone. He begged me to come with him and said that he would personally drive me to Glasgow. For a moment I felt myself floating. I felt hope soar through me and at that moment I really wanted to go home. So what stopped me?

That happened two weeks ago, and I'm still homeless!

I don't know why I refused to go. I don't know if it was my pride or my shame, but I think deep down it was me, like my dad, trying to do things on my own terms. I watched him walk towards the train station as I sat with his smiley face badge pinned on my jacket and my hand clasping the poem tightly and I wanted to go with him, but I didn't.

This morning, I went to an internet cafe to keep warm and saw an Indian girl crying as she sat in front of a computer. Ten minutes later I watched her wipe her tears and leave. I went over to the computer she had been using to see if there was any unused time left. I did this from time to time as it was a way to get online without paying for the service. People paid for an hour and would log in for thirty minutes then leave. When I sat down in front of the computer, I noticed that she hadn't logged off so I opened what she had been looking at. I

saw some symbols and the letters which formed
UREDRUMU, which didn't make sense until I read more.

On my way to the hospital, I gave a homeless boy I saw
sitting at a bus stop the poem and the £100 my stepfather had
given me. I told him about a charity that catered for homeless
teenagers in central London. And told him to get over there
now as they would help him get off the streets and change his
life – I watched him run across the street and jump on a bus
heading towards central London, he must have thanked me a
thousand times. Then for reasons no one, not even I, can
explain, I went to the hospital and became the Unidentified
Homeless Boy in the hospital suicide pact.

The Room

Elle calmed down and peered into the darkness, the sound became louder and seemed to float towards her. Suddenly a sort of hologram image of a boy appeared right in front of her. He looked confused and frightened.

"Are we dead?" He asked her.

"No, I don't think so. I believe that we're in some sort of limbo place . . . wait I heard you. My name is Elle, can you hear me?"

"Yes, I can hear you, and I can see you, but I can't see myself. I don't know what's happening to me."

"Do you remember what happened before you came here?"

"I remember following Aisha Patel from the internet cafe. I went to primary school with her and Gia, one of her friends told me that my dad was really mean to her so I wanted to find out what happened. I followed her into the hospital and then I lost her. Next, I saw a little boy-"

"About 8 or 9 years old, I saw him too!"Elle said.

"I followed him to the third floor and into that room, I saw you in that room, I saw that man holding you, I saw what was going on and told the boy to run . . . I told him to run then I tried to help you."

"I saw the boy come in then the person hit me, and everything went black."She turned and pointed, "Some of the people in the hospital room are now in that room over there staring at something," Elle told him.

He looked past her at the people, "Hello, we're over here, can you see us?"

"I've tried that, I don't think they can see us or hear us."

"How do we get out of here?"

"We need to work together, what's your name?"Elle asked.

"Paris Haughton, my name is Paris."

CHAPTER 72

Fulham Road was cordoned off; only police vehicles were being allowed into the taped-off area. Traffic was backed-up all the way to Sloane Square in one direction and near Hammersmith in the other. Paul Dayo-Johnson and his children had abandoned their car at Earls Court and were now walking swiftly towards the hospital. JJ was texting on his phone as he strode quickly to keep up with the others. Some other people were heading in the same direction, and Paul repeatedly found himself checking to make sure all three children were nearby. As he walked swiftly, he picked up dribs and drabs of conversations, all saying the same thing, all shocked whispers of a loud occurrence – a mass suicide had taken place in the local hospital! Children were dead, murdered by their own hands!

When Paul arrived at the hospital, he saw that it was sealed. The reporters and TV crew had been banished to the front of the hospital and had set up shop as they waited to hear some more breaking news which they could furnish the World with.

JJ's phone vibrated, and he opened the text message and read it. "David, look, Paris just sent me this text!"

"What! Are you sure it's from him?" David asked, grabbing his brother's phone, he read the message. Shocked, he showed the text to his dad.

"I don't understand what does 'tweet tweet' mean?" Paul asked his son.

"It's a joke we shared with him," JJ replied.

"David! David! Over here!"

David turned and saw Paris' dad pushing towards him.

"Have you heard anything about Paris, Mr Haughton?" David asked him.

"No, and they won't let me into the hospital without clearance. I'm waiting for someone called Sergeant Kelleher to clear me."

"JJ just got a text message from Paris-"

"They said that Paris was dead! Are you sure?"

"I'm sure. It's something to do with a joke we told Paris."

They both turned as they heard some commotion. A police officer came out of the hospital and called out for Gregory Haughton to step forward.

"Come with me, David, we need to let them know that Paris is alive. Please come with me!" Gregory Haughton begged.

"Dad, Dad we need to go in with Mr Haughton!" David called out to his father.

Reunited, Paul and Grace Dayo-Johnson sat in the investigation room with their children, Paris' father and the people investigating the incident. JJ's phone was connected to the computer system, and they were trying to track Paris' phone via JJ's phone using the Global Positioning System (GPS). Information from both phones flashed on the screen.

"You did a good thing young man, from the look of your phone I see you've sent Paris nearly 50 text messages," Inspector James told JJ.

"It wasn't just me, my brother's phone died so he used my phone to help send some text messages telling Paris to get in touch and Maria sent some from her phone as well."

"You all did a good job," Inspector James told them, "now let's hope that we can locate Paris. The tech guys think he may have jogged his phone somehow which is how you received the text from him. Whatever the case at least we now have hope that he might still be alive."

Some have described racism as a fear of the unknown. People not being able to relate to someone different because they don't know them, fear them, and this fear turns to hate. Some other people describe racism as a lack of love. They say the racist has a cold heart and therefore is unable to love anyone, not even themselves. This lack of love for self, manifests in hate for self and reflects in hate for/of others.

Gregory Haughton sat next to Paul and Grace Dayo-Johnson and prayed like he had never prayed before for good news. He tried to still his shaking hands. He closed his eyes as tears welled up in his eyes. He was scared, and he didn't have anyone to confide in. Mrs Thakur and her husband had gone to identify Aisha Patel's body in the mortuary. And he was scared because he knew that he could be doing the very same thing right now. He could be in the mortuary identifying Paris' body but, thanks to all the relentless texting that had gone on, the police believed that Paris might still be alive and were actively searching for him. David and JJ had insisted that no one but Paris would understand the 'Chirpsing' joke so they weren't dealing with a phone thief. He stared at his hands. They trembled like an alcoholics hands. He clenched and unclenched his hands, closed his eyes and bowed his head as his tears burst through and flooded his face. He felt a hand take hold of his and squeeze. He opened his eyes and looked at the hand as words flooded his mind – words he heard not long ago:

I believe that one day, one day soon, all men will be one man.

All love will be one love. Hate will be hated and love embraced.

One day, one day soon, the love of God will flow, touch, change and uplift all.

One day, one day soon . . . and that day shall be called –
Today!

He looked at the kind face of the owner of the hand.

"Hang in there," Grace said and squeezed his hand harder.

"Thank you, thank you both and God bless you and your children for what you've done today. I know how happy Paris is when he goes to your home. I think he's happier there than he is with me. I've really messed things up, and he probably hates me for it."

"Paris doesn't hate you. He's a good boy, and he loves you, hold on to that."

He nodded and squeezed her hand, "Thank you."

The Room

*They both saw it at the same time when it suddenly appeared.
A Rainbow – red, yellow, pink, green, orange, purple and
blue colours held on to each other and formed a magnificent
sight. They noticed that the people in the room either ignored
the Rainbow or couldn't see it. They were still standing;
transfixed by whatever it was they were staring at in front of
them.*

*"They know, they know you're still alive, Paris," Elle
suddenly said.*

"How?"

*"I don't know, but you have to get back and get them to
help the others."*

"What others?"

"There are names on Jessica's computer . . ."

"What is it, Elle?"

"Can't you hear the voices?"

"No."

*"Over there by the Rainbow . . . you need to go over there,
Paris, quick go over there that must be the way out."*

"Let's go together!"

*"No, I have to help Jessica and the others, I have to get
them out of that room."*

"What if they're dead? What if you can't help them?"

"What if they're not dead? And what if I can help them?"

"I'm not leaving you here by yourself-"

*"You have to go now, Paris! You're running out of
oxygen!" She mustered all her strength and pushed him
towards the Rainbow – then everything went black.*

CHAPTER 73

A screen on the wall flashed blue several times then red laser lines appeared from several points on the screen and crossed each other at a central flashing point as an alarm sounded.

"What's going?" Inspector James asked.

"We've just picked up Paris Haughton's mobile phone signal. It just came on, and it's in this hospital!" One of the tech guys called out.

"Location?" Inspector James and Police Commissioner Pike asked at the same time as they both hovered.

"Basement of this hospital!" The tech replied.

*

"PARIS! PARIS! Where are you?"

"Paris Haughton, if you can hear me make some noise!"

"Paris, where are you?"

He heard his name and turned towards Elle just as she pushed him towards the Rainbow. He felt himself falling and gasping for air at the same time. He couldn't breathe, and his brain felt like it was shutting down.

"PARIS! PARIS! Where are you Paris?"

"Paris Haughton, if you can hear me make some noise!"

"Paris, where are you?"

He felt something hard in the back pocket of his trousers then he heard Elle's voice telling him to open his eyes before it was too late. *'Open your eyes, Paris, and move your legs'*, she whispered softly, her voice seemed like it was right next to his ear. He turned, she wasn't there, and he was in a small confined space. He moved his legs. Something clicked, and an alarm suddenly sounded. He heard footsteps running and then he heard voices and felt something above his head move then light flood onto him.

"He's in here! He's in here! We've found him! He's moving! He's alive!" A police officer shouted. He gently removed the gag from Paris' mouth and together with another officer helped him out of the boot of the car which had been sealed with carpet tape to stop air from entering. "We need a trolley right now, he can't walk, his hands and feet are tied! Get a trolley!" They both saw the gash on his head at the same time and then the pool of blood in the boot of the car he had been locked in. Feet ran away, and feet ran back with a trolley. The bonds holding his feet and hands were cut, a drip inserted into his arm and a wad of sterile gauze pressed firmly against his bleeding head as they loaded him onto the trolley.

"Cover him up and take him to the investigation room right now!" Sergeant Kelleher told them then ran ahead of them into the hospital.

"He has a concussion. His blood pressure is very low, and he's lost a lot of blood, but he's young and healthy. I have no doubt that he'll be fine," the doctor said as he removed the blood pressure cuff from Paris' arm and rechecked the large plaster on his head, and the drip which was feeding him fluids. "He'll need an MRI scan later, and his blood pressure monitored every thirty minutes, but his vitals are looking good."

"Thank you, Doctor," Gregory Haughton told him, tears poured down his face as he looked at his son. "Thank you God for giving me a second chance," he whispered.

Paris reached into his back trouser pocket and pulled out two items. He held up the stone with his initials on it and showed it to David and JJ. He told them how he had felt it pressing into him as if keeping him alive. Suddenly he became agitated, "I need to see Elle! I need to see her now!" He told them.

Anna took hold of his hand, "Paris, Elle is still in a coma, she's been in a medically induced coma since this afternoon."

He calmed down and nodded then held up the second item and lifted it up towards Grace Dayo-Johnson. "I took this from your picture frame on the wall. I was going to get an enlarged copy made for my room and then return it."

Grace took the picture from him, "I was looking for this," she smiled as she thought of the time she had spent searching for a picture she knew was missing but not knowing which one it was. She looked at the happy faces of Maria, David, Paris and JJ in the photograph, "did it help?" She asked.

He nodded, "It kept me going. It kept me wanting to get back to when I was happy like in the picture. I would think about it and pray that I didn't die. Are you angry I took it?"

"No, Paris, I'm not. I was talking to your dad and if you want you can stay with us for a while. He's going to see your mum in America, and you're practically at our house nearly every day so you can stay with us while he's away."

"I'd like that, thank you," Paris told her as she hugged him.

Unable to hold back any longer, Sergeant Kelleher asked Grace if he could talk to Paris then quickly pushed the trolley he was on to one side of the room, "What happened, Paris? Do you remember what happened?" He asked.

"I followed Aisha Patel here. I heard from Gia Mishra that my dad had said something to her, and she was upset. I wanted to apologise to her . . . I followed her from the internet cafe to the hospital . . . I lost sight of her and then there was a little boy acting strangely. I followed him, and he went to that ward where all those kids were drinking stuff from plastic cups. Someone handed him a cup. He dropped it, or I knocked it out of his hand. I grabbed him and told him to run . . . you need to make sure he's okay!" Paris rubbed his forehead and winced.

"Are you okay to continue, Paris?"

"Yes, I'm fine. A man was a man holding Elle, I tried to help her, he hit her, and she fell. I moved to help her up then he came at me . . . I need to see Elle, where is she?"

"She's in a room on ITU," Anna told him.

Sergeant Kelleher frowned, "Paris, who was this man? Have you seen him before? Did he say anything to you?"

"I don't know who he was . . . I've never seen him before," Paris replied.

"I'll take you to see Elle," Anna told him and helped him into a wheelchair. "Is that okay, Mr Haughton?" She asked his father.

"Yes, of course, please take him . . . anything he wants is fine with me."

Anna pushed Paris in the wheelchair towards the door. Maria, David and JJ followed. Gregory Haughton stood rooted to the spot, held by the shame of knowing something he had done and something he had failed to do had resulted in 14-year-old Aisha Patel killing herself.

Paris remembered something, "Wait! Jessica's computer, Elle told me the password, she thinks more kids are going to do the same thing tomorrow."

"What's the password?" Sergeant Kelleher asked.

"The password is 'mysister', lower case and no spacing."

"Sister!" Sergeant Kelleher froze momentarily then turned to Genny who had heard and was typing frantically on her computer, "Anything?" He asked her.

"Info is coming through," Genny told him, "okay, her mother remarried, and she took her stepfather's name, which is . . . coming through now . . . Brownlow!"

Images from Genny's computer appeared on the screen just as David opened the door and Anna was about to push the wheelchair out of the room.

Paris felt a sudden chill and turned, he looked at the image of the man on the screen. The man was smiling and had his arm around a girl. "That's him!" Paris shouted, "that's the man who tried to kill Elle and who hit me on my head when I tried to stop him!"

All eyes went to the image of a smiling Inspector Patrick Carmichael on the screen.

CHAPTER 74

ITU Room

"Elle come back to us, sweetheart, please try. If you can hear my voice, move towards it and come back to us, Elle. We love you," Clarissa said as she held Elle's hand tightly.

"What's going to happen?" Ruth asked Steve.

"I've stopped the drug that was keeping her in the coma, sometimes the longer you keep someone in a medically induced coma, the harder it is to get them out. Now we just have to pray and wait."

The Room

Elle felt weak. It had taken all of her strength to push Paris towards the Rainbow, and now she could barely focus on anything. Jessica and the others in the room were no longer there. She was by herself now, and she felt scared. She heard words around her and tried to listen:

"For God has not given you a spirit of fear but of power, love and a sound mind Elle!"

ITU Room

Madeline Stapleton stood at the back of the room and prayed, "God has not given you a spirit of fear, Elle, but of power, love and a sound mind! Elle, you have a spirit of power, love and a sound mind. Don't be afraid, Elle, stay focused and come back, don't be frightened," she said over and over again.

The Room

Light from the Rainbow suddenly fell on her, and she felt the warmth spread through her and strengthen her. She took some deep breaths as she tried to focus.

ITU Room

David knocked on the door, pushed it open, and JJ moved

forward and held it open. Anna pushed the wheelchair into the room followed by Maria.

"My name is Paris Haughton, and I'm here to help Elle just like she helped me. We were in the same place, and she saved me. She thinks that Jessica and the others might still be alive. She doesn't know they're all dead. I need to tell her."

Anna pushed the wheelchair right next to the bed. Clarissa, desperate, said nothing but her eyes spoke – they pleaded, they asked him to do whatever he could.

Paris took hold of Elle's other hand and squeezed it, "Elle, can you hear me. I made it back, I'm here right next to you, come back, move towards the Rainbow, Jessica and the others are dead, Elle, you need to come back."

Clarissa felt Elle's hand move and gasped, "Elle, baby, please come back, do what Paris is telling you Elle and come back to us." Her hand tightened around Elle's.

The Room

"Elle, you need to get out of here, sadly, Jessica and the others are gone," a man's soft voice said.

"Who are you?" Elle asked

"My name is Payne Holister, and I'm here to help you, Elle. I help people like you who shouldn't be here, to get out. On the count of three move forward and grab hold of the hands that are reaching out to you, okay."

Elle felt something cold engulfing her, pulling her down, pressing her into coldness. She closed her eyes.

"Elle, focus, open your eyes and concentrate," Payne Holister said.

"Something's pulling me down. I can feel it."Elle told him.

"The Lord is your Shepherd Elle. You shall not want. Though you walk through the valley of the shadow of death, you shall fear no evil, for the Lord is with you. No weapon fashioned or formed against you will ever prosper, okay."

"Okay," Elle said.

"On the count of three, move, I am with you."
"Okay, on the count of three, one-two-three," Elle said.
She felt a force push her forward as she lunged forward
towards the Rainbow, she felt hands holding hers and
pulling her forward – into something solid.

ITU Room

She opened her eyes slowly and saw Paris' face, "Paris," she
whispered, "you made it back."

Paris smiled at her, "Hi."

"Elle, oh my God, Elle you're back, baby you're back,"
Clarissa sobbed.

Elle lifted her hands up and like when she was a baby and
used to do the gimme-gimme sign by opening and closing her
hands quickly for something. She did it now desperate for her
mother's hug. "Mummy, Mummy, I love you so much, I heard
you. I heard everything you said, everything you all said, even
what Dr Park said. Sometimes it felt like I was standing over
there and sometimes I could see you all!"

"She's woken up!" Maddy squealed and rushed over to the
bed and hugged her sister. "Josh said you'd wake up soon cos
his dad is the best doctor ever!"

Elle hugged her sister then held her arms open, "Hi, Josh, I
heard your jokes, the ones about your grandmother were
hilarious, thank you for making me smile."

Josh moved forward and hugged Elle. She kissed his cheek.

Then as if all at once everyone moved in and hugged and
kissed her.

Happy that she was back and wanting to give her time with
her family Anna indicated to Paris, David, JJ and Maria that
they should leave. She patted Elle's arm and was about to
leave when Elle grabbed hold of her hand and pulled her
towards her. Elle whispered something in her ear, and Anna
froze and stared at her. Elle smiled and nodded, and Anna
nodded in response and smiled. She kissed Elle's cheek almost

as if to acknowledge that they shared the same connection – they had both been helped back to the land of the living by a man called Payne Holister. Amazed but undaunted, Anna left with the boys and Maria.

One by one Elle embraced her family.

"Grandma, thank you and thank everyone for praying for me," Elle whispered as she hugged her grandmother tightly. "I love you so much, Grandma, so much."

"Aunt Ruth, I found the oil you hid in your bag and put some in my smoothie when you went to the bathroom," she giggled. "Then, I had two muffins for breakfast cos the oil made the muffins taste so good. I love you. You're the best Godmother ever. You look out for me even when you're not looking out for me," she told Ruth as she hugged her.

"I hate what you did to our family, but you're my Dad and I love you, plus you only did what you know, you were never taught anything better," Elle whispered to her father as he held her and sobbed.

Surprised at her energy levels and her ability to talk fluently with no dents in her cognition or language, Dr Park did some high-level stimuli-based tests as Elle chatted away.

"Mum, Mum, guess what, we're going to New York with Grandma, Dr Park and Josh!" Elle said to her mother.

"What? How did you know we're going to New York? Mum, did you tell her?"

Madeline Stapleton usually told her granddaughters secrets then swore them to secrecy in the same breath, "No, I didn't tell Elle about New York," she protested.

"Dr Park told me," Elle said, "He said that he used to love you, and he still does and that when I woke up, he would take us all to New York."

All eyes fell on Dr Steve Truman aka Dr Park as he occupied himself with checking Elle's vitals and avoiding the questions he sensed were in their looks.

"Yeah! We're going to New York, Maddy you'll like it there, we can go to the Empire State Building and the Statue of Liberty, and we can go to Uncle Toney's joint and hang out. We can help my dad do his clinics there on Tuesdays and Thursdays. Dad, it is Thursdays as well as Tuesdays isn't it?"

"Yes, it is."

"Looks like we're all going to New York then," Clarissa said.

Steve looked up and smiled at her, "Looks like we're all going to New York then," he counter-said.

CHAPTER 75

A police courier clad from top to bottom in black leather walked in and handed Inspector James an electronic pad for him to scan his thumbprint and sign. He waited for the green authentication light to come on. As soon as the green light came on, he handed the sealed file to Inspector James and walked out of the room. Inspector James opened the file looked through the papers then walked past Sergeant Kelleher who was studying the footage of interview which took place earlier with Inspector Carmichael and showed the paperwork to Police Commissioner Pike.

*

"She's my daughter. I was only trying to protect her! I'm her dad! I have to protect her!"

Sergeant Kelleher slapped the desk hard, "There it is, staring us right in the face. Things don't happen in isolation. He sat there and told us that she *is* his daughter, and he *has* to protect her. He wasn't talking about Jessica, she was already dead at the time of the interview, he was talking about his other daughter! Get him in here, now!"

*

Inspector James walked over to Sergeant Kelleher and showed him the paperwork then told him to hold up a hand while Commissioner Pike swore him into office. Slightly dazed, he stared at both men who looked at him with pride.

*

Inspector Carmichael observed his adversary with complete contempt. He was untouchable, in his mind, the sergeant couldn't touch him. He had awards and commendations for his work and no one beneath him could touch him.

"Inspector Carmichael, we pulled Paris Haughton out of the boot of the car you dumped him in after you knocked him on the head and left him there to die-"

"You can't prove I did anything, I was with my wife, she'll swear to it. This is some conspiracy to make me look bad so that I don't sue the hospital isn't it? Well, you won't succeed, you hear me!" He stood up and turned to leave the room.

"You didn't tell us you had another daughter, Inspector. Danielle, isn't it? Just so that you know, Danielle is being picked up as we speak."

Inspector Carmichael froze then turned around, "You can't do that. How dare you bring my daughter into this!"

He ignored him, "Danielle C. Brownlow, 20 years old, studying architecture at university. I guess the C is for Carmichael? You must be proud of her. Were Jessica and Danielle close?"

"I don't have to put up with this, you have nothing on me plus you can't interrogate me, you're beneath me in rank. Get Inspector James to question me-"

"Sit down, Inspector Carmichael!"

"Get your superior officer to give me a call. I have nothing to say to you, Sergeant!"

"She's my daughter. I was only trying to protect her! I'm her dad! I have to protect her!" Inspector Carmichael's earlier words played over and over again on a loop through speakers.

Inspector James wandered over and sat on a chair next to the one a now shocked Inspector Carmichael had vacated. "Just so that you know, Patrick, John here isn't a Sergeant anymore, he's just been sworn in as an Inspector two grades above you, and he can question you, arrest you and hold you in a cell for as long as he sees fit." He patted Patrick's arm, "Just thought I'd let you know." He wandered back to the paperwork he had been looking through.

Inspector John Kelleher stood up and pushed Inspector Carmichael onto a chair and held him down, "You are responsible for the deaths of Victor Jenkins, Kelly Albright,

Lisa Goldstein, Samantha Simpson, Aisha Patel, Jimmy Duncan, Terry J. King, An Unidentified Homeless Boy and Jessica Carmichael! You tried to kill Elle May Williams and Paris Haughton! You stand for everything we at TTS are against, and you're going to prison. And, if I find out that your other daughter, Danielle, is involved, she's going to prison as well, do you hear me?"

"I don't . . . look I, um, you can't prove anything-"

"Yes I can, look at the two people over there, recognise them? It turns out a complaint was filed against them by an Inspector who said they failed to treat his daughter with due diligence and their neglect put his daughter at risk and nearly cost her, her life. It turns out this Inspector is suing the Emergency Medical Services. The EMS was forced to put the paramedics on suspension pending an investigation and had to seal their report regarding Jessica, which is why we couldn't find it. I told you we'd find the paramedics and their report didn't I? You think you can sue or threaten to sue people, and they keep quiet don't you, well not this time. You're going to prison for a long time Carmichael."

"She's my daughter. I was only trying to protect her! I'm her dad! I have to protect her!" Continued to play on a loop.

CHAPTER 76

11.25pm

"We have the list from Jessica's computer. We can flood the system with the Talk To Someone messages now and stop things going further. Are we cleared to proceed?" Dr Lewis asked Inspector Kelleher.

Inspector Kelleher knew that he didn't have authorisation to say yes to flood the internet with material using an international government server and government files containing firewall breakers. But he thought of his father's last words, *'Johnny, make every minute of your life count, help those who can't help themselves and enjoy your life'* he thought of the lives they could save and without blinking gave the go-ahead to go live. He stood and watched with everyone in the room as suicide, and self-harm chat rooms were wiped clean then overridden with the TTS messages and contact numbers to call for immediate help. The computer program also picked up IP addresses of trolls and shut their computers down, alerted local authorities where they were and sent out a national 'Apprehend and Detain' message.

Within minutes the TTS Anti-Suicide Campaign was live!

The Bit in the Middle

Many years ago a little boy used to sit with his father and listen to music on his father's record player on Sundays after lunch. Ray Charles, Nat King Cole, James Brown, Gladys Knight, The Temptations, Billy Holiday, Dionne Warwick, Jim Reeves. Sammy Davis Jr., Frank Sinatra, Elvis, Sam Cooke and Tony Bennett would all sing to him as he sat back and wondered how the music got into the round, black vinyl discs in his father's record collection.

One Sunday while changing a record his father handed him the record he had just taken off the player. The boy looked at the black vinyl disc; he turned it this way and that as he studied it.

"Dad, why does it have a Side A and a Side B?"

"Because Side A has the first part and Side B has the second part," his father told him as he took the record from him.

"So what does the bit in the middle do?"

"The bit in the middle holds both sides together son, the bit in the middle is what makes everything make sense."

"So, it's important?"

"Absolutely. Listen very carefully, son. Without the bit in the middle, there wouldn't be a Side A and a Side B."

CHAPTER 77

San Francisco

Jeremy Buchanan counted the money again then smiled at his father and thanked him as he tucked the cash into the pocket of his chinos.

"These pictures are good, son, email them to me with the contact details for the girls. You can earn a bit more if you bring me some full frontal shots. I'll pay you a lot more and hey maybe I might even just look into that new set of wheels you mentioned the other day."

"Dad, these chicks are young, I can get tits, but they don't wanna take anything else off for the camera, believe me, I've tried."

"I'm talking about 10-"

"Ten thousand dollars, are you serious?"

"Did my granddaddy come from Alabama? Am I not one of the richest men this side of Frisco? Sure I'm serious, son."

Jeremy smiled at his old man, 'ten grand and the new car he wanted – sweet', he thought to himself. He could see himself driving to school in the car. He could see himself hooking up with chicks because of the car, and he could see himself selected as the Prom King because of the car.

Candice Buchanan stared at the police officers on her doorstep. She had only opened the door because it was the maid's day off and her husband was in his study with the invisible do-not-disturb sign on the door, and Jeremy was in his room and never answered the door anyway.

"Mrs Buchanan?" The female officer asked.

"Yes."

"We need to talk to your son, Jeremy, Ma'am."

"Why do you need to speak to Jeremy? What has he done?"

"Can we come in, Ma'am?" The male officer asked.

"What is this about? Why do you need to talk to Jeremy?"

"Let us come in and we'll explain everything."

"Candy, who is it?" Her husband asked, his voice emerging from his study before he appeared moments later.

"It's the police, Frank, and they say they want to talk to Jeremy-"

"Talk to Jeremy? What do they want to talk to Jeremy about?"

"I don't know yet. I was just trying to-"

"Well, let them in Candy sugar, let them in."

She cringed, she hated the way he mockingly condescended and the way he never let her finish her sentences. He treated her like she was an 'eager-to-do-anything' farmer's daughter and he was a big-ole-banker about to foreclose on her daddy's land. He told her often that he wasn't to blame for her family's penury, that fate made her daddy poor and his daddy rich, and there was no sense crying 'bout it. He often joked in the presence of their wealthy guests that his floor was her ceiling and her cosmetically-enhanced looks and breasts were bought by him to do as he pleased. She forced a smile on her face, "You heard him. Please come in, officers," she told them and opened the door wider.

Seated on a love seat in the living room Candice watched as her husband beguiled the police officers. They had been in the house for ten minutes now, and Jeremy had not been summoned. He told them jokes about their boss and the times he had helped support the police charities and how his granddaddy had been a big-ole-police-man in Alabama. He offered them liquors from Paris that they couldn't pronounce, which they declined, then he told her to rustle up a plate or two of some refreshments for them, which they also declined.

The female officer coughed and the male officer cleared his

throat as if on cue, "Mr Buchanan, we need to talk to your son, Jeremy," he said.

"What about, officer? You sure I can't interest you in a drink now? You absolutely certain?"

"No thank you, Sir, we need to talk to Jeremy about some pictures he took of a young lady called Kelly Albright."

"Kelly Albright, I don't recall anyone with that name, Candy honey, you ever hear Jeremy talk about some gal named Kelly Albright before?"

"No, never," Candice replied, but she had spoken to a Kelly Albright several times on the phone and at Jeremy's insistence had told Kelly he was studying – she said nothing.

"Ma'am, is Jeremy at home?"

"Yes, he's upstairs in his room doing his homework-"

"What has this girl got to do with my son, officer?" Frank asked.

"Your son took pictures of this girl and put them on the internet, we need to talk to him right now," the female officer said, she stood up suddenly and walked to the door as if her spoken words reminded her why she was here.

"Candice go and get Jeremy down here," Frank told her.

"Jeremy, did you take these pictures?" The female officer asked as she held some pictures of Kelly up in front of him.

Jeremy looked at his dad. His dad looked away, "I don't think so, I . . . um, I . . ."

"Jeremy, don't look at him, look at me, son, did you take these pictures of Kelly Albright?" The male officer asked.

"I don't know, I don't remember taking them, maybe she took them and sent them to me, I don't know."

"These aren't self-taken pictures. Someone standing over Kelly took these pictures. Was that person you, Jeremy?" The male officer asked.

"I said, I don't remember taking them."

"Why is that, Jeremy? Is it because you've taken so many

semi-naked pictures of fourteen-year-old girls that Kelly is a blur?" The female officer asked.

"Don't answer that question, son, I'm calling my lawyer, this is harassment. He said he can't remember. He's a seventeen-year-old kid himself. He's a minor!"

"He's old enough to groom girls to take their tops off, Sir!"

Frank stood up, "You need to leave my house, officers, we don't have to put up with this. Do you know who we are? Do you know who I am?"

The female officer moved towards Jeremy and made to take hold of his arm when suddenly Candice Buchanan lunged forward and hit her in the face then grabbed hold of Jeremy and like a mother hen, pushed him behind her then shielded him with her body. She screamed at the female officer to get out of her house. Shocked by her sudden outburst no one moved for what seemed like several moments as they stared at her crazed face. Then everyone moved at the same time.

Jeremy grabbed the car keys on the table and tried to run.

The female officer grabbed Candice.

The male officer grabbed Jeremy.

Frank grabbed his drink.

"Everyone calm down," the female officer said, "Candice Buchanan, I'm arresting you for assault." She pulled out her handcuffs asked Candice to put her hands out in front of her and then bound her hands together with the handcuffs.

"What the hell are you doing?" Frank shouted.

"Your wife just hit a police officer, that's an offence," the male officer told him. He turned to his partner, "Take her into the other room and read her her rights. I'll deal with Jeremy."

The female officer marched Candice into the huge, immaculate kitchen and read her her rights as the male officer continued to question Jeremy.

"Please help me," Candice whispered. "Please help me, my children are upstairs, and he won't let me take them if I leave him. He has all the money, and everything is in his name. I'm sorry I hit you, officer, but something inside me snapped and I saw a chance I had to take. Jeremy's not a bad kid. His dad makes him take those pictures. That's the only way Jeremy gets any money from him. You have to arrest my husband. Jeremy gives him details about the girls, and my husband grooms them online, he blackmails them, and I think he may have met up with some of them at hotels."

The female officer looked at Candice, "Does he hit you?"

"Yes, he um . . . he looks at porn on the internet and has all these pictures of naked girls on his laptop. Some nights when he can't get an erection he gets frustrated and hits me. I tried to leave, but he won't let me take my children."

"Where are they exactly?"

"Upstairs in their room, they share a room . . . they're good boys."

"How old are they?"

"They're five-year-old twin boys, Clinton and Paxton. Please help me. I don't want him to do to them what he's done to Jeremy. I need you to lock Frank up and throw away the key, do something, anything to keep him away from us. I tried to be a good mother to Jeremy. His mom left Frank when Jeremy was ten and never came back. Frank is like poison. He controls Jeremy with money and gifts. You need to arrest Frank, but you can't let him know I told you anything or he'll use his money and power and take my boys away from me."

The female officer studied her for a few moments. She noted her shaking hands and the almost crazed desperate look in her eyes. "Okay, but to make it look legit, I'm gonna have to take you to the station and book you. Do you have anyone to corroborate your story and watch your kids for a few hours?"

Candice placed a shaking hand over her mouth as she held back a scream of relief. She quickly composed herself, "My cell phone is the pink one on the table in the other room. Call my mom, her number in on speed dial on my phone."

"Okay. Ready to go back in?"

"Yes, you'll call my mom right, no matter what I say in there, you'll call my mom? Please just tell me you'll call her no matter what!"

"I promise you I'll call her before we take you in."

"Thank you . . . thank you so much." She started to cry.

When they walked back into the living room, Jeremy was crying. The picture of Kelly, dead, taken in the hospital room in London was on the table next to him, and the male officer was looking at emails on Jeremy's laptop. Frank was on his cell phone telling his lawyer what was going on. He hung up when he saw Candice and the female police officer.

"Mr Buchanan, I'm taking your wife to the station, you need to come down with Jeremy-"

"Why can't Candice go with him? Y'all are heading in the same direction anyway."

"Because she's been arrested for assault and as you pointed out Jeremy is a minor, we can't question him without you being present."

"I'm sorry officers, I sure would like to help you out there, but I have two small children asleep upstairs, it's the maid's day off, I can't leave them alone and I sure as hell am not going to wake them up."

"Is there anyone I can call to watch them?"

"No, there isn't anyone you can call to watch my children."

The female officer picked up a cell phone, "Whose is this?" She asked.

"That belongs to my wife. You can't touch that."

"Well seeing as your wife is under arrest for assaulting me, I *can* touch this. Mrs Buchanan, is there anyone I can call to watch your children?"

"My mother," Candice replied not looking at her husband.

"On no, there is no way that old gospel preaching maniac is coming into my house, no way in hell!"

"Mrs Buchanan, can I call your mother to watch your

343

children?"

"My husband said no, so don't call her," she replied.

"That's damn right. I said no! Look, this here is my house, I pay the bills and what I say goes. I said no, so no it is!"

The female officer put the phone down and shrugged, "Well if you both say I can't call her then I won't."

Candice panicked. She tried desperately to control her sobs.

"My house and my rules," Frank said, smugly confident.

"That may be so, but this is how I see things, you have to come down to the station, you don't want to wake the other children so we don't have a choice." The female officer picked up Candice's phone, pressed some buttons and checked the contacts on speed dial. She pressed a button and spoke to the woman who answered then she hung up and put the phone down. "Your mother-in-law is on her way," she told a vexed Frank, "it's either that or I call Social Services and have your children sent to a foster home."

"Well, what do we have here?" The male office said as he opened one email after another and looked at the attachments.

"What is it?" The female officer asked.

"Looks like Jeremy here has been sending pictures of topless underage girls to daddy for a while. There's a picture of Kelly Albright here."

"I don't know anything about any emails!" Frank said.

"But Dad, you asked me to email-"

"Keep your mouth shut, don't say another word, Jeremy. Like I said, officers, I don't know anything about any emails or what my son has done."

The female officer looked at the confused, betrayed look on Jeremy's face and the look of self-preservation on his father's face. She knew Jeremy would talk if she made him scared enough. "Mr Buchanan, I'm arresting you for the possession of indecent pictures of minors and the assisted murder of Kelly Albright!" She told him.

"Murder!" Frank Buchanan squealed, "I didn't murder

anyone!" He moved towards the door.

The female officer pulled her gun out and aimed it at Frank, "Stop!" She shouted. "Stop or I will shoot you!"

He froze, "But I didn't murder anyone," he told her.

"Put your hands behind your head and lace your fingers, do it right now Mr Buchanan!"

He protested but complied, "I said I didn't murder anyone-"

"If a person is driven to suicide it is murder!" The female officer said.

"Dad, I'm scared, what do you want me to do?"

"Don't say anything, Jeremy-"

"I've had just about enough of this. You had better start talking Jeremy, or I will shoot your dad for resisting arrest!"

"Okay, okay, please don't shoot him, I took the pictures, he gives me money and stuff in exchange for them. Don't shoot! I'll tell you everything!"

"Backup is here," the male officer told her.

She lowered her gun, "Okay, read those two their rights and take them to the station. I'll wait with Mrs Buchanan for her mom to get here so she can hand her kids over then I'll bring her down to the station," she told her partner.

CHAPTER 78

Dylan - Orlando, Florida

Do you know what a dream-seller is?

No

I'm a dream-seller.

My name is Dylan, and I moved to Orlando a few months ago to make a new life for myself. I grew up in Essex, which, since the making of the TV show depicting fake tans, fake boobs and white teeth with nothing much else to offer, has put Essex on the map (not sure if that's a good thing, though). My twin brother Ryan was doing well as a Sales Rep for a company which supplied microbiology testing kits to microbiology laboratories back home, and I found myself drifting around doing one thing after another but not connecting with anything. My dad made a lot of money in the building trade, and we lived well, expensive house, several big cars, swimming pool, tennis court and a mammoth garden – we didn't have to keep up with the Joneses because we were the Joneses! My brother and I went to private schools and were supposed to be destined for big things. I remember my favourite teacher saying that Ryan had the gift of the gab, and he could sell snow to Eskimos and coats to keep them warm in the same transaction. I remember waiting for him to say something equally witty about me, something like *'Dylan you're going to change the World!'* or something like *'Dylan you're going to make a difference!'* But he never did. He didn't even look in my direction. Instead, he turned back to the board and continued the lesson. I remember trying to focus on my textbook and not let anyone know that I was hurt. I would have settled for a smile of encouragement if he felt there were no words he could spare me but for him to not even look at me when I worked so hard in his class hurt me. I wasn't jealous of my brother, but I couldn't understand why I worked so hard and never got any credit, yet he never did anything but loaf around, and he got all the praise. It wasn't just at school; it was the same at home. Our parents would tell him to be serious and work hard like me but then heap all the praise on him – how sick was that. Did they think that I didn't need any praise or encouragement? Didn't they think that the same thing that made Ryan shine was required to keep me shining? We are twins! Formed from the same egg! It made Ryan mad sometimes, and he would shout at our parents and tell them to treat us the same but the more he shouted and rebelled the more they seemed to pacify him with more praise and ignore me. One day I overheard my mother on the phone to her cousin, she said that she needed to pay more attention to Ryan because I was so much easier to deal with. I was malleable, and I always did what I was told. She said that I was lovely but bland, and Ryan was colourful so needed more attention. That made me mad. I started taking drugs soon afterwards. I initially justified it as being part of a coping mechanism but in fact, after some psychiatric interventions I soon found out it was a way of getting back at my parents for what I called their emotional neglect. I went to rehab so many times that I was there more than at home. I liked it there, the people there were encouraging, and they paid attention to me, they tried to break the hold the drugs had on me. They gave me weaker versions of the drugs to wean me off them, they talked to me and told me I had a future, and they coached me to want to reach for the best. I realised that being around my parents was my problem. It was like being in a cesspit in the middle of a drunken outdoor rave – I was constantly pissed on. I moved out of their house. My dad set me up in an apartment near town but then he and my mum came round every day to visit me. My dad would look around my apartment under the guise of helping me fix things, but I know he was looking around for drugs and that made me mad.

I saw the advert for dream-sellers in a local newspaper one

day. It said that successful candidates would be living and working in Orlando, Florida, the Sunshine State and all training would be given. I didn't think twice. It meant moving far away from my parents and their weird sense of love – I applied for the job that day and within weeks I was a dream-seller.

This is how dream-selling works, just for the record, I don't intend to hold anything back so to the faint hearted timeshare sellers who might get offended, look away now ☺.

I sell a week of residency in a five-star apartment, which is also viewed as a paradise home, to the poor or average. Don't get me wrong. Some well-off people have also bought from me, but they have the finances which attract 'Freebies'. Rich people are always getting free things that they can afford. My parents were typical examples. They got free flights, free clothes, free jewellery – all as part of a promotion deal of some sort but all free.

The apartments are gorgeous, and most of them well maintained – not all of them, though. People or 'targets' as I call them swarm to me and my co-workers like moths to a flame, lured by the promise of cheap amusement park tickets. They are supposed to do a tour, get fed cheap food and hopefully be blown away by the luxury of the apartments and the thought of owning something so beautiful, albeit, only for one week of the year. We are trained to try and get them to buy from us on the spot. We are trained to spurn out one sob story after another to get these people to buy our timeshares, people who probably had to save up for years just to come to Florida for a holiday. Some of the people from the UK tell us stories of having used their redundancy money or pension lump sum payout to pay for them and their families to come on a 'once-only' holiday of a lifetime. The aim is to get these people to part with a deposit of thousands of dollars as a down payment. Sometimes I think to myself that these people might not have thousands of dollars stashed away because they used all their savings just to get here and see Mickey Mouse! Some of the people might have to pay utility bills and car payments and feed themselves and their families and might not have an extra two hundred and fifty dollars to hand out each month to pay for a timeshare mortgage in Orlando. I don't know if my colleagues feel the same as most of them have their eyes focused on selling more and more and more and getting a new ring. You can tell the big sellers (who are usually old), by the amount of bling on their fingers. Somehow that much bling-bling on wrinkled old fingers looks vulgar and off-putting to me but to them, it's seen as a sign of prestige. Then you have the covetous young ones; the young female sellers, the eye-candy, who look like they're all hungry for a kill, and the 'Miami-Vice' looking young bucks who look like they're waiting to do a drug deal. Sell, sell sell, they're told because the more you sell, the bigger the ring you'll get, so buddy, sell, sell sell to the poor suckers. Don't give a damn that they might not be able to afford the timeshare, don't care that if they buy it, they might have to work until they are ninety-nine years old to pay for it and could drop dead the day after they retire.

For those 'targets' who were strong and able to resist the hard sell tactics, they sent in the old-timers who could barely walk. They were designed to make you feel that if you didn't buy a timeshare, you would deprive them of feeding their family or helping their grandkids and as a result personally send them to an early grave. The old-timers told you friendly stories and told you how they had a timeshare and how their whole family had benefited from it, how if it were put into a bottle it could be sold as a wonder drug. It was here that some of the hard-hearted 'targets' caved in and bought one of the dreams. It was here that some of the 'Owners', people who had purchased a dream in the past, were again targeted to buy another week or upgrade to acquire more bedrooms – get a bigger apartment.

Two things really irritated me about the whole process. The

first were the calculator people. Usually, a man because maybe they felt that women were unable to handle a calculator and it was all part of their sexist attitude, (women were mainly eye-candy). Anyway, these men went to a table the 'target' was at, introduced themselves then started banging away at the keys on their calculator as if their lives depended on it. They would write numbers down indicating how much you would pay and over how many years. They usually spoke over you and made you feel that you either had to be one of the dumbest people in the World for not buying a dream or one of the dumbest people in the World for having no ambition to want to own a dream. Either way, if you didn't succumb to them, you were too dumb for them to deal with you. If you didn't succumb to their calculator charms, they quickly exited leaving you feeling guilty, battered, bruised and vulnerable. Leaving you open to the second thing that irritated me – the ladies with the power (usually middle-aged ladies). These are the ladies who are supposed to stamp your form so that you can go down to the ticket area and pick up your cheap park tickets. Their job was like a TV-money lender's job, to reel you in, gut you and bleed you dry. Their aim was to get you to buy 'a fantastic', 'one-time-only-deal', 'an amazing offer' of three days and four nights of timeshare – nothing more and nothing less. They usually got the 'target' to buy something because by the time they came on the scene the 'target' just wanted to get out.

I always feel sorry for them, the 'targets'. They merrily walk around the cheap buffet bar in glee, happy in the free food they pack onto their plastic plates – always more than they can eat. Always food of no nutritional value whatsoever, they never seem to realise that they will pay for the food a thousand times over when they bought a dream (most of the 'targets' bought something, even the amusement park tickets they bought were overpriced). It always amazed me how the 'targets' quickly gave into the swing of things, how they would stop what they were doing when someone picked up the microphone and informed the room that another 'target' had just purchased a timeshare property. They would announce that the family blah blah of blah blah had just bought a week, and the other sellers were to remove that week off their inventory list. Then family blah blah of blah blah would be welcomed into the timeshare family, and the entire room would clap for the new family members.

I am a dream seller, and I hate myself for being one. Sometimes the only thing that gets me through the night are my drugs, and I hate that. I started mixing some toxic stuff with the drugs I take in the hope that one day I might not wake up, one day I might not hear the sound of the alarm clock in the morning. I spoke to Ryan yesterday, and I think that he sensed something was wrong with me. I could hear the concern in his voice, but I pretended I couldn't. If I told him how I felt about my work and the life I was living he would tell my parents and I'd have them all down here trying to take care of me but not listening to me - what's the point of that?

CHAPTER 79

Dylan Part 2

I did two things that ostracised me from my Orlando work buddies. The first thing I did happened at the movies. A group of us (a bunch of us as I'm often corrected here) were at the movies watching this film and in the middle there was a scene shot at a restaurant. The main characters were in focus having this major discussion, and there were loads of other people seated at tables all around them, background extras. Anyway, all these other people were talking to each other, and I wondered what they were talking about. I could see them in the background facing each other on various tables which were laden with plates indicating the different stages of their meals. Some people were moving their hands as they spoke, others were looking at each other and talking, and I wondered what they were all talking about and if they had their own scripts. It was a crucial part of the movie where the main characters were discussing something that was vital to the plot, something that would make sense of the one hour and five minutes we had already invested in watching the film. I thought I was only thinking it but I actually said it out loud, I said, *"I wonder what those people in the background are talking about? Do they have scripts that they're reading from or what? I mean come on how fake is that? Look at those two on the table in the corner. They probably can't stand each other!"* Apparently, I didn't just say those words I said them really loud. I said them so loud that everyone in the theatre heard me, turned and stared at me. And, Security came and escorted me out.

The second thing, according to my Orlando work buddies was even worse (I killed a sale). It involved a lady called Minzie Baxter who was just about to buy a three-bedroom timeshare property when I stopped her. Minzie was eighty-five years old and from Arizona. She had never been to Orlando and had saved up for thirty years just to get here. She was a widow and had worked in the same place since she was eighteen years old. She had married Stan Baxter, her high school sweetheart who had also worked in the same place all his life. One of the things Minzie and Stan had dreamed of was coming to Orlando. It was a dream they had for nearly thirty years but children, grandchildren and life happened and each year they told each other 'Maybe next year' or 'Definitely next year' and each year came and went with their dream being pushed into the next year until Stan died. The sad thing was, they could have come if they had really wanted to but it was like their dream was only real while they were dreaming and taking that step towards its manifestation would have left them 'dream-less' and given them nothing to look forward to. It was as if they lived in fear of their dream coming true and if it did come true, they would die. So each year they pushed it into the next year and then grabbed on to it and held it like a rope that helped them get through that year until the next year when they pushed it on again – it gave them something to live for, something to look forward too. 'Next year we're going to Florida!'

The 'unattainable life-chain', my dad called it and said it was a disease among the poor. They lived to dream, scared that if their dream came true, they would have nothing more to live for! He said the concept of getting another dream was not something poor people perceived.

Minzie reminded me of my grandmother. She had eyes that spoke of years of trusting. I came across her as Raoul, a calculator guy, was banging away on his calculator and churning out numbers and repayment plans and Minzie was looking at him with her big trusting eyes believing everything he told her. He was acting like he was some genius and kept on waving his hand with all his bling-bling on it as if he were trying to dazzle her or blind her, either way, he was doing his best to confuse her. I looked at Minzie and listened as Raoul talked about investing and a twenty-year repayment plan and I wondered how he could do this knowing that she probably wouldn't live for two more years and even if she did, she wouldn't be able to travel from Arizona to Orlando for much longer. So, when Raoul ran off to get some papers to clinch the deal, I sat next to Minzie and whispered in her ear that she shouldn't buy the timeshare because she couldn't afford it and that she shouldn't tie her money up in this but enjoy Orlando and go back home. She told me she loved my accent and that her great-grandfather had come from England on a ship that nearly sank while crossing the ocean. She listened to what I said and told me that she didn't really want to buy anything and just wanted the park tickets, but the nice young man had insisted that she buy something. She told me that she had told him several times that she didn't have any spare money, and he had told her that he could organise a loan for her and that her children and grandchildren would love her even more. Can you imagine the emotional blackmail these people use!

Long story short, Raoul came back with the papers and Minzie pointed at me and told him that the nice English man had told her not to buy anything, and she was going to listen to me because her great-grandfather had come from England. And that was it, two strikes and I was out! My timeshare buddies ostracised me. Would I do it again? The first thing, speaking during a movie, probably not but the second, telling an eighty-five-year-old widow not to buy a timeshare she'd probably never use – yes, I absolutely would!

So, ostracised, I had to plan my next move. I had no job, and no friends in Florida and I needed to make plans. I could go back home to England and die slowly under the suffocating watch of my parents, or I could die now and not put myself through the pain.

I started mixing more of the toxic stuff with the drugs hoping I will sleep myself away. I act like I don't care but the pain of the rejection I feel is deep down in my soul, and it's like its roots run too deep to destroy. I went to a church in Kissimmee yesterday and spoke to a man there who said he was an Assistant Pastor. He asked me to let him pray for me, and I said I didn't need his prayers.

What I don't understand is why I went there if I didn't need prayers – I'm getting confused nowadays. I just took six pills and some whisky ten minutes ago but when I was swallowing them it suddenly hit me that I took some pills less than an hour ago and did some cocaine then as well, or I think I did . . . I'm losing time. I can't remember things, and I'm feeling sleepy all of a sudden – can't sleep at night so better get some shut-eye now. Last night I had a dream about her and the words I said to her last week, I'll call her tomorrow. I should have let that man pray for me . . . who was he again? I need to lie down. I'm feeling woozy and sleepy . . . remember the words I said to her last week. I need to call her tomorrow . . . the words I said to her last week were, um. Why is the TV on? Why is the TV so loud? Was it so loud before? What were the words I said to her last week? I remember . . . I wrote them down somewhere, did I write them down or didn't I? I'll write them down now . . . . .

Two weeks later

The police had been called to the scene because neighbours had reported a weird smell that they described as clinging and pungent – one not familiar with this plush part of Orlando where some of the residents earned six-digit salaries. The police knocked on the door; they could hear the TV which was on and knocked louder. No one answered. Their office was in downtown Kissimmee, and they knew the smell well. They smashed the front door open and walked into the house. The smell of death claimed their nostrils completely.

One of the officers looked around the property while the other went to check the body. Next to the decomposing body, the officer saw a rectangular shaped, small piece of paper. He put on some latex gloves then picked the paper up, suspecting it to be a suicide note. He read the words written on it in what looked like shaky almost childish handwriting and frowned:

> *Your laugh – Arrested me*
> *Your giggle – Put me in jail*
> *Your smile – Threw away the key*

CHAPTER 80

Samantha walked through Heathrow airport confident that her life was about to change. Dylan had been found dead a few weeks ago, and she was not coping very well. Her parents had agreed for her to take a year out of university where she was studying English Literature and do another around-the-World 360 package work and travel holiday. They hoped that by doing this she would meet new people and get over Dylan, but more importantly she would live a real life and not the fairytale one spurred on by characters in the English Literature books she studied. They both knew that she was manic-depressive and although they didn't fully understand they didn't hide it like some parents. Far from it, they talked about it openly in public then tip-toed around her in private so that she wouldn't have one of her emotionally, at times violent, eruptive episodes.

"Our Sammy has bi-polar," her mother would say at the dining table to guests.

"Sammy is normal, she may act a little weird or despondent sometimes when she doesn't take her meds, but she's coming along," her dad would offer at a party.

Eyes would secretly fall on Samantha and wonder just how crazy and violent she was. Words were never spoken, but the looks said more than words ever could and Samantha hated it. She hated the sympathy she got from her parents, family and friends. She tried to tell people that she had been a little depressed years ago when she'd been bullied at school and instead of things being managed properly, she'd been put on anti-depressants and her Aunt Matilda's nerve-calming tea. If she had been given a bit of proper counselling, she would probably be right-as-rain now. Instead, she had been put on drugs (and tea) and only months later given counselling. So, to cope with things she created a persona of perfection which she used to fool everyone.

Everyone that is apart from Dylan, he got her. From their first meeting they clicked. He saw beneath the facade of the perfect person she had erected, and he wanted to be with her. Now, he was dead, and she saw the long road she had to travel and felt that she couldn't go it alone. She had phoned some bereavement organisations and asked for help but after describing her feelings, the help they offered involved them talking to her parents. Which, she figured would include her parents talking to her doctor and her doctor talking to a psychiatric counsellor who might section her – so she hung up each time and didn't call them back. Instead, she started visiting websites looking for help. It was in a chat room that she started talking to Jessica Carmichael (Jessy James 6) and Kelly Albright (KeLi) – she didn't know their real names. What she did know was that they understood her and seemed to care about her.

They chatted for weeks and arranged to meet in London. Travel arrangements got expedited when she found out that Jessy James 6 was being treated (as an outpatient) in a hospital. She knew that things were meant to be when she changed some of the dates of her work and travel holiday, and KeLi was able to come on an earlier student exchange holiday. Samantha was sure that the signs were everywhere telling her that she should meet up with her two new best friends. (She had to pay 500 Australian dollars to make the changes to her travelling arrangements, and KeLi had missed her flight but was able to catch a later flight and still get to London twenty minutes before she did). She saw everything that was thrown at them to prevent them meeting as signs that they should meet – as a unique language which the stars spoke.

The Meeting
On the pretence of needing to go to the bathroom, KeLi had slipped away from her travel group at the airport and located Samantha at the luggage carousel as agreed.

Jessy James 6 was waiting for them in Arrivals. She had cards with their online names on in her hands as she jumped up and down, excited to see them.

Just before they headed to the underground KeLi's phone rang. It was her mother checking to make sure she had arrived safely and she was feeling okay.

On the train, KeLi talked about Jeremy Buchanan and how he had made her depressed and her life miserable. Both Jessy James 6 and Samantha listened. Samantha told them about Dylan and how his death had left her distraught and gasping for air, which was sparse, stale and lifeless. And, Jessy James 6 told them that she wasn't Jessy James 6.

<u>CHAPTER 81</u>

The Tenth Person

Shane Nelson read once that thousands of children under the age of 10 were depressed. He asked his mother why this was, and she said it was because they didn't think of anyone else but themselves. That these children were being raised not to care about anyone but just what they could get from everyone and when they couldn't get something they became depressed. She said in her day she had one doll and a few colouring books when she was his age, and she was happy with her lot. Shane wasn't sure if he was depressed, he knew he got things his brothers and sisters didn't get, but he was unhappy. His father gave him everything and the rest of the family nothing. He knew his brothers and sisters hated him, and his mother was always scared. He was torn, he loved his mother, but he also loved his father. He had tried to hate his father for his siblings' sake but found he couldn't. His home was a time-bomb, and he hated living there. The only thing that made him happy now was talking to Jessy James 6 online.

On The Day Of The Suicide Pact
Shane had tried to get away from his brothers and sisters earlier but for some reason, they kept watching him. They made him go on the roof with them, and they shared their chicken and chips with him – something they had never done in the past. In the past they usually relegated him to wherever they were not, it didn't matter where; he was 'Daddy's favourite' and a snitch, as such he was the enemy.

Robbie, Shane's eldest brother, gave him some money and asked him to get two bottles of cola from the local shop as there was a 'buy one get one free' offer there. Robbie wanted to smoke and didn't want Shane to see him and take that information back to his father. Eager to leave, Shane took the money and left his siblings on the roof.

Shane Nelson ran as fast as he could with Robbie's money in his hand. Jessy James 6 had given him specific directions to where she was in the hospital, and he was determined to get there on time. He had never ventured further than his school, which was less than a ten-minute slow walk from his home, by himself before but today he was going to get to the hospital using the map on his phone for directions.

Shane walked through the hospital reception without being stopped by anyone. Jessy James 6 had said that security wasn't that tight. He walked right to the back of the ground floor and took the lift to the third floor following the instructions she had sent him. He saw an Indian girl looking at a notice board for directions then he saw her walk with confidence towards the direction of Livingston Ward. Shane waited a few moments then followed her.

As soon as he walked into the room on Livingston Ward, he noticed that there were more people that he thought there would be. Suddenly he felt scared and wanted to leave. He felt something in his hand and looked down. It was Robbie's money. He put it in his pocket. He looked around gingerly; the Indian girl he had seen earlier was writhing on the ground, an empty cup next to her. Jessy James 6 handed him a cup. He looked at her cold eyes and thought that she looked different from how he had imagined her. Shane took the cup and was about to drink from it when he saw the reflection of a man in the mirror on the wall. The man was hiding behind the dark, floor-length window curtain. He had his hand around a young girl's mouth, and she was struggling against him. Someone knocked the cup out of Shane's hand, or the cup slipped, he wasn't sure which. A boy grabbed him and told him to run away. He looked up at the boy who was pushing him out of the room then turned and quickly ran out of the room.

On exiting the hospital, Shane ran as fast as he could away from the hospital. He ran across Kings Road and was nearly hit by a double-decker bus. He ran towards the River Thames and stood midway on Battersea Bridge looking down at the murky river below. He ignored the joggers, the dog walkers and the pedestrians who passed him. He was afraid to go home and even more afraid to return to the hospital. His mind was twirling, and he wanted to go back and help the boy who had helped him and help the girl who he had seen in the corner with the man holding a hand over her mouth but he was scared. He had to do something, but he didn't know what. He pulled out his phone and stared at it then pressed 999 and told the police to get to the hospital. He refused to give them his name or his address but told them to send urgent help to the Livingston Ward to save the children then ended the call and turned his phone off.

It was cold and dark. Shane climbed over the railing of the bridge and stood looking down at the murky waters beneath him. He was about to jump when he heard a voice telling him not to do it . . .

Hours later when Shane got home the police (who had traced his phone) and social services (who the police had called) had been and gone. Cold and scared, he rang the bell and waited.

Robbie opened the door and as soon as he saw Shane he grabbed him and hugged him tightly. "They said you might be dead, Shane, that you went to the hospital to kill yourself. Mum fainted, and Siobhan has been screaming and crying for hours. The others are all upset. Sure we tease you and pick on you cos Dad likes you best, but it doesn't mean we don't love you." Robbie started to cry.

"Robbie, Luv, who was that at the door?" His mother asked her voice hoarse from crying for her 'missing, presumed dead' last born child. Robbie turned, and she saw Shane. She screamed and fell to the ground crying and beating her chest as she thanked God that her son was alive. She opened her arms and gathered Shane to her. Her trembling hands touched his face, his arms and his legs; making sure that he was real.

She was determined that she would keep her children closer more than ever now that Murray had been arrested for fencing stolen property (she had given all the evidence she'd secretly stashed away over the years to the police). She had also, finally, taken out a restraining order against Murray and pressed charges against him for domestic abuse. He couldn't come near the family unless he got help for his post-traumatic stress disorder caused by his time in the army. Social Services had arranged counselling sessions for the whole family, and they were to be re-housed with immediate effect.

"Shane, I love you so much, how could you think that I could go on living a normal life without you? How could you think that Shane? I love you so much. I love all of my children. I love all of you so much. I can't lose any of you."

"Shane's home, Shane's home!" Robbie called out to his other siblings.

Siobhan rushed into the hall as did the other children. They saw their mother and Shane and hugged them. They cried tears of disbelief that their baby brother had wanted to die and tears of relief that he was alive.

CHAPTER 82

"Danielle is nice."
"Danielle is a good girl."
"Danielle will go far."
"Danielle is so pretty."

I've listened to those words and words similar to them for years, and they make me sick. If I was so perfect why did my dad abandon me when I was five years old? Why did he walk out on my mother, my brother and me and go and shack up with that rich posh bitch, Eloise? 'My name is Lady Eloise, but you may call me Aunt Eloise', were her first words to me when we met. I thought of some things I would like to call her but just smiled and let her kiss my cheek. It used to make me laugh when Eloise would tell Jessica to be more like me, nice-good-an achiever-and pretty. I used to think that Jessica shouldn't even be here, that, if my dad hadn't gotten Eloise pregnant during their sordid affair then he would still be married to my mum, and Jessica Carmichael wouldn't exist.

It was actually Eloise dearest who gave me the idea about forming the suicide pact thing. Well, she didn't actually say to me 'Danielle, go out and set up sites and chat rooms online that people will visit and end up wanting to kill themselves!' What she did was encourage Jessica to be more like me and that gave me the idea to pretend to be Jessica online. I got her to set up some sites because I convinced her that she was depressed and that her mother was a nymphomaniac drunk (actually that part is true), I convinced Jessica that she needed to connect with like-minded people who self-harmed and wanted to die. Jessica was so gullible. She was going through the normal hormonal stuff teenagers with no Godly guidance or parental intercessory prayer go through. Things like - mood swings, being lethargic, feeling unloved and feeling depressed. But, I was able to convince her that her issues were mega-serious. I would sneak alcohol into her room when I visited and pretended to get drunk with her, and when she passed out, I would log onto her computer and chat online and make her think that she had done it while she was drunk. I forged a close friendship with Jessica that a lot of people couldn't understand. When Ryan and I dated he found it strange that no one voiced the obvious where Jessica was concerned – My dad had once been married to my mum and had abandoned his family to shack up with Jessica's mum and produce the spoilt brat that was Jessica. And I the 'abandonee' child (as he called me) was trying to play happy families with the 'usurper' child.

Even my mum wasn't happy that I visited Jessica. She had remarried years ago, and my brother and I had taken my stepdad's surname as we both thought that he was more of a father to us than our real dad. My mum was happy when I got a place in a university outside London, and she had no idea that I visited Jessica when her parents were out – it was Jessica's and my secret. Sometimes I would visit when her parents were in – hide in her bedroom where we plotted, planned and drank in secret – and they never knew I was there, they thought she was talking to herself. Eloise or Dad would knock on her door, and she would unlock it and open it with me hiding behind it and talk to them as they secretly scanned the room. She never invited them in and for some reason, they never insisted on coming in or were too scared to come in – it was priceless.

Why do people, especially teenagers, so readily believe lies? I visited one of those demon-worship-type websites one day. The site displayed evil paraphernalia like skulls, bones, knives, dripping blood, death signs and strange words like UREDM and EDICUS on its main page. I remember it had this flashing sign asking if people wanted to make easy money. It said all we had to do was set up a website using their server (and promoting them) and get people to log on to it using one of three symbols they would issue. They would pay handsomely for everyone we got to log on to the website. Once a person visited the site the host site would have access to that person's online accounts and be able to bombard them with evil-depressing addictive information (I didn't bother to find out what this information was). The host site sent me three symbols:

∞ - the infinity symbol

Ω - the end symbol

Θ - the death symbol

Armed with these symbols I quickly set up my site, and I started telling lies online, and people bought into my lies. I would say I was depressed, or people didn't understand me or I was being bullied. Or I had just broken up with my boyfriend. Or I had just broken up with my girlfriend. Or I enjoyed self-harming, or I was bulimic, or I was anorexic. Or I was hopeless, guilty, angry, unloved, worthless, irritable, had warring parents going through a divorce, had warring parents already divorced or my family wanted to marry me off to someone I didn't know. Or everyone hated me, or I was homeless and unloved, or I was suicidal. It was so easy to connect with people when I told these lies and the more lies I told, the more people I connected with and the more money I made. I will never know why it is that when you want to talk about good things no one wants to listen but tell someone you're depressed, or suicidal, and you have their full attention.

Synopsis of a true story – A young man wanted to get married but only had one eye so none of the available young girls wanted to marry him. Crying he goes to his mother and tells her that no one wants to marry him because he has one eye. He asks her why he only has one eye (not clear why he waited that long to ask – that part was never told). Anyway, he goes to his mother and asks her why he only has one eye. The mother looks at her crying son and tells him that when he was a little toddler, he wanted to play with a dangerous toy that had a sharp pointy bit, and she had said no and hidden it. He cried and cried for it, and she gave in and gave it to him. He was running around with the toy in his hand and fell. The toy poked out his eye, and this is why he only has one eye. I kid you not. That was the story she told him! On hearing the story, the man said that his mother should have taken control and never have given him the toy. That at most he would have cried for a while and forgotten about the toy, now, because he only has one eye, no one wanted to marry him, and he would cry for the rest of his life. Wow, what a story. The moral of the story, parents, is, Take Control - Step Up And Be Parents! You pay the bills, so check what your kids are doing online and throw out the computers and mobile phones if you have to! They may cry or moan, but they'll thank you one day! That way they won't end up talking to someone like me and reading the lies I and my demonic friends put out there to steal their souls. The soul is the single most valuable asset a person has, and it really is all about getting souls you know. There are demons and evil spirits out there trying to kill, steal and destroy, and they tell me that the harvest is ripe because people don't pray anymore. People have left the security of God's shelter and live God-free lives. The demons laugh at the stupidity of unbelieving human beings. They call them names, they say *if only they knew the secret, if only people would search God's Word, the Bible, they would see that all they had to do was repent and stop sinning, let God be the centre of their lives and truly believe. God loves them, but they live in ignorance, doubt and unbelief, limiting God, instead of accepting the Truth they believe our lies! They focus on how big their problems are instead of telling their problems how big JEHOVA JIRA, The Provider, the One True God is.*

We say things like:

It will be better if you leave this World – Lie!

If you kill yourself, the pain will stop – Lie!

This problem is so big nothing will solve it – Big Fat Lie!

Parents, a word in your ears, this is something I heard once –

It's not just what you leave for your children that really counts, it's what you leave in them! Teach your children to value life – theirs and other peoples!

Apologies for digressing. So, I set up several suicide chat rooms and got Jessica to be one of the main participants. I convinced her that she would be better off dead, and she believed me. Just like all the others, I convinced online. Kelly started talking to me when she was in America and mentioned that she would be in London, and I arranged to meet her at Heathrow Airport. Samantha was a lost soul. Everything was stopping her from coming to London when she did but did she listen? No, she kept pushing and pushing to come and end her life. She paid out more money to change her plans so that she could meet Kelly at the airport and I could meet them. I had to say that I was an outpatient because Kelly wanted to know how I could meet them at the airport if I was admitted to the hospital. Samantha never bothered to ask any important questions, even though she was older than Kelly.

It was weird watching Jessica read emails and chat room conversations then proudly show them to me claiming she wrote them, with my knowing that she didn't, because I did. A bit like telling a joke with all the fanfare, as if it's yours, to the person who shared the joke with you in the first place – very weird.

By the time my dad realised the kind of person Eloise was, Jessica had been born and my mum remarried so he couldn't get mum back. My brother wanted nothing to do with him so I was the one who got all his attention and I hated him for too much too late. I wanted to destroy what had destroyed my family – that's the reason I did it.

I stole the pills. I mixed the pills with the chemicals and orange juice, and I poured the poison into ten cups because nine other people were expected. I set up fifty suicide pact groups all over the UK, and Jessica's group was scheduled to be the crash before the explosion. Elle was never meant to be part of the suicide pact. She was collateral damage. I didn't know that Jessica had sent Elle text messages (what was Jessica thinking?), it's not like she didn't know the suicide pact was taking place that day. I can only assume that she wanted to say goodbye to Elle in that bizarre sick way of hers.

I poured the poison into the ten cups. I made sure Jessica's cup had the most in it. One person was missing, but I decided to go ahead, and he could have his when he turned up. Jessica gulped hers down in seconds and the others followed suit. I don't know how my dad figured things out. I saw him rush into the room. His face looked torn, and I waited to see which of his daughters he loved the most. He rushed over to Jessica, but she was already dead. Then things happened fast. Elle came in. My dad had his back to her, and she didn't seem to see me. I saw her in the mirror and turned away. I watched as she looked at the people in the room who were either dead or dying, she was about to scream when my dad hit her then grabbed her from behind and held his hand over her mouth. He pulled her over to the window and hid there. A small boy came in, and I gave him a cup, he was about to drink the contents when an older boy rushed in and knocked the cup out of his hand then told him to run. My dad hit the older boy on the head from behind with something, and he fell to the ground hard. Elle seemed to have fainted, and dad poured the remaining poison from the bottle I had mixed it up in, into her mouth and made sure she swallowed it. I grabbed the empty bottle and ran out of the room and went home leaving my dad in the room with the dead bodies, one of which was the child he should never have had.

*

Inspector Kelleher looked through the one-way glass at Danielle who seemed to be staring at the wall opposite her. He turned to Dr Geeta Singh, a Psychiatric Consultant who worked with TTS as a counsellor. "Any change?" He asked.

"No, she's still just sitting there," Geeta replied.

"Did she say anything about the suicide pact?"

"No, not a word, it's as if . . . as if she is . . . " Geeta paused.

"As if what, Dr Singh?"

"From her facial expressions, her smiles and frowns it's as if she's staring at a screen and watching her life play before her. I've seen people do this before, just sit and stare at the wall in front of them like that, living and reliving their lives moment by moment as a means of disassociating themselves from their current environment. It's almost like how people were trained to beat the lie-detector tests, by focusing their minds on other things that really happened and remaining calm."

"Has she said anything about her mother and brother yet?"

"No, but I think she still believes they're alive, she talks about them in the present tense. Twice while I was talking to her, she said that she was waiting for a call from her mother, and she said that her brother hates her father and wouldn't have anything to do with Jessica when she was alive."

"I've listened to your sessions with her. How come she is clear about Jessica being dead but not about her mother, brother and step-dad being dead?"

"I think she has a form of suppressed death-disassociation syndrome, somewhere in the depths of her mind she has managed to keep the people she loves alive but realises that Jessica and the others are dead. I've never come across this before, and I've sent an email to a colleague of mine who deals with death-disassociation syndromes to see if he can shed some light. I can't help feeling that Danielle's is selective."

"You think she's faking it?"

"I'm not sure. Her mother, brother and step-dad died in a car accident recently, and I think that she blames her father for this. She feels that if her father hadn't abandoned them, her mother and brother would both be alive. Some studies have shown that when a person hates and fails to forgive tormentors are released into them. Other studies have shown that when a person hates and is unable to forgive they are a good candidate for murder or suicide. Danielle, however, is complicated, she is unable to kill herself so has directed her suicidal thoughts to the murder of others-"

"Including Jessica!"

"No, especially Jessica. Jessica is the catalyst in all of this!"

"Her father has told us everything."

Dr Singh looked at Danielle, "I suspect that's only everything he knows, and there are a lot of unanswered questions in his mind. I spoke to him earlier, and he has expressed a lot of guilt. I think that he might try and take the blame for her."

"Anna still thinks there are other websites we haven't found, and I need Danielle to open up and tell me where they are."

"She's a tricky character. I don't know if she'll do that."

He studied Danielle through the glass, "Can I borrow your computer Doctor?"

"Sure," she handed him her tablet computer.

Inspector Kelleher walked into the room, seemly distracted by what he was searching for on the computer in his hand. His mobile phone and some papers were tucked under his arm. He noticed Danielle didn't turn to him or acknowledge him; she continued to stare at the wall. He pulled up a website and placed the computer on the table, asked her if she wanted a drink, waited for her to respond and when she didn't, told her he was going to get one for himself then left.

Danielle saw the man come in but pretended that she didn't see him. She stared at the wall in front of her and embedded herself in her 'happy' memories. Moments later she saw the man put the computer on the table, heard him say something which she ignored then saw him leave. She frowned when she saw that he hadn't taken the computer, her frown deepened when she saw that he had left his mobile phone hidden under the papers on a table by the door. 'He must think I'm stupid', she thought to herself. 'If he thinks I'm going to tell him anything then he must think I'm really stupid!' She looked at the clock on the wall and smiled. It was nearly midnight and soon the next set of suicides would take place. She looked at the computer on the table and frowned, one of her sites was on the screen. The screen went dark, and she quickly reached out and moved the computer closer and touched the screen – it jumped back to life. She read that her site had been shut down, and she smiled at the stupidity of the so-called investigators. They knew nothing about technology; if they did they would know that the site they shut was a dummy site. They would also know if they were smart that she would never let them trap her by getting her to log onto anything from the computer which could be traced. She looked around the room to make sure there were no hidden cameras. The walls were all white plaster so she knew that there couldn't be a one-way glass system in place (she had no idea that one of the plastered walls was fake and really was a one-way glass, and there were several concealed cameras in the room recording her every move). She got up and moved quickly to the phone, she pressed the button on the side and smiled when she saw that there was no password and the phone, an Android, was ready to use just by touching the screen. She logged onto the internet and then onto the mainframe of her sites and entered a code to open up all the firewalls and activate her suicide chat rooms. 'Those kids are going to be dropping like flies,' she thought as she entered a chain of commands instructing the readers what to do and when. Finished, she carefully logged out of the chat rooms and put the firewalls back in place. She turned the screen off and left the phone exactly where she had found it. She sat down and stared at the wall in front of her.

The man walked in with two cups and placed one next to her then sat down. Moments later she saw that the man was still sitting there, she took a deep breath, "What do you want?

What did you hope to achieve by coming in here?"

"A confession would be nice, Danielle."

She studied him coldly for a few moments. "Okay, I did it. I arranged everything because I wanted Jessica and her mother to pay for making my dad abandon me when I was five."

"No remorse?"

"Should I have any?"

"Nine people are dead Danielle! Your father tried to cover up your crime and tried to kill two innocent children. You'd have to be a dangerous sociopath to show no remorse."

"You know, when you put it like that and when I think about everything, I have absolutely no remorse."

"Why?"

"Because I'm a product of my environment."

"What?"

"People always blame Frankenstein, but the real monster was the doctor who made him. Frankenstein, like me, was the product of someone else's messed up actions!" She looked at him with cold, dead eyes then turned back to the wall – and as if watching her life play before her on a screen, smiled.

Deep in thought Inspector Kelleher headed towards the main incident room. Genny came rushing out, she saw him and pulled him along with her as she quickly strode with some police officers.

"Now I know why Inspector James wanted you to run things. You're not just handsome you're pretty smart as well. It worked, by getting Danielle to log onto her site using your phone with the computer in the room we were able to locate her mainframe computer, hack open her firewalls and find all the other computer users who were logged on and waiting for her to give them the green light. Excellent work."

"So you think I'm handsome?"

Genny stumbled. She quickly corrected herself, "That's all

you heard? Really?"

He smiled, "I have this thing where I hear important things, like me being handsome, first."

"Oh, I get it, that was one of the jokes you promised to tell me," she increased her pace, and he had to walk fast to keep up. "So, tell me how did you know she would go for the phone and not the computer?"

"She thinks she's smart, and everyone else is stupid, sometimes you have to think like the criminals to solve the crime and catch them."

"Good thinking, Batman, it worked."

"Where are we going?"

"A group of children who logged into one of Danielle's chat rooms have been located by the assisted GPS system picking up signals from their mobile phones. They're all at a single location, a warehouse in East London. Cars are waiting downstairs, and Police Commissioner Pike has insisted that all the children be apprehended safely and brought in for questioning and counselling. Anna and Peter are getting some more counsellors organised. Tristan is working with Inspector James and Dr Chang Lin on finding the locations of any more suicide pacts and Police Commissioner Pike is bellowing out orders so I thought we could get over to the warehouse."

"Good thinking, Robin," he jogged ahead of her. "You need to take it up a gear slowcoach, look alive, put some grease in your cogs and move it, we have urgent business to see to," he said and smiled.

CHAPTER 83

The following Day

Inspector Kelleher, Anna, Dr Steve Truman, Clarissa and Ruth sat in the back of the government vehicle as it sped towards the Houses of Parliament. TTS was now viral, but they still had to convince the lawmakers of the United Kingdom that national laws had to change to validate TTS.

They passed through security checks and were each issued with a 'Visitors' badge, instructed that it must remain visible at all times then escorted to a waiting room.

Born and bred in London, Clarissa had only ever driven past the Houses of Parliament and Big Ben; she had never been inside until today. She was nervous and once inside the waiting room, promptly excused herself and went to get some fresh air. Clarissa paused for a moment and looked around the large hall which was Westminster Hall, where monarchs had laid in state and where Winston Churchill had been laid in state. She wandered around. She looked at some of the brass plaques set into the floor. She read a leaflet which said that Westminster Hall was still used for ceremonial events today, and it was here that the Queen had addressed both the House of Commons and the House of Lords and the hall had been used for meetings with Nelson Mandela and President Obama in the past.

"Excuse me, Madam, are you okay?" A man asked her.

She turned and smiled nervously at him and immediately noticed how immaculately dressed he was and the large gold emblem hanging from a chain around his neck. "I'm fine, thank you. I needed to get some fresh air and get my thoughts together for a meeting."

"I know who you are, can I say that I am proud to be able to talk to you. I read about what you did to save your daughter's life, and how you fought for the truth, I wish more parents were like you."

Tears flooded Clarissa's eyes, "Thank you."

"My Mrs said if you hadn't fought to save Elle then insisted the police investigate things other children could have died. How is Elle doing?"

"She's doing great. I left her eating a huge triple chocolate chip muffin."

He smiled. "Glad to hear that, I'm on a well-earned break, do you want me to give you a quick tour of the place?"

"That would be nice, thank you. What do you do here and why are you wearing that huge gold thing around your neck?"

"I'm a messenger here and get to wear this 14 carat gold emblem to signify that. My dad was a dustbin man, he worked for the City for 25 years and never once stepped foot in here. And here I am working in the Houses of Parliament. To think, the son of a dustbin man from East London working in the Houses of Parliament and wearing this. He must be looking down from Heaven and shaking his head in amusement."

"Your dad would be very proud of you, I know I would," Clarissa told him.

He blushed and nodded his head, knowing that his dad would be over the moon. He cleared his throat, "This is one of the most famous buildings in the United Kingdom. It used to be a palace that housed kings and queens, the Palace of Westminster it was known as back then. It was granted to the politicians as a permanent home in 1550." He told her that the word parliament was derived from the French word 'parler', which meant 'to talk'. He told her that Big Ben, as it was fondly called, was actually the Elizabeth Tower and people could go on tours inside Big Ben where they would get to climb the 334 steps to the top. He showed her St Stephen's Hall and told her that it used to be St Stephen's Chapel, where monarchs and their families worshipped when they stayed at the palace in the old days. He talked about the statues which lined either side of St Stephen's Hall and about the murals which were on the walls. Passion and pride emitted from him and engulfed Clarissa. It made her proud to be British and share this history with him. He took her to the Chapel of St Mary in the undercroft and told her that it was here that members met and said prayers in the morning and even though there was a lot of diversity of faiths among members, the Houses of Parliament were established on Christian foundations. Clarissa looked around the chapel and took in its beauty. They both heard heavy footsteps coming down the steps leading to the chapel and turned.

"They're ready for you now, Mrs Williams," a doorkeeper said.

CHAPTER 84

"The children drank a mixture of hospital drugs, potent cleaning chemicals and orange juice. The result was that their internal organs dissolved within minutes and they must have died in excruciating pain," Dr Steve Truman told the members of parliament.

"How did they get hold of these drugs and chemicals?" A member asked.

"We believe that they were stolen," Inspector Kelleher answered.

"We think that this whole unfortunate matter is something that should never have happened but what you are asking will impinge on the freedom of speech laws and we have come a long way and don't want to go backwards," another member said.

"We're not asking that you go backwards. What we're asking is that things are monitored more stringently," Anna insisted passionately. "We want trolls arrested. We want every bully, every bigot, every racist who uses abusive or racist language to intimidate or insult anyone online to have their account closed immediately and their details handed to the police so that they are monitored. If the host site fails to close these accounts because of advertising or for whatever reason they may have, then they get hit with a minimum of a £20,000 on the spot fine. We want all self-harming sites and suicide sites closed immediately!"

"And I would like World Peace, Mrs Lewis, but it doesn't mean that I'm going to get it now does it," an elderly member said dismissively.

"My daughter, Elle, could have died, her friend and eight other children died. Because of TTS going viral, the other suicide pacts which should have taken place today were stopped. In less than four hours of TTS going live, hundreds of calls have come in from vulnerable children asking for help.

When are you, the lawmakers of this country, going to help them? If the 'freedom of speech' law supersedes the law of common decency and love, then our children have no hope. My daughter could have died, don't you get it-" she stopped unable to contain her emotions.

Ruth stood up and walked to a whiteboard; she drew two symbols on the board and looked at them for a few moments, "These two symbols stand for the word 'Crisis' in Chinese. These symbols are two words joined, the word 'Disaster or Danger' and the word 'Opportunity'. There is a crisis happening in this country and some other countries in the World! The disaster is that young people are living without hope and they can't or won't take charge of things unless they see that we - the adults - are fighting in their corner. This is an opportunity for you to do something and stop this senseless taking of one's own life! Put these new laws into place immediately and keep them there. We already have the support of millions of people including several World leaders, actors, athletes, musicians, singers and teenagers." Pictures of thousands of people carrying Talk To Someone placards appeared on the screen. "Give us your support, gentlemen, help us to stop this crisis!"

Inspector Kelleher's phone vibrated, he read the email and opened the attachment then got up and said something to Ruth. He asked for the lights to go down and linked his phone to the computer. Suddenly images appeared on the walls, pictures of young children and teenagers and messages they had either read or sent online in previous weeks.

The silence was interrupted by gasps and exclamations which filled the air followed by outbursts.

"That's my granddaughter's picture, where did you get that? Why did she visit that suicide chat room?" A member said.

"That's my daughter's picture. That's her online account! Isn't that a self-harming site?" Another member said as he stood up and pointed at the screen.

"That's my grandson, how the hell did you get access to that?" The dismissive elderly member said. "Why did he log into that suicide chat room? My grandson isn't suicidal. He's only twelve and his parents give him everything!"

New laws were introduced immediately, and TTS was not only live, but it was also legal and validated and ready to flood every receptive country in the World!

*

"How did you get all that information?" Ruth asked as they drove away from the Houses of Parliament.

"Genny hacked into some personal files," Inspector Kelleher replied.

"But I thought it was illegal to hack into government files."

"It is but she didn't hack into government files. I sent her a list of names of the MPs we were meeting with today and she traced their families and hacked into the accounts of their children and grandchildren to see if any of them had previously visited any suicide or self-harming sites. It was a long-shot, we weren't sure we would get any hits but looks like we got lucky."

"It's true what they say," Clarissa said, "most people will move heaven and earth to protect their own!"

CHAPTER 85

Two Weeks Later

Ruth laughed as she listened to Elle tell her about New York and how 'eye-bulgingly' big the muffins were. She heard Maddy and Josh laughing in the background and Steve and Madeline telling them to be careful and not get too close to the horses – they were in Central Park. Clarissa came on the phone and told her to tell Bryson she had got him both the *Nets* and the *Knicks* jerseys that he wanted. Clarissa also told her how many teenagers TTS had helped so far and how the numbers were growing daily and also that Anna had said that Ruth shouldn't forget what they talked about in the police car that night. Ruth smiled - she had completely forgotten that conversation.

"Bryson, Jermaine, can I speak to you for a moment?" Ruth asked her sons.

"What's up, Mom?" Bryson asked.

"Your dad and I want to talk to you, come into the den and sit down."

"This isn't about the birds and the bees, is it? We covered that topic years ago at school, and Dad tried to talk to us a couple of years ago and ended up confused," Bryson joked as they followed Ruth into the den. He ducked as the cushion his father threw at him sailed past his head.

"Dave, stop that," Ruth jokingly warned.

"I wasn't confused, I was trying to explain things, and you guys kept asking unnecessary questions," Dave said.

"Okay, a lot has happened recently, and it's occurred to me that we tell you guys to tell us everything that's going on and sometimes you don't realise that we went through what you guys are going through once upon a time. We didn't just pop up one day on this planet as Mom and Dad, we were young once, we had fears, secrets, good times and bad times."

"Did I do something wrong?" Jermaine asked.

"Yeah, did Jermaine do something wrong again?" Bryson asked.

"You know you could have done something wrong, Bryson," Jermaine said.

"Boys, hush, listen. I want to tell you something about me when I was growing up. I was about nine years old, and we were staying in North London one summer, and I didn't know anyone. One evening my mom sent me out to buy something from one of the local shops and on my way back home I met a group of kids and we talked for a few minutes then I went home. The next day about six in the evening there's a knock on the door. We were just about to sit down and eat dinner so my dad went to answer the door. I heard some voices and went to stand just out of sight by the sitting room door," she paused.

"Who was it?" Bryson asked.

"It was the group of kids I met the day before."

"What did they want?" Jermaine asked.

"They came round to ask if I could come out to play with them," she smiled as she recalled that day.

"What happened? Why are you smiling like that?" Dave asked.

"They asked my dad if Sonia could come out to play with them."

"Who's Sonia?" Dave asked.

Ruth pointed at herself, "Me, when I met those kids the day before I told them my name was Sonia."

"Is Sonia one of your names?" Bryson asked.

"No, it isn't."

"I don't get it, why did you tell them your name was Sonia if it isn't?" Jermaine asked.

"When I was young I hated my name. It was a big deal for me because I didn't want to be called Ruth and it made me really angry and sad and sometimes I would get depressed and moody and, not being able to explain why I was sad, I would blame it on my name. I thought it was old-fashioned and not cool. Everyone was either Sandra or Maxine or Jackie or Janet, and I didn't know anyone called Ruth."

"Did you know anyone called Sonia?" Jermaine asked.

Ruth frowned as she tried to remember, "Actually, no, I didn't," she giggled.

"So what happened?" Dave asked.

"So they asked if Sonia could come out to play and my dad told them that there wasn't anyone called Sonia in our house. They insisted there was, and she had told them she lived here and then they described me. My dad called me, and I kind of hung back by the sitting room door then went slowly round the corner towards the front door. As soon as they saw me, they shouted 'There she is! That's Sonia!' I had my head down because I was embarrassed as I had lied about my name. My dad saw me and said, 'no that's my daughter Ruth, her name's not Sonia' to which one little boy said 'no she's Sonia, she said her name was Sonia yesterday', then he said loudly, 'Hi Sonia' and waved at me."

"What did you say?" Dave asked.

"I said 'Hi' back and waved."

Dave, Bryson and Jermaine stared at her then started laughing; she looked at their faces and started laughing as well. It was magical – pure unadulterated laughter.

After a few more moments of being laughed at and laughed with she continued, "My dad looked at the kids and then at me and said, 'no this is my daughter, and her name is Ruth'. He told them that we were just about to sit down and eat dinner and that I couldn't go out to play that evening. They said they would call for me again another day. Just before they left one of the girls said 'Bye Sonia' and waved at me, and my dad looked at her as if to say something like 'Didn't you hear me say that her name is Ruth?' or 'Weren't you listening to me?' But she probably didn't get it."

"What did you do?" Dave asked.

"I gave her a big smile and said 'Bye' and waved at her."

Again the laughter erupted as her husband and sons laughed at her comical embarrassed expression.

"Guys, I was nine years old, come on give me a break here," Ruth said.

"What happened after they left?" Bryson asked

"My dad asked me why I told them my name was Sonia, and I told him that I didn't like my name. I thought he was going to get furious and tell me off, but he didn't. He told me the meaning of my name. He told me that his sister had been called Ruth and that they were close when he was younger and that she had died young, before I was born. He said that when I was born, he loved me so much that he wanted me to have her name. He also said that Ruth was the name of a Moabite woman in the Bible that married a Jewish man who died, but she remained loyal to her mother-in-law Naomi and followed her back to Bethlehem. Her loyalty was rewarded by her marrying a man called Boaz who was the grandfather of King David who was a direct ancestor of Jesus Christ the Messiah. When your Grandfather told me all of that I felt honoured to have my name and never told a lie about it again."

"Wow," Jermaine said, "that's awesome."

"I just wanted to share that with you. I know that teenagers nowadays have so much more compared to when I was growing up but I think that you guys are also exposed to so much more as well, there are so many pressures out there trying to get you to conform to standards set by people with no morals. Your dad and I love you both so much, and we want you to know that you can come and talk to us about anything. We may not have gone through everything that you are going through or will go through, but we have our 'toolboxes', and I'm sure that there's always something that we can do to help you out with whatever it is you're going through in life. Don't keep anything inside that has the potential to take you to unhealthy places, talk to us okay."

Bryson and Jermaine nodded.

"Okay, now that Sonia has got that off her chest, let's go get some dinner," Dave said as he struggled to conceal his smile.

The boys laughed openly.

Ruth was about to follow her sons into the kitchen when Dave stepped forward and pulled her towards him, "I love you, Ruth," he told her.

"I know, sweetheart, I love you too baby," she told him.

Bryson: "Can you believe that, Mom actually waved back when they called her Sonia, hahahahaha."
Jermaine: "And, and she said 'bye', don't forget that, hehehehehe."
Bryson: "She's great, both Mom and Dad are great."
Jermaine: "Hahahahaha, 'bye', that is so classic."

"Are those two laughing at me?" Ruth asked Dave as they stood by the kitchen door watching their sons set the table.

"No baby, they're laughing with you. That's the best story you could have shared with us. Now they see you as being human not just as Mommy."

Later that day

"Mom, do you have a minute?" Jermaine asked.

Ruth closed the book she'd been reading, "Of course I do, Jermaine, come and sit down," she patted the space next to her on the sofa.

He sat down and fidgeted with the tassels on the edge of a cushion. "What do you do if someone says that they want to kill themselves?" He murmured.

Ruth's heart started to pound. She felt as if every nerve in her body had suddenly jumped to attention, sparked by the words her nearly fourteen-year-old son had just spoken. Suddenly she remembered what Anna had told her and saw the significance. She took a deep breath and willed words into her head, "You tell someone, sweetheart, you never keep that sort of information to yourself because you can't handle it."

"What if they've asked you not to tell anyone, if they've begged you to keep it a secret and not to tell anyone?"

"Sweetheart, if you don't tell anyone, and you can't talk the person down, and they go on to commit suicide then you'll feel bad for the rest of your life. It isn't something that anyone of any age should have to deal with especially a teenager. It's not your secret to keep, and you shouldn't have to deal with the pressure of trying to keep it. You've taken the first step of telling an adult now we need to get a school counsellor, or the person's parents involved as soon as possible, okay."

"Okay . . . I wasn't going to say anything. I've been struggling with this for weeks, Mom. She's been cutting her arms, drinking and then she started giving her stuff away like she didn't need it anymore. I only found out cos she forgot to wear long sleeves under her school blazer, and I saw her arms. There were all these old and fresh cuts she did to herself with a razor blade – they looked nasty. I didn't know what to do. She begged me not to tell anyone about it. I just told Bryson now, and he said to talk to you, he said after the story you told us today and with what happened with Elle you're relatable, and you'd know what to do."

Ruth hugged her son to her and kissed the side of his head, "I'm so proud of you, Jermaine, so incredibly proud of you. I just want you to know that you and your brother can talk to me or your dad about anything." She thought for a few moments then said, "This is what we're going to do . . . "

CHAPTER 86

New Town, Mississippi

He saw the man sitting on a cloth foldable chair by the side of the river. The man had tanned skin and looked like a Native American. His eyes were kind and ageless, and his smile was one that reached deep into his eyes as if to announce to the recipient that it was genuine. He whistled as he moved the fishing rod in his hand gently. The boy figured the man was in his thirties, but he wasn't sure. He stopped studying the man and approached him.

"Hello, Mister. What are you doing there?" He asked.

"I'm fishing," the man replied.

"My mom said there isn't any life in this river. She said that all the fish have died, and the river is now like the Dead Sea."

"Is that so?" The man said, opened the ice box by his leg and pulled out three fishes that were still alive and wriggling. "I caught these not long ago so looks like the fish are back."

"Wow, are those real?"

"As real as you and me," the man replied and chuckled.

"Wow, real fish in this river, I bet my mom's gonna be shocked when I tell her, I bet she's gonna say the fish must have lost their way and ended up down here."

Again the man chuckled. "What's your name, son?"

"Simon," the boy replied.

"How old are you, Simon?"

"Eleven."

"Did you tell your mom that you were coming down here?"

"No, she's mad at me cos I wouldn't play with my little brother. I ran down here to be by myself."

"What about your dad?"

"He's in the army. He's away."

"Is he a soldier?"

"No, a doctor, he's helping people. I miss him."

The man studied the boy, "You want to see if you can catch

anything?"

"I don't have a fishing rod."

"Here take this net and throw it into the water," he handed Simon a net attached to a pole by a rope. "Throw it out with all your strength."

Simon did as he was told then sat on the riverbank next to the man and listened as the man whistled softly, the sound calmed him. "What's your name, Mister?" He asked after a few moments.

"My name is Payne Holister."

"I have a Hollister T-shirt, so does my brother, are you the one who made them?"

Payne Holister smiled at Simon and shook his head.

Suddenly the pole in Simon's hand began to move erratically, and he struggled to hold it steady. He followed the instructions that Payne gave him and firmly pulled the net out of the water. The captured fish struggled against their restraint as Simon stared at them. He stared at the different colours, shapes and sizes of the fish; his mouth opened in shock, his breathing laboured from the exertion of pulling the net in.

"Put three fishes in this, take them home, show your mom then come back for the rest, I'll put them in a bucket for you."

"Honest Mister? They're all mine?"

"Yes but on one condition."

"What?"

"I need you to do three things for me, Simon."

"What?"

"I need you to tell your mom where you're going, to look after your brother and play with him when she asks you to, and not get mad about things anymore. Your dad will soon be home."

Simon looked at the fishes then nodded, "Okay."

"Go home, Simon, take the fishes with you."

"Thanks, Mr Holister," Simon said then ran home with the three fishes.

*

"He was here, Mom, right here! He was sitting in a fold-away, and he had a fishing rod in his hand and three fishes in an icebox, and he gave me a net attached to a pole."

"What did you say his name was again?"

"Mr Payne Holister."

"Payne Holister, 'Pain Healer', that's an unusual name."

"He said I always need to tell you where I'm going and to look after Andrew and play with him when you ask me to, and not get mad at things. Oh, and he said that Dad would soon be home. He also said I could keep all the fishes."

"He said your dad would soon be home?"

"Uh-huh," Simon nodded.

Her heart needed to hear that, it soared, she had secretly been losing hope for weeks. Two medical doctors and three nurses were recently killed in the attack on a base next to where her husband was stationed, and she was scared that he might not come back alive. She wiped her tears away and looked at the river, "You know what the darndest thing is? Your dad and I were told that there were no fish in this part of the river. It all seems like a fairytale, so unreal."

"I didn't make it up, and these fishes are real. I'm not gonna eat them, Mom. I'm gonna grow them. I'm gonna harvest them like they do on fish farms on the Discovery Channel, and when Dad gets back the river will be full of fish again, and we can go fishing like he promised."

"Payne Holister?"

"Mom, did you hear what I said?"

"Yes I did, little man, you're going to harvest the fish and get more and more and more, and you're going to play with Andrew and tell me where you're going and be good."

"No, that's not what I said just now, but I'll do all that stuff, and I won't get mad like I used to over silly things."

"That's good to hear. Come on, let's go home, boys."

"Can I carry a fish, Simon?" Andrew asked.

Simon hesitated but only for a moment, he looked around and saw a small glass jar. He filled it with water from the river then took one of the little fish out of the bucket and put it in the jar then handed the jar to his brother, "be careful."

"I'll be careful, Simon, I promise I will," Andrew said.

Their mother looked on in pride. Her son had had an encounter with someone called Payne Holister, and it was evident to her that he had changed – his anger had gone. She looked around for a sign that the man had been there and saw something leaning against a tree. She walked over to the tree and reached for what she thought was a fallen branch.

"That's his fishing rod, Mom. That's the rod he was using when I saw him. Maybe he's gonna come back for it."

She looked at the smooth piece of wood in her hand, "Thank you, Pain Healer," she whispered almost to herself but not quite and put the rod back. "Come on, boys, let's go home."

Simon carried the bucket of fishes and Andrew carried the jar with a small fish inside. All three walked back up the path towards their home.

"Are they fish or fishes Simon?" Andrew asked.

"Well, fish is the plural of fish. But I reckon fishes is for different fish all in one place, and fish is for the same type of fish in one place. But it doesn't matter Andrew, we can call them fish or fishes, you can choose what we call them, we're in this together."

"You're gonna let me choose, Simon? Wow, Mom, Mom, Simon said I can choose. That's the first time you let me choose something, Simon . . . gee thank you."

EPILOGUE

Chicago, Several Years Ago

She stood in The Room and again watched her life play
out on the screen in front of her, she saw her husband
clutching their daughter as he cried out, "No, no, no . . .
not my baby! Not Anna Lee! Think of all the things she
could have done with her life . . . all the good things she
could have done, think of all the people she could have
helped!"

**What would have happened if Anna Lee hadn't survived
that day?**

THE END

Note from Author

Most people, like me, will know someone who committed suicide or know someone who knows someone.

When I finished my MSc in Medical Microbiology at University, I got a job in a renowned London hospital's Microbiology Laboratory, and it was there that I met him – my work mentor. He wasn't that tall, was balding, of slight built and told me once that he bought some of his trousers in the children's section of clothing shops. He took me under his wing and taught me the difference between studying Medical Microbiology and working in a laboratory and how to put my theory know-how, into practice. He used to wind me up by calling me 'Gladiola' instead of Gladys – he told me it was the name of a beautiful flower, and I believed him (we didn't have the internet back then for me to check if it was true or not).

I worked with him for nearly seven years; two of those years were spent on maternity leave having my children. When I went back to work each time he brought me up to speed and made sure that I was okay with all the new methods.

The things I remember most are his willingness to always help me when I needed help at work, and how when we had a slight misunderstanding I would frown at him, he would frown in return, we'd smile, and things would go back to normal.

Once, I found and identified a rare parasite in a patient's sample and he confirmed what it was then got everyone's attention and made everyone aware that I had found it. And, he heaped so much praise on me that I was chuffed.

I don't know why he decided to commit suicide. I don't know what was going on in his mind or what led to things happening the way they did. I do know that even now, even years after the event, I still miss him. I named one of the male characters in my first novel after him . . . in memory of him.

Sometimes I wonder why he didn't Talk To Someone. They say it's the people left behind who suffer when you go. They do you know. They really suffer when you go. They constantly ask themselves what they could have done to stop you, what they could have done to change your mind and help you see that everything looks different in different shades of light. A Proverb says – *Weeping may endure for the night, but Joy comes in the morning*. You may think that you have no one to talk to, you are so wrong. Your mother or father, a relative or a friend will ask themselves some questions when you die, one of which will be, why didn't you talk to them?

Some faiths believe that when you kill yourself, you go to hell. Some psychiatrists believe that no situation should ever result in you committing suicide. Some people believe that to get through the weeping, you have to perceive the joy.

Here's A Suggestion: Pray to the God of Peace, JEHOVA Shalom. Then take 15 minutes and make a list of some of the good things in your life, include the people who love you and who you will be leaving behind, heartbroken and shattered – because you are precious to them – you matter!

Don't be a statistic – Don't be a sad memory, a hidden picture, a dark shadow, a name whispered by people with heavy hearts. No matter what you're going through right now know this - **you are precious, you are unique, your life is valuable, and you are irreplaceable to your family. You can get through the darkness and into the light beyond** – I say this in the voice of your mother, father, sister, brother, relative and friend. You can get through whatever situation you're in. Talk through the pain, let that be your release – committing suicide is like saying to hell with the life you've been given because things will never change, but change happens when things are done differently.

Tomorrow is whatever you make it . . . you have free will, the God-given power of choice . . . choose life!

Finally, many organisations have been set up to help people deal with problems so don't ever suffer in silence or alone - **Talk To Someone!**

Talk To

Someone!

U MURDER U (SUICIDE)

A Story
A story is told of an elderly man standing on a bridge trying to
talk a young person down from committing suicide. Seeing
that the young person was moments away from jumping into
the murky waters below, compassion so filled the elderly
man's heart that he paraphrased some words he remembered
from the Scriptures (words God had spoken to mankind):

"**Listen, your life is not meaningless neither is it through**
I have so many great things I need you to do
I have placed in your heart desires that you must fulfil
So, Seek Me, Trust Me, live, and see all your dreams come
true.

I have always known you
I have always cared
Even when you ignored Me
I was always there

People have hurt you. I feel your pain
You did things wrong, and I see your shame
But, in a blink of an eye restoration can start
So trust in Me, and I will protect you and renew your
heart.

Why?
Because
I have always loved you
I have always cared
So don't ignore Me
Because . . . I AM . . . right here

Nothing can take away My Love for you
I Love You – Full Stop."
"Those words saved my life" – Shane Nelson